RESURGENCE

Nicole M. Ahles

NAB
Publication

This is a work of fiction. The characters, organizations, and events portrayed in this novel are either products of the author's imagination or are used fictitiously. Any resemblance to actual events, places, or persons, living or dead, is entirely coincidental.

RESURGENCE
By: Nicole M. Ahles
Paperback – 1st edition 2023

NicoleAhles.com

NAB Publication
Cover design copyright © 2022 by Britani Christenson, Casey Christenson
Image copyright © 2022 Eezy Inc. All right reserved
Interior design by Nicole Ahles
Printed by Ingram Spark

ISBN 978-0-9911126-7-8

For my daughter, Seylah.

Much like Tala, you, my darling, have fire in your veins
and love in your heart.
And both are needed to change the world.

RESURGENCE

ONE

Tala let her feet wander the vacant corridors. The lights above were dim and cast a silver hue around her, meant to have the same effects as moonlight even though she was deep underground, the real moon nowhere to be found. She glanced at the time on her new palm pad. The sun would be up in only a few hours, and the daytime lights would return. Artificial sun. People needed natural light, or so she'd been told, for proper sleep, immunity, and mental health. For those who never left The Village, the engineered lighting meant to replicate the conditions of the actual sun was essential to daily life.

It was quiet, most people still nestled in their beds, though she didn't sleep in the same living quarters as The Village's general population. The long hallway opened to a large room, a lounge with sofas, two tables, and chairs to match. The oversized virtual windows around the room were a live picture of the outside world. Snow was coming down, lightly, softly, a mere dusting on the ground. She shivered at the sight of it. Or maybe she shivered from a different kind of cold.

There was a tug at her heart as she thought of Kane. It had been over a week since they'd said goodbye, but it may as well have been a lifetime. Her mind conjured an image of him, remembering the pained look in his stoic eyes before she lay down in the secret compartment of the truck.

"Take some time to rest. To recover your mind," Vulcan had said, not unkindly, when he introduced her to The Village. "This is your new home. Get to know it. Get comfortable in it."

Tala took a seat on a sofa, sinking into it, her back to the virtual windows. She pulled her knees to her chest, hugging them, grounding herself. She found herself awake at this time every night. While Cara slept away on the top bunk in their unit, she slipped out and came to the same spot.

Her mind was full. Mila, lying in a hospital bed in Stoughbour, over twelve hundred miles away. Still unconscious, according to the latest update from Cara. She was still in contact with Avery in the city. He had kept his word. Though little could be done for Mila, he had people looking out for her, people operating in secret in the hospital system. The Unified Rebels, or the Unified Revolutionaries as they referred to themselves, the Revos, had people on the inside all over Columbia City. Maybe it was better she was still unconscious. It meant she knew nothing of what had happened. The assassination, the massacre. A death toll nearing three hundred. Tala envied her. She thought of Max, whom she was relieved to have no contact with. How would she ever explain to him that she'd left Kane? That she'd lost Kane.

Despite herself, she thought of Thias. She found herself frequently wanting a glance inside his mind, just so she could know what he thought of her now. What he thought of her defiance. Would he concede that he'd underestimated her? Most of all, though, she feared she would only find he didn't care about her. That she meant nothing. After everything, how was it that she could hang on to this small hope that there was something in him that grieved the loss of her?

She closed her heavy eyes, dropping her forehead to her knees. Most of all, her mind was filled with Kane. She thought about him day and night. It was only now and then that something would distract her enough that for a fleeting moment, she'd think of something else. But that was rare. He was on her mind and in her heart, and she felt an ache in the void he once filled.

Where was he? Was he safe? It had taken Vulcan longer than expected to get a contact to Clara City, where they'd left Kane, to look for him. By then, the service on the temporary palm pad they'd given him was expired, and when the contact went to the clearing in the woods, Kane was gone. Disappeared without a trace. He'd left the tent behind, but his personal belongings were also gone. Tala let that knowledge help keep the worst thoughts at bay. If his things were gone, maybe he just moved. Though that didn't explain why. He'd been instructed to stay where he was. It was the only way for them to be together again. So, why would he ever leave?

She should never have left him. In a tiny bathroom somewhere in the Appalachians, they had sworn to each other they wouldn't separate. They'd had no time to make a real plan; if they had, then maybe they could've come up with something else. But instead, she left, and the weight of that decision was heavy on her shoulders, heavy in her chest. She deserved every ache her choice left behind.

She missed him. She missed him in ways she didn't know existed. But there was no one she could tell this to. No one who would understand. She kept to herself, going simply back and forth between the City Center, the large and open atrium in the heart of the underground compound, and her living unit on the secured fifth floor, away from practically everyone.

A loud noise caught Tala off guard, and she jumped. Likely a janitor. They came around this time most mornings. She glanced back at the time on her palm pad. It was after five. People were going to start waking up, The Village would soon come alive. She rose from the sofa and made her way back to her unit where Cara was still sound asleep. Quietly, Tala eased into the bottom bunk bed and wrapped the blankets tightly around herself. Her fingers brushed the edges of the two photos she kept wedged between the mattress and the wall, and she tucked them in farther to keep them safe. Even if she wanted to look at them now, it was too dark in the room. Rolling onto her side, she curled her body up and closed her eyes.

She waited. Kane's face lingered in her mind. And then, like she did every time she slept, she imagined his arms sliding around her, pulling her close.

She'd imagined it so hard that if she pushed her mind enough, she could almost feel those arms like they were really there. And then she was finally able to fall asleep.

Tala woke to a quiet room, which was louder to her than the bustling streets of Columbia City had ever been. She rubbed her eyes and reached for her palm pad under her pillow, glancing at the time and sighing with relief. She'd actually slept. She missed breakfast entirely, but she'd slept, and that was everything.

There was a sudden click from the unit door as it unlocked, and a moment later, it slid open, Cara strolling into the room.

"Good," she said. "You're awake."

Tala sat up, her grogginess ebbing.

"Vulcan wants to see you."

Tala felt her body tense. She had seen him a few times in the City Center, though they hadn't spoken since her arrival. And she knew her time to rest had now come to an end.

She nodded at Cara as she slid the blanket back and rose from the bed. "I need a few minutes, then I'll be ready."

"I'll wait," she said. "I'm escorting you to his office." Cara would disappear during the day for hours at a time, to where, Tala didn't know. She knew lots of people who lived in The Village. But she always returned to their unit at night. She'd been assigned to Tala as a security detail. Tala was free to move about during the day, but after dark, it had been made clear to her that she was required to have an escort. Though many residents of The Village didn't know her face, most of them knew her name. Many saw her new alliance with the Revos as a victory, but for some of the ex-pats from the Republic of Columbia, she wasn't a welcome addition to their community. When they looked at her, they saw an Alexander, they saw Thias. And too many had suffered under his authority.

Tala went to the dresser, grabbing a pair of black jeans and a blue t-shirt. She had brought few belongings with her during her escape, and Vulcan had given her enough money when she arrived to buy the essentials, including new clothes from the two clothing stores in The Village. If she wanted more options, she'd have to go above ground into Hatfolk which she was prohibited from doing. But it didn't matter, her wardrobe was the last thing on her mind.

Stepping into the small bathroom, Tala washed her face with cold water, pushing the last of her sleepiness away. She loved this about The Village, no water restrictions. No coordinated blackouts for electricity conservation. She ran a brush through her hair, which was finally blond again after the brown hair dye had washed out. She pulled it into a pony, then quickly dressed. When she was ready, she emerged from the bathroom.

Cara was sitting on their sofa, picking at her thumb nail. "Ready?" she asked as she rose to her feet.

"Yes." Tala nodded. It was time to be put to work. It was the entire reason she was there. Maybe a sense of purpose and a mission would help her melancholy.

Tala followed Cara out of their room, down the long corridor and past the empty lounge she found herself in every night. They passed through the security doors of their living quarters, then rounded a corner, officially leaving the east wing. They passed a block of elevators and the stairwell, then turned down a corridor in the south wing that Tala had never been down before. Not that it was surprising. The Village was huge, relatively speaking, and because of her self-imposed isolation, she hadn't seen even a fraction of it.

They came to a reinforced glass doorway where Cara pressed her hand to a security pad that lit up at her touch. The door clicked, unlocking, then opened, and the two of them stepped through. The hallway widened, with glass walls on both sides that looked into an empty conference room. They passed what looked to be a control room, with a dozen or more people sitting at large desks with hologram computer screens. None of them looking up as they passed.

At the end of the hall was a waiting room with a tall desk in the center and a woman behind it, mostly obstructed from view until she stood. She was portly, with heavy brown curls and dark eyes hidden behind a pair of thick-framed glasses. She gave a silent nod at them as they passed.

Tala followed Cara down another corridor. Its walls were lined with horizontal panels of glossy wood, and their feet echoed loudly on the tile floor. They passed one door and approached a second, and Cara gave a hard rap on it before stepping through it.

"Ahh, you're here," Vulcan said as he rose to his feet.

Tala, suddenly unsure of herself, hesitated in the doorway, taking in the spacious office. She was slightly surprised by its stylish design, though she didn't exactly know what she had been expecting. Vulcan stood behind a white, C-curved desk with two gray upholstered chairs sitting in front of it. Behind him, protected behind a glass panel, was a large map. It was worn, the edges frayed, with obvious creases and folds in the paper. She didn't recognize what it was a map of however.

To her left was a small seating area. Four armchairs sat facing each other, a coffee table in the center. One wall was made of floor-to-ceiling virtual windows. The clouds outside were low and gray. The snow from the night before was now melted, leaving the browned and wilted grasses exposed and ugly. The adjacent wall was tinted light blue, a digital wall, though with nothing to show on it at the moment.

Tala stepped into the office, Vulcan carefully watching her take it in. He quietly studied her, his long dreadlocks hanging over his shoulders, his left arm a sleeve of black ink, his golden nose ring catching in the light.

"Sorry," she said, realizing she'd been quiet too long.

He cleared his throat as he motioned to the seating area. "It's no problem," he said, his face impassive.

Tala took a seat in the deep chair, sinking into it. Cara sat beside her, Vulcan across from them. Vulcan – Addox, she reminded herself, thinking of his real name – had obvious dissimilarities from his brother. Where Kane's skin was a rich, caramel brown, his was fair with faint freckles across his cheeks, and his eyes were hazel while Kane's were dark brown. But Tala couldn't help but see Kane in his other features. His jaw was a defined line, his cheekbones were high, his brows thick with a small peak at the top. Like Kane, he had full lips and an intensity in his gaze that was unsettling. It only made her miss Kane more.

"You've had some time to decompress," he said. "Though I imagine things are still hard."

Tala swallowed rising emotion and gave a solemn nod. She wasn't about to let him see how deep her heartbreak ran. He couldn't possibly understand.

"But there's work to do. And I need you. It's why you're here," Vulcan said. He stood, making his way to the digital wall. He tapped it, waking it up, then pressed his hand to it, unlocking it biometrically. With a few taps, a map appeared before her, the same one behind his desk. He swiped his fingers around, zooming in on the eastern side, and it dawned on Tala what she was seeing. She could clearly make out the Republic of Columbia with DeSoto to the south.

He continued to zoom in to the northeast corner of DeSoto, bordered by the Republic, to an area where the Atlantic coastline was highlighted in red.

"You see this?" Vulcan asked, turning toward her, pointing to the colored area. "This is what the Republic is in control of in DeSoto. DeSoto's President Pierce has positioned her troops along the coast south of this region to hold off farther encroachment, but her numbers are nothing in comparison to the Republic's. With air support, Republic Militia Forces pretty much walked in and took over.

"The Republic claims DeSoto is responsible for the attack in Columbia City and the assassination of President Royer, but Pierce has repeatedly denied these allegations. Mazanada to the south of DeSoto is already intervening on their behalf, and Pierce has requested military support from the Central Colonies, Tahari, and Pacifica as well. But without proof that they weren't responsible, no one is eager to act," he continued.

"No one wants to fight the Republic," Tala said. Thias knew this. "But isn't that what I'm here for?"

"To fight our fight, the Revos', not DeSoto's," he said, pursing his lips. "But it still might be in our interest to help. If MF continues to gain control farther down the east coast, the Republic will also control major shipping hubs, giving them control over imports from around the world that we rely on. If the Republic can get across all of DeSoto, it would interrupt the flow of resources like food, medicine, cotton, and even petroleum in the Gulf. And that definitely would affect us."

"What do I have to do with any of this?" Tala asked, glancing at Cara as she sat quietly in the chair beside her. Her ink, a closed red fist with a stem that resembled a rose, shown near her collarbone as she brushed her dark hair aside.

"You're the only one who knows the truth about what happened that day in the city," Vulcan said, folding his arms across his chest.

"But I don't have physical proof of anything," she said. She'd only seen the documents of the massacre plans, the payments to the shooters, to the sniper, on Thias's computer. But she'd been unable to download or copy any of them. Though she was there when President Royer was assassinated. She'd failed to stop that.

"It's still worth it for you to say something," he said.

"To who?" She screwed up her face.

"To the leaders of our neighboring countries. We appeal to them with your knowledge. And then decide together how to proceed," he said.

This took her by surprise, that the UR collaborated with the other North American countries. Vulcan was right, she was the only person who knew, unequivocally, what happened, what her brother had done, and she nodded in understanding. She had to at least try. Giving the Republic any amount of power or control was out of the question.

"Good. I'll set something up," he said.

"Is there any news?" she asked before she could stop herself.

Vulcan gave a furtive glance at Cara before looking back at Tala, his eyes meeting hers. "No," he said with a shake of his head. "We're doing what we can. But the situation inside the Republic is deteriorating daily. My people have to be careful about how they go about looking for him. But they are looking."

Despite herself, her heart still fell. "Is there anything else?" she asked, rising to her feet.

"Make friends. Part of influencing people is having connections with people," he said. *Influencing people.* He sounded like Thias.

But she knew he was right, though she hated it. The last thing in the world she wanted to do was put on a happy face and pretend everything was okay.

"Got it," she said, knowing this wasn't up for debate.

Tala collapsed onto the small sofa in her unit, Cara sitting on the armrest beside her. They had walked in silence back to their unit, Tala replaying Vulcan's words in her head, wondering if this had been Thias's goal all along.

"I'm going to be leaving soon," Cara said after a moment. "As soon as a new security detail is assigned to you."

Tala sat up as she looked at her.

"My work is in the Republic. Not here," she said.

"How will you get back? Getting out was hard enough," Tala said, recalling an image of Cara dressed in a Republic MF uniform for her escape.

Cara laughed. "That won't be a problem. This isn't the first time I've done anything like this."

Tala considered this. As lonely as she was now, it would only be worse without Cara. Cara knew Kane. Which meant that for one other person, Vulcan excluded, he was real, they were real.

"I know you're worried," Cara said, her voice kind.

Tala tried to feign surprise as she looked at her.

"I hear you leave every night," she said.

"Oh," Tala said, her gaze falling, her shoulders slumping.

"It's okay to be worried. But don't give up hope. Hearts don't have clocks or calendars, and distance can't stop what's meant to be," Cara said. "Right now, you have to do everything in your power to help our cause, to help unify the people. It's why you two separated in the first place. And if you give up now, all of that will have been in vain."

Tala dared to meet Cara's eyes, and she could see both compassion and determination in them.

"Tala, you have the power to make a difference. But that'll never happen if you hide away in here forever," she said.

TWO

Tala slept through breakfast for the tenth day in a row. Three meals a day were served in the City Center to all the citizens of The Village. She rose from her bed, tucking the blankets neatly around the sides. She glanced briefly at the photos she kept between the mattress and the wall: one of her and Mila, toasting martinis in the Met Lounge in Stoughbour, the second of her and Ronin in uniform at an MF awards dinner. She pushed back a surge of emotion, then put them back into their safe place.

It was time to get out of the room. She couldn't stay locked away forever. Pulling up the map of The Village on her palm pad, Tala searched the five levels of all four wings, knowing exactly what she wanted to do. And there, on the third level, she found it. The shooting range.

Tala set off, leaving the secured living quarters, and made her way to the south wing, pausing at the open railing, glancing briefly down at the City Center below. It seemed to always have people in it, despite the time of day. The height was enough for her to catch her breath. She bypassed the first set of elevators, instead taking the stairs which also overlooked the large atrium down to the third floor.

Following the map, Tala wound her way through the corridors of the south wing, the virtual windows on the walls showing a shining sun outside. She passed an ink parlor, the tech department, and an accounting office as she made her way deeper into the labyrinth until she finally reached the double doors of the shooting range.

Inside, she was met by a lone man at the counter in a tiny lobby. She showed her credentials on her palm pad, and he lingered on her name, glancing up at her twice, a brow raised.

"Don't have no plasma guns here," he said in a gruff voice.

"And that's exactly why I'm here," she said, not breaking his eye contact.

"And what kind of gun are you looking to use today?"

"Just a handgun," she replied curtly.

"Semi-automatic?" he asked.

Tala nodded. He didn't need to know she didn't have a clue what her options were. But a semi-automatic sounded like a good place to start.

"I'll grab one from the vault," he said as he turned away from her, then disappeared through a secure door behind the counter.

Tala waited in the silent lobby, the only sound coming from her foot tapping the floor. She couldn't understand her nerves. She'd fired a gun many times. And sure, this wasn't a plasma gun, but the concept had to be the same. It was her MF training, however, that had taught her that any gun other than a plasma gun was second-rate. They were illegal in the Republic, used by criminals and the Rebels. And here she stood, waiting her turn to learn how to use one.

"Here you go," the man said, returning with a gun in one hand and three magazines in the other. He set them on the counter. "It's not loaded. You'll do that back there," he said with a nod toward a door behind her. "And here's some extra magazines. Wasn't sure how many shots you wanted to take."

She looked at him blankly.

He sighed loudly. "First, rack it," he said, picking up the gun, holding it in his left hand, then he pulled back the slide to reveal the empty chamber.

"Then," he said and grabbed a magazine. He pushed it hard into the magazine well with his palm. "Activate the slide release to put a round in the chamber," he demonstrated, then quickly unloaded the gun, putting the pieces back on the counter. He reached below and pulled out a pair of shooting muffs, setting them down with a thud.

Tala reached for all of it, the gun, the magazines, and the muff. The gun was cold in her hand. It was heavy.

"Pick any available bay inside. There are safety glasses in a cubby in each one. And don't forget to disengage the safety," he said with a smirk.

Tala's eyes narrowed, and she bit back her retort. The handgun might be new to her, but she wasn't completely ignorant. She turned toward the secure door to the range, and he unlocked it with a code from behind the counter. Tala stepped into the indoor range just as a shot was fired, the loud boom reverberating through the room.

Despite the cacophony inside the range, Tala had heard nothing outside of it. She strode across the room to an open bay beside a woman, her back to Tala as she fired a shot. Tala set the gun and ammo on a small shelf in the bay, then secured the muff over her ears and put on the safety glasses. She loaded the gun, just as the attendant had, disengaged the safety, then took aim at the target on the wall opposite her. Sucking in a breath, she pressed the trigger, the gun kicking back hard, jerking up, and she knew she hadn't even hit the target.

Tala steadied herself as she took aim a second time. Firing, the gun jerked again, and she missed the target completely. She sighed in frustration as she made a third attempt. But the kickback was proving to be too much. She missed again. And again, and again.

Tala jumped as she felt a tap on her shoulder. She turned to see the young woman who'd been in the bay beside her. She was striking, with baby blue eyes, her lips punctuated with bright red lipstick, and long locks of dark hair that hung to the middle of her chest.

Tala slid the muff off her ears.

"Sorry," the woman said with a smile. "I saw you struggling a bit. First time?"

Tala's shoulders slumped. "Just with this gun."

"Maybe I can help," she said.

"I just need to get the hang of it," Tala said, trying to hide her embarrassment. She was a trained MF agent. How could she not know how to shoot a gun?

"I'm not too bad," she said, motioning toward the paper target on the opposite wall, the shape of a person drilled repeatedly across the chest.

"Sure," Tala conceded after a moment. The woman was no doubt a good aim.

"Okay," she said, grabbing her gun from the counter in the bay beside Tala. She quickly double-checked the safety. "Get into position. Like you're going to fire a shot."

Tala squared her hips and outstretched her arms, the muzzle aimed down the line at her target.

"Bring your body forward more," the woman said as she got into position, her arms outstretched in demonstration. The inside of her left forearm was covered in a detailed blue and purple mandala in the shape of a lotus flower. "Lean into it. Push your shoulders forward, bring the tip of your head down."

Tala adjusted her body into the aggressive stance as instructed, mirroring the woman as she stood beside her.

"It's your recoil that's getting you."

Tala already knew this.

"Bring your left foot back just a bit, so you can press your body forward, countering the kickback," the woman continued.

Tala slid her foot back and adjusted her grip, bringing her left hand high on the side of the handgun, her thumb parallel with the barrel.

"Whenever you're ready," she said as she stepped back, away from Tala.

Lining up her rear and front sights, Tala pressed the trigger, her bullet penetrating the corner of the target.

"Hey!" the woman gasped with a smile. "Nice work. Can I give you one more tip?"

Tala relaxed her body and turned toward her.

"You're small, like me. We naturally have less power in our stance. You've got great coverage on the gun with your hands. I find that if I extend my arms, then roll my left elbow in, just slightly, that I have more leverage over the recoil."

Tala turned back to the target as she considered this. Raising her arms, straightening them, locking her elbows and wrists, she took the woman's advice, rotating her elbow just slightly inward. She took aim. Sucking in a breath, she fired, her bullet piercing through the shoulder of her target.

She let out a breath of exhilaration and turned toward the woman, unable to hide the smile on her face.

"You're clearly no rookie with a gun," she said with a laugh. "That's no beginner's luck."

"No, I'm not," Tala said quietly but didn't elaborate. The last thing she wanted this woman to know was that she was former Militia Forces. "I appreciate the help," she said.

"No problem! There's rarely another woman in here. Figured we should stick together."

Tala gave a small laugh. That had been true in her former world too.

"I'm Vi. Well, Violet, if you ever meet my mom. But to everyone else, I'm Vi," she said as she outstretched her hand.

Tala swallowed as she reached for it, taking it in hers. "I'm Tala." She waited for the dawning on Vi's face, but instead, she just smiled.

"You're new around here. I've been here for the better part of ten years," Vi said. "I know practically everyone in The Village."

Tala nodded. "Yeah. Not quite two weeks."

"Well, when we're done here, want to grab lunch? It's about that time," she said as she pulled a palm pad from her back pocket, glancing down at it.

At the mention of food, Tala felt her stomach rumble. It would be nice to know someone, to not eat alone. "That'd be great," she said, forcing more enthusiasm than she felt. But she had to start somewhere.

Vi returned to the bay beside Tala, and they both continued with their target practice. With every shot, Tala mentally walked herself through the new stance. What she'd done for years with her plasma gun was so deeply ingrained in her that it was like fighting an old habit. By the time she'd fired through all three magazines, she was finally beginning to get comfortable with the gun and the change in her body, even though she hit the target a fraction of the time. It was a start.

A light sweat had formed along her hairline, and she returned the safety glasses to the cubby.

"Well?" Vi asked as she stepped around the partition between their bays. "I'm starving."

Tala smiled, feeling the same way. They returned their muffs, guns, and empty magazines to the attendant in the lobby, then set off toward the City Center.

"You've lived here for ten years?" Tala asked as they walked the corridor.

Vi nodded. "My family is from the Republic," she said. "My dad left when I was eleven, and it was too hard for my mom to support us there. A few years later, we left, made our way to Hatfolk, and then when she pledged to the Revos, we moved down here. She's pretty skilled with computer code. That's what she does for The Village."

"Is it just you and your mom?" Tala asked, stealing a look at Vi. Tala couldn't help her curiosity but silently wished Vi wouldn't reciprocate the questions about her life. For once, there was someone who didn't know her. Or at least think they knew her. Someone who didn't already have their mind made up about her.

"I've got two brothers. Jackson's seventeen, still a minor. He lives with us. And my brother, Huck, is with the UR military," Vi said as they emerged from the corridor, the City Center before them, loud commotion and conversation from the lunch crowd echoing around them.

"I pledged when I turned eighteen, which is why I'm still here," Vi said as they made their way to the elevators.

"And what do you do?" Tala asked, knowing every adult in The Village had to work.

"By day, I'm a tailor, which isn't all that exciting. But at night, I make my own clothes. My boss gives me access to everything in the shop afterhours. I just buy my fabrics."

Tala was surprised. She hadn't thought a Revo would be an aspiring clothing designer. But she was learning that being UR had less to do with being a kind of rogue freedom-fighter, like she'd thought them to be, and more about living in a free world, contributing to a greater society. The Village was a full-fledged city, and everyone played a part in keeping it alive.

Together, they emerged on the main level, the atrium filled with tables, nearly every chair at each one filled with people eating and conversing. The smell of food wafted in the air, and Tala's stomach rumbled eagerly. The bagels and granola bars she kept in her unit for the mornings she missed breakfast were doing little to sustain her.

Vi gave a nod to someone across the room as they joined a long line of people. Despite the vast number of people waiting to be fed, it moved quickly and efficiently as kitchen personnel dished helpings of food onto plates.

Soon it was Tala's turn, and she took a small helping of turkey, mash potatoes, gravy, fresh fruit, and a salad. As she made her way through the tables of the City Center behind Vi, she felt exposed, people's eyes on her, even if it was just in her imagination. She focused on the back of Vi's head as they wound their way to a table near the koi stream that snaked through the atrium.

Vi took a seat beside a man who sat alone with his plate of food and motioned for Tala to take a seat across from them.

"Tala, this is Declan. Pretty much my best friend in the world," Vi said.

Declan smiled, showing off a perfect set of white teeth. He was slender but fit. His eyes were a pale hazel, and the dark hair on his head matched the goatee on his face.

"Tala?" he asked, and she felt her chest tighten, waiting for her moment of exposure. "You're new here," he said.

Tala took a seat in the chair, her plate of food in front of her, beckoning to her. "Yeah. Almost two weeks," she repeated to Declan.

He nodded. "Well then, welcome to The Village."

Tala looked between Vi and Declan, their eyes bright, with genuine smiles on their faces, and for the first time since she'd arrived, she felt herself take a real breath, her body relaxing.

"So, tell us about yourself," Vi said between bites of turkey.

Tala shifted in her chair. How could she tell her story without giving away too much?

"Umm," she said, her mind racing over the possibilities. "Not a lot to tell. My parents are dead. They died in a fire a long time ago. And I have a brother. But we're not close," she said. Thias's face appeared in her mind, and a chill ran down her spine, his steel blue eyes staring at her with disappointment.

"From the Republic," Declan said.

"Is it that obvious?" she asked.

"That's where most come from these days," he said.

Tala couldn't help but nod. She wondered how people were getting out with the borders closed and heavily guarded. But she'd managed, so she knew it was possible.

"Do you have a job here yet?" he asked.

"I've been working with Vulcan," she admitted. Even if she didn't want them to know the details of her life yet, she refused to start a new relationship with anyone based on lies. Lies had ruined too much already.

Both Vi and Declan nodded between bites of food, and she was relieved when neither pressed for more. Just then, Tala caught sight of Vulcan on a small bridge spanning the koi stream, as though she'd conjured him by saying his name. Their eyes locked for a brief moment, and he waved his finger at Vi and Declan, then tipped his head and looked away.

"Vi told me about herself," Tala said, looking back to Declan, eager to redirect the conversation. "How about you?"

He shrugged. "Not a very exciting story. My family was recruited before I was born, and we moved from Pacifica to The Village when I was ten. My dad is the head of maintenance here, my mom works above ground in Hatfolk, and I'm at the tavern. I don't serve drinks, though. I'm in the back, stocking, ordering, organizing. That kind of work. It's no dream job, that's for sure. But for now, it works."

Tala nodded. What was a dream job, really? She only knew Militia Forces.

"Is it that easy to get into The Village? Your families just moved across the country?" Tala was fascinated by the novel underground city.

Declan shook his head fervently. "Not even close. There's an entire application process. Counterintelligence around here doesn't mess around, and the vetting procedures are intense and extensive," he said. "You have to have a citizenship ID just to get past the secure entrance above ground. And all visitors need pre-approval to come down. Basically, we don't have friends over that don't already live down here," he said with a chuckle.

"You know," Vi said, straightening in her chair. "It's Friday. We have game night in my unit. Trivia. You should come."

"Trivia?" Tala couldn't help but laugh. "I'd be terrible at that."

They both smiled at her. "We'll go easy on you," Vi said.

It seemed wrong to be making friends, to be going to game nights, which she'd never done in her life. It seemed wrong to feel comfortable around people, to laugh. But this was a new beginning, and the only way to let go of her old life was to embrace a new one.

Reluctantly, she nodded. "Okay."

A new realization dawned on her. For the first time in her life, she was completely on her own.

Tala sat on her bed watching the time. It ticked by slowly as she debated whether to go to Vi's unit, even though she said she would. She'd asked Cara to come, if only to have someone she knew there, but she'd turned her down.

"Sorry. I'm meeting people at the tavern. Besides, game night? Not really my thing. But message me when you're done. You can't go wandering the corridors after dark on your own."

Tala wasn't surprised. She wasn't sure game night was her thing either. But it had been nice to have people to talk with. Though they had no idea who she really was. The truth was that she didn't seem to have any idea either. Leaving the Republic, joining the UR, it had stripped her of her identity. She was torn between who she used to be and who she wanted to be, though she still wasn't sure who that was. If she didn't want people to see her as MF, as a Republic founding father's granddaughter, as Thias's sister, then who did she want them to see?

Maybe, she thought, it was best to start small, with only a room of people playing game night rather than with an entire movement. She would never connect with anyone if she wasn't willing to put herself out there. If she wanted to learn to fly, she'd have to also be prepared to fall. That thought was both thrilling and terrifying.

Just after eight, her mind mostly made up, she left her unit and headed for the second-floor west wing with Cara in tow. She hated feeling like she needed a babysitter but was thankful Cara never seemed to be put out by it. The City Center was loud, bustling with people as she passed, the revelry echoing through the corridors of the living units. When she came to number 2218, she stopped, unable to reach her hand out and knock. She stood, immobile. She could neither go forward nor backward. Instead, she stared at the white, windowless door in front of her.

In the back of her head, she heard the faint whispers of Kane's voice urging her on, to knock on the door, to build her first bridge. There was a tightening in her chest as she recalled their last night together, his words as fresh on her heart as when he had spoken them to her:

You have to continue to move forward…

"Tala," Cara said firmly. "You need to get over yourself. This isn't the Tala I escaped the Republic with. There's nothing scary about game night."

Tala eschewed eye contact with Cara, knowing she was right. She swallowed hard and knocked. She waited only a short moment, and when the door opened, Vi was standing on the other side.

"I wasn't sure you were coming," she said with a wide smile, her lips still painted crimson red. "Come in." She stepped aside to let Tala pass.

"Message me when you're ready. See ya, Tala," Cara said as she nudged her, pushing her closer to Vi.

Tala stepped inside. The unit was larger than hers, but not by much. To her right were a full-size bed and two bunks in an L above it, a quad-family unit. Like Tala's, there was a sofa and a chair to make a small living area and a door in the corner that led to the bathroom.

Declan was already there, seated on the sofa beside a boy that looked like Vi. Jackson, she assumed. Declan smiled and gave her a small wave of his hand. "We might be the lamest party on a Friday night in The Village, but that doesn't stop us from having a good time," he said with a chuckle.

"Tala," Vi said as she motioned to the boy and then a middle-aged woman in the chair beside him, "this is my mom, Jana, and my brother, Jackson."

Tala smiled at the woman. She, too, resembled Vi. She was slender, with curvy hips, and dark brown hair. Her skin was pale and her eyes a striking blue, like her daughter's.

"Welcome," Jana said with a warm smile that met her eyes. "Violet said we would have a new face tonight. I'm glad you could join us."

"I take it you do this often?" Tala asked to no one in particular as she took a seat in an empty folding chair.

"Pretty much every Friday," Vi said. There was happiness in her voice that Tala envied as she dropped to her knees beside her. "Okay," she said as she reached for a box, then opened it to reveal a thick stack of cards. "Ever played trivia?" she asked, turning toward Tala.

She shook her head. "No," she admitted sheepishly. Games hadn't been anything her family had done before her parents' death, and they definitely weren't anything she and Thias had ever done either.

"We're playing guys versus girls. One point per correct question. First one to twenty wins," Vi said.

"And we go first," Declan said, sitting up straighter, as if his body had an ideal position for his mind to think in.

Jana reached for the box from Vi and pulled out a card. "Oh, easy," she said with an eye roll. "How many oceans are in the world? Name them."

"Five. Atlantic, Pacific, Indian," Declan said, ticking each one off his fingers.

"Southern and Arctic," Jackson added.

"Correct," Jana said as she placed the card at the back of the deck.

Jackson took a card from the pile and smirked. "Tala, I hope you're better with geography and world history than my sister is."

Tala glanced at Vi, letting out a small laugh under her breath. "I'm pretty terrible."

"Name the former North American country that is known today as the Hudson Territories and Great Lakes Federation," Jackson said.

Tala's eyes widened as she repeated the question in her head, her mind coming up blank. She looked at Vi, who gave her a small shoulder shrug. They both turned to Jana as she sat with her hands folded neatly on her lap.

"Canada," she said coolly.

"Aww," Jackson said as he slapped his knee, then placed the card back in the deck, Declan frowning beside him.

Vi took the box of cards from Jackson, and she laughed when she read it. "No way will you get this. Who is credited as the father of the computer?"

"What? Of course we don't know this!" Jackson gasped. "They probably lived like a million years ago."

"You're not dramatic at all. No, not even close to a million years ago," Vi said. "Charles Babbage in the early 1800s."

"So, like a million years ago," Declan said.

They continued their game, going card by card through the deck and laughing with each turn they took. Tala found herself without much to contribute to the game, but the jovial atmosphere around her was infectious, and she caught herself genuinely laughing more than once. For the first time since she'd arrived at The Village, she didn't feel the weight of her old life bearing down on her. She felt lighter than she had in a long time.

"Okay," Jana said, taking the box. "Tie game at nineteen. Boys," she said as she glanced at the card in her hands. "Which planet in our solar system has the most gravity?"

"Damn. I don't know," Declan said as he looked to Jackson. "You're the one still in school, you should know this."

"What?" Jackson asked with a slack jaw. "You're the one who finished school, you should know this!"

"Sorry, I don't find myself doing much planetary work at the tavern," he said.

Tala and Vi swapped glances, and Tala laughed under her breath, though she, too, had no guesses.

"I seriously don't know," Jackson said, deflated.

"So, pick one. We've got a one in eight shot," Declan said.

"Venus."

Declan cocked his head to the side. "Venus?"

Jackson nodded. "That's my guess."

"Okay," he said, turning to Jana, "Venus."

A smile curled at the corner of Jana's mouth as she glanced briefly at Tala and Vi, then back to the boys. "Incorrect. It's Jupiter."

"Aww!" they both yelled in unison as they threw their bodies into the back of the sofa.

"Okay, okay, okay," Declan said as he composed himself, his expression turning serious. He pulled a card from the deck, and a moment later, his shoulders sunk. "Last question, for the win," he mumbled under his breath. "Name the three founding fathers of the Republic of Columbia."

"Ah man," Jackson said. "Tala's got this one in the bag."

Everyone's attention settled on Tala, and she felt her chest restrict, heat rushing to her cheeks. The room suddenly seemed to be closing in on itself. Of course they knew who she was. She'd only kidded herself thinking otherwise. The silence in the room was deafening, and she swallowed hard, her eyes meeting Vi's which seemed to be filled with anticipation rather than judgment.

"Weston Allen, Viktor Royer I, and Miles Alexander," Tala said quietly.

"Yes!" Vi yelled as she jumped to her feet, high-fiving her mother beside her.

Jackson and Declan scowled in defeat.

"Way to pull through for us," Vi said with a smile as she nudged Tala in the arm.

Tala forced a grin, hoping it didn't look as fake as it felt.

"I should get going," Declan said as he rose to his feet. "I've got to work in the morning." He tapped Jackson's forearm with his, then turned to Jana, pulling her into a hug, giving her a small kiss on her cheek. "Nice game."

With his back to Tala, she noticed the lines of black ink creeping up along his spine from under the neckline of his shirt. She wondered what it was. It was surreal to be surrounded by people with ink. It was the pledge to the UR, and Tala had never had any affiliation with anyone in her former life who was inked. Except Kane, she thought, as he surfaced in her mind.

"Next time, you really should try being on a winning team. That's your, what, sixth loss in a row?" Jana asked him as she hugged him in return.

"Seven. But who's counting?" He turned to Vi, wrapping his arms around her and squeezing hard, lifting the heels of her feet off the floor. "I'll see you tomorrow," he said with a laugh. When he dropped her, he turned to Tala, a smile still on his face. "Beginner's luck?"

"Maybe," she said, putting her palm pad back in her pocket after sending Cara a quick message.

"Next Friday, I expect a rematch," he said with a nod. "I'm out!" he called over his shoulder as the door opened. A moment later, he was gone.

Tala shifted awkwardly on her feet as she turned to Vi and her family.

"Tala, I'm so glad you could join us," Jana said, her voice was soft and light. "You're welcome back any time."

She gave her a small smile in return, thankful for her hospitality. Jana had nothing but kindness in her eyes.

"I can walk you to your unit," Vi said as she slipped on a pair of shoes.

"Actually, my escort will be here shortly," Tala said.

"Then I'll wait in the hall with you," Vi said with a casual wave of her hand as she opened the door.

Tala was about to object, but Vi was already out of the unit, waiting in the dim corridor, the moonlight lighting casting a silver glow over her pale skin. Small, soft lights along the floor lit the walkway.

"Thanks for everything," Tala said warmly to Jana, then stepped into the hallway beside Vi, the door closing behind her.

The corridor was empty and quiet as Vi leaned against the wall.

"How long have you known?" Tala finally asked. Her voice sounded loud in the stillness around them.

Vi shrugged. "Since I saw you standing in the bay beside me at the shooting range."

Tala squared her body to Vi. "Then why did you ask who I was?"

"Well, I was introducing myself, and yeah, I knew who you were, but it doesn't mean I knew you. So, I treated you like any other person I'd just met," she said, her eyes meeting Tala's. "I didn't want to come across like some fan-girl. Or some creeper. And I figured you'd tell me who you were when you were ready."

Tala wasn't sure how to respond. Her whole life, everyone seemed to know her better than she knew herself. No one had ever just let her be Tala Alexander, without all the baggage. Until now.

"I didn't mean for you to get put on the spot back there," Vi said, her voice sincere. "My stupid brother. I —"

"It's fine," Tala said, interrupting her. "You have nothing to apologize for. Thank you," she added quickly, "for giving me the chance to just be me, without everyone else's opinion weighing in."

Vi smiled gently. "I can't imagine what you've been through. I think everyone should have the chance to make their own name for themselves, without all the prejudice. That's all I was doing. And now that I know you a little bit, well, I can't help but think maybe you could use a friend."

Tala smiled. In that moment, she couldn't help but feel that Vi was exactly who she needed at the very time that she needed her. She was shifting to a new resonance, and it was the idea of having someone like her in her life that suddenly made it possible to think she could let the old begin to fall away.

Tala swallowed rising emotion and nodded. "I'd like that."

THREE

Tala still wandered the corridors in the middle of the night, finding her way to the same familiar lounge every time. It was beginning to feel like her sanctuary. Kane's absence was heavy, and with every passing day without word from him, it only grew heavier. She was living two lives. During the day she was beginning to find a new routine, she was beginning to feel purpose again. But at night, she grieved alone in the dark.

It had been almost three weeks. There wasn't so much as a footprint that Kane left behind, wherever he went. But if anyone could hide in the shadows, it was him. He'd done it for years after he'd escaped Stanger Research Lab.

Mila was still unconscious. A medically induced coma. Details were finally coming out of the Republic. She'd been shot in the chest, nicking her heart, a second bullet had lacerated a lung. In the chaos that had erupted when the shooting in Quarry Square began, she'd fallen to the ground and was trampled on by the fleeing crowd. In addition to her gunshot wounds, she also had a fractured skull and some broken ribs.

It was early morning, and Tala sat at the same table in the City Center that she did every day, beside the stream that flowed through half of the atrium, bright orange koi swimming back and forth. She pushed her breakfast absentmindedly around her plate: her blueberries to one side, her strawberries to the other, half of her French toast growing cold.

"You okay?" Vi asked over the hum of the people around them.

Tala glanced up, shaking herself from the fog in her mind. "Sorry," she said quickly as she straightened in her chair.

"What's on your mind?" Declan asked, lowering his voice and leaning in.

Tala looked between the two. She was incredibly grateful for both of them. They took her in without hesitation, without judgment. She wanted to tell them about Kane. She wanted to celebrate him and who he was. But she also wanted to keep him close, deep in her heart. If she said his name aloud, she'd have to admit what she'd done. She'd have to tell them she'd left him, and now he was nowhere to be found. She feared that putting those words out there would make them real. And as well as she seemed to be holding it together, if there was one thing that would break her, it would be losing Kane.

"It's nothing," she said after a moment, offering them a tired smile. "Just stuff. I'm fine."

They were quiet, and she knew they were unconvinced. But it was all she could bring herself to say.

Tala's palm pad vibrated in her pocket, and she pulled it out to see a message from Vulcan, requesting she come to his office. He seemed to disappear, then reappear in her life. She hadn't seen, nor heard from him in a week, not even in passing around The Village. Last she knew, he was trying to coordinate a meeting with other leadership, but who they were, Tala didn't know.

"I've got to go," she said, looking up at Vi and Declan. They knew she worked with Vulcan, just not any specifics.

"How about a drink this evening, after we're done with work?" Vi asked.

"We'll see. I'm not sure what my day looks like," Tala said.

"Fair enough. I'll check in later," she said.

Tala nodded as she stood. Grabbing her tray, her breakfast half unfinished, she headed toward the garbage.

"Oh!" a woman said as she abruptly cut in front of Tala, a cunning smile on the corner of her mouth. "I wondered if I'd ever get to meet the infamous princess of the Republic," she said with a mocking chuckle.

Tala could hear the bite in the woman's voice and felt a charge of instant animosity. "Well, here I am," she said sharply. "Though hardly the princess you imagine."

"I'm not so sure about that. I've seen you in the Republic. You've got no place in The Village," she said, her dark eyes narrowing on Tala. "You made a mess there, and you should've stayed to clean it up."

"My mess? Excuse me, but you don't have the first clue about what happened. And you don't know the first thing about me," Tala said, raising her chin, squaring her shoulders to the woman. She looked younger than Tala, by maybe a couple of years, but stood several inches taller. And with a head full of wild, curly black hair, she looked even taller.

"What I know is that you don't belong here. You ran away like a scared little girl," she said.

"Like I said, you don't have a clue. It sounds a lot like you're from the Republic too. Maybe you're the one who ran away," Tala said. She sidestepped the woman and dumped her leftover plate of food, then slammed the tray on top of the stack beside the trash. "Go complain to someone else and stay out of my way. I have work to do," she snapped.

"You're just as nasty as I imagined," the woman scowled.

Tala rolled her eyes as she turned on her heel, then headed for the stairs. With her irritation seething, she made her way to the south wing on the fifth floor. At the secured door, she pressed a notification button on the security pad and waited until the office administrator's face appeared on the screen.

"Credentials," she said in a dull voice.

Tala held her identification on her palm pad up to a small scanner, and after a second, the door unlocked and opened. She made her way down the hall, passing the empty conference room and the control room where, again, no one so much as looked up from their desk.

"Vulcan requested to see me," she said as she approached the administrator at her desk.

"You'll have to wait a minute," she said with a nod toward the seating area.

Tala sat, the chair stiff and uncomfortable, still irritated with the woman in the City Center, whoever she was. She saw the occasional looks some people gave her around The Village, those who didn't approve, but no one had ever said anything to her. Until now.

"Tala, you may go back," the woman said with a nod. "Last door on your left this time."

She rose to her feet, her brows raised. Vulcan's office was the second door on the right, and she'd only ever met him in there.

Tala turned down the hall, passing Vulcan's office, the door closed, and made her way to the last door, as instructed. As she stepped into the room, her breath hitched, taken aback to find it was a group of people that waited for her and not just Vulcan.

"Tala," Vulcan said, his voice deep. "Thanks for coming."

Tala's heart rate quickened as her eyes moved from one person to the next. Vulcan's face was the only one she knew. A man stood beside him, tall and thin with narrow shoulders, though she could see the lines of definition in his arms. His skin was olive-brown and his hair was dark and thick, shaggy, hanging past his ears and brushed haphazardly out of his face. He wore a short beard and mustache, both as unkempt as the hair on his head. The ink of a green serpent wrapped around his left wrist and over his hand, the tail winding down his thumb.

Beside him was a woman, striking, with defined brows and high cheekbones. Her hair, the color of black coffee, was cut short, the right side nearly shaved, the left hanging sleekly around the side of her face, just past her eye. The last person in the room, in the far corner opposite Tala, wore an upturned frown on her face. She was short, despite her chunky heels, with thin eyes, full lips, and a complexion that shined. Her long hair was dark at the roots, gradually blending into an aqua-blue color at the tips.

"Let's all sit," the woman with the cropped hair said, motioning to the many chairs and two sofas that filled the room. It was a casual environment.

Tala nodded, finding a chair similar to those in Vulcan's office. In the sudden presence of the strangers, her nerves were coming to life, and she folded her hands neatly in her lap to keep their quiver at bay.

"Tala, these people are important for you to know. Sorry it took so long to bring us all together. Things have been… complicated lately," Vulcan said. "This is Jasper Colson," he said, a nod toward the other man in the room, the one with the serpent ink. "Gemini Chabert," he said, motioning toward the woman with the dark, short hair. "And Ash Song," he said, nodding toward the woman with the blue ombre hair.

Ash Song, Jasper Colson, these were names Tala recognized immediately. She'd heard them before from Thias, always with irritation. Whenever they were mentioned, there was trouble in the Republic.

"This is UR leadership," Vulcan said.

Tala took a slow breath. These were not the people she imagined leading a rebellion. They all seemed so young. None of them could have been older than their mid-thirties.

"It was time to show you who we are," Ash said, her voice soft, though not small. "Jasper and I function as the public leaders for our organization. You've likely heard of at least one of us."

Tala nodded silently.

"And Vulcan and I work behind the scenes," Gemini said. "We don't like to show all our cards, so to speak."

"We're here today to get an account of what happened in the Republic. Of what you know," Jasper said, leaning forward, his elbows resting on his thighs. "We can't plan our next move until we have a better idea of the big picture."

Tala cleared her throat as she sat up straight. "Well," she said, not sure where to begin. The last thing she wanted to do was to relive any of it, but she knew it was necessary. Her silence helped no one but the Republic. "I can tell you the shooting that day in Quarry Square wasn't DeSoto, like the Republic is claiming. The gunmen were citizens of the Republic. Convicts escaped from Jerez Island Prison. And I can tell you that President Royer's assassination was the work of a sniper named Palmer, hired by my brother."

The room was quiet, everyone's eyes on Tala. She swallowed hard, steeling herself. The last thing she wanted was to appear small in front of these people.

"And how do you know these things?" Gemini asked, breaking the silence.

"I saw documents, money transfers. And I was in the room with Thias and the sniper when Royer was killed."

"How did you access these documents?" she asked with a raised brow as she pushed the sleeves of her shirt up her arm, exposing the black ink covering her forearm, a lion's head with dazzling, cerulean blue eyes.

"I broke into Thias's home computer," she said, drawing her eyes away from the ink. "I had the help of a couple friends." She felt an instant tug in her chest. "And while at Royer's birthday party, I overheard a private conversation between President Royer, Thias, Chancellor Adams, and Chief Justice Murdo," she continued, recalling the night of the lavish celebration, when she'd secretly wandered the halls of the upscale museum. "I was in a gallery room at the Larabee that I shouldn't have been in. They didn't know I was there," she said, remembering the panic she'd felt as she'd hidden behind the small wall partition.

Her hands were growing clammy as she spoke. "They were discussing a plan. Something about payments made to inmates, that they were all under clear orders that no one was to be taken alive. They were issued cyanide pills in case they were captured. Then the chancellor confirmed they had ceased all trade negotiations with Pierce and DeSoto.

"President Royer stressed that their action be seen as a reaction, not an instigation. Those were his words. I saw the list of inmates on a document on Thias's computer, along with money transfers to each of them," she said.

"Thias is claiming the guns used in the massacre came from DeSoto. Which is how he's pinned the shooting on them," Jasper said, cracking his knuckles, sending a shiver down Tala's back.

She shook her head with fervor. "No. They're old Republic of Columbia guns. I found them in a raid I conducted weeks before the shooting. I took one without anyone knowing. There were things not adding up, and so I decided to take matters into my own hands. My friend was able to pull the serial number from the gun I took. Most of them were scratched over to make them untraceable, but he was able to digitally recreate it. It was undoubtedly a Republic gun."

"These friends," Ash said, "who are they? Where are they now?"

Tala frowned. "Max is still in Columbia City. And Kane, I uh… we don't—"

"We don't currently know the whereabouts of Phoenix," Vulcan said, using Kane's codename, his gaze catching Tala's.

"He's the one you were escaping the Republic with, isn't he?" Jasper asked, his voice kind and with a hint of sadness that made Tala cringe. She didn't want to be pitied. "The one we weren't able to get through the checkpoint at the border."

Tala nodded soberly.

"Are we looking for Phoenix?" Ash asked.

"Yes," Vulcan said firmly. "But there have been some unexpected complications. We're doing our best."

Tala's brow furrowed as she looked at him, but he averted his gaze.

"You don't have any physical evidence," Gemini said, a statement rather than a question. "It's your word against the Republic's. Against your brother's."

"Yes," Tala said, hating the demure sound of her voice.

The room fell quiet again.

"President Pierce is adamant DeSoto had nothing to do with this. But parts of your story are consistent with hers," Gemini said after a minute had passed. "Mazanada is already providing military support. And I think we have enough information to at least call a summit with the other leaders of our neighboring countries."

"We have to be careful wherever we go with you," Ash said, her gaze settling on Tala. There was an intensity in her golden-brown eyes that made the hairs on Tala's arms raise. "The Republic has named you a person of interest in the attack. There's a reward for information leading to your apprehension. Despite this, however, some people see you as a beacon of hope. But you have to understand, Tala, that even though there are people who don't believe the accusations against you, there's always going to be someone in the mix who only sees you as an Alexander. People have suffered greatly at the hands of the Republic's regime. For some, you're going to be guilty simply by association."

Tala understood this. It wasn't fair, but she was quickly learning that the world was anything but.

"Freelancer is leaving us soon. She has a job in the Republic to get back to. You'll need a permanent detail once she's gone," Gemini said.

"I'm taking care of that," Vulcan said.

Tala didn't want to see Cara go, but she knew it was coming. She'd warned her weeks ago.

"We don't believe your brother knows where you are or who you're with," Gemini said.

"He thinks he knew everyone in my life," Tala said. "The UR are likely the last people he'd think I had any connection with. Let alone an allegiance."

"Chances are he thinks you're in hiding somewhere in the Republic. You and Freelancer made some noise trying to get out, but no one knows with any certainty that it was you. And anyone who did is now dead," Gemini said casually.

Tala's mind went back to her escape, the shipping yards, the car chase. There was blood on her hands.

"I think it's time," Jasper said, his voice commanding as he turned toward Tala. "No one knows your side of the story. It's time you tell it. It's time we tell it. We're going to make an advocacy propaganda video, an advoprop, and we're going to stream your message from Pacifica to the Republic. From coast-to-coast people will finally know what you know."

Tala took a deep breath. "I know not everyone is going to believe me," she said, straightening in her chair, her voice steady. "But my people were slaughtered that day. I lost my partner that day. My best friend is in a coma. And the person I love most in this world is nowhere to be found. All I have left is the truth. It's my only weapon. And I will fight until everyone knows it," she said with every ounce of fervor in her body.

She scanned the room, from Vulcan to Ash to Gemini to Jasper, seeing the unmistakable gleam in each of their eyes, the corner of their mouths all turning up in satisfaction.

Tala read the script she wrote for her advoprop for an hour straight, carefully memorizing every word. She sat nervously in a chair outside a recording room, her foot bouncing rapidly on the floor. This was her ultimate stance against Thias. Once her video was broadcast throughout the Republic, there was no going back. Her job was to plant a seed of doubt in those who believed him. It was to stir the defiance of the dissidents throughout the Republic. Her statement was a call to action for her country.

She glanced down at herself and smiled knowing that Mila would approve. No one had objected when she asked Vi to help get her ready. After everything, she was still hopeless when it came to style. But unlike the Republic, who had decided for her what she'd look like in her National Statement, no one here cared if she didn't look perfect. Tala didn't want to be perfect. She wanted to be real.

They decided on a pair of black, ribbed denim jeans, and a pale blue-gray shirt with a dark red leather jacket. Aside from a small braid that hung on one side, her long blond hair draped freely down her back. For once, she felt content with the reflection in the mirror. In the Republic, she had been seen as either masculine in her MF uniform or pretty in a dress and heels. *Delicate.* That's how Vaughn described her once. All of it discounted her, no one seeing who she really was. She was resolved to make this new life different, refusing to be predetermined by those around her.

Tala looked up from her script as the door to the recording room opened and a middle-aged man with a thick, peppered mustache gestured for her to come in. He gave her a small smile as she passed, stepping into a large and spacious room with an oversized green screen in front of her, bright lights and a camera directed at it.

Gemini came in hurriedly behind her, followed by Jasper, and Tala took a shaky breath, nervous that they'd be watching her. She suddenly wished she had asked for Vi or Declan to be there. Or at least Cara.

"Relax," Gemini said, as if reading Tala's mind. "We're just here to watch and give any feedback we can."

"I'm Callum," the man who'd let her in said, the door shutting behind him as he strode across the room. "You can stand on the X right there in the middle," he motioned with a nod of his head toward the green screen background.

"We can superimpose you anywhere in the world," Jasper said. "Anywhere in particular you'd like to be?"

"Oh," Tala said, taken aback. "Anywhere?"

He nodded with a small laugh under his breath. "We can worry about that later."

Tala folded her script and slid it into her back pocket, taking her position as instructed. She turned toward the camera and took a breath.

"Stay relaxed. We don't want you to look forced. Genuine," Gemini said. "I watched your National Statement, as well as when you spoke to cameras at Royer's birthday. I know you're a natural."

"Pressure's on then," Tala muttered to herself.

"You had some fire in your speech to all of us just a while ago. Channel that anger, your sadness, but mostly, your conviction," she said.

Her conviction. Suddenly, Tala realized she wasn't looking for validation from anyone. It didn't matter if people liked her. Her job was simple, to tell the truth, to expose the lie that so many people had been fed. It wasn't her job to single-handedly take down the Republic. She simply had to fan the flame.

She took a deep breath, letting it fill her lungs, then released it slowly, feeling her chest relax, and her shoulders fall.

"I'm ready," she said after a minute.

Callum adjusted the lighting on her, then stepped behind the camera.

"We can do this as many times as you need," Jasper said as he folded his arms across his chest.

But Tala knew she was only going to need just the one. She closed her eyes, letting all of it consume her: her parents's murder coverup, Thias's gun aimed at her, the sounds of gunfire on the crowd, the screaming and chaos, the bloodied and desperate people who ran past her on the street, the light in Ronin's eyes going out as he died in her arms, her goodbye to Kane. Her blood became gasoline in her veins, and every emotion surged together, becoming the spark to light her fire.

She opened her eyes and gave a single nod of her head.

Callum started a countdown from five, then fell silent, fingering the last three numbers, then pointed at her.

She took a sharp breath.

"Hello, fellow Columbians, and anyone else who is watching this. I am Tala Alexander. Many of you know who I am. And most of you likely know the accusations that I've had something to do with the awful attack on our people and the assassination of our president during the Annual Address. I'm here today to tell you they are lies." Tala felt a rush of energy course through her, the very tips of her fingers beginning to tingle.

She kept her focus on the camera before her, as though she were looking directly into the eyes of every citizen of the Republic.

"The truth is that President Royer was murdered by a sniper, hired by my brother, Thias Alexander. That the gunfire that was opened on the crowd in Quarry Square was done so by our own citizens, hired by the Republic government, then made to look like an attack from DeSoto. I saw the orders and money transfers for myself. This is what the leadership of the Republic of Columbia has come to… to lies, to murder, to coverups. Our people deserve better."

Her breath caught for just a moment. "I took an oath to protect all of you, and that is exactly what I am doing now. I'm arming all of you with the truth. We will only overthrow this corruption by coming together with a shared vision for a better tomorrow.

"I've seen the facts and know the lies my brother tells. But the truth is irrefutable. It will be derided, it will be denied, but that doesn't change what it is. We are all suffering at the hands of Thias Alexander and the Republic's corrupt leadership. And we are forever going to be doomed to repeat what we fail to repair. That is why I am here now, to let the truth speak for itself and to call on my people to fight. Don't live the lie."

Tala took a breath, hardening her face, her hands shaking under the adrenaline pulsing through her.

"I am Tala Alexander. I am for my people. I am a Rebel."

The room was silent, and Tala held her breath until Callum gave her a thumbs up. Jasper clapped slowly, loudly, while Gemini smiled, and Tala felt a wave of relief wash over her.

"Well done," Gemini said.

"Do we need any more takes?" Callum asked as he turned toward Gemini.

She shook her head. "No, I really don't think so."

"I think Vulcan was right to bet on you," Jasper said, a glint in his dark eyes.

"Tomorrow is the Republic's weekly National Statement," Gemini said, a hand on her hip. "We'll pirate their satellites and be able to broadcast our encrypted video of you through their system. It's a complete advantage that they use state-run media. It all comes out of one operations center, transmitted across the entire country. They're not the fortress they believe themselves to be."

"It's short, less than two minutes, so hopefully they don't figure out how to get past our signal intrusion before it's finished," Jasper added. "We've got the best people working on this."

Tala smiled. For the first time in her life, she felt in her bones the certitude that she was truly doing something for her people. Her grandfather helped create the Republic during a time of anarchy, when the world was nearly lost from the ravages of the Great War. Her mother had been the one to set all those children in that medical lab free, giving Kane the very chance at life that he had. Maybe rebellion was in her blood.

In that moment, though, her smile faded, quickly falling away as she thought of Kane. Sadness flooded her, filling her up, and she could hear his voice in the back of her mind:

"I'll be with you wherever you go."

He was all she needed, yet she was without him, and she felt the return of her ache deep inside as her heart clung to him. If only he could see her now.

FOUR

It had been raining for four days straight, the wind blowing hard and whistling through the dense cover of the surrounding trees. There was a biting chill in the air, and it seemed Kane was never able to truly warm the cold in his bones. A single bulb dangled from the rafters of the ceiling, the only light in the room. He quickly replaced the full aluminum pot catching the stream of water coming in from the roof for an empty one, then went to the door and poured it out.

Burke poked at a small fire in the stone fireplace while Gerrit sat across the room, taking inventory of their diminishing food supply. No one spoke. There was nothing to say. They all knew how dire their situation was, and how quickly it was deteriorating. So instead, the only sounds came from the crackling fire, the drip of water, and the wind rattling the old windowpanes.

Kane had been hidden away in the small hunting cabin for weeks now. He knew Addox would've sent someone to look for him by now, but he'd had to get out of Clara City abruptly. And now he didn't know how to make contact with anyone. He wasn't entirely confident Addox was still looking for him. Things in the Republic were growing worse by the day. Preferreds against Standards and Substandards, families divided in their support for or against the country. More MF patrols. People simply disappearing. Other nationals arrested on the spot if discovered. And if by chance, Addox was still looking for him, he'd never find him. That was the point though. He had to hide from the MF. Which also meant he was hiding from the UR. But Tala, she'd never give up. It was in her that his hope lay.

Every day he racked his brain for a plan. It kept him up at night, and it distracted him from the mundane during the day. But it wasn't just about getting across the Mississippi and out of the Republic, which presented its own problems. Even if he could get into the Central Colonies, where did he go from there? He had no way to get to Hatfolk, only knew vaguely where it was, and winter was now here. To go north meant he'd have to cross the Ozark Mountain range and then the rolling hills of the northern plains where the elements alone would be his demise.

He sighed as he took a seat on the rickety wooden furniture and glanced between Gerrit and Burke, two brothers he'd met in a small grocery store in Clara City two days after Tala left. He had watched them watch him as they made their way through the aisles until one finally had the nerve to approach him.

"This you?" he asked, his voice hushed, holding out a palm pad for Kane to see, a picture filling the screen. It was a digitally created image, not a real photo, but it was unmistakable who it was. Kane. Above his head was a red banner: **Person of Interest - $25,000 Reward.**

Kane looked up at the stranger, studying him. He could hear his racing heart, could spot the faint beads of sweat gathering at his hairline. The second man approached Kane from behind, pinning him between them. Overpowering them both wasn't a concern, but the last thing he needed was to make a scene. It was more pertinent than ever that he not draw any added attention to himself.

Kane was silent, stealing a glance over his shoulder at the second man, then back to the one still holding the palm pad.

"It was issued by Chancellor Adams. Got the alert about ten minutes ago. So, tell us, what'd you do to piss him off?" he asked Kane.

Of course, it was Vaughn. Who else would know about him? Who else would want him? The fact that he didn't have a photo, no name either, was a mild source of relief. It meant he hadn't identified him. Max helped cover his tracks years ago, and in that moment, he was overwhelmingly grateful for his friend.

Kane's eyes narrowed as they met the stranger's. "His girlfriend and I are in love," he said, his voice steady. He had nothing to lose by being honest. And it felt like a pure act of defiance to say it aloud.

A smile curled at the corner of the man's mouth as he shoved the palm pad into the pocket of his jeans. "I guess that's good a reason as any to hate you."

"Isn't his girlfriend that Alexander girl?" the man behind Kane asked, speaking for the first time.

Kane turned, looking at him, but said nothing. He knew the answer was written across his face.

The man nodded. "That's what I thought. We spotted you over by the produce. And after seeing that alert, I thought, *maybe*. You've proven to be far more interesting than I imagined."

"What do you want?" Kane asked, his irritation rising as he tried to decide if the two guys would mean trouble for him. "$25,000 is a lot of money. Isn't that what you're looking for?"

"Oh, we'd never be able to collect on that without exposing ourselves in the process," the first man said with a breathy chuckle. "Although, yeah, that money could go a long way for us. More and more MF troops are arriving here every day. So we've got to get out of here, and fast."

"You're DeSoto nationals," Kane said. As it dawned on him, he realized the traces of their southern accent. Though they hid it well. If this was true, it was as dangerous for them to be in the Republic as it was for him now that he was a wanted man.

"I'm Burke," the man before him said, sidestepping Kane's question altogether. But he didn't need confirmation. "This here is my brother, Gerrit. Got stuck in the city by accident when the borders all closed. Didn't think things would fall apart as quickly as they did."

"What's this got to do with me?" Kane asked.

"Know a guy who's friends with my sister's husband. He's got a hunting cabin 'bout thirty miles north of here. That's where we're headed until we figure out how the hell to get out of here. We're headed to the Colonies. That's where our sister is."

Kane cocked his brow at the mention of the Colonies, looking briefly between the two. "I still don't know what this has to do with me."

"Look, my brother-in-law lives across the border in Ozark Colony and was in Clara City for car parts. Then one day, my sister lost all contact with him. He just disappeared. That's why we came. To look for him. Next thing we know, DeSoto and Republic are on the brink of war. If we're discovered, it's off to a work camp, or worse, a plasma charge to the head. And we figured if you're on a Republic bulletin, you've got just as much to lose as us. So why not work together?" Burke said with a shrug.

"Safety in numbers," Gerrit added. "You got a plan, a way out?" he asked.

Kane wasn't about to say either way until he knew what he was dealing with, though their reasoning did make sense.

Just then, a woman started down their aisle, and the three men fell silent. She glanced nervously at them, and Kane turned away to hide his face. There was no one left to trust these days, especially with $25,000 on the line.

The woman didn't linger, just grabbed what she needed and swiftly left the way she'd come.

"You're extending me an offer to come with you just because?" Kane asked. If ever there was a time to tap into his heightened senses, it was now. The body always had physiological reactions when lying: fluctuations in the voice, fidgeting, a narrowed and distant look in the eyes, sometimes a flicker to the left, tension in facial muscles, swallowing, sweating, increased heart rate.

"Like my brother said, safety in numbers," Burke said. "There's no catch. And you certainly don't have to come. We can all walk away right now."

Kane studied him intently, measuring every movement of the stranger, then finally exhaled a slow breath, relaxing. If he was lying, he was damn good at it. Better than anyone he'd ever met. He tipped his head to him. "And how would we get to this cabin?"

"My sister got us in touch with the guy who owns it before we lost contact with her. He said he'd take us," Gerrit said. "But we've got to get going soon before it gets dark. A car on the roads after dark will attract attention."

"How do you know you can trust him?" Kane asked. He couldn't afford to blindly place his life in the hands of just anyone.

A man turned down their aisle, a slight limp in his walk. He paused at the sight of the three of them, then hurried past, averting his gaze. Everyone was on edge, it seemed.

"If Marina says we can trust him, then we can trust him. Don't really have any other options," Burke said. "Marina's our sister. And we trust her with our lives."

Kane crossed his arms over his chest as he considered this. Being wanted by the Republic changed everything for him. Patrols were heavy, and he hadn't heard even a whisper from the Rebels since Addox left with Tala. His only lifeline was the palm pad he left him with, which had just one percent battery life left on it. He only hoped it would hold out long enough to pay for the last of his food. If there was a nationwide alert that went out with his face on it, not even the small clearing in the woods would protect him for long. He was on his own now. "I'm in," he finally said.

"Get what you can for supplies. Meet outside in ten," Burke said.

Kane's gaze lingered for a moment, then he turned on his heel and headed for another aisle. Even if he didn't think the brothers were lying, it didn't mean he trusted them. But at this point, what option did he have? Just about everyone in the country would've seen that bulletin alert with his picture. Clara City wasn't safe anymore. Nowhere was.

Despite this, leaving exponentially complicated getting to Tala. She was torn up when they said their goodbye, hanging on by a thread. And it nearly killed him to watch her go. But staying alive was the only way he was going to get to her. And if it meant leaving Clara City with Burke and Gerrit, then that's what he had to do. He'd find a way to get to her. He wouldn't ever stop trying.

Tala stood between Vi and Declan along the fifth-floor railing, the bustling City Center far below. There was a buzz of energy that was almost palpable as the people around The Village waited eagerly for her advoprop to be broadcast throughout the atrium, across the country, throughout the Republic.

She stole a glance at the time on her palm pad. Just minutes now. She closed her eyes as Thias appeared in her mind. Her pulse quickened as the look in his cold blue eyes put her on edge. Even with over a thousand miles between them, he could still get a visceral reaction out of her. She reached out, grabbing hold of the railing, and steadied herself. She couldn't help but want to know his reaction to her message.

There were a million memories between them, and that tugged at her heart. But maybe, she told herself, not every story was meant to be a good one. Even between a brother and a sister. Perhaps some stories were meant to strip you and tear you down, not to ruin you, but to give you a chance to rise as a stronger, better version of yourself.

Like a phoenix, she thought. Then her mind immediately went to Kane. She would give anything to feel him beside her, his hand firmly holding hers. He walked into her life so unexpectedly and in the most extraordinary way, and suddenly she couldn't remember how she'd lived without him. Yet here she was, doing just that.

Tala inhaled deeply, her breath shaking. Her nerves were taut.

"Hey, it's going to be good," Declan said, nudging her with his elbow.

"No, it's going to be great," Vi said. She reached out, covering Tala's hand with her own.

Tala nodded as she glanced between each of them.

"Good evening, people of the Republic of Columbia." Wynn Davison's voice rang out, the screens around the City Center coming to life, filling with her face. All that thick brown hair, her lips punctuated in pink, the triangle of the Republic behind her. Tala knew the podium she stood at, having stood at it herself. Wynn, the Republic's spokesperson, was beautiful as ever. Perfect. Exactly what the Republic wanted.

Boos erupted from the crowd below as Tala's chest tightened with anticipation. Any moment.

"You okay?" Vi asked quietly, leaning in closer.

Tala nodded, not trusting her voice. The truth was that she was equally terrified and excited. There was something empowering about being able to share the truth.

"Unbridled violence continues to erupt around the country following the attack in Columbia City," Wynn said. "Ensuring public safety, President Alexander is once again amplifying the presence of Militia Forces along the borders and in all major cities around the country. Arrests continue…" Tala's ears fell deaf. She cringed, the pep in Wynn's voice in direct contradiction with the words that flowed from her mouth.

Hello, fellow Columbians, and anyone else who is watching this. I am Tala Alexander." Tala's voice boomed throughout the City Center, her face appearing before them all, cutting Wynn off. The crowd below fell instantly quiet as her video played.

Tala drew in a breath at the sight of herself, superimposed in Columbia City with Quarry Square behind her, the site of the city's massacre. Her memories of that day still too fresh, she turned away. Her heart hammered in her chest as she listened to herself echo throughout The Village.

"I'm arming all of you with the truth. We will only overthrow this corruption by coming together with a shared vision for a better tomorrow."

Tala brought her hand to her face and was surprised to find she was smiling. A light static played over the audio, and Tala turned back to the atrium, the video of her fading in and out. The Republic trying desperately to cut her transmission.

Her body tensed knowing it was almost over. If only their computer techs could hold on a little longer.

She watched on the screen as her face hardened, the look in her eyes intensifying. She sounded so certain of herself.

"I am Tala Alexander. I am for my people. I am a Rebel."

The video over, Wynn immediately reappeared on the screen, her jaw slackened, her eyes wide. She opened her mouth to speak, but not even a whisper escaped her lips. She glanced side to side, then back to the camera, then the screen went instantly dark.

There was momentary silence, then suddenly cheers erupted from below, people hollering in excitement, people clapping.

Tala felt it deep inside her. It was out there, the truth, a storm forming like a mass across the ether.

"That was awesome," Declan declared as he clapped with fervor.

"If you weren't famous before, you are now," Vi said with a smirk.

Tala turned at the sound of approaching footsteps to see Ash making her way toward them in high, chunky heels, her black and blue ombre hair cascading over her shoulders in waves. She smiled, small crinkles forming at the corners of her eyes.

"You aired everywhere," she said. "The Republic, DeSoto, Pacifica, Tahari, the Great Lakes Federation, and throughout all four Colonies. Hell, maybe even in the Hudson Territories."

Tala's fingers tingled at the idea of her message spread across most of North America. She took a breath, slowly exhaling. The energy around her was contagious and filled her up. She'd done it. She'd done what she promised Thias she would do.

"The truth will come out, it will tell its story."

He underestimated her, and that was his mistake. She would make him regret it for the rest of his life. That was the silent promise she made to herself. She wouldn't be small for him ever again.

Kane rolled to his side, pulling his leather jacket tighter around himself. Between the cold and the constant circulation of thoughts in his head, he couldn't sleep. He could hear the slow, rhythmic breathing of Gerrit, the nasal snore of Burke. Normally he was irritated by it, but tonight, it didn't matter to him. He knew he wasn't going to sleep.

He'd seen her, her video that had hijacked the Republic's National Statement. All this time, he wasn't sure if she'd made it. But that broadcast meant she was safe. Together, he and the brothers had watched in silence from Burke's palm pad. Between the three of them, it was the only device that had a power cord, the only device with any life left in it.

Never imagining they'd get stranded there, Gerrit never brought a charger into the Republic, and Kane had never been given one. With no charger, the dated palm pad was incompatible with Burke's, and the battery was completely dead. He was on his own. But a power cord would be useless to him now anyway. The palm pad was only good for three days before service expired, a security failsafe, and he'd been gone for weeks.

Tala was even more beautiful than he remembered. There was a change in her. He'd always seen the spark in her eyes, but now there was full fire in them. Seeing that made their goodbye worth it. As hard as it was, making her go on without him had been the best decision he could've made. And while he was filled with sorrow, he had no regrets.

Seeing her fortified something in him. He had to find a way back to her. It didn't matter anymore what it took.

He rose from the hardwood floor where he slept, his blankets thin. Practically useless. Stepping outside, he sucked in the cold air. The rain had stopped, but the lingering humidity seemed to only make it colder. He shoved his hands deep into his pockets as he shivered.

With no destination in mind, he started to walk. The forest was dense, thick with tall, mature trees. Many had dropped leaves for the winter. The wind bared the branches high above his head as they swayed in the darkness, creaking loudly, testing their strength in the quiet night.

Twigs snapped and leaves crunched beneath each step he took until, finally, he could hear the rushing of water in the distance. The river. The air was rich with the smell of musty, wet earth. Kane approached a large, downed tree, the scent of decomposing wood overwhelming to his heightened senses which had no filter following all the rain.

The woodland was dark, gray and brown, wilting and bare, the gloom in synchronicity with his melancholy. There was something about all of it that was calming.

The Mississippi River came into view, the border between the Republic and the Colonies. It was swollen and full, and a barge slowly crept its way south, most likely to the river port in Clara City. Across the wide expanse of water, Kane saw the shadowed embankment of the Central Colonies. His freedom in sight but out of reach. He sighed as he ran his fingers through the hair on his head that had grown in over the last few weeks. What he'd give for a good shave. And a hot shower. Anything but an icy bath with river water.

He glanced up, a few stars visible through patchy breaks in the cloudy nighttime sky. Once upon a time, the stars had given him hope, but now they were nothing more than small specks of light to him. They were dull and without the luster he once saw in them.

Looking away, something moving in the distance caught his attention. He took a small step out of the tree line, closer to the riverbank as he strained his eyes in the black of night. There was something there, in the dark, gliding across the water.

Slowly, he moved along the bank, following it as it moved north against the current, sticking close to the shoreline. A boat. Then he heard the whispers. Two men, their hunched over bodies tucked low in the boat as two oars pushed it along.

Kane followed quietly, stepping back into the shadows of the trees, keeping pace with ease as it glided along. The whispers had fallen quiet, only the sound of the river now in his ears.

He wasn't sure how long he'd followed it for, but as they approached a clearing in the trees, Kane spotted a small house. The boat slid onto the sandy bank in the clearing, and he watched from the cover of the woods as two men jumped out, pulling it up, out of the water.

One of the men grabbed something from the boat, then tossed it aside. A bag of some kind. With a man on each side, they rolled the boat over, then lifted it above their heads, carrying it toward him to the tree line.

Kane quietly slunk farther into the woods, keeping the men in sight. Behind a row of large tree trunks, the men set the boat down, then threw a tarp covered in leaves and branches over the top to hide it. They turned and headed for the small house, grabbing the bag they'd tossed aside as they passed.

He watched them disappear into the house and waited another several minutes, then slowly crept over to the boat, lifting the corner of the tarp to take a peek. Squatting beside the small boat, an idea began to form in his mind.

Anticipation sprouted somewhere inside him, excitement growing of its own accord, waking him up. He dropped the corner of the tarp, covering the boat once more. Turning on his heel, he retreated the way he'd come, taking off into a sprint. Then instantly blurring into the night like only he could, he made his way back to the small hunting cabin.

Tala, Vi, and Declan sat in a row at the bar. Tala had more congratulatory drink offers than she could keep track of, much less drink. Across the tavern, Cara sat at a corner table with people Tala didn't know. She only knew Cara as serious, with a tough exterior, and she thought it was nice to see her laughing. She was without her usual edge, just like anyone else in the tavern.

"So, this is what it's like to be friends with a celebrity," Vi said with a smirk as she took a drink from a pink martini, a lemon peel curled inside the glass. "Free drinks."

Tala couldn't help but laugh. The whole mood around The Village seemed to have shifted. And for the first time since she'd arrived, she felt she had real purpose. She felt she finally had a place among them. There would always be people who didn't like her, who didn't want her, but in that moment, she was okay with that.

"Any news about how the Republic responded to your message? Your brother?" Declan asked, shaking the ice in his drink.

Tala shook her head. "No clue. Though I already know how Thias responded." It didn't feel right referring to him as her brother anymore. Her brother was who she'd played pirates and climbed trees with when they were kids. He was the young man who stepped up and raised her in the absence of their parents. Her brother was a completely different person than Thias. "If blood could actually boil in your veins, that's what he's experiencing," she said.

"I think about my brothers," Vi said. "I can't imagine any of them doing what yours has."

"Tip of the iceberg," Tala said, then swallowed the last of her vodka drink.

"We need a new topic," Declan proclaimed. "This one is a downer."

"Agreed!" Tala exclaimed as she raised her hand in the air to get the bartender's attention. Her body felt warm all over as she pushed her empty glass away.

The tavern in The Village wasn't anything like what she was used to in Columbia City. Those all had plush barstools, colorful lights, modern art and furniture, chandeliers that refracted light like raining diamonds, and typically live music. This place was simple and minimalistic. Wooden stools along a black bar with a slick surface. It was dim, fixtures casting dark amber hues around the room. Banquet tables with red vinyl covers lined the perimeter, tall pub tables filled the center, and the music played over a speaker system. There were bars like this in the city, she had just never been to any of them.

She was far away from her Preferred citizen lifestyle in the Republic, and she couldn't help but think she liked this better. There was no ostentation anywhere she looked. It was just people enjoying themselves.

"Oliver from the bank asked me out," Vi said, launching them into a new conversation.

"I have no idea who that is," Tala said. "Ah," she turned to the bartender as he approached. "Can I get another one of these? I don't know what it was."

He nodded with a smirk. "Sure thing. I got you."

"So, what'd you say?" Declan asked before taking a swig of his whiskey.

Vi shrugged. "I said no."

A new drink was set in front of Tala, her empty glass taken away. She took a sip, the alcohol stronger in this one, and winced.

"Really? I thought all you women around here liked him. He's a good dude," Declan said.

"I'm not saying he isn't. I just don't feel anything when I'm around him. I want butterflies or *something*," Vi said.

"I think that's fair," Tala said, nodding. Her head felt fuzzy, and she made a mental note to herself to slow down.

"You and I, we're going to our graves single," Declan said wryly, then waved to the bartender. "Hey, Julian. I need a refill," he said. He turned toward Tala. "How about you? Will you die alone with us?" he asked with a laugh.

Tala's heart seemed to come to a stop in her chest with that question, her hand coming to a halt as she was bringing her drink to her mouth. She swallowed hard, then looked between them at their quizzical faces. Taking a breath, she set down her drink.

"You okay? You're white as a ghost," Vi said quietly, leaning in. "You know he was just joking?"

Tala met her gaze, her bright blue eyes looking back at her with concern.

She wasn't ready for this conversation, but it felt wrong to keep Kane hidden away like a secret. It just hurt to think about him, even the happy memories.

She took a large drink from her glass, feeling it burn on the way down, and tapping into her liquid courage, she shook her head. "No, I have someone."

Both Declan and Vi sat up straighter.

"Seriously?" Vi said, looking taken aback. "All this time and you never said anything."

"It didn't end well," she said quietly, not wanting eavesdroppers.

"So, you're not with him?" Vi asked.

"I am. We are. Together, I mean. There's just a whole world in between us right now. I don't even know where he is." She drew back her rising emotion and quickly took another drink. "We tried to make it into the Colonies together, but we had to separate."

"Oh, Tal," Vi said, reaching for her hand.

"But," she said with a steady breath that was stronger than she felt, "we'll find each other. And all will be right again."

Vi and Declan were quiet.

"Don't look at me like that, please," Tala begged, hating the pity in their eyes, even though they meant well."

"Does he have a name?" Declan asked.

"Kane," she said with a small smile at the sound of his name on her tongue.

"Well, a toast," he said, holding up his refilled drink. "To Kane getting his ass here. And fast."

The three of them clinked glasses. Yes, she thought, to getting there fast.

"What are we saying cheers to?" a woman's smooth voice asked from behind Tala.

She turned, her eyes finding the same woman she'd run into in the City Center after breakfast the day before. Irritation instantly flared inside her.

"What'd you want, Wren?" Vi asked sharply.

"My, aren't you in a mood?" the woman said coolly and then laughed. "I just wanted to know what our princess was celebrating. I'm Wren, by the way. You left yesterday before I could introduce myself," she said with a sly smile. "Are we toasting to your new-found celebrity status here in The Village? As misplaced as it is."

"I don't know what your problem with me is. But at any rate, what I'm toasting has nothing to do with you, so you can just keep walking," Tala said, suddenly feeling sober.

"You seem to be in a mood, as well. Unless you're always like this. Then I guess you're in good company," Wren said with a nod at Vi. She took a step closer to Tala, leaning in. "I still meant what I said. You don't belong here. This is the real world. And I'll cheers when you're finally gone." She turned quickly on her heel, then swiftly headed across the tavern, a sway in her hips and a bounce in her step that made Tala cringe.

Vi was on her feet in an instant, but Declan was faster, grabbing her by the arm and pulling her back down onto her seat.

"She's not worth it," he said, his hold still firm on Vi's arm.

"Who's that?" Tala asked, still watching her walk away, an acrid taste in her mouth.

Vi's eyes were wide, her teeth clenched.

"That would be Wren. She came here about a year or so ago with two guys, Gage and Hunter," Declan said as he glanced across the tavern at her, his eyes narrowing. "She's no one special but sure thinks she is. Came from the Republic. Her dad is in prison there. Don't know what for. But she's out to get the world over it."

"That explains a few things," Tala mumbled. Guilty by association, that's what Ash had said.

A little after midnight, Cara and Tala walked in contented silence back to the secure living quarters on the fifth floor, Tala's head thick from one too many vodkas. While Cara readied herself for bed in the bathroom, Tala crawled under the blankets in her bottom bunk. She reached for the familiar photos wedged between the mattress and wall. They were only a snapshot of a millisecond in time, but they had been proof that her life hadn't always been so complicated. The person she was in those photos was happy. Even if naively so.

But she had no photos of Kane. It was like he never happened, though, in her heart, she knew some of the most perfect moments of her life were spent with him.

She had fun tonight, with Vi and Declan. And that was something to be thankful for. Despite everything, it was good to talk about Kane, even if it was equally difficult. Her heart felt the still distance between them, but saying his name aloud made him feel real. And she needed that more than she knew.

Tala woke with a headache, the daylight from her virtual windows making her temples throb. Sluggishly, she made her way to the convenience store on the main level for a pain reliever, then reluctantly dragged herself into the City Center and joined the line for breakfast. Declan and Vi were sitting at their usual table beside the koi stream when she sat down, her head nearly hanging in her food.

"You look rough," Declan said.

"I don't drink like that," she said with a forced half-smile. The clamorous noise echoing throughout the atrium was doing nothing for the pounding inside her skull. It was Saturday and The Village always seemed livelier on the weekends. Though this one seemed to be even more so.

"Eat my bacon," Vi said, sliding four strips onto Tala's plate.

Tala grimaced as she looked at the meat, her stomach churning.

"Really, it will help. I don't know why, but greasy food is always good for a hangover," she said. "Eat your eggs and banana too."

Tala picked up the bacon, still warm but not hot, and began to nibble. A few tables away, she spotted Wren beside two men she could only assume were the friends Declan mentioned. She still didn't entirely understand her animosity toward her and quickly looked away before Wren could notice her watching her.

Tala ate quietly, listening to Vi and Declan banter back and forth about what movie they wanted to watch that night. Declan wanted to go to the theater, Vi wanted to watch one from the comforts of her unit.

Tala couldn't help but feel like everything around her was just so ordinary. But it was an illusion. The reality was that there was little about her life that was normal. She was fighting with her brother, not in a small, petty way that most siblings did. No, their fighting had them standing on the precipice of war. She didn't doubt that if they ever came face-to-face again, he wouldn't hesitate to kill her. That reality was far from the seemingly ordinary existence she was living in at the moment.

"What'd you think, Tal?" Vi asked, looking across the table at her.

Tala felt a tug in her chest at the nickname Vi was adapting to. That was always what Ronin had called her. She took a breath, meeting Vi's gaze. "Movie?" She wondered if they ever left The Village, if they ever went above ground.

"Yeah," Declan said. "Where'd you want to watch one?"

She shrugged. "It doesn't matter. I honestly haven't seen a movie in ages."

"What did you do with your life in the Republic?" Vi asked with a laugh. "No bars, no movies, no game nights. Probably no dancing or concerts."

"It's a good question," Tala admitted. "I worked. All the time. I was at my brother's beck and call. All the time. And then once I found Kane, well, I lived for every moment we could be together," she said wistfully.

Vi and Declan were quiet as they looked at her, and Tala shifted her body on the chair.

"Okay, so our job is to show you what a little fun looks like," Vi said. "You are allowed to have fun, you know?"

"I've been having fun," she said. "Really."

Tala's pocket vibrated. She fumbled in her chair as she reached for her palm pad. A simple message from Vulcan stared her in the face:

My office.

She looked up at her friends and couldn't help but smile as they continued their debate.

"I'm not sure about the movie," Tala said, rising to her feet, "but I'm being summoned, so I've got to go. I'll keep you in the loop." Vi had been right about the food. Between a partially full stomach and the pain reliever that was kicking in, she felt the sharp pangs of her headache beginning to dissipate.

On the fifth floor, Tala scanned her credentials and was let into the secured offices.

"You can just go in," the administrator said with a nod. This was not the same woman who usually sat at the desk during the week. This one had a kinder smile.

Tala approached Vulcan's office and knocked on the open door. He looked up from the hologram computer screen, and for a fleeting moment, she couldn't help but see Kane in him.

"Take a seat," he said with a curt nod as he reduced the hologram.

"Everything okay?" she asked, then immediately regretted it. Of course things weren't okay. Nothing was okay.

"Your video sure is making an impact. I was able to make contact with Boy Scout in Columbia City this morning. People are in a frenzy. They've flooded the grocery stores, clearing the shelves of anything and everything they can stock up on. People know this is about to get worse before it gets better."

Tala couldn't imagine the mayhem that twelve million people in the capital city alone created. There was no way to undo what she'd done, and she hated the idea of inciting panic, but she regretted nothing.

A moment later, a knock came at the door and Tala turned to see Cara stroll into the room, taking the seat beside her.

"Right on time," Vulcan said. "I was giving Tala a brief update."

Cara nodded. "I hear your message is making some noise," she said, looking at Tala, the corners of her mouth turned up.

Tala gave her a tight smile.

"I was telling Tala I spoke with Boy Scout. Says people are fired up right now," he said.

Tala thought about Boy Scout, Avery as she first knew him, and his role in her escape. It was because of him that she'd gotten out of the city.

"Fired up?" Cara said, her eyes narrowing as she looked across the desk at Vulcan.

His lips pressed into a straight line as he nodded.

Tala couldn't help but think there was more to their conversation just then but knew it wasn't her place to ask, despite how much she wanted to. Columbia City was the only home she'd had before The Village. She knew people there and hated the thought of any of them being caught up in everything. Mila was still hospitalized, but she couldn't help but wonder about Max.

She also thought of all the MF agents back at Command that she'd worked with. Things had to be a nightmare. She could see Captain Kole's furrowed brows in her mind. Mostly, she wondered who believed her rather than Thias after her advoprop. Surely not everyone bought into his lies.

"Now, what I called you here for," Vulcan said, bringing Tala's mind back. "We're going to be leaving The Village."

"Leaving?" Tala asked in surprise.

"Not for long. A few days," he added. "But there are some things you need to see, some people you need to meet. I've called a summit. And I'll be assigning you a permanent security detail. Cara, we need to get you back into the Republic."

"Barrington's plane?" she asked casually.

Vulcan nodded.

"Barrington? As in Elias Barrington?" Tala asked, recalling him from the president's birthday party.

"You know him?" Vulcan asked, his eyes widening, his head cocking to the side.

Tala couldn't help but think she said something she shouldn't have, she just didn't know what. "I met him and his wife, Victoria." She could never forget Victoria, who had sought out Tala to introduce herself. All that copper-red hair and those stunning green eyes. She was like no one she'd ever met. And she knew her father. It had caught her off guard at the mention of him that night.

Vulcan and Cara were quiet, exchanging a furtive glance at each other that didn't go amiss by Tala.

"Yes, Governor Barrington," Vulcan said after a minute. "You need to pack a bag. It'll be cold where we're going. We leave tomorrow at one. We have to take a little longer route to avoid a snowstorm, so without stops, it's about a sixteen-hour drive. Remember, warm clothes. I suggest a stop at the clothing outlets here in The Village. Sorry, but you can't go above ground."

Tala nodded. It hadn't even crossed her mind to leave The Village to go into the city of Hatfolk. Life above ground seemed like a distant memory.

"We'll be gone a few days, so pack enough," he added.

"Okay," she said, unsure of what to expect with her upcoming outing. "Is that all?"

"Yes," he nodded.

Tala rose to her feet, ready to leave, then turned back to him. "You mentioned the other day that there were some complications with the search for Kane."

He looked up from his desk, his eyes meeting hers. "It's nothing you need to worry about."

"Have you found something? Any traces of him?"

His lips pursed as he shook his head. "I'm sorry."

"But you're still looking for him?" she asked. Her faith was beginning to waver.

"It's part of why Cara is heading back into the Republic. She's going to take over the search," he said.

Cara nodded fervently. "We'll find him."

Tala glanced between them both, but with nothing left to say, she turned to leave. She had some packing to do. And apparently, some shopping too. Outside Vulcan's office, she pulled out her palm pad and sent a quick message to Vi. Though this was a job that should've been Mila's, she knew she'd be more than happy to help.

FIVE

Kane led the way through the woods, his duffel strapped across his body, with Burke and Gerrit following on his heels. It was pitch black and raining again. He could see his breath with every exhale. But the last two things on his mind were getting wet or being cold.

Twigs snapped beneath their steps, their feet squishing into the saturated ground. They were leaving tracks, but they intended to be long gone before anyone could find anything. Anticipation surged through his veins like fire. His freedom was so close he could almost taste it. But making it into the Central Colonies was just one step in the long journey he had yet to make. According to Burke, he estimated his sister Marina's house was still another fifty-five or so miles away, and without a vehicle, they'd have to take it on foot. Once he made it to Marina's, then he would make a plan on how to get a message to the UR.

The rain was coming down harder now, and somewhere in the distance was a low rumble of thunder.

"Shit, it's cold," Gerrit cussed under his breath.

Kane ignored him, simply pulling the collar of his jacket higher and forging ahead.

After an hour's trek through the dense forest, Kane spotted the house in the clearing, relieved to find it dark. Either no one was home or they were sleeping. It was early, some time after three in the morning.

"Over here," Kane whispered under his breath as he approached the covered boat. He lifted the corner of the tarp, showing its bow to Burke while Gerrit stepped around the large trees, checking the clearing.

"Looks quiet," he said with a hushed voice, stepping back into the cover of the tree line.

Burke and Gerrit carefully removed the tarp from the boat while Kane grabbed the oars, then cautiously stepped into the clearing to stand watch, his eyes straining for any movement, his ears on alert for any noise. He glanced over his shoulder at the now exposed boat and couldn't help but smile.

"Coast is still clear," he whispered as he waved them over.

The brothers lifted the boat above their heads, and when Kane gave them the go-ahead, they stepped out of the cover of the trees, the dark of night their only protection. They made their way the short distance to the river embankment, and turning the boat onto its belly, they slid it into the water.

Kane tossed his bag onto the bench near the bow, then carefully handed the oars to Gerrit after he climbed aboard.

"Get in," Kane whispered to Burke. "I got this."

Burke glanced over his shoulder at the house, then climbed in. Kane gave it a hard push, then quickly and with ease, he hopped over the bow and inside the boat.

Gerrit and Burke each took an oar, and the three men lowered themselves to the floor of the boat as they gradually pushed themselves into deeper water. The bank of the Colonies was a good two miles across the river, and they would be completely exposed once in open water. Kane was thankful for the rain, which meant two things for them: there was no moon, better hiding them under the cloak of night, and there were likely to be fewer MF patrols out and about. At least, he hoped.

They eased the boat downstream, past the clearing to where the river narrowed, the current easily taking it along. But they couldn't go too far south. That only brought them closer to Clara City, which was crawling with MF.

Rounding a bend in the river, they all exchanged silent glances, having an entire conversation without a spoken word. Burke and Gerrit nodded at each other, then turned the bow of the boat. Aimed for the Colonies, they began to paddle.

Kane stayed vigilant, his head on a swivel, his ears on heightened alert, the sounds of the heavily falling rain and the rushing of the river louder than he expected.

As they paddled through the open water, time seemed to stand still. Even with every row the brothers made, the opposite river embankment never seemed to get any closer. And despite their westward paddling, the current was slowly taking them south.

The sky seemed to suddenly open up, the rain pouring down on them, and Kane was no longer able to keep it out of the collar of his jacket. Water ran down his neck, down his back, and he shivered from the cold. He eventually lost all concept of time, and after what felt like an eternity, they finally passed the halfway point in the river. The distance behind them proved that they were, indeed, making progress. Suddenly, lights appeared in the distance, just north of them, catching even Kane off guard. Something was heading in their direction, but it was too dark to see anything other than the bright, white beams cast out from it.

Kane's pulse quickened and he, Gerrit, and Burke exchanged nervous glances.

"Let me row," he said hurriedly as he stood, only long enough to step over the bench and into the middle beside Burke. The boat rocked under the movement, and unsteadily, Burke climbed into Kane's vacated spot.

Crouching low, Kane took both oars. Though he wasn't about to reveal his true strength, he knew he would be more effective than the brothers.

Flexing his arms, he began to row, feeling the boat glide across the water's surface. He stole a quick look at the lights up the river, then focused his eyes ahead at their destination. He couldn't think about anything else, there was too much on the line. And he knew he wasn't about to get a second chance at this.

Blinking the rain out of his eyes, Kane pulled hard on the oars, rhythmically, as they began to close in on the embankment. Less than two hundred yards now.

"Aren't you tired, man?" Burke whispered in astonishment as he watched him.

Kane shook his head. Technically speaking, he should be tired, but he didn't care enough about pretenses at that moment, he just kept rowing. His heart was in his throat as he glanced over his shoulder at the lights in the distance. Fortunately, they didn't seem to be approaching them with any great speed. In the blackened night and through the rain, its shape still didn't take form.

"I think it's a barge," Gerrit whispered.

"I'd rather not find out until we're safely on shore," Burke said.

Kane ignored them and continued to row, trying to find a balance between going quickly while not revealing his abilities. His life depended on both. His mind filled with Tala. This was the only way to get to her. He wasn't about to give up or surrender now.

Less than a hundred yards. His fingers began to tingle as a surge of energy ran through him. He no longer cared about the lights in the distance, barge or not, and just kept his eyes on the shore.

"I think we're gonna make it," Burke exclaimed under his breath.

"Shut up," Gerrit said. "You can't say shit like that."

Then Kane heard it, a deep voice calling out to them as a spotlight lit up the darkness, quickly finding them, blinding Kane in the eyes. A boat sat hidden in the shadows, not far from the shore of the Colonies, south of them by a few hundred yards.

"Halt!" The words seemed to boom in his ears as his chest tightened. "This is Republic Militia Forces. You're in restricted waters. You are ordered to desist and identify yourself!"

Kane didn't so much as glance at the boat as its engine fired to life. He pulled vigorously on the oars, his determination filling him up, pushing him harder.

"Get down," he instructed through gnashed teeth, the rain running down his face.

Burke and Gerrit ducked below the side of the boat while Kane raised his body up onto his knees for better leverage. There was no point in hiding anymore.

"I gave you an order!" the angry voice of the MF yelled out, their spotlight following them across the water.

His heart hammered in his chest as he rowed, adrenaline pumping through him. The sound of an electrical blast cut through even the rain, the plasma charge hitting their boat, slicing through the wooden side. The boat rocked from the force.

"We're taking on water," Gerrit said.

They were close now, and Kane kept his focus. He couldn't afford to think about the MF. He couldn't afford to think about the water that was filling their boat, soaking through the knees of his jeans.

"Kane, did you hear me?" Gerrit asked breathlessly.

"We're almost there," he said, his voice deep, strained.

A second plasma charge went past him, Kane feeling its heat as it narrowly missed his head. But he still didn't break his concentration. This was only going to end in one of two ways: by reaching the riverbank of the Colonies or with his death.

The water continued to rise in the boat as more plasma charges hit its side, each one taking Kane's breath away. Their boat was quickly breaking apart. Burke and Gerrit kept crouched low, their hands over their heads.

Suddenly there was a rumble as the bottom of their boat glided over the shallow, rocky bottom of the river.

His jeans now soaked to the middle of his thighs, Kane stood and reached for his bag, still dry from the bench it sat on. He smiled, his relief nearly palpable.

"We're here," he said. He threw his bag over his shoulder, then hopped the edge of the sinking boat. The icy river water went up to his knees as he trudged through it toward the shore. Gerrit and Burke splashed behind him, abandoning the remains of the boat as it caught in the current.

Reaching dry land, the three of them took off in a clumsy run, bogged down by heavy, wet jeans, their feet sinking into the silty ground from former river floods. The MF continued calling out orders to them, and Kane could hear their approaching boat, but he knew they wouldn't reach them now.

They ran hard, for what seemed like forever, and Kane was surprised to find even he was exhausted, if only mentally, just as much as Gerrit and Burke. Finally reaching a fringe of trees, stepping into their darkened cover, they slowed to catch their breath.

Kane glanced over his shoulder but saw nothing. His ears strained to listen for any traces of sound from anyone who might still be pursuing them. Confident they were alone, he turned to the brothers and let out a hearty laugh. "Welcome to freedom."

Through heavy breathing, Gerrit and Burke exchanged glances of relief, then looked to Kane, their smiles as wide as his.

"Man, how?" Burke exclaimed as he looked at Kane, slightly slack-jawed. "That was incredible."

Kane felt heat rush to his face. "Adrenaline can make you do more than you can imagine," he said coolly with a shrug as he turned away.

"I'm just glad we made it," Gerrit said.

"Don't celebrate yet. We've got a long way to go still," Burke said.

With the rain giving way to a light sprinkle, Kane changed into a dry pair of jeans, though there was nothing he could do about his soaked shoes, leather boots that would take forever to dry, especially in the cold. His jacket too. All he could hope for was a relatively dry rest of the night and the sun to come up in the morning.

"We've got to keep moving," Gerrit said. "MF isn't supposed to be here, but they've likely got patrols in the area anyway."

"Marina lives near Edmond, southwest of where we're at. We'll have to keep the highway in our sights but stay far enough off the road to keep from drawing attention to ourselves," Burke said, slinging his bag over his shoulder and starting up a steep hill. "We've got a haul."

While it had been densely wooded on the east side of the river, the landscape on the west side quickly gave way to wide-open fields, their crops chopped down after being harvested, offering them no protection or coverage.

"Cotton country," Burke said, gesturing to the empty field.

Kane was used to corn and wheat fields, soybeans too, having grown up in the north. He'd never seen a cotton field before, even if there were no cotton bolls to look at. All that was left to see were brown, wilting rows of the crop's remains.

They followed along a dirt road while it was still dark, walking for miles. Eventually, the rain let up to a light mist, then stopped altogether. Kane's feet were frozen and chafing in his shoes, and every step he took was painful. He was sure there were raw blisters on his heels. But he tried not to think about it, keeping his attention ahead.

While his body was able to heal itself after an injury, all thanks to the lab rat he'd been turned into by the Republic years ago, the constant rubbing of his shoes was preventing his body from doing just that. He shivered, his teeth nearly chattering as he shoved his hands deep into the pockets of his wet jacket.

As dawn began to brighten the sky in the east, the night giving way to the brilliant colors of the morning sun as it crept over the land, he felt relief spread deep inside him. It was perhaps the first real invitation of a new day since his goodbye to Tala. And while it was still cold, the traces of the rainy night hanging in the air, he could feel the faint warmth from its rays.

Kane had no idea the time when they came to a copse of trees, taking cover, nearly collapsing on the damp earth. They had been walking for hours, with occasional chatter, cold, damp, and without sleep. In the distance, Kane could make out the scattered outlying buildings of a town.

Propping himself against a downed tree, he let out a sigh, instant relief in his feet from being off them.

"Any idea where we are?" Gerrit asked. "There's a town ahead. We need water."

Burke opened his sack and pulled out the last of their food supply, spreading it out across the ground: half a loaf of wheat bread, a sleeve of crackers, and three pouches of tuna. "This is all there is, boys."

Kane's stomach growled at the sight of it, as bland as it all was. It's what he'd been living on for weeks. Burke opened the sleeve of crackers, taking a few in his hand, then tossed it to Kane. It wasn't much, but it was better than nothing, and with dirty fingers, he took some, then passed them along to Gerrit.

After twenty minutes of rest, they rose to their feet. Kane's had the chance to heal while resting, though he knew they would be torn up again as soon as he began walking, all the constant rubbing on the wet leather.

They made it to the outskirts of the small town, which couldn't have a population of much more than a few hundred. The homes were small and rundown, and many of the businesses were closed, with boarded windows and spray-painted walls.

They wandered the poorly maintained main street, more gravel than pavement, until they found a convenience store.

"You know I've got nothing," Kane said. He hated that he had nothing to contribute. Without Burke or Gerrit, his provisions would've dried up weeks ago. He was living on their generosity. But now everything was running low, food, money, the battery life in their one remaining palm pad. There would be nowhere to charge it on their journey.

"I've got it," Burke said, stepping forward. He pulled his palm pad from his pocket, powering it on. "You two wait outside. Nothing makes people nervous more than three strangers walking into a small store together these days."

"Figure out exactly where we are," Gerrit said.

Burke nodded as Kane and Gerrit sat down on the curb across from a vacant lot of overgrown weeds that swayed in the breeze. Two cars drove past, all eyes on them, and Kane quickly looked away. He wasn't taking any chances. Colonies or not, there was still a hefty price tag on his head.

"Talk about the journey from hell," Gerrit said after a few minutes.

Kane let out a low, breathy chuckle as he kicked at the loose gravel at his feet. "That's an understatement."

"Marina's gonna be devastated when we show up without Corban," he said.

"That's her husband?" Kane asked. They'd spent weeks hiding out together, but they tried not to make anything personal. Kane knew little about them, and likewise, them about him. It was safer that way. "Still can't get a call out to her?"

"I've tried calling her two dozen times or more, but the reception towers must be knocked out. The data connection is weak, going in and out. No voice connection, and not strong enough to send a message out. Probably didn't help we were in such a remote area either. How we managed to get that National Statement is beyond me."

"I'm betting the Republic is limiting reception, interfering with the network transmissions. We saw that Statement because they let that transmission through," Kane said, recalling something Max described to him about it once.

Gerrit shook his head. "Fuckers. She was pregnant. Maybe she still is." He shrugged. "All I know was Corban went to Clara City to buy car parts. It's the closest major city to them. That's it, damn car parts. Then just disappeared into thin air," he said, snapping his fingers near Kane's face.

"Your sister from DeSoto too?" Kane asked.

He nodded. "Met Corban when he came to our hometown for a tractor auction. He's a cotton farmer. They ran off and got married couple months later, and she moved into Ozark Colony with him."

"That's where we are, right? Ozark Colony?" Kane asked.

Gerrit nodded. "In the delta, southeast of the Ozark Mountains. Not much to this area but small towns and farmland."

Kane looked around at the town they sat in the middle of. Its state of disrepair. It was what he imagined his hometown of Bedley might look like these days. It was never anything special. Just a small fishing town on Lake Michigan.

The best maintained buildings in sight around them were the convenience store they sat in front of, a small medical clinic a few doors down, and a church down the street, its steeple high above everything else, as if on lookout over the town. It looked almost new, maybe freshly painted, and this caught Kane by surprise.

There were people who believed in a higher power, though no one seemed to agree on what it was exactly, and it wasn't a particularly popular belief to have. Widely organized religion was hard to come by. At least in the Republic where the state was expected to come above all else.

"You think the UR will find you here?" Gerrit asked with hesitation.

"Sure as hell hope so," Kane said with a loud sigh, turning toward the sun which felt good on his face. It was the warmest it'd been in a while, and Kane shed his jacket, draping it over his duffel. "One way or another, I'm going to get back to her." They both knew who he meant.

Gerrit was quiet, silence settling between them that Kane didn't feel the need to disturb. A few minutes later, Burke emerged from the store, a plastic bag in one hand and a folded paper in the other.

"Got us six bottles of water, some peanuts, and chips. They didn't have much and shit was expensive," he exclaimed when he came up beside them. "Trust me when I tell you that place isn't as convenient as the sign says."

"And what's that?" Kane asked as he tipped his head toward the paper in his hand.

"Oh. A map. I don't know how long my battery will hold out on my palm pad. It got wet in our sinking boat, so I mapped out our route the old fashion way," he said.

"Didn't think 'bout that," Gerrit said, rising from the curb, brushing the gravel from his jeans.

"We don't know how long we're gonna be walking. Maybe we'll have better luck with reception here than we did in the Republic," Burke said. "Though I still got nothing yet."

"How far do we have to go?" Kane asked.

"It's about a mile and a half to the interstate highway. That way," Burke said, pointing west. "Then we go south for a while before heading west again. It's about forty miles to Marina's if we stick to the roads. Give or take."

Kane exchanged glances with each of them before sighing. "Time to get going."

"You called it Ger. The guy inside warned that MF have been spotted along the main roads. The Colonies' National Guard is trying to push them all back. Governor Blakely is up in arms. But MF just does whatever the hell they want," Burke said as they all stepped away from the curb and began down the street.

"I'm past giving a shit about MF," Gerrit spat.

"You'll care if you come up against a plasma charge," Kane said. While he could do incredible things, he wasn't infallible, and a plasma charge could just as easily be the end of him as anyone else.

They fell silent as they walked in stride beside each other until the interstate highway came into view, half a mile ahead.

"We should still stick to the fields," Kane said. "Shouldn't get too close. Just enough to keep it in sight."

Gerrit nodded in agreement, and the three of them turned south, skirting a field of haystacks.

"And what happens if we do stumble on MF?" Burke asked. "I think we should have a plan."

"We fight like hell," Kane said.

"About all there is to do," Gerrit said.

"No matter what, I'm not going back," Kane said, keeping his eyes forward. "I'm just not."

Their conversation waned, Burke humming a tune to himself, the only other sounds coming from birds overhead and cars on the road in the distance. Nearly an hour later, their fears were confirmed when three MF patrol vehicles came into sight, heading northbound. Gerrit was the first to spot them, and they all dropped to the ground, their faces in the dirt until long after they passed.

Back on their feet, they continued south. Kane looked at the sun high in the sky, squinting at its brightness. He could feel the warmth on his skin, and he breathed a deep breath of fresh air.

"Let me see that map," Gerrit said after a while.

Kane wasn't sure how long they'd been walking in silence, but the interruption seemed suddenly loud.

"This has us going right into Riverdale," Gerrit said sharply, looking up at Burke. "That's literally just on the west banks of the damn river, across from Clara City."

"There's no other way to get there," Burke protested. "Follow the highway."

"MF are sure to be everywhere there," Gerrit snapped. "Give me your palm pad."

Burke reached into his pocket, pulling it out. He powered it on, then handed it to his brother.

Pulling up a map, their GPS pinging them, Gerrit zoomed in on their location. "Look, we follow the highway until here. To Jordan. Then we go west on county road fifty-one."

Burke took the palm pad back, Gerrit pointing to the small dot on the map.

"We'll end up backtracking," he argued.

"Not more than a few miles. We're not going into Riverdale," Gerrit said flatly.

"I agree. That'd be suicide," Kane said.

Defeated, Burke sighed in frustration. He powered off the palm pad and returned it to his pocket while Gerrit folded their paper map and shoved it into a side pocket of his duffel, then quickly walked ahead.

By mid-day, they had all slowed their pace. They'd been going for almost eleven hours and awake for over twenty-four.

"I can't keep going like this," Gerrit finally said, the first one to say what was on all their minds.

"There's a town way ahead," Kane said, looking into the distance. Even he was fatigued. Tired, the sun on him all day, the sheer distance they'd gone. His body needed to recover after extreme physical exertions, like rowing them across the river. And he had no skills against mental fatigue. "We get there, and we find a place to rest."

"It better be a good place. An actual bed would be nice," Burke said. "I can barely keep my eyes open as it is."

Kane's shoulders slumped forward, his body heavier with every step. He focused on simply putting one foot in front of the next. It occurred to him that now that he'd finally reached the Colonies, he was going south. Tala was north. He was no longer sure what he was doing. His mind was delirious from a lack of sleep, and nothing seemed to make sense. North, south. Riverdale, Jordan. Republic, Colonies. It all blurred together. There was a certain point where exhaustion and insanity seemed to equate to the same thing. And if he wasn't there already, he almost was.

He turned his face skyward and inhaled slowly. He thought of the church he'd seen earlier in the day. Religion, faith, it had never been a part of his life. In fact, if he had an argument of the existence of a higher power, it would've been in opposition of one, based simply on life experience. But in that moment, his desperation had nothing left but to turn to it. Whether he believed or not didn't matter. Tala had never felt further away. There was nothing left but misery, and if there was even the smallest chance that something greater than mankind existed, this was absolutely the time to call upon it.

He wasn't even sure how to ask for help. Was it something he said aloud? Was it something he needed to hope for in his heart? Was it an image to conjure in his mind? He didn't know. So he decided to try all three.

In his mind, he saw Tala. He saw her running into his arms, and as he imagined it, he felt joy spread through him at the thought of them together again. She was his home.

Then his heart spoke, a faint whisper asking for the will and strength to continue. And the wisdom he knew he would need to make the right decisions.

"Whoever you are," he said quietly under his breath, "sustain me for this journey. Guide me. Give me the fortitude to go on even in the bleakest of circumstances."

"What'd you say?" Burke asked, glancing over his shoulder.

"Nothing," Kane said with a shrug as he kicked a rock. "Just doing a little praying is all," he admitted.

"Didn't take you for one of those types," Gerrit said without irony.

"I'm not. But I figured it's about all there is left to do right now," he said, his eyes fixed ahead on the town they were approaching.

"Well then, say one for me," Gerrit said.

Kane glanced at him and gave a solemn nod of his head.

On the outskirts of Fairhaven, the county seat according to the welcome sign, was a grove of trees, and the three of them wound their way deep inside, shielded by the dense woodland. Finding a small clearing, they dropped their bags, Burke and Gerrit letting out deep groans of relief from releasing the excess weight they'd been hauling.

"I'd say that one of us should stay awake, take turns sleeping," Burke said. His southern accent was thicker when he was tired. "But I think we're all past that."

"Sleep. Just stay alert," Gerrit said, and Kane nodded. It was true that none of them would be able to stay awake for long.

Kane lowered himself to the ground near some gnarled roots, and propping himself against the trunk of a tree, he folded his arms across his chest. Birds squawked loudly from high up in the branches. His head falling back, he closed his eyes, Tala briefly lingering in the back of his mind. But even she wasn't enough to keep him awake, and before he knew it, the world went dark.

❖

Leaving promptly at one, as Vulcan said, they had been on the road for eight hours, stopping once for a short food and restroom break. The van they drove was large, Vulcan up front with their driver, Shep, Tala in the middle row, and Cara in the back third row. And there was still room for their bags.

It had felt good to get out of the van, to stretch her body, but she was eager to get to their destination. Wherever that was. With nothing else to do on the drive, Tala had dozed on and off for the first half, but her mind was now awake, even if it was dark outside. Nightfall came so early in the winter months. She sat up in her seat, the row completely to herself, then leaned her body against the door, her hot breath fogging the glass of the cold window. She wiped it away, clearing her view of the passing landscape. All around her were wide-open fields, small groves of denuded trees in the distance, the land covered in a heavy blanket of snow, putting the world to bed. The moon, high in the sky, cast a radiant silver glow across the perfect white landscape, untouched by man. Mother Nature's winter masterpiece. But despite its beauty, it was seeing the world in black and white, and Tala couldn't help but find it cold and uninviting.

While Vulcan and Shep kept an ongoing conversation during the daylight hours, there was little talk now. It was mostly just the sounds of Vulcan's low, steady breathing from the front, the ragged, nasally sounds of Cara asleep behind her, and the hum of the van on the road. After weeks of sharing a room, she'd grown accustomed to Cara in the night. Once again, Tala felt the pangs of loneliness. And that only seemed to make the void between her and Kane that much greater.

In the dark silence, he filled her brain, and she couldn't help but wonder about him: where he was just then, what he was doing, if he could see the same nighttime sky from wherever he was. By leaving The Village, she couldn't help but feel the more miles she was putting between them, and it stole the breath from her lungs.

It had been nearly a month since they'd said goodbye, the hardest goodbye she'd ever had to make. There were too many people she'd had to say goodbye to, and too many people she'd lost without one at all. None of it was easy, no amount of time and distance filled those voids. She simply had to find ways to live around them.

She knew no decision in life could be undone. And she was filled with regret. But she had to keep going to make it worth something, to mean it wasn't in vain. And she knew that Kane, wherever he was, was fighting to make it back to her. Her heart clung to that certainty.

After a while, all the quiet around her, the monotony of the landscape, Tala felt her eyes grow heavy. Just like every night, her mind summoned Kane, and slowly she drifted off.

Kane woke, his body shivering. The sun was long gone, and he breathed into his hands to warm them, his breath visible in the dark. Putting on his jacket, he stretched his body to wake it up, then woke Gerrit and Burke. Both were slow to stir, their exhaustion etched across their faces despite their rest. They each ate a tube of peanuts and the tuna, drank some water, then headed out of the woods and back toward the highway.

Unlike the last several nights, there were stars high and bright in the sky, and Kane couldn't help but sneak a peek. He looked for the few constellations he knew. They were the flicker of a thousand lights on the backdrop of night. He thought of the ten-year-old version of himself, lying on the rickety remains of the old fishing docks in Bedley, looking up at each of those stars with wonder, believing in his heart that each one was a possibility for the future. A new sense of serenity came over him, and he felt a rejuvenation deep inside. Maybe it was because he'd finally gotten sleep.

Maybe it was because he'd prayed. Though he had no way to know either way.

The moon overhead was luminous, casting a glow on the ground below. Because of the conditions in the Republic, few cars were found on the roads after dark. It was a sure way to attract attention. But here, the cars drove freely, their headlights bright beacons in the darkness.

Kane knew their advantage was the cover of night, but it was also the advantage of any Militia Forces in the area. He had to stay alert. Keeping the highway still in their sights, they walked mile after mile, stumbling here and there over rocks and the uneven earth of the empty fields.

"I gotta ask," Burke said, not long after they passed the outskirts of another small town to the east. "How'd you end up with Tala Alexander? I mean, isn't she kind of a big deal? An Alexander. The princess of the Republic or something?"

Kane grinned to himself. Theirs was his favorite story. "Not such a princess. She was working alone one night when some guys jumped her. I was nearby, so I helped her out," he said, leaving out the finer details, including the fact that she'd been MF.

"Were you something big in the Republic too? Until you got your face plastered across the news alerts," Gerrit said.

"Nah. I was a nothing as far as the Republic was concerned," Kane said.

"Classic star-crossed lovers' story," Burke said with a chuckle.

"I'm not sure it's quite as dramatic as that," Kane said. The night they met played like a movie in his mind. He knew from the very beginning that meeting her was going to change things for him. He didn't know how, but he knew she would. And that's exactly what had happened. She changed everything.

As they continued into the night, the temperature continued to drop, and neither the pockets of his jeans nor the pockets of his jacket did little for his frozen hands. They all picked up their pace, tired as they were, trying to keep themselves as warm as they could.

The fields eventually gave way to rows and rows of railroad beds, trains both coming and going. They were careful to stick to the shadows, avoiding crews on the clock as they hopped over the lines of the railroad terminal until finally, it was far behind them.

Just after midnight, they arrived in Jordan, a small city, yet large enough to still have a few businesses open at that late hour. Burke restocked their food and water supply at another convenience store, and the three of them took a seat outside a twenty-four-hour liquor store, eating soggy, pre-packaged sandwiches and chips and downing their water. Kane's quench was insatiable.

"Figure about another seven hours or so," Burke said between bites of food. "About twenty miles."

"My legs are going to fall off," Gerrit said. His teeth chattered in the cold. "I really don't think I can make even another two."

Kane sighed in understanding. The few hours of sleep they got was good, considering he'd been propped up against a tree, but it was wearing off, leaving more exhaustion in its wake. And the cold didn't help anything. It wasn't cold like in Columbia City this time of year, it wasn't below freezing, but Kane was certain it wasn't far off.

"We could find a place around here and sleep again," Burke suggested.

Gerrit took a quick look around. "I'm not sure a nap here's a good idea."

"Well, if we do, we're better off heading out of town and finding something remote again," Kane said after finishing his last bite of food. Then he took a long swig of water, emptying the bottle.

"It's too damn cold to sleep anywhere out here," Gerrit said.

"True," Burke said quietly, then sighed. No one seemed to be eager to get back on their feet.

Kane reached for his bag and pulled out a dry pair of socks. Untying his boots, which were still damp, he slipped them off his feet. Changing his socks felt like a small piece of heaven, and he quickly put the boots back on before his feet had a chance to swell.

"Good idea," Gerrit said, doing just as Kane had.

A haggard truck pulled into the parking lot, so dated that Kane couldn't help but muse that it looked like an old gas-powered vehicle like in the old movies, though he knew that was impossible as gasoline as a transportation fuel was completely obsolete. A man well into his sixties hopped out of the cab, heading for the liquor store. He glanced at the three of them, then quickly went inside.

"That might be our cue," Burke said.

Gerrit let out a heavy exhale. "Just a few more minutes."

Kane leaned back onto his elbows, in no hurry to move. Seven hours was seven hours. A few more minutes delay wasn't going to hurt anything.

"I'm thinking we should steal the truck," Gerrit said with a nod toward the vehicle in front of them.

"Yeah, and I'm thinking running from MF is hard enough. Let's not add the local police to that list," Burke said.

The door of the liquor store opened, the man reappearing as though conjured by their conversation, bypassing them as he headed straight for his truck. Opening the driver-side door, he put his paper bag into the truck, the glass bottles of alcohol inside clanking together. Then he turned, carefully eyeing the three of them.

"Who're you? And what're you sitting out here for? It's damn near freezing out. You look plenty old to buy booze for yourselves," he said, his eyes narrowing as he approached them.

"Just passing through," Kane said with a furrowed brow.

The man nodded, his eyes lingering on each of them, then he looked around the empty parking lot. "On foot?" he asked.

"Yep," Gerrit said coolly.

Kane knew immediately where this was going and cast an uncertain glance at Burke.

"You come from the Republic?" the man asked bluntly as he hooked a thumb through a belt loop on his jeans.

"Is it that obvious?" Kane asked, hearing the sharpness in his tone. He knew they looked out of place. Disheveled after weeks in a cabin with no plumbing and a full day of walking. Probably smelled as bad as they looked.

"Well, where you headed? Maybe I can help you out," the man said.

Kane eyed him dubiously. "What's in it for you?"

"What've you got?" he asked as he tipped his head to the side.

"Not much," Gerrit said.

"Well, I ain't gonna turn you into MF, if that's what you're thinking," he said. "But I'll give you a ride if you've got some money."

Kane rose to his feet, towering above the man, his jaw clenched as he studied him. "How far?" he asked, his gaze not dropping from the man's. He could hear the nervous irregularity of his heartbeats.

"Depends how much you've got," he said in an uneven voice.

"Edmond," Kane said.

"That's 'bout twenty miles," the man said. "Hundred bucks?"

Kane let out a laugh. "I don't think so. I think I could use the walk." Kane took a small step closer to the man, his eyes holding his.

"Okay," he stammered. "How 'bout fifty?" He nervously looked between Kane and the other two.

"I can do that," Burke said.

Kane still didn't break his gaze, letting his eyes bore down into the man. "Anything but the ride to Edmond and I'll make you regret you ever met us."

The man swallowed hard.

"We'll pay you afterward," he added sternly.

"How do I know you'll pay up?" he asked with a small quiver in his voice.

"You don't," Kane said flatly. "But we will. And if we don't, well, then you can go looking for MF."

"I'm not looking for no MF," the man said sharply.

"Good. Neither are we. Doesn't change anything though. We'll pay you when we get to Edmond," Kane said with finality. He grabbed his bag, Burke and Gerrit rising to their feet. "We'll ride in back," he said coolly as he tossed his bag over the side of the truck bed, then slung his body up, hopping inside.

Within minutes, Gerrit and Burke beside him, they were getting on the highway, westbound, Kane watching the road signs to make sure they were on track.

The world went by in a blur, and soon they had left behind the lights of Jordan entirely, heading into a dark abyss of night. Despite the biting cold, it was exhilarating to be moving again, and Kane once again felt a resounding placidity take hold deep within. *Tala,* he thought, *I'm coming.*

Like it had been their entire journey, the landscape was flat with mostly bare fields, a few trees here and there. At some point, they passed a field of wind turbines, at least a hundred of them, the giant blades rotating in the dark, reflecting the moon.

Burke powered on his palm pad, watching the red dot marking their location as it moved along the highway, and eighteen miles later, he gave a solid bang with his fist on the back window of the cab. "We can walk from here," he said to Kane and Gerrit.

When the truck came to a stop, the three of them jumped out, their feet landing on the ground with loud thuds.

Burke went to the driver's side window as the man rolled it down. "Fifty?" he asked.

The man's eyes caught Kane's, and he shuddered as he nodded.

"Give me your palm pad," Burke said impatiently.

The man handed it to him, careful to avoid Kane's gaze. Burke scanned a barcode on the man's palm pad, instantly transferring the money to him, then handed it back.

"Th… thank you," the man said, and before anyone could respond, he quickly rolled up his window and peeled out, the bald tires of his truck screaming loudly in the still of the night.

"Wasn't sure about him," Gerrit admitted as he hoisted his bag over his shoulder.

"He just wanted the money," Kane said.

"You sure made him nervous," Burke added with a laugh.

A smile tugged at the corner of Kane's mouth. "Come on. Let's go."

"Guys, I've got service!" Burke announced triumphantly, looking up at them. "Should I call her?"

"It's late and we're almost there. We've come this far. No sense in dragging her out into the night," Gerrit said.

"Okay," Burke said with a resigned sigh.

The three set off, once again on foot, though the mood among them had shifted dramatically, their exhaustion ebbing for at least a short while.

Half a mile down the road, they turned onto a gravel road, their shoes kicking up dust with every step, the gravel crunching beneath each footfall. They walked in silence, drenched in silver moonlight, side-by-side, for another mile. A farmhouse set back from the road came into view. Burke was the first one to come to a stop, the others following him a moment later.

He looked down at the palm pad in his hand, then glanced up at each of them. "We're here," he finally said.

Relief settled on each of them as they stared up the drive at the darkened house, white with black shutters on the front and second-story windows. To the right of the house stood a large barn, a silo beside that, a tractor and a tractor on steroids parked between them.

"Well, let's go," Gerrit said, interrupting the silence.

In unison, they stepped forward, slowly at first, then quickly picking up their pace until they were in a near sprint, headed for the front door.

Breathless, Burke was the first one onto the small porch, Gerrit behind him while Kane lingered on the bottom step.

Burke knocked, the rapping of his fist on the wooden door sounded loud, almost menacing at that late hour. He knocked a second time, harder.

A crash from somewhere in the house was heard, and the men exchanged glances.

"Marina?" Gerrit called out.

There was silence.

Burke knocked again.

"Who is it?" a woman called through the closed door, and Kane heard the trepidation in her voice.

"Marina, it's us! It's Burke and Gerrit!" Burke yelled, his voice booming in the quiet.

There was a brief moment of silence, then slowly, the door opened with a creak. Burke tipped his head to the side, and the door was suddenly thrown open, a woman with a head full of brown curls lurching through the doorway into Burke's arms.

"You scared me!" she yelled while she cried, clinging to Burke like her life depended on it.

"Sorry, we didn't mean to," he said gently. "We've been walking for almost twenty-four hours now."

Marina pulled away, wiping at her tears as she looked at Gerrit, then threw her arms around him, crying harder.

"I can't believe you got out," she said, her voice muffled, buried in the collar of Gerrit's jacket. When she pulled away, she looked sheepishly at him. "Corban?" she asked, her voice thick.

Burke and Gerrit exchanged a silent glance, then looked at Marina.

"I'm sorry, Mare," Gerrit said quietly with a shake of his head. "We couldn't find him."

"But it doesn't mean he's not somewhere," Burke added quickly.

Marina's breath caught, but after a moment, her face hardened, and she exhaled slowly. "Okay," she said, her voice quiet but steady. "We can talk more about it later." She turned, her eyes finally finding Kane. "Who're you?"

"Oh," Burke said, clearing his throat. "This is a friend of ours. We've all been hiding out together."

"I'm Kane," he said, his voice low and gruff, full of exhaustion.

Marina's eyes flickered between her brothers, then back to Kane. "What're you looking for?"

"He's trying to connect with the Rebels," Gerrit said.

"The Rebels?" she exclaimed as she took a step back.

"I don't mean any trouble," Kane said.

"He's trying to get back to his girl," Burke said, and Kane was thankful he kept Tala's name out of it. "We'll vouch for him. He just needs a place until he can connect with someone. He's come all this way with us."

Marina studied Kane for a moment, then took a breath. "Fine. If you vouch for him," she said, nodding at Burke.

"Thank you," Kane said, though it sounded feeble.

"I've got beds for all of you. The baby's sleeping. So you better keep it down or you're gonna be up with her," she said, stepping into the house.

"You had her," Burke said joyfully.

"Of course I had her. Do I look pregnant?" she said with an eye roll. "Don't answer that," she snapped quickly as she turned on her heel, both Gerrit and Burke taking defensive steps backward.

"Didn't say a word," Gerrit said in amusement as he held up his hands.

Marina's eyes narrowed as she looked between them, then she finally cracked a smile.

Kane was the last one into the house, stepping into a cozy living room with a couch and a loveseat, thick curtains hanging beside the front window.

"There's a bedroom upstairs with bunks," she said with a nod at her brothers. "You two work that out," she said, more like a mother than a younger sister. "And you," she said, turning to Kane. "I'll grab some sheets and blankets. There's a couch in the den. Though I can't guarantee you won't hear baby Iris from in there, and it can be loud right off the kitchen. But it'll give you a bit of privacy."

Kane gave her the best smile his exhausted self could muster. The idea of a warm place to sleep sounded like bliss. He couldn't care less that it was a couch. "Thank you for this."

In less than thirty minutes, Kane had taken his turn showering in piping hot water, then crawled into his make-shift bed on the couch in the den. The sheet beneath him was soft and the blanket Marina gave him was thick and heavy. Lying back, his head sinking into the down pillow, he thought of Tala. One step closer, he told himself. With a smile lingering on the corners of his mouth, he rolled to his side and closed his eyes. And until his body finally shut off for the night, she was going to be the last thought to fill his mind.

SIX

Tala woke with a start by the slam of a car door. Her eyes shot open, and she sat upright, taking a glance around. They were at a convenience store, Shep now gone from the van. The lights outside the store were so bright that she winced as she looked out the window. They were surrounded by city, glowing lights in the darkness as far as she could see. She peeked at the time, five-thirty in the morning, and yawned, reaching her arms out, stretching her body.

She noticed the hydrogen pumps behind them. Though not the most economic source of fuel, many vehicles still ran on it. "Don't we need to refuel at any time?" Tala asked Vulcan who was now awake and busy with his palm pad in the front seat.

Vulcan let out a low chuckle. "You assume because our van isn't new that it's antiquated. No, we converted all our vehicles to plasma fuel. It's better for long drives. We're frequently going cross-country distances."

"Oh," she said. She hated how little she knew of the world outside of her former life in Columbia City. "Where are we?" she asked.

"The eastern edge of the Rocky Mountains."

Tala looked out the window, turning in her seat until she saw them. Even through the darkness, the snow-covered raised mass of land made her breath hitch. Starkly contrasted with the night sky, they were more magnificent than she'd ever imagined, and she stared in awe out the rear window at them.

"That's where we're headed," he said with a nod toward the mountains. "Hope you don't get car sick."

Tala turned back forward. "I guess I wouldn't know. Never driven through anything like that."

His lips pursed as he looked over his shoulder, no doubt thinking what she felt. She was like a child seeing the world for the first time.

Shep opened the door with a yawn and climbed back into the driver's seat, handing a cup across to Vulcan. Tala knew the smell from anywhere, and her mouth salivated, instantly craving it. Coffee.

"You can just buy coffee at a convenience store around here? Not a coffee house?" she asked, her disbelief obvious. In the Republic, it was a sometimes limited and always expensive commodity. "That smells incredible," she said quietly to herself.

Shutting the door loudly, Shep started the van back up. "Sorry," he said. "Should've gotten you one."

"Most coffee comes out of South America," Vulcan said between sips. Steam rose from the small vent to drink from. "The Republic doesn't have the greatest relationships with those countries. It's a far more common good than you think. You can easily get it pretty much anywhere outside the Republic."

Her ignorance once again felt conspicuous. But she was thankful that Vulcan wasn't condescending when he spoke to her. If he thought it, he didn't show it.

"You know, there's a small coffee shop in The Village," he said.

"Where?" she gasped, wondering how she never knew this.

"Second floor, south wing. We don't serve it with breakfast in the mornings to support the shop's business," Vulcan said casually. "The Bean."

She would be looking for The Bean as soon as they returned to The Village.

Getting back onto the highway, they headed west, directly toward the mountains. Suddenly, Tala's world fell away. She couldn't take her eyes off their grandiose beauty, a white, overpowering silhouette in the night, and she was filled with anticipation.

Reaching the foothills, they began their ascension, and Tala watched as the snowy cliffs grew steeper and steeper, the urban landscape in the valley quickly giving way to a dense forest of evergreen trees.

Tala lost all track of time, their van eventually leaving the main roads for narrower passes, the snowpack deeper and deeper with every mile they climbed. They weaved around bends and sharp corners, and a queasy feeling deep in Tala's belly began to form, starting out small, then quickly growing. She let out a groan as she swallowed hard.

"You okay?" Vulcan asked with a look back at her. "You don't look so good."

"You called it," she said weakly. "My stomach can't handle this."

"Here," he said, handing her a small packet and a bottle of water. "Those should help. But will take about ten minutes to kick in. Small sips of water."

Tala took them from him, tore the packet quickly, then swallowed the two pills. She only prayed she could keep them down long enough for them to work.

"I know it's cold, but open your window a bit. The fresh air will help too," Shep called back to her, addressing her in the rearview mirror.

She pressed the button on the inside of the door, the window lowering, the biting air from outside rushing into the van. Tala reached for her jacket, throwing it over her chest and arms. Cara woke with a start, sitting bolt upright. Her eyes met Tala's, and she seemed to understand. She quietly slid across her seat, away from the draft.

Tala lifted her chin, taking in deep breaths of the fresh air. The cold stung in her lungs but the nausea was beginning to subside, and after fifteen minutes, she closed the window.

"Better?" Cara asked as she yawned.

"Much," she said, nodding. She caught a grin on Shep's face in the mirror.

They continued their climb. And just when Tala thought they had reached the summit, another new peak emerged before them, cloaked in snow and ice that glimmered in the moonlight. They wound their way up the narrow roads, high walls of snow on both sides from plows. She'd never seen so much snow in her entire life. They would get copious amounts in the city after a winter storm, and when there was no place for it, the plows would pile it in the middle of the streets. But that didn't compare to this in the slightest.

Just after six-thirty, they turned down the narrowest road yet, a layer of snow and ice covering the ground, and just wide enough for one vehicle, a steep cliff dropping off to the side of the van. Tala stole a glance below, and even with her limited visibility in the dark, her heart caught in the back of her throat. She quickly looked away, then slid across the seat to the opposite side, catching her breath.

Shep was unfazed by the cliff, navigating around the snowy bends and curves with ease, though Tala wished he would slow down. Their drive taught her two things she hadn't known about herself: that she got car sick, and that her small fear of heights was actually a huge fear of heights. Being in tall skyscrapers in the city with walls and windows, and even railings, had given her a sense of security. But out here, there was nothing but a few feet of clearance between them and the cliff edge. This was a whole new experience of heights.

In the distance, a ribbon of orange from the rising sun crested along the top of the mountain ridges, brightening the world around her. After winding for another half hour, the road suddenly widened as they reached a summit, shallow canyons and valleys in the distance. Just ahead was a looming concrete wall and security gate. To the right of the gate, in oversized black letters that were lit up brightly from behind were the words *Camp Washington*.

Tala sat up, leaning forward for a better look. The concrete wall, at least fifteen feet high with curled razor wire strung across the top, seemed to go on as far as her eyes could see in both directions. Whatever was inside that gate wasn't meant to get out, and whatever was outside wasn't meant to get in.

Four soldiers stood in two booths at the entry point on both sides of the gate. They wore dark gray camouflage fatigues and a heavy black vest across their chest, the words Military Police in bold white letters. Each carried an automatic rifle slung over their shoulder and a handgun holstered at their side. It reminded her strongly of the Militia Forces Academy where she'd done her training.

Both Shep and Vulcan rolled down their windows as two soldiers approached their vehicle, each with a small device in their hand.

"Morning," the one said to Shep as she stepped up beside the window, a white fog in the air from her breath. Even from the backseat, Tala felt the frigid bite in the air as it flooded the van. "Identification," she said. The other soldier stood alongside Vulcan's side of the van.

Shep and Vulcan handed over their palm pads, and each MP used the device to scan them, then handed them back.

"How about those two?" the soldier at the driver's side asked as she peered into the back of the van.

Tala pulled her palm pad from her pocket, opening her identification app, and Cara passed hers forward. She handed both to Shep who gave them to the soldier at his window.

Tala shivered, though no one else seemed bothered by the cold, least of all the police standing outside.

"Tala Alexander," the woman said, looking up from the palm pad. "I know she's an expected guest, but she still needs to register. You'll have to take her to the security office."

"Yep," Vulcan said with a nod. "I know the drill."

"I know, Captain. Just doing our job," she said.

"Keep it up."

Captain?

Both officers raised their right arm, their fingers grazing their brow in salute, their faces hardened and stern. They held their position for a few seconds, then both relaxed, dropping their arms. They retreated from the vehicle, returning to the booths, then the dual doors of the gate separated, retracting from each side. A moment later, Shep drove onto the base and immediately turned right into the security office parking lot.

"You guys wait here," Vulcan said as he zipped his jacket and opened his door. "Tala, you're with me."

She grabbed her coat which she'd been using as a blanket just as a rush of cold filled the van. She quickly slipped her arms into it, the inside fleece lining soft on her skin. She zipped it up and cinched the waist, then pulled the faux fur-lined collar high around her neck. Vulcan was a dozen steps ahead of her, and she had to jog to catch up.

"What is this place?" she asked, falling in stride beside him, her two steps to his one. It was like trying to stay caught up with Kane all over again.

"It's a specialized military training base," he said, glancing sideways at her.

"The Rebels? I mean, the Revos?" She still wasn't used to the different name.

"Yep. Among others. We run coordinated military operations through here."

"Coordinated? Like, other governments?" she asked. The chill was so cold that she felt ice forming on her top lip.

"I told you," he said coolly, "the Republic thinks we're just a nuisance. But while we may not be huge in numbers, not compared to them, we've got strong backing. You're about to see for yourself."

She was relieved when they finally reached the door of the building. The security office was quiet, one man in fatigues sitting behind a counter watching something on a tablet. With chairs around the perimeter of the room, it looked like a small waiting room at a doctor's office. Most importantly, though, it was warm.

"Need a clearance pass," Vulcan said as the man stood up.

"Captain," he said, saluting him as the military police had. She couldn't help but steal a glance at Vulcan. With his cargo pants and t-shirts, usually the cuffs rolled to his shoulders, and his dreads that hung to the middle of his chest, he seemed the most unlikely military captain. She thought of Captain Kole back at Command in Columbia City. Always in a suit, always a stern expression, always a furrowed brow. Trimmed hair, clean-shaven. While he was a loyal servant to Thias, he was a strict leader to the MF that worked at headquarters.

"I need your identification credentials," the soldier said to Tala.

She handed him the palm pad, and he scanned it, then went to a computer with a holographic screen like the ones in The Village.

"Please step over here, in front of the screen," the soldier said to her, motioning to a large blue screen against the wall.

She stepped in front of it, and he took a quick photo of her. He returned to his computer, then scanned her palm pad once again before finally handing it back to her. "Here you go," he said. "You have temporary Delta Code security clearance. You are prohibited from carrying a weapon. It'll expire in ninety-six hours." He sounded tired, and she wondered how long he'd been sitting at his desk.

"We'll get checked into Anthem House, then grab something to eat," Vulcan said once she took her palm pad back. "After that, I've got your permanent security detail assigned to you, so we'll get you two set up."

Tala followed him as they left the building, stepping back into the cold. As they walked back to the parking lot, the sharp bite from the cold returned in her lungs. She was sure it was something she could never acclimate to.

Shep drove their van across the base, its own city perched high and alone in the mountains. They passed formations of soldiers dressed in heavy fatigues in a large open square of gravel, snow, and ice, buildings surrounding it on all sides. While all the buildings they passed looked similar to one another, with red brick and concrete exteriors, one, in particular, stood out among the others. It was several stories high and made of gleaming glass with three levels of balconies overlooking the square on the second, third, and fourth floors. Snow-covered hedges and ornamental pines decoratively lined the ground around it.

"That's the Mirari building," Cara said as Tala gazed out the van window at it. "It's the command center, the heart of the base."

They drove down paved roads lined with tall evergreens, the snow sprinkled on the needled branches turned to ice. Tala read the signs in front of every building they passed, the Indy Dormitory Complex to the left, the Lincoln Training Center and the T. Allen Logistical Center on the right. Rounding a bend, the Nicholls Administrative building came into view, and then finally Anthem House.

They stepped into the building's foyer where a short woman in camo fatigues met them at the door. "Captain," she said as she saluted at the sight of Vulcan. "You're right on time. Here are your keycards, each of your rooms is ready."

"Meet here in thirty," Vulcan said, his eyes sweeping the room.

Tala took the white plastic card and turned it over in her hand, a barcode on the back.

"Room 203, up the stairs and to the right," the woman said to Tala. The others seemed to know exactly where to go and set off for their rooms.

Clutching her bag, Tala ascended the large staircase off the foyer, just behind Shep and Cara, to the second floor, her fingers dragging across the smooth, oak railing. At the top, she turned right and found her room around the corner.

It was small but tidy. Bright white walls and large windows, a small dresser along a wall between two of the windows, a chair in the corner, and a double bed with a thick, light gray comforter spread across it.

Her sleepless night catching up with her, Tala stepped into the small bathroom just off the room and splashed cold water over her face. She glanced at her reflection and sighed at the exhaustion in her eyes. She didn't know what the day had in store for her, but she knew she needed to be prepared for anything. She wasn't about to look as tired as she felt.

She rummaged through her duffel, finding her makeup and a hairbrush, then went back to the bathroom. The loud rumbles of military jets suddenly filled the quiet. Tala could feel their power in her chest and knew they were close. She counted ten fly overhead before it fell quiet again.

Tala finished her makeup, just enough to freshen her face. There was no reason to be glamorous now. She brushed her hair and pulled it back into a tight pony, then went back to her bag, pulling out a change of clothes. She was relieved to get out of the clothes she'd traveled all night in, putting on a fresh pair of jeans and a thick sweater. She now understood why Vulcan told her to dress warmly. Looking at the time, she grabbed her coat, then headed for the foyer.

Right on time, Tala, Vulcan, Shep, and Cara left the guest house on foot down the snow-packed street. The morning sun was eclipsed by the mountain peaks in the distance, and despite its bright rays, it offered no relief from the chill in the air. It was a cold like nothing Tala had ever felt. It seemed to go straight to the bone. She pulled her collar higher, then shoved her bare hands into her pockets, wishing she had gloves. Tucking her chin into her jacket, she followed quickly behind the others, her eyes wandering curiously from building to building.

Just ahead, something caught her attention, high above the tops of the buildings. There seemed to be a ripple of color in the air, like a soap bubble. Then it disappeared as quickly as she'd seen it. Tala glanced around, spotting a second small ripple in the sky to her left, the same faint wave of colors that quickly disappeared.

"Cara," she called ahead. "Do you see something in the sky?" she asked, her eyes darting rapidly from left to right. Soon she was spotting them everywhere.

"They're holoshields," Cara said, peering over her shoulder at Tala.

She raised a brow in confusion as they passed a formation of soldiers, their chins and mouths covered by a balaclava, their cheeks pink from the cold.

"See the tower?" Cara pointed to a tall signal tower reaching above the surrounding buildings. Tala quickly noticed the same towers scattered all around. "They project a holographic image above the base. They shield it visually from the air."

Tala's eyes lifted skyward in disbelief as she smiled. "No prying eyes from satellites."

"Or reconnaissance jets and drones," Vulcan added.

They passed another dormitory complex, another logistical center, and a row of training centers. Tala's teeth chattered as she walked, taking each step cautiously across the icy ground. Her eyes watered, her tears freezing on her lashes, making them stick to each other when she blinked. When finally the mess hall came into view, her relief was palpable.

Cara let out a chuckle as she glanced at Tala. "A little cold, are you?"

"I didn't know cold like this existed," she said as they made their way inside. Tala took a deep breath of the warm air, though she didn't remove her coat until halfway through their breakfast, after she finally felt the ice in her blood thaw.

When they were finished, they dumped their trays, then bundled back up, Tala bracing herself to go back into the cold.

"Cara, Shep," Vulcan said as they made their way across the mess hall toward the door, "I presume you can handle yourselves for a while. Tala and I are going to meet her new detail."

"Really?" Cara asked with a dull expression. "Of course we can manage on our own."

Vulcan chuckled. "Then I'll see you later."

Outside the mess hall, Cara and Shep headed back toward the guest house while Vulcan turned left. Rounding a corner, the Mirari building came into view across the square, or the yard, as Vulcan referred to it during breakfast conversation. The building lit up crystal blue like the sky, the sun gleaming brightly off it. Vulcan paid no attention to Tala as she wondered at the sights around her, taking it all in. They walked in silence, mostly because it was too cold to talk.

They took a flight of stairs to the first tiered balcony, the largest of the three, of the Mirari building, and Vulcan used his security credentials at the door. She followed him inside where she was met with a wave of welcomed warmth. She glanced around, finding herself standing in an expansive lobby with four floors of windows above her and a large staircase rising to each floor. Small seating areas scattered the room, and on a far wall hung the focus of the large atrium. It was the same shape as the map in Vulcan's office, painted with black and white swirled lines, much like strata lines in a rock formation, she thought. Though she wasn't sure what it was or what it meant, she couldn't help but think she would soon find out. The foyer's modern look took her by surprise. It was the last thing she expected to find on a military base where all the other buildings were so simplistic.

People moved about the room, paying no attention to them, most in fatigues or dress military uniforms, though some wore civilian clothes.

Without pause, Vulcan headed for the stairs, passing an administrative desk, Tala following closely behind, though her eyes wandered. Although she was surrounded by walls of windows from each floor above her, she could see nothing through them but warm, golden light.

On the third floor, Vulcan used his credentials to access a set of double doors, and Tala quietly followed him through. They were met by two military police who nodded at Vulcan as they continued down a long corridor, passing security-protected doors, walking in silence. Tala once again had to hurry beside his long strides. They rounded a corner, and Vulcan looked at her.

"Sorry Cara can't stay," he said.

"I just want her to find Kane," she said. "And I know she's the best for the job."

He nodded, saying nothing as they turned down another corridor. The bright lights above seemed to illuminate the white walls and ceiling. From somewhere in the distance, Tala could hear laughter as they passed two men in conversation, one in an officer's uniform, the other in a suit and tie. They both tipped their heads at them in hello as they went by.

"You know you're here to make a difference, right?" Vulcan said. "It's a big spot to fill, and you need to figure out a way to do it without Kane. Until we find him, that is."

"And what if you can't?" she asked, speaking the words she hadn't dare say until now.

He looked at her quietly, his lips pressed in a straight line. His silence was like a heavy weight pressing down on her chest, and she looked away from him, her emotion rising. She swallowed hard, telling herself this was not the time to consider any of this.

Finally, they came to a stop at one of the many doors along the hall. Vulcan opened it and held it for her while she stepped into the room. It was a small lounge, with two sofas and two large windows overlooking more brick buildings, a formation of soldiers marching in unison down the street below.

"Wait here. Your detail will be here in a few minutes," Vulcan said, then closed the door, leaving her alone.

Tala quickly shed her jacket, laying it over the armrest of the couch. Across the room was a refrigerator cooler filled with water bottles, and she helped herself to one, then perused a bookshelf beside it. Four shelves of books. She thought of Kane. He'd liked to read. It was how he passed the time during his years at Stanger.

She took a large gulp of water; it was cold on her teeth and she sucked in a breath. All the books, she realized, were history books. Some United States history, some world history, both before and after the Great War. As her eyes roamed over the titles, the door to the room opened, and Tala turned quickly, a man in uniform appearing before her.

Her heart suddenly dropped, the air in her lungs turning solid, her body frozen in place.

"Hi, Tala."

SEVEN

"Maverick?" she gasped, her eyes wide as she stared at him.

He gave her a sheepish smile. "It's me," he said with a small nod of confirmation.

There he stood, only feet away from her, dressed in gray camo like every other soldier on base. It had been over five years, and he looked different, yet so much the same. His brown hair still had natural blond wisps, and while it was still cut short on the sides, the top was longer than she'd ever seen him wear it before. There were creases around his hazel-brown eyes that she never remembered, but she still saw the familiarity in them. She saw Mila in them. He was still tall, that would never change, but he was more filled out, his chest and shoulders broader, stronger.

"You… you…" she stammered, unable to say the words. Tears rushed to her eyes and she fought to blink them away. "I went to your funeral. I spoke at it," she said, hearing the accusation in her voice.

"I know," he said gently. He stood near the closed door, keeping the distance between them. "I didn't want any of it, all the hurt for my family, for you."

Despite herself, a tear rolled down her cheek, and she quickly brushed it away. "This whole time you've been with the Rebels? The Revos," she quickly corrected herself.

He nodded, frowning.

She took a sharp breath, bringing her hand to her head, a headache taking hold.

"I was recruited by the UR right out of secondary school," he said.

"So, Militia Forces… you were a double agent?" she asked.

"Yes," he said quietly, though his voice was strong. "I was tasked to locate and plant a bug on server twelve, the Republic's government server. A series of non-lethal attacks were to be carried out so that the UR could then observe government emergency response protocols."

"Were you successful?" she asked, folding her arms across her chest, her tears drying. She was filled with conflicting sadness, shock, and anger.

He shook his head. "The mission was compromised. The UR monitoring the situation picked up a tail MF had on me. We didn't have time for an alternative exit strategy. The Revos made a public display of abducting me. And it was all reinforced when they had a body identified as mine wash up in the bay."

Tala's mind swarmed with his story, and feeling dizzy, she moved to the sofa. "I… I need to sit," she said taking a seat on the stiff cushion. "No," she said a moment later, "I need to stand." She started pacing as she rubbed at her temples. She felt a hysterical laugh bubbling up inside her, and she swallowed hard to keep it at bay. It was too much to process.

"You can't imagine how painful it was to leave you and my family like that," he said.

"Oh, I can imagine," she snapped. "I was just on the other side of that."

Maverick went quiet, crossing the room and taking a seat. "Tala, I'm so sorry. I know that probably means nothing, but I am," he said as he looked up at her.

She moved to the sofa, though kept distance between them as she sat. Her tears reappeared, filling her eyes. She lifted her head, catching his gaze, seeing him through the pools in her eyes. Those eyes she had known so well.

"Our friendship? If you were with the Revos all along, what was our friendship? Was I just an in?" Her heart hurt just asking the question.

"No!" he asserted, his voice rising. "You and I, that was all real. In the beginning, I didn't want anything to do with you. Because you were an Alexander. But in the academy, I saw something in you that just drew me to you. I'd never known anyone to work as hard as you did for your place with MF. Our friendship was real in every way. I'd never had a friend like you."

Another tear ran down her cheek, but she couldn't take her eyes off him. He'd been her best friend, her safe haven when she had no one else. No one but Thias. But Thias had never been to her what Maverick had. She swallowed hard, unsure what to believe. Her heart told her it was all real, but her mind doubted everything.

"I swear to you on everything that you were never part of my mission," he said. "I would've refused if you had been."

"You don't understand how many lies I've been told, by the people who mattered most to me. I just don't know how to believe," she said, looking away, her gaze dropping to the floor.

Maverick fell silent.

"Do you know about Mila?" she asked quietly. She thought about his sister, her best friend, so far away.

He let out a slow exhale. "Yes. They told me. They also told me that you asked for protection for her. You have no idea what that means to me."

"Well, she stepped into your shoes in my life," she said, hearing the thick emotion in her voice. "She was my only link to you." She lifted her gaze, meeting his once again. "She is everything to me." And with that thought, she felt herself break. It was all too much. Thias. Ronin. Her parents. Mila. Kane. And now Maverick. Her heart didn't know how to hold it all.

Her tears spilling down her face like the breaking of a dam, her head fell into her hands, her breath ragged. One by one, the fortification walls she'd built around herself were crumbling. She couldn't understand how a heart as broken as hers could still beat. If only her tears could really drown her sorrows, could extinguish the searing pain she felt so deep inside. Maybe then she would finally be okay.

Then she felt them, warm and strong, as Maverick slipped his arms around her, pulling her close. Her face was on his chest, her cheeks hot and wet. She didn't know how to stop crying, her body heaving.

"I'm so sorry, Tala," he whispered sadly into her hair.

Despite herself, she wrapped her arms around him, then she let herself just be held.

That night, Tala sat on the edge of her bed in Anthem House, the dim light from the lamp on the nightstand glowing throughout the room. Maverick was now in the room across the hall. It was dark outside, snow beginning to fall. Though her tears had stopped hours ago, she still felt like a fragmented version of herself.

She thought about Maverick, her mind still processing him. How was it that in the blink of an eye she had lost so many people and now suddenly had one back?

She felt embarrassed that she'd fallen apart in front of him. But seeing him again, it was all too much for her. Everything in her heart and in her mind had converged and she couldn't stop herself. She bled every emotion, every burden she had been carrying with her for so long.

They had eaten dinner in the mess hall, catching the tail-end of it when most of the soldiers had cleared out. With so many things on her mind, Tala hadn't eaten much, and it was catching up to her now, her stomach growling.

It was surreal to sit across from him. She'd been without him for five years and though there was so much to tell him, she found she didn't know what to say. So instead, there was an uncomfortable silence between them, one that didn't go amiss by Cara. Though she said nothing, she was gentler with Tala, her voice softer when she spoke to her. Tala cringed, not wanting to be coddled.

Maverick was just as quiet around Tala, but she knew it wasn't because he didn't know what to say to her. It was because he was trying to read her. Would he still be able to after all this time? Knowing him seemed like a lifetime ago. She hardly recognized in herself the person he'd once known. Yet somehow, in some strange way, she couldn't help but think that he still could. Once upon a time, he knew her thoughts sometimes before she did. He'd known her in the least superficial way, though never romantic. She'd let him in. And there had to still be some of that woman left in her. At least she hoped that not everything about her was different. She didn't want all that had happened to have broken her, to have changed what was at the core of who she was. She hoped it didn't have that much power over her.

Now, all she craved was sleep, but despite her fatigue, there were too many thoughts in her head to be quieted.

A soft knock came at the door, and Tala went to it apprehensively.

"It's Cara," the voice on the other side called quietly.

She unlocked it to see Cara standing before her, still in the jeans and long-sleeve shirt she'd worn all day, her red ink just peeking out above the collar.

"I was hoping we could talk," she said.

Tala lingered quietly in the door for a moment, then stepped away, letting Cara brush past her.

"I'm sorry Maverick was such a shock," she said with contrition as she took a seat in the chair across the room. Tala took a seat on the bed, folding her legs beneath her.

"Shock is one word for it."

"I'm leaving tomorrow. Back to the Republic." Cara leaned forward, her elbows on her thighs. Her dark hair was pulled into a loose pony, a few stray strands falling around her face. "And I wanted you to know I'm going to do whatever I can to find Kane."

Her words were like music to Tala's ears.

"But I need you to do something," Cara said, her eyes shadowed in the faint light of the lamp. "I need you to keep fighting," she said steadily. "You can't be a victim. I know you're tougher than that. Your advoprop was good, but it doesn't stop there."

Immediately, Tala wanted to defend herself, but she held her tongue. Somewhere deep inside, she knew what Cara was talking about. She was letting circumstance control her. If she couldn't learn to control her emotions, she'd be doomed to ride their roller coaster forever.

"You've lost more than any one person should," she said gently, "but this is war now. And the heartache it leaves behind is never fair. You have to find a way to keep going. Kane was right when he said you were strong. I see it in you too. You need to stop underestimating yourself and what you're capable of. You'll never beat your brother otherwise."

Her words were like a reality-sucker punch to the gut. "Kane, Mila… they gave me something to fight for," Tala said. "And now I have neither."

"You still have to fight for them," Cara said. "They're both out there, and they need you to be the Tala we know you to be. And now you have Maverick back. I don't know anything about your friendship with him, but I can see it in the way you look at each other that there was a time when you both mattered to each other."

Cara held her gaze, and Tala wanted to look away. But couldn't. She nodded slowly. She was right, about all of it, and she hated that. Not because she didn't want Cara to be right, but because she felt it in herself, that she'd all but given up. She'd let her grief, her regret, her loneliness all take over her.

"It's just hard," she admitted after a minute, "reconciling what I thought I knew with everything I know now."

Cara nodded, seeming to understand. "The way I see it, you have two options. You can let it break you, or you can let it wake you up. Who're you going to be?"

Things seemed so insurmountable. But she told herself that anything was possible if she could just have the nerve to break the walls of conformity she'd lived within her whole life. She wasn't in the Republic anymore. She wasn't her brother's puppet. She wasn't a Preferred citizen or an MF agent. All that was left now was just Tala. It was time to create her own identity.

Who did she want to be?

In the Republic, she'd been afraid of the limits that society, that the legacy of her name, that her brother put on her. But here, she had no limits to restrain her. She could be as powerful as her will and determination would allow her to be. She could either let her fear stop her, or she could let it fuel her.

Kane would find her, just as he promised. And Mila had made it this far, she didn't have a reason to believe she couldn't make it further.

"Strong people aren't born, Tala," Cara said with a steady voice. "They're built on the foundation of struggle. They're created by the darkness they've conquered."

As she sat there, looking across the room at Cara, she felt something shift inside her. She hadn't come this far to only come this far. Her mind began to clear, and she felt a resolution taking hold.

Tala felt a light come on in her eyes.

"Make your brother regret ever doubting you," Cara said with a firm nod. She rose to leave, crossing the small room in only a few short strides, and as she reached for the doorknob she paused, turning back to Tala. "Vulcan wants us in the foyer at 7:20 tomorrow morning. Reveille is at seven."

"Reveille?" she asked.

There was a smirk on Cara's face. "Guess you'll find out at seven tomorrow morning," she said. "And Tala, I promise. I'll do everything I can to find him."

If there was anything to believe, anything to put her faith in, it was that.

Then she was gone, and Tala was left alone. The vortex in her mind had stilled. After locking the door, she crawled under the heavy blankets on the bed. Turning off the light, she rolled to her side, her mind summoning Kane's arms around her. But unlike all the nights before, when those arms were there to hold her together, this time they seemed to fortify her.

It was still dark when Tala woke the next morning, the moon casting a silver luster across the snow outside her window. Just as she was getting out of the shower, a loud sound rang out, a horn playing a tune she didn't recognize. She glanced at the clock to see that it was seven. The blaring tune was full of energy and quick in tempo, and she could only assume this was Reveille. A wake-up call.

At exactly 7:20, as Cara said, Tala met everyone in the foyer, and they quickly left Anthem House. Tala's breath caught as she stepped outside, the morning cold instantly shaking away any lingering sleepiness. She buried her face in her jacket as they set off on foot down the street. Vulcan and Shep were deep in conversation as they walked ahead of the group. Maverick was five steps ahead of Tala, Cara beside her.

They kept a brisk pace, and Tala felt the inside of her nose begin to freeze. Passing the Indy Dormitory Complex, soldiers dressed in the same fatigues Maverick wore, a heavy jacket and cargo pants, combat boots, a balaclava, and a cap on their head, moved in droves as the yard came into view, filling the vacancy with more people than she could begin to count.

"Keep up," Vulcan called over his shoulder as they pushed their way through the sea of men and women in uniform.

Tala quickened her pace, the cold burning in her chest with every breath. They crossed the yard and headed toward the Mirari building that overlooked it. Tala was on Maverick's heels as he took a flight of stairs to the first tiered balcony. Standing between Cara and Maverick, Tala looked out at the soldiers below as they swiftly organized themselves in neat rows from one side of the yard to the other. Off to the side, she spotted a flag flapping in the breeze.

"I forget how cold it gets up here," Cara said to Vulcan, her body giving a hard shudder, her breath appearing in puffs in front of her mouth.

"What's the elevation up here?" Tala asked, her body shivering despite her best efforts. She tried hard to think about anything other than how cold she was. The air even smelled cold, if that was possible.

"About nine-thousand feet," Vulcan said.

"That's high," she mumbled into her coat.

Maverick cast a sideways glance at her and smiled. "You get used to it."

She looked up at him. "I really don't think I ever would," she said. She looked out at the soldiers in the yard below, making up perfect square formations: ten squares across, ten squares down.

The crowd fell quiet, every person in uniform standing at strict attention facing the balcony where Tala stood. Even the breeze seemed to stand still.

A moment later, footsteps echoed in the frozen silence, and Cara gave Tala a quick elbow to the side. She turned her back to the yard, mirroring the others. She straightened her body, brought her hands behind her back and raised her chin. Her eyes suddenly grew wide and her jaw slackened as she watched a woman appear on the balcony above her.

Dressed in a long, black wool coat, she looked out over the yard that was now completely filled with military soldiers, her copper-red hair glowing in the light of the rising sun. There was no mistaking her. Victoria Barrington.

Tala took a breath in confusion while Victoria held the attention of the crowd, then a moment later, a loud and booming voice called out, slicing through the silence.

"Attention, left!"

In a swift, unison motion, everyone turned over their left shoulder, Cara reaching out her arms to turn Tala's body on command, and she was thankful for the assistance. A trumpet sounded, playing a melodic tune that

Tala had never heard, and it took her a few seconds to realize what every person in the yard was staring at: the waving flag.

The tune played on while the flag flapped in the breeze, the sun lighting up its red and white stripes. No sound but that of the trumpet echoed through the yard. Not even the birds overhead dared chirp or caw.

At the commencement of the song, a voice rang out, calling attention back forward, hers included. Tala watched as Victoria raised her right arm and saluted the troops below. A moment later, she turned and walked away, retreating into the Mirari building.

Tala's face screwed up, she turned to Cara. "I don't understand," she said under her breath.

A grin curled at the corner of Cara's mouth. "What don't you understand?"

"Victoria Barrington."

"Well, you may have met her as that in the Republic, but here we know her as President Victoria Merritt."

"President?" Tala asked, her head cocked to the side. "Of the Unified Revolutionaries?"

"No, Tala. Of the United States."

"What?" she gasped.

"Come with me, Tala," Vulcan said as he turned, walking away. Tala hurried after him, Maverick beside her. They stepped into the familiar lobby of the building, and Tala let out a sigh of relief to once again be indoors.

Vulcan opened a door near the main staircase, the lights of the small room automatically turning on as they detected their motion.

"Hang your coat in here," he instructed as he took his off, putting it on a hanger in an open closet. Both Tala and Maverick did the same, and despite the thick sweater, Tala rubbed her arms, still cold from being outside.

Taking a brisk pace, they left the coatroom and made their way to the staircase. Vulcan led them to the fourth floor where he used his credentials to open the doors. Then they made their way down a wide and long hallway, silently passing military police standing like sentries every ten yards, the sound of their shoes echoing with each step. Tala wanted to ask questions. Where were they going? How was Victoria Barrington president of a country she thought had been dead for nearly a century? But she knew she'd get nothing from him, so she instead continued to follow him in silence.

At the end of the hall, they came to large mahogany double doors where two military police stood at attention on both sides, one of whom put up a hand to halt them.

"Commander," he said into the comm just inside his ear, so small and discrete that Tala hadn't noticed it at first, "Captain Vulcan, Sergeant Sanders, and your guest have arrived."

They waited in silence outside the doors, Tala's heart beating in anticipation with every passing second. Then with a nod of his head, the officer entered a security code, opening the doors for them.

Tala stepped into a spacious room. A polished marble floor that reflected the light from the chandeliers above, a seating area with two red sofas that faced one another, an oval coffee table between them, then beyond that, a large desk set in front of five large windows overlooking the yard. But despite the grandeur of the room, Tala's eyes focused on only one thing.

Victoria.

She smiled as she rose from her chair across the room and rounded the desk. She looked as fashionable in her black pantsuit and stilettos as she had in her emerald gown at the president's birthday. But it wasn't her clothing that was striking, it was all her gorgeous copper-red hair, and those mesmerizing green eyes that were unlike anyone's Tala had ever met.

"Tala, it's so good to meet you again," she said kindly. "Please, sit," she said, making a sweeping gesture toward the oversized sofas.

Tala followed Vulcan, taking a seat between him and Maverick, sinking into the plush cushion as Victoria sat across from them.

"I had no idea when we met that—"

"That this is what I really did?" she said, finishing Tala's thought with a grin. "That was the point though. As a governor in the Colonies, Elias provides me a good cover."

"I guess I don't understand what's going on," Tala said. Everyone around her seemed to have all the answers while she had none.

"Tell me what you know about the former United States," she said.

Tala's brows furrowed. "Not much. They crumbled late in the Great War, invaded and bombed by former overseas allies that also assassinated their president. I think," she said, trying to recall the history lesson she'd had so many years ago. Her education never focused much on the United States. They were taught about the Republic.

Victoria nodded as she crossed her legs, her right ankle tucking neatly behind her left. "At that time, it was a multipolar world with many international states competing for influence and dominance in world affairs. It wasn't just the U.S. that collapsed during the Great War. Leading up to it, the fight was mostly abroad. With many overseas alliances and interests, the U.S. was a key player in that conflict, so when they were attacked on their homeland, their military ambitions proved to be too expensive and unsustainable, and they were unable to launch an effective counteroffensive. With the assassination of both the president and vice president, pervasive cyber-attacks, the failure of critical infrastructure, and the military destruction of many of their major cities, chaos erupted. The nearly instant crash of the financial sector left the economy in ruins, the health care system failed, and basic necessities became scarce. A savage black market was born. It became every man for themselves."

"Until my grandfather," Tala said, the picture clearing.

"Yes," Victoria said, folding her hands neatly in her lap. "In the beginning, it was Miles Alexander and Viktor Royer I. They earned the support of the people by amassing a militia army that provided protection and order, easily taking control of the northeast. They eventually combined efforts with Weston Allen, who operated similar control in parts of the Midwest."

This, Tala already knew. It was her family's legacy.

"They were highly supported by the people and therefore appointed themselves as the de facto government until an election could be instituted and a government decree created," Victoria said.

"Appointed themselves? They were elected," Tala argued.

Victoria pressed her lips into a line. "Never in the history of the Republic of Columbia has there ever been an election. They appointed themselves based on the assumption that they were the choice of the majority. And that's how they declared themselves a republic. Unable to recruit the south and the region west of the Mississippi, they drew the borders of what is the modern-day Republic, and the country was established."

"This isn't quite what I was taught," Tala said.

"No, it wouldn't be, now would it? You don't have to take my word for it. There is extensive documentation of this," she said. The room fell silent, Victoria watching Tala with patience. When she said nothing, Victoria continued. "The Republic's ascension to power was a rapid one. Not only was the region highly devastated by the war, but it also had the largest population of displaced people. Born of this were industrialization for rebuilding, science, technology, and innovation for advancement. Though there was great inequity in all of it. And while the country was taking off, people were heavily taxed. The vision was to have the most powerful country, which at the time meant it required the most powerful military, a costly endeavor at the expense of the people.

"In the midst of this, the people became divided on the direction they wanted the country to go in and dissension started to build. There were people who thrived in the new order. But the country was also built on the backs of many of its citizens, overworked and underpaid. It was those people who pushed for a change in leadership. It didn't take long for fighting to once again ensue, and as a result, Royer, Alexander, and Allen revoked all free elections indefinitely, permanently declaring themselves in their government positions. The hierarchy of citizenship was established, aimed at avoiding further division among the people. There were no longer political parties. For the country to run peacefully, they had to be one people for the Republic. This is, of course, an abridged version of history."

"They taught us that the Republic was successful in the beginning because it brought prosperity for the people. But I suppose that's all relative," Tala said quietly. "I imagine it's easy to define yourself as prosperous during a time of such ruin and desperation."

"How true," Victoria said, tipping her head to Tala.

"I don't see how the U.S. fits into any of this after its demise," Tala said.

"The United States was severely maimed, yes, but it didn't die entirely. You see, it was more than just a country, it was an ideal just as much an ideology. It was a way of life, a democracy that gave power to the people while providing constitutional protections. The principles at the core of the American identity were freedom, equality, liberty, and justice. Diversity doesn't have to mean division. Even as a politically polarized nation, the founding values of the country were widely and strongly believed in by most," Victoria said, sitting a little taller.

"Despite all the global unrest," she said, "the U.S. managed to maintain some organization. Being driven out of the nation's capital, they moved to the great plains. Slowly, while other countries were being born, what was left of the U.S. essentially became nomadic. It had no home. In order to preserve what was left, to rebuild, it went underground and began to call itself the Unified Rebels, later the Revolutionaries. Today, countries like Tahari in the northwest, Pacifica in the southwest, and the Central Colonies have limited resources to support their ever-growing populations and sustain their governments and economies. Independently, anyway."

"Are you saying that these countries have all partnered with each other?" Tala asked, her mind trying to keep up.

"Precisely. An organizational breakthrough."

"And the Republic?" she asked uncertainly.

"As you know firsthand, the Republic rules with an iron fist, both domestically and internationally. And they know that a divided North America keeps them strong. Republic hegemony ensures enough military force to systematically defeat any one of us on our own. So as the North American countries started coming together, we took our cause to the table, and we united under one vision. Our strength stems from our unification. While we operate under individual names and through an interstate system of government and leadership, a treaty amalgamated us as a whole. I've been elected by the other leaders as the overseeing president."

"And DeSoto?"

"With much support from Mazanada to their south, they've always tried to maintain their own nation and boundaries. Their availability of certain natural resources has afforded them their independence on an international level, but they have limited economic and military durability. Republic imposed tariffs and embargoes are crippling them. And now they're fighting the Republic over land rights and control of shipping ports along their east coast. The survival of DeSoto relies on financial and military patronage to both mobilize and maintain a military force in opposition of the Republic."

"That's where this summit I've been brought here for comes in, isn't it?" Tala asked. "You all want my testimony on the Republic, on Thias, to decide how to approach DeSoto. They either join you or they're left on their own."

"And you said you didn't understand politics when we first met," Victoria said with a small laugh. "In order for this to work, we need all of us to come together. We need to return to our roots, a democratic republic, where the people elect their leaders in free elections, and where those leaders uphold the governing laws via a just constitution. No one person with the power.

We're stronger together than we are divided. And it's the only way we will take down the Republic of Columbia, to restore the freedom and liberty of the people."

Tala was at a loss for words. The real world was not what she had known, nothing was as she'd been taught.

"Tala, there is division and unrest in the people in the Republic. Much of the country outside the major cities are low-income and oppressed, the government taking and taking and never giving. These people have no voice. But they see something different in you. Even Thias knows this, which is why he's labeled you a person of interest with the attack in the capital. He knows that if he vilifies you, he reinforces himself," she said steadily, her eyes fixed on Tala. "But believe it or not, you have just as much influence as he does. Especially following your advoprop."

Tala felt uneasy. She had never wanted to be a leader. She wanted to be a protector. But maybe they weren't mutually exclusive.

"Your father was one of the fairest leaders the Republic ever had. Thias, he was the demise of all his work. You, you Tala, you're an Alexander, people know you as MF, the good kind, the kind that protects its people. You made it out of the fire, people know you as a survivor. Yours is a name that has been whispered throughout the people, spreading like ripples in a pool. And now, your advoprop is making waves of those ripples.

"We're not asking you to march into Columbia City and singlehandedly take down your brother. We're asking you to be a catalyst for the change we're seeking. Pacifica, Tahari, and the Central Colonies are the force behind it. Our three militaries, along with the UR, have leagued together as the Unified military. But we need to ignite the passion in the people inside the Republic, help them find their voice. The two greatest motivators are fear and hope. There's already fear. Now we need hope. We need to unify people, not continue to divide. And that's where we need you."

Tala thought of Lilian, whom she met on her escape out of the Republic. She believed so firmly in what Tala represented that, despite her limited resources, she'd willingly given them her car when theirs had been destroyed by the MF. Her husband had been ruthlessly murdered at the hands of the MF, their income drastically reduced by the government, and yet she still managed to have a fight left in her. Tala admired that strength and fortitude, but listening now to Victoria, to all the intricacies involved, all the strategy, she wasn't entirely sure she had what it would take to be what they wanted her to be.

But this was her true test, wasn't it? Like Avery said,

"I'm giving you the chance for us to fight together, for the bigger picture, to help bring about the change that I think you want."

That bigger picture, she now understood, was far bigger than she ever could've imagined. Thias had warned her that he would hunt her, that he had the army to destroy her. But now she had much more of an army behind her than she'd known.

Her fear was rising up inside her, afraid of the uncertainty of tomorrow. History was finite, but the future is not. A quiet voice whispered from somewhere inside her that when everything is uncertain, anything is still possible. She could help write the future. She just had to be brave enough to step outside of the boundaries of fear.

"I'm sorry the world isn't what you've known," Victoria said with contrition.

"No, it's not," Tala said. "It's just, I'm only one person." She let her eyes rise to fully meet hers.

"You may not feel like the beacon that you are. But I assure you that you are. A star cannot be seen in the light of the sun, but rather only in the darkness. And it takes just one to light the way."

Tala wasn't sure she entirely believed that, that she was a beacon. But maybe this was just one more way she was underestimating herself. There was so much at stake. As a Militia Forces agent, there was little that she had feared. She dove into dangerous situations regularly, all without a second thought. That was the job. Now she understood real fear because, for the first time, she stood to lose so much. In that moment, she knew she didn't have the choice but to step into this new role. Not because of Victoria, not because of Vulcan or the Revos. She didn't have a choice because of who she was. She wouldn't walk away from her people now.

"I'll do whatever I have to," she finally said, her voice steady.

A smile curled at the corner of Victoria's mouth, a gleam in her bright green eyes. "I'm very glad to hear this. We are convening with our other leaders the day after tomorrow. My apologies to have to drag this out, but there's been a travel delay with Pacifica's President Walker. I'm looking forward to hearing your story in detail. We all are."

Tala swallowed a lump rising in her throat as she glanced at Maverick, suddenly glad he was beside her. Vulcan she was still uncertain of. But Maverick, even after all this time, was still her ally. There are some things that time is simply unable to alter.

They all rose to their feet, Victoria giving small smiles to both Vulcan and Maverick. "Thank you for bringing her," she said, then turned to Tala. "I'll see you very soon," she said as she outstretched her hand.

Tala straightened, then reached out and took it. An eagerness began to sprout deep inside. Of all the things she'd look back on and regret in her life, deciding to act wasn't going to be one of them.

EIGHT

Kane had been on Marina's farm for three days and already was feeling constricted. The nearby town of Edmond was small, most of the surrounding area farmland, located in the southeast region of Ozark Colony, and all of twenty-three miles from Clara City. Despite Governor Blakely's increased National Guard presence near the border, MF were still found in the area with two goals in mind: to keep people from fleeing the Republic and to bring back anyone who'd managed to make it out.

Marina insisted it wasn't safe for Kane to leave the farm. He could be recognized by anyone. The bounty on his head wasn't motivation just for Republic citizens, MF would pay anyone if it meant bringing him back. So, despite what he wanted, he stayed put.

To make himself useful, and to at least get out of the house which was comfortable and he was grateful to have the place to stay in, he helped with the chores around the farm. The first day they rested, then on their second morning, they all rose before the sun. Marina made them a hearty breakfast of fried ham steaks, eggs, and toast, then she bundled up two-week-old baby Iris, tucking her snuggly into a wrap across her chest, and set out to feed the animals.

Marina had six beef cows and two Holsteins, Lucy Sue and her calf Pepper who was only a few months old. Lucy Sue required a special diet separate from the others because Marina was milk-sharing with Pepper who was still nursing and only needed to be milked once a day. While Kane quickly got the hang of the feeding process, he was thankful that Gerrit was familiar and efficient with the milking machine.

The beef cows, each contained in their own quarters, were fed with a combination of forage, grains, and supplements twice a day. And on his second day of chores, Kane mucked the stalls of all eight cows. Like the cows, the chickens were also fed twice a day, though throughout the day, Marina would toss some of the table scraps into their trough.

Then there were the hogs that Kane couldn't help but find both the ugliest and the most odorous of them all, and when it came to filling their automatic feeders in the morning, he did so as quickly as he could.

Marina also had three empty, sprawling cotton fields, but as it was winter, they wouldn't need any attention until the spring. Cotton was their livelihood, even though they didn't gin it themselves. It was the bulk of their income, and it was Corban's work. Though no one said anything, Kane knew what was on their minds, each one holding out hope that he'd make his way home in time for planting.

In the meantime, Marina sold most of her milk supply to a local market in Edmond. Every other day, she would drive into town, bringing roughly three gallons each time to the processor for pasteurization. Twice a week, she brought her collection of eggs from her hens to the market as well. An added boost in income would come with the upcoming butcher of one of her cattle and three of her hogs, all of which were nearing finishing, teetering on the edge of reaching their goal weights.

By the end of the day, Kane collapsed onto the couch in the den, the house going to sleep. His body wasn't physically exhausted from the work, but his brain was. He knew two things for certain. The first was that he wasn't getting any closer to Tala. He had no idea how to get a message out, and if he wasn't allowed to leave the farm, no one was ever likely to find him. And the second was that he never wanted to be a farmer.

He thought of Marina, who had been on her own for two months, with no word on her husband. She'd had a baby in that time, and because the world didn't stop, she was out every morning and evening doing what needed to be done on her farm. And while she was younger than both Gerrit and Burke, she ruled the two of them.

His eyes open, gazing out at the moon through the window above his feet, he couldn't sleep. He thought of Max, back in Columbia City. He'd known Max longer than he'd known anyone, and it didn't feel right to not have him nearby. He didn't necessarily miss their pod back in the city, with the built-in bomb shelter that served as Kane's bedroom, but he found he was homesick for Max. For Tala. He didn't know someone could be homesick for a person rather than a place. But it made sense. Places were just that, spaces that existed. But Max and Tala, they're where he had connection. They were the places he called home.

Now he was with a house full of strangers. What had linked him with Gerrit and Burke was now gone. They'd made it to where they needed to be, but Kane was nowhere near where he was going. And his mind raced. How could he get word out? If only telepathy was a real thing, he thought foolishly. His desperation was getting the best of him now.

Sighing, he rose from the couch and made his way through the dark den and into the kitchen where he grabbed a glass and filled it from the tap. He turned at the sound of footsteps to find Marina standing in the doorway, Iris swaddled in her arms.

"I hope she didn't wake you," she said quietly.

He had been so preoccupied with the million thoughts in his head that the baby's cry had gone unheard. "No. Just thirsty."

Marina sat in a chair at the dining table, tossing a blanket over her chest and shoulder, then began nursing Iris. "I appreciate your help around here," she said as she looked up at him. "It's nice to have extra hands to help me."

Kane set the empty glass down and leaned against the counter. "You know," he said quietly, "if I make it out of here, I know people that might be able to help. With Corban."

She was quiet as she studied him.

Kane shifted on his feet.

"You mean the Revos," she said, a statement rather than a question.

Kane would have to get used to referring to the UR as the Revos now instead of the Rebels. He wasn't in Republic territory anymore. "I know you don't want to get involved but—"

"It's not that I don't want to get involved," she said sharply, cutting him off. "I can't *afford* to get involved."

He understood. Her husband was gone, and she had a farm to run, a baby to raise.

"Everything costs something," she said. "And your friends looking for my husband would be no different. Especially if I'm not eager to join their cause."

"And you don't think you're building credit by helping me?" he asked.

She was quiet, and he could tell she was considering this.

"You don't have to take me up on my offer," he added with a shrug. "I just thought I'd help the only way I know I can."

"And I am grateful for that," she said gently. "Tell me, what's in Hatfolk? Burke said your girlfriend?"

He exhaled slowly. "She's more than that. She's my whole world."

"But you're not married?" she asked, her head tipping to the side slightly. "You look plenty old enough to be married. Older than me anyway. No offense."

"None taken. And no, we're not married. That's never been an option for us," he admitted with a shake of his head, thinking about their secret life back in the city. Hiding in the shadows, stolen moments. Having to watch her on the arm of another man, broadcasted across the nation. He cringed at the thought of Vaughn ever having touched her.

Silence settled between them, the only sounds now those of Iris suckling beneath the blanket.

"I promise I'll do what I can to help you," she said, her voice filling up the silence. "Just give me time."

"Thank you," he said quietly. "I appreciate all you're doing for me." He turned, setting the water glass in the sink, then crossed the kitchen toward the den. "Goodnight, Marina."

"Goodnight, Kane."

Being awake for much of the night made it hard for Kane to find the motivation to get up the next morning. Even with the curtains drawn, he knew it was still dark. It was the smell of bacon wafting through the air that finally gave him the needed incentive to rise. He stretched his body, then sat slumped over for a few minutes. He could hear the conversation in the kitchen just as clearly as he would've if he'd been standing beside everyone.

"Those boards are rotten, Mare," Burke said. "I'm going to go into town to get some wood."

"Think you could stop by the feed supply store and the market? I need a few things and to drop off the eggs," Marina said. "It'd save me a trip."

"Just make a list of what you need," he said.

The conversation went quiet for a moment, and Kane stood, reaching for a clean t-shirt from his duffel. He never realized how grateful he was for a washing machine until he hadn't had one for a month.

"Are you sure you don't know anyone we could talk to?" Gerrit asked, his voice low. "I know he's fine here for right now, but we told him we'd help. And right now, we haven't done a damn thing for him. He's pretty much the only reason we got out of the Republic. He found the boat and rowed us halfway across the river, hauling like no one I've ever known could."

Knowing they were talking about him, Kane sat back down, sinking into the sofa.

"Why's he wanted by MF in the first place?" she asked. "You told me to trust you, so I am. But he's got to have done something."

"It's his girlfriend," Burke said with a sigh.

"I don't understand," Marina said.

"Damn. He'd probably kill me if he knew I told you this," he said.

Kane closed his eyes, recoiling even before the words were out of Burke's mouth.

"Tala Alexander," he said, his voice low.

"What?" she gasped. "Why didn't you tell me this sooner? This… this changes everything."

"How so?" Gerrit asked.

"I saw the broadcast. I know her declaration," she said. "If MF find him, they'll make a spectacle of it so they can get to her. You're putting all of us at risk by hiding him here. I haven't been running this farm, raising this baby all on my own to throw it away over this," she snapped.

"Relax," Gerrit said calmly.

"No one knows he's here. And he won't be leaving the farm," Burke said.

"Things are changing, Mare," Gerrit said. "It's either the Revos or it's the Republic. Take your pick."

Marina let out a frustrated grunt. "I know what people are saying about her. That no one would dare go up against Thias Alexander unless there was no other option. That that reason alone gives her all the credibility she needs. And maybe I do believe her. Her brother's a tyrant."

"It's because of him that Corban is missing," Burke asserted.

"You don't think I know that?" she asked, her voice thick.

"So I'd think you'd want to do anything and everything you can to fight him, to fight the MF. And helping Kane is part of that," Burke said.

"Fine," she conceded. "Poke around. But if MF show up on my porch it'll be your lives at risk. And if MF don't get you, I will."

The kitchen fell silent, only the sound of bacon sizzling in a pan.

She was right, his presence caused complications. Had he anywhere else to go, he would. He had to stay alert, keep his mind sharp, he had to be ready at a moment's notice to protect this family, Marina and Iris. He wouldn't let something happen to them.

Kane took the lull in the conversation as his opportunity to leave the den. He knew he had to do whatever he could to stay in Marina's good graces. Staying useful to her was the only reason she'd hang on to him.

"Morning," he said with a yawn as he opened the door to the kitchen. A sideways glance out the window showed it was raining, which was going to make the morning chores twice as miserable.

"Breakfast is ready," Marina said in a calm voice.

"I'm heading into town this morning," Burke said. "Anything you need?" His eyes met Kane's, and he knew he was trying to read him, to see if he'd overheard their conversation.

"Nope," he said with a lazy shake of his head. "Got nothing to give you if I did."

"Come eat," Marina said, carrying a plate of hot bacon in one hand and a plate of French toast in the other.

As Kane took a seat, he spotted Iris in the baby swing in the corner of the room, sleeping through all the conversation around her.

"Don't worry about the morning feeding," Kane said, looking up and catching Marina's eyes behind her full head of curly ringlets. "I think I know well enough what I'm doing. Gerrit and I can take care of it."

She screwed up her face as she looked at him.

"Ever heard of maternity leave?" Gerrit asked with a laugh.

"Well," she said, "I have some canning I could do. Thank you." Her eyes held Kane's gaze for a moment, then she looked away as she took the chair between her brothers.

After breakfast, Kane and Gerrit headed out into the rain. It was heavy and cold, and they jogged to the barn for cover. Even the animals wanted nothing to do with the rain. The hogs were huddled in the pig house in the corner of their pen, the chickens inside their coop.

Kane fed the cows while Gerrit brought Lucy Sue to the milking stanchion and hooked her up to the milking machine. Bracing himself, he headed back into the rain, his feet sinking in thick, muddy puddles, water sloshing up his legs. He fed the hogs their allotment of grain and the leftover vegetable scraps, then the pellets for the chickens. In a matter of minutes, he was soaked, the cold drops that were coming down in sheets catching behind his head and dripping under the collar of his jacket, sending a chill down his spine.

After all the animals had been fed, he checked and refilled their water troughs, though it seemed pointless with all the rain. The last thing to do was reach into the coop and retrieve any eggs he could find. The hens all clucked in a frenzy as he struggled to fit in the narrow doorway. He managed to pull out eight, holding them carefully in the hem of his shirt, then headed for the house.

Burke returned an hour later in Marina's small car. Without Coban's truck, the boards stuck out from her trunk. The three of them went to work repairing the hog pen, and despite the pouring rain, Kane was thankful to have something to occupy his mind. He found that whenever there was a lull in activity, his mind wandered to Tala, and sometimes even their happy memories depressed him.

They tore the rotting boards off the posts, Gerrit making sure the hogs didn't escape the gaping hole in their pen while Kane and Burke pounded the new ones into place. The rain saturated the ground, and the smell of live animals and manure was stirred up, giving Kane a headache. No, a farm was definitely out of the question for anyone with senses always in overdrive. But he put his head down and focused on the task at hand, reminding himself once again that he had to be useful.

As they were pulling off the last rotted board, a pickup truck drove up the long driveway and the three of them all paused their work to watch it come to a stop near the house. A man climbed out of the cab carrying four heaping cloth grocery bags. He gave them a glance, and Kane could've sworn he'd seen a small flare in his eyes when he looked at him. But the stranger turned away quickly, heading for the house.

"No idea," Gerrit said with a shrug as they exchanged nervous looks. The wrong kind of stranger could cause a lot of trouble for them.

While holding the board steady against the post, Kane strained to listen through the loud rain to the conversation the man and Marina had from the covered porch.

"Got our pigs back from the slaughter and got way more than we thought. Thought I'd share with you. With Corban gone and now a little one, I figured not having to go to the grocery store all the time would make things easier for you," he said to her, holding out the bags. "Got about ten pounds of ham, two loins, and about another ten pounds of bacon in there. I think Jessilynn put in some sausage too."

"This is awfully nice of you, Bridger," she said, taking the bags from him.

Bridger. Kane made a mental note as he watched him from the corner of his eyes.

"Not to be nosy or anything, but who're your new farmhands?" he asked with a nod across the yard toward Kane, Burke, and Gerrit.

Kane struggled not to look up, instead focusing on the nail that Burke was driving through the board. Though his ears picked up every word.

"Oh, my brothers," Marina said, her voice tight.

"I thought you only had two."

Kane felt his chest tighten. Not that he looked anything like any of them.

"You've got a good memory," she said with a nervous laugh. "The other one is just a friend of theirs. He's passing through town on his way north."

"Ahh," Bridger said as he looked over his shoulder, his eyes meeting Kane's just as he'd stolen a glance his way. "Well, anything comes up, you know how to reach me."

"Absolutely," she said with a smile. At that moment, Kane heard Iris's crying scream ring out, and he was thankful for their interruption.

"Guess that's your cue," Bridger said with a chuckle.

"Thanks again," she called out as he turned away, unfazed by the rain, his gaze lingering once more over Kane and the others before he finally crawled back into the cab of his truck.

Once he was out of sight, Kane took a deep breath, not realizing he'd been holding it.

With the hog pen properly repaired, all three men made their way back into the house. Marina had Iris swaddled against her chest in a wrap as she stood over the stove stirring a large stockpot, the sweet smell of fruit filling the room.

"What're you making?" Burke asked eagerly.

"Jam," Marina replied without a glance at any of them.

"I claim the shower first," Gerrit said. All three of them were cold, soaked, and dirty. Kane's pants covered in a thick layer of mud.

"Throw those nasty clothes in the washing machine. I'll start it when you're all finished showering. And nobody better have traipsed through my house in your filthy shoes," she said.

"Never dream of it," Burke said, catching Kane's eyes, smirking as his sister stood with her back to them.

"Marina, you got a razor I could use?" Kane asked. "I don't typically have this much hair." He ran his fingers through the coarse hair growing in on his head. He couldn't remember the last time he'd let it get this long. Not that he'd had much choice in the matter now.

"You can use Corban's. He's got an electric clipper in the middle drawer and I'm sure there're some disposable razors in the closet in the hallway bathroom," she said. "Use whatever you need."

They each took turns showering, Kane going last since he knew he'd take the longest. The hot water was refreshing, warming him deep into his bones, the steam rising and fogging the mirror. He hadn't realized how cold he was until he was suddenly warm again. He stayed under the stream of water as long as he could, until it began to run cold.

Using a towel to wipe clear the mirror, he stared at his reflection, the large phoenix inked over the left side of his chest, up to his shoulder and just around his side, across his ribcage. Seeing it now made him think of the first time Tala had seen it. He was terrified to show her, unsure how she'd react. Showing her the ink proved his affiliation with the Rebels, a group she'd been trained to fight against. Yet she had only looked at him with wonder in her eyes, likely shocking her as much as it did him. He could almost feel the tips of her fingers on his skin now as they smoothed across the black stain.

This was what happened when he didn't have something to do; he thought about Tala. But the reality was that she never truly left his mind. He was just able to distract himself from time to time. But in that moment, thoughts of her filled him up. Her smile, her long, blond hair, her eyes as blue as the sky on a clear day, the sound of her laugh. She consumed him entirely.

Taking a deep breath, he tried to shake away the images that brought both joy and ache inside of him. He reached for the clipper in the drawer, finding it exactly where Marina said he would. Glancing back up at his reflection, he turned it on, then brought it to his head. Twenty minutes later, his head was smooth again and his facial hair was trimmed short with clean lines. Aside from the gaping hole that lived inside him, he felt a little more like himself.

NINE

Under heavy cloud cover and falling snow, Tala and Maverick made their way down the evergreen-lined street, passing the dormitories and across the open yard toward the Mirari building, leaving fresh footprints with every step. They had spent the entire day before together as he gave her a tour of Camp Washington. It was a specialized training base with only active-duty military and civilian contractors stationed there. No families. Not every soldier for the Unified military went through the camp, but for those who did, it was a year-long assignment.

The base was far more extensive than Tala could've imagined. It was large and sprawling, rising and falling in elevation with its peaks and valleys. There were remote training camps and both indoor and outdoor training courses, as well as an extensive outdoor shooting range, and the entire east side of the camp housed two complete air defense squadrons. She watched, one by one, as the fighter jets were launched for exercise, then heard them return hours later. Being so high in the mountains afforded them privacy, however, it didn't give them much room for a runway. Tala had watched them take off vertically, through the power of fusion plasma, rather than race down a runway for a horizontal liftoff. According to Maverick, they had the capacity to do both.

During the many hours they'd spent together, Tala felt her tension relax with him, though they spoke little of anything personal. It surprised her how easy it was to talk with him. It was his laugh that brought her back to another time, transporting her to their years at the Militia Forces Academy. But letting her mind wander back only reminded her of his deception, a cloud that hovered over them. It may have been aimed at the Republic, but she'd been a casualty of it. Since her parents' death and until Kane, she had been more real with Maverick than anyone else in her life, and it stung knowing there had been a lie between them from the beginning. She couldn't help but feel cautious as she tested how to let him in again after so long. They shared a thousand memories, and while he was practically a stranger to her, she could feel the familiarity of their friendship between them. It was still there. *Time*, she told herself. It would just take time.

Overhead, the rumbles of the nearby jets taking off brought her mind back. She could feel their power hammering in her chest, pounding like thunder, even if she couldn't see them above her. It wasn't as cold as it had been since she arrived, and the heavy snow that was falling created a veil of white, obscuring the world around her. The big, wet flakes landed on her cold, bare cheeks and caught in her eyelashes.

They stepped inside the Mirari building, Tala now understanding why Cara described it as the heart of the base. It seemed to be the heart of everything: the base, the government, the entire movement. Vulcan was already there, waiting for them. She brushed the snow off her sleeves and ran her fingers through her now damp hair. Though she knew she should be nervous to meet with the leaders from the Colonies, Pacifica, and Tahari, she felt surer of herself than she had in a long time. Like Victoria had said, she had a role to play, and she was prepared to play it. What the others decided to do with her information was up to them, it was out of her hands.

As ridiculous as it was, what made her nervous was how she was dressed, in jeans that hugged her hips and a thick, cable knit sweater. She wished she would've made a better effort. It was ingrained in her to look a certain way in front of people of position and influence. In the Republic, it would've mattered greatly what she looked like for something of this magnitude, but

Vulcan assured her that here it was less so important. They weren't interested in her outfit, they wanted to know what she knew. If there was anyone who was the epitome of casual, almost grunge, it was him. And he had no reservations about being in anyone's presence.

Tala slipped out of her wet coat, hanging it in the coatroom, Maverick's just beside hers. She stole a glance at him, dressed in his fatigues like all the other days. She couldn't help but think he looked sharp. Being a soldier suited him. Just as being a Militia Forces agent had. If heroic had a type, he fit it.

Vulcan led them to a secure conference room on the second floor, the length of which had floor-to-ceiling virtual windows like in The Village. Each chair around the long, white table was filled, Victoria sitting at the head, a digital wall behind her like in Vulcan's office.

Everyone stood as Tala stepped into the room, Maverick leaving her at the door. She wanted to reach for him, to keep someone she knew nearby. She peered up at him, and he tipped his head closer to her. "You've absolutely got this," he whispered under his breath before the door closed between them.

Vulcan strode across the room and rounded the table, taking a seat between Gemini and Ash. Tala walked to the only open chair on the end, opposite Victoria. She counted twelve people, including herself. With everyone's eyes fixed on her, she straightened. She refused to look small and insignificant.

"Thank you for joining us," Victoria said, her voice soft but strong. It was commanding. "Tala, I speak for all of us when I welcome you to the table today."

She nodded and gave a half-smile. "Thank you." It was then that Tala began to feel her nerves standing at the threshold, and she swallowed hard as she pushed them away. She set her hands in her lap to keep them steady and took a slow breath. It was warm in the conference room, and she hoped her cheeks didn't look flushed.

"A quick introduction," the woman to Tala's immediate right said. She had a slight accent that Tala couldn't quite pinpoint, maybe southern. "I'm Teagan Blakely, governor of Ozark Colony." She had full lips painted dark red and heavy eyelids accented with long lashes, a small mole beneath the corner of her right eye.

Tala tried to summon a map in her mind. She was fairly certain Ozark Colony was where she had crossed the Mississippi into the Colonies from the Republic.

"I assume you know all the Revos," Teagan said, her head tipping to the side toward Jasper beside her. They were all, by far, the youngest people in the room. Along with Tala.

"I'm President Lana Xavier of Tahari," a small woman beside Victoria said as she lifted her hand, catching Tala's attention. She had dark auburn hair with side-swept bangs, large eyes and a narrow nose. She gave Tala a warm, wide smile full of perfectly straight teeth.

"Graham Walker of Pacifica," the man beside her said. "President," he clarified as he cleared his throat. He was large, both tall and wide, with a round, clean-shaven face. "I'm glad you could be here today." Even his voice was big and deep.

Tala, of course, didn't know President Walker, but she was familiar with his name. Thias had very strongly disliked him, which was about all she knew.

"While we've never officially met," Elias Barrington said next as they went around the table, his voice low and steady, "I think we're both familiar with one another. I'm, of course, the governor of Lakewood Colony in the north." There was a serious intensity in his golden-hazel eyes as he looked across the table at her. He also had broad shoulders, but not in the same way as Graham Walker, his face buried behind a heavy, well-trimmed black beard, his hair combed to the side, oiled. Looking at him and his wife now, there was a unique dichotomy between them. He looked hard and stern, much like Thias, while Victoria looked stately and assured. She was young, somewhere in her forties, while he looked in his fifties.

The man beside Elias looked small in comparison as he gave Tala an agreeable smile. "I'm Governor Otto Fulton of Lincoln Plains Colony. The Village where you've been staying is in my territory," he said. He was neatly dressed in a black blazer and tie, with wavy dark hair that hung past his ears and a short beard that was more gray than black. "I've worked with your brother many times. It's a pleasure to meet you. You've got a name I've been familiar with for many years."

Tala felt a subtle tightening in her chest. She never understood what it meant when people said that. A sweeping glance around the room though showed no one seemed surprised by his revelation.

"And I'm Governor Fischer Hutton of Mountain Range Colony, where we are currently. Home of Camp Washington. We border Lincoln Plains to the east and split Pacifica and Tahari to our west," the last man at the table said. The tallest in the room, he sat with good posture, his eyes hidden behind thick-framed glasses, with defined lines around his mouth and eyes.

"The Central Colonies are made up of four separate colonies," Victoria said, her voice taking over the room. "With four provinces in Tahari and five in Pacifica, our thirteen regions combine to make up the United States. With the small exception of DeSoto's western region, we make up almost all of the territory west of the Mississippi River. And Camp Washington is the base of operations for the Unified military, a joint effort between our nations."

Tala tried to piece the map together in her head.

"We've all been watching the precarious situation in the Republic of Columbia very closely," Lana Xavier, Tahari's president, said. "We understand that you have a different account of what transpired in Columbia City than what your brother is claiming."

"We're all aware of his purported version of events," Teagan Blakely said.

"If you don't mind," Tala said, "I'd like to just refer to him by his name."

"Understandable," Fischer Hutton said as he gave his glasses a nudge. The simple gesture reminded her of Max.

"You've walked all of us through it," Vulcan said, his arms stretched out comfortably on the table. "Now it's time to share it with them."

Tala took a breath, gathering her thoughts, then began, starting with the discovery of the cache of guns.

"But you were only able to confirm that one gun was registered to the Republic," President Graham Walker interrupted as he shifted his body in his chair which looked too small for him. "How do you know the others weren't DeSoto guns?"

"I don't," Tala admitted. "But they were made untraceable. Maybe they got serial numbers off a few like I had, but it wouldn't have been many. And as soon as the guns were discovered, evidence began to be fabricated. I hardly think it's a coincidence."

"Fabricated in what way?" he asked in his booming voice.

Tala's mind raced. How could she give an account of everything that had happened without revealing too much about Kane? The last thing she needed was to spark curiosity over him.

"There were four men who were found dead at the scene where the guns were discovered," she said. "I confirmed at the crime scene that the men had no ink on their bodies. But the autopsy revealed large ink markings on all of them. They were classified as Rebels, and the case was closed. Later, however, I discovered their real identities in documents I found on Thias's computer."

"And these men, they were not Rebels?" Graham asked.

"No," Jasper interjected. "We had no connection with them."

"These men who were accused of being Rebels, how were they killed? Was that investigated? Why were they at your crime scene to begin with?" Lana asked.

"After they were classified as Rebels, there was no further investigation into them or their deaths. Thias closed the case," Tala said, taking a slow breath through her nose. While that was the truth, it was only one part of it. It had been her and Kane who killed those men.

"You said you accessed Thias's computer?" Fischer asked with a raised brow.

Tala nodded. "But that's getting a little ahead in the chain of events."

"Go on," Lana said.

Though her hands still felt unsteady, wedged beneath her legs, her mind was clear. Tala continued with her story, explaining the deaths of her C.I. who had tipped her off, Gep Masters from the first arrest that had set everything in motion, and Agent Mills who had revealed confidential information about Masters's interrogation by Thias and Vaughn. She then recited the conversations she'd overheard at the president's birthday party. They were so ingrained in her memory she couldn't have forgotten them if she tried.

"Wait a moment," Otto Fulton interrupted. "Are you saying that Chief Justice Murdo and Chancellor Adams are involved in this too?"

"Absolutely," she said with a firm nod.

"Were you in a romantic relationship with the chancellor?" Teagan asked, her expression sober, though Tala suspected by the look in her eyes that she already knew about her and Vaughn.

"Not in the way you're thinking," Tala said, a chill running down her spine. She hadn't thought of Vaughn in weeks, not since she'd gotten out of the Republic, and the thought of his hands on her left her unsettled. "It wasn't real. My relationship with him," she said. She saw the curiosity in everyone's eyes as they fixed on her.

"It was an act. I led him on to get more details about the case. Between the evidence I knew was fabricated and the small details that didn't add up, he was a good source of information. He would reveal tidbits here and there about things while over dinner or in casual conversation. Though I didn't know what I'd stumbled into at that time. In the very beginning, he and I were set-up, yes romantically, but nothing real ever came of it. I used him for the case," she said. She hoped none of them judged her the way she judged herself for the flirting, the kissing, all of it. Then she thought of Kane, how unfair it had all been to him. Even if he tried to convince her otherwise.

"Back to the party," Graham said, and Tala was relieved to move on.

Tala returned to the two conversations she'd listened to from her hiding place inside the art gallery.

"Just so I'm understanding correctly," Otto said, his beady eyes on her. "There were two separate plots. One for the shooting in the square which the president was a part of, and the other for the assassination of Royer led by Thias?"

"Yes," Tala said. "It's after those conversations I overheard that I broke into Thias's computer."

"His work computer?" Otto asked, brushing a strand of hair out of his face.

"His home computer," she corrected. "In the conversations, that's where he mentioned keeping his files." Tala felt her palms beginning to sweat. She was starting to feel more and more like she was on trial. She glanced at Ash, not sure what she was expecting, but would take any backup she could get. They knew her story.

"How were you able to access it? I would imagine he has security measures in place," Fischer said calmly but with edge in his voice, a challenge that maybe she hadn't had it in her to accomplish such a task. Everyone always seemed to think Thias was indestructible. But Tala had gotten through, she got past him.

She couldn't help but see the look in everyone's eyes that said parts of her story seemed improbable, even preposterous. But it was all the truth, and she wouldn't back down. Maybe they thought they knew her, from whatever source – Thias, Vaughn, the Revos – but none of them really knew her. None of them knew what she was fully capable of.

"Not just anyone could've gotten into his house, but I wasn't just anyone. And I had help," Tala said, trying to keep her voice level. She explained how Max had made her bugs, and how she was able to plant them throughout Thias's house. Every one of them seemed to perk up when she described the documents on his computer. The bank accounts and money transfers, the list of inmates and their accompanying photos, the map of the park, the orders for the hit on Royer. She was relieved not to have any further questions about Max or Kane.

"And you identified four of the men in the photos you found on the computer as the four dead victims at your crime scene in the beginning?" Lana asked from across the table.

"Yes," Tala said, hoping her voice sounded strong and steady because she was beginning to feel anything but.

"And the day of the attack, what happened then?" Graham asked. He folded his hands, his fingers making a steeple as he rested his elbows on the table.

This was the part she hated to recount the most. It's when she'd lost Ronin. It's when she'd let Thias get away. The sounds of gunfire and screaming, the images of innocent people, bloodied and distraught, running from the scene. And Tala completely helpless in all of it.

"Did you ever consider going to anyone with what you knew before it all happened? Did you really think you would've been able to stop all of it?" Teagan asked, her eyes fixed on Tala.

A pulse of anger surged through Tala as she realized the accusation. "And who should I have gone to?" she asked, hearing the bite in her voice. "My

MF captain, Kole, who I'm sure was in Thias's pocket, likely participating with the fabrication of all the evidence? Or maybe the media that is government run?" She swallowed hard, fighting to keep her anger in check. "If I'd have gone to MF, I would've been reported. Detained at best. If I'd have gone to the media, I wouldn't have made it out the front doors alive. Thias killed the president. He hired people to open fire on his own people. Do you think he would've hesitated to do something to me to keep me quiet?"

The room fell silent. Tala's nerves had been transformed, and now she felt fire inside her.

"I did the only thing I could," she said sternly. "There was nothing I could do to stop twenty-six gunmen in the square. And I knew my chances of keeping President Royer alive were slim, but I still had to try everything I could to keep Thias from taking power," she said, reigning in her voice, her eyes darting from person to person around the room, challenging them to question her. She caught Governor Otto Fulton's eyes, dark and small under thick brows, and she was taken aback by the small curl at the corner of his mouth. Was he smiling at her?

"No one here is accusing you of not trying," Victoria said, her voice like velvet as it carried through the room. "We're simply trying to get as many answers as we can."

"I don't like the insinuation that I could've saved all those people, that their blood is on my hands," she said, her voice steady.

"Of course not," Otto said. "Tala, you were one person in a very extensive and elaborate plot. Personally, I don't fault you for any of it. Including the assassination. If things are as you've described, Thias likely had fail-safes in place. He wasn't going to let anything ruin what he had set in motion."

Tala took a slow breath, relieved that at least one person in the room wasn't judging her for her failures. Even if she judged herself for them.

"If Tala didn't have information detrimental to Thias's image and mission in the Republic," Gemini said, speaking for the first time since they'd sat down, "then he wouldn't have taken the measures he has to silence her. He put out a hit on her. His own sister. He's afraid of her."

"You're what stands between him and a war with DeSoto and a civil war within his own country," Lana said, a grim expression on her face. "Nobody would want to be where you are."

Tala wasn't sure how to respond to this. It was true though. She certainly didn't want to be where she was. But no one had asked her. Fate put her there anyway.

"His motivations seem pretty clear to me," Graham said, once again readjusting in his chair. Tala thought he looked incredibly uncomfortable. "He wasted no time invading DeSoto. And he went right for their shipping ports. It's not just imports and exports for the Republic and DeSoto that will be in jeopardy if the Republic seizes control of all coastal areas around DeSoto. I don't doubt that he wouldn't try to seize control of the entire region, all of the Caribbean and central America, including the Panama Canal, because then he would control all shipping from east to west," he argued.

"And that undoubtedly would impact all of us," Lana said. "We have a lot of goods that come to us through DeSoto. The Republic too. If the Republic controlled what came from everywhere else as well, there would be devastation in all of our countries. Those are small countries in that region that wouldn't be able to put up much of a fight against the Republic's Militia Forces."

"DeSoto is likely a very small part of his plan," Teagan said. "This is a threat to all of us. One by one, he could systematically destroy each of us on our own."

A pit opened inside Tala at the sudden realization. She'd never understood the full depths of Thias's greed until just then. And where would he stop once North America was conquered?

"Our only advantage is that we're a united front," Victoria said. "And it's crucial we converge with DeSoto, and I don't mean just as allies." She pressed her lips into a firm line as she looked around the room.

"If we can get the people within the Republic to also intervene, well, he can't fight us on all sides," Fischer said. He took his glasses off and pinched the bridge of his nose.

"Things are deteriorating quickly inside the Republic," Lana said, her voice sharp. Everyone's head turned in her direction as she stood, walking to the digital wall. With a tap of her fingers, it woke up, and she pressed her hand to it, unlocking it. A large home screen appeared before them. With a few swipes and taps of her fingers, a map of the Republic appeared.

"Here," she said, pointing with her finger to a region west of Lake Michigan. "And here," she said, moving her finger toward the center of the map, near the city of Alexandria where her grandfather had been born. "Forced labor camps have been setup. We have people inside the Republic who have been able to get messages to us. Anyone they arrest as dissidents, anyone they find from DeSoto, they're being sent there. A rearmament is creating work force shortages. The people in these camps are compensating for it."

Victoria rose to her feet as Lana resumed her seat at the table. "Your advoprop has been very effective," she said with a pause, squaring her body with Tala's, her eyes lingering on her from across the room. Then she turned to the screen, tapping it like Lana, dragging her finger around. Photos of crumbled concrete and steel appeared before them. "These images," Victoria continued, stepping to the side to give everyone a clear view, "were taken two days ago after explosives were detonated in the intermodal transit hub in Michigan City. This is a hard hit against the Republic. While destroying it will surely affect the people, it is a huge disruption of the transport of MF supplies throughout the country." Using her finger, she swiped through a small gallery of images, all showing the complete decimation of buildings, and three of what looked to have been cranes. Michigan City was the second largest city in the Republic. It's location along the Great Lakes made it a prime location for shipping goods throughout the country by boat, truck, or train.

"Since the bombing, there have been riots throughout the country. Those for and against the Republic clashing. But this," Victoria said, motioning over her shoulder, her eyes once again finding Tala. "This wasn't us. This was you. Your message, to *your* people. This is the flame you fueled from the spark of your advoprop."

Conflicting emotions surged through Tala's body, her cheeks flushing. "Were there casualties?" she asked.

"There most always are," Victoria said, though she didn't elaborate. "One star to light the way," she said, talking directly to her, referring to their previous conversation. Victoria closed the images on the screen, then took her seat at the head of the table once more.

"If she has this kind of influence, we need more from her," Elias said, and Tala realized that he'd been quiet throughout the conversation. "Thias uses his own newspeak with his people. We counter it."

Tala swallowed. Thias had made her small because that was how he wanted her. And she couldn't help but wonder, if it was true and he was afraid of her now, had he seen a threat in her long before she saw it in herself? It was time to show him what she was made of. "I'm ready for whatever," she said firmly. The days of submitting to him were over.

Victoria pressed her lips into a small smile. And then Tala saw it, it was in her eyes. She was poised and graceful and kind, but there was fire in her. The intensity she saw in Elias's stern face matched what thrived inside Victoria.

She just wore it differently. She was a woman who was never going to back down to the Republic. And Tala wasn't going to either.

Thias's biggest flaw was that he was so focused on his primacy and his craving for dominance that he underestimated people. He scoffed at the Rebels, he believed that if he oppressed his people that they wouldn't have any fight left in them. He was ignorant to the unity between his neighboring countries, and he thought Tala to be the woman he tried to mold, demure and insignificant. All of it, his underestimation, would be his demise.

"Is there anything else you'd like to say or add at this time?" Graham asked.

Tala sat a little taller. "Just that I hope you believe me."

"You have given us plenty to further discuss," Teagan said.

The other leaders nodded as Tala's eyes circled the room. She'd given them everything, and now all she could hope was that it was enough.

"There is something else for you, something that you should see," Victoria said, her eyes catching Tala's, then swiftly moving to Gemini.

Gemini nodded as she rose from her chair. "Come with me," she said as she passed Tala, heading for the door.

She quickly stood, unsure of what was happening.

"Tala."

She paused, her eyes catching Otto's as he stood as well, looking sharp in his blazer.

"Thank you for your testimony," he said as he tipped his head to her. There was something in his eyes just then that caught her off guard. A gleam that she hadn't expected. Almost a smile. She hadn't come to the summit in search of validation from any of them. She knew what she had, what she'd done to get it. But in that moment, as he gazed the short distance across the table at her, she couldn't help but feel that she'd found it anyway, in him.

She offered the room a half-smile, then turned to follow Gemini out the door.

Maverick straightened as Tala stepped into the hall, his eyes catching hers, and she couldn't read them. She felt a small pang inside. She'd always been able to read them. It was just another reminder that they weren't what they once had been.

Together, they followed Gemini down the hall. They turned three corners, each corridor looking exactly like all the others, doors and doors, all numbered, most with security panels. They finally came to a stop at a secure door. Gemini opened it and stepped aside to allow them in.

Tala stepped into a small room, a sofa and a chair facing a large TV screen on the wall. It looked like a cozy living room. She looked at Gemini with a raised brow. "What's this?" she asked.

"We received a transmission this morning," she said. "It's meant for you."

"I don't understand," Tala said, her eyes moving to Maverick as he shrugged.

"You will." Gemini picked up a small remote from the table beside the sofa and turned on the TV. She tapped the remote a few times, then finally Tala understood. Her heart fell as she looked up, Thias's face filling the screen.

"Press play when you're ready," she said, handing her the remote.

Tala took it gingerly in her hands, not trusting them as she felt the quiver in her fingers.

"Have you seen it?" she asked.

Gemini nodded, her mouth turned down at the corners. She turned toward Maverick. "You're cleared for this information. You can stay or leave," she said. "It's up to her."

His eyes met Tala's. "Stay," she said without hesitation. She didn't know what was in the video, but she was certain she didn't want to be alone when she watched it. "Please."

"I'll come back for you," Gemini said. Silence unfolded in the room as she left, and Tala rounded the sofa, taking a seat, Maverick beside her. There was something that felt safe about having him with her for this. Though a video message couldn't physically harm her, she knew better than anyone that words had power.

Tala looked at the still image of Thias's face, the video paused, and suddenly all the reasons not to watch it came crashing over her, taking the breath from her lungs. Did she really want to know what he had to say? Did she care?

She hated the answer that whispered faintly in the back of her mind. *Yes.*

She took a deep, steady breath, letting it fill her up, fortifying her. She reminded herself that Thias only had the power over her that she gave him. This was her mind preparing her heart. She had stopped liking him a long time ago. But despite herself, there was a part of her that loved him still. And maybe that was okay. Maybe the fact that she could still love him as a brother after everything said more about who she was than it did about who he was.

She stole a glance at Maverick.

"As hard as this might be to watch, I know you'll regret it if you don't," he said, nodding encouragingly.

Her hands clutched the remote, and after a moment, she pressed play, the video before her coming to life.

Thias sat back in a chair, his elbows propped on each armrest, his hands folded together. She recognized the room immediately from the National Statements President Royer had made. He was in the cynosure in the Central Government building. He was in the president's chamber. He wore black slacks and a gray dress shirt, though no jacket, no tie, the top of his shirt open, the button loosened. It was an odd look for him. He looked… *comfortable*, she thought. This was a side of him she didn't know.

His blond hair was longer than she remembered, thick tendrils starting to curl at the ends as they were tucked behind his ears, the top combed lazily back off his forehead. By all accounts, he was handsome. It was his eyes that hadn't changed. They were a striking steel blue, cold and hard, and they made the hair on the back of Tala's neck stand. They were the one constant as he sat before her.

He let out a loud sigh of emotion, his head bobbing slightly like he was struggling to find the words to speak.

"Tala," he finally said, then paused for several seconds. "This is hard for me, talking to you as though you are right in front of me. When in reality, you're likely somewhere far away. Where? I can't say, but I'm guessing you're not in the city anymore." He took a breath as he sat up, his elbows now on his thighs, his head dipping, though his eyes never dropped from the camera.

"It hurts me that we are so divided. It hurts me that after all these years, after everything I've done for you, raising you on my own, giving you everything, that you could turn against me. Turn against your people and your country. And for what?" He kept his voice steady and calm, and Tala felt her anger beginning to simmer, her fingers tingling. It was almost laughable that of all things, he was accusing *her* of being the traitor. Like he hadn't ordered the assassination of their president, like he hadn't conspired to kill hundreds of his own people, like he hadn't shot her friend in cold blood.

"The division that is between us is setting a terrible example for our people, for the world. People see you and I at war with each other and suddenly they feel it's justified to go to war with everyone else. Your broadcast that hijacked my system broke my heart," he said, his voice cracking as his eyes fell briefly to the floor.

Tala glanced away and willed herself to take a deep breath, exhaling slowly through her nose. She noticed the shake in her hands, then a moment later, Maverick slid his over them, gripping them enough to still them. She looked back up at the screen.

Thias's eyes bore into the camera. "I don't know where I could've gone so wrong that you would think it okay to join the Rebels." She heard the rising tension in his voice. "That act alone is tantamount to treason. You know how the Republic handles Rebels and their schisies," he said, using the slang term for Rebel sympathizers. "And though you should be no exception, I'm offering an olive branch to you. You're my sister, and all I want is for us to be together again. As a family. I want you and I to stand before our people as a united front, honoring the legacy of our family that came before us. Our father. Our grandfather. I am willing to pardon you for everything, if you just come home. That's all I want, for you to come home," he said with sadness, a pained expression on his face.

She was buying none of it. For the first time in her life, she saw through him. Through every lie that spilled off his tongue. He was a master, and she was convinced that even he fell prey to his own manipulation and deceit. The truth and the lies blended flawlessly together, making it impossible to know where one ended and the other began.

"The one good thing that came from your broadcast," he said, "was that I could see that you were okay. I don't believe you're safe," he said with a firm shake of his head. "But at least I could have the peace of mind that you're okay." He fell silent, his head dropping, and she saw his ragged breaths from the rise and fall of his shoulders. The fact that he thought she'd fall for any of this was a slap in the face.

"I will rescind the notice that you're a person of interest. Come back to Columbia City. Together, you and I can do great things. If we cannot come together, our battles will be fought at the expense of the people. And I know you don't want that. All that blood on your hands. I know you don't want to lose one more person close to you. It doesn't have to be like that. Come home. You and I can repair what has been torn. Vaughn's heartbroken and only wants to mend your relationship. You're like a sister to Nina, and the children miss you terribly."

Tala felt a pang in her heart as she thought of her nephew and niece, Jax and Millie. Far too young to ever understand any of it.

"I know you think you believe in what you're doing. But you're wrong. Look around you. Dividing the people weakens us as a whole, and we can never have peace amid that kind of discord. Think of all the lives you could spare. There's already been enough destruction left in your wake. Keep in mind," he said with a pause, his eyes fixing on her through the screen, "there is still more that you stand to lose."

She suppressed a shudder as a chill ran down her spine, realization dawning on her. She swallowed hard as she stole a glance at Maverick who was too absorbed in the video to catch his guileful threat. At least that was something to be grateful for.

"You come back, and I will forgive everything." His jaw set in a hard line, his lips pursing. "Whatever your next move, heed my warning. The Republic of Columbia was built out of the ashes of war, and it will not crumble under the petty threats of the Rebels. You choose them and you will have chosen wrong. I will destroy anything that stands in my way. Please don't make that be you. I couldn't bear it. I know that the particulars of politics are new to you, and so I understand your ignorance. And I leave you now with this. There is an old, proverbial saying that to know your enemy, you must become your enemy. Do you, Tala, have what it takes to do this?"

Tala's body stilled as the video ended and the screen went black. While his face was no longer before her, she could see him clearly in her mind. She was torn between her fury over his galling attempts to put everything on her shoulders, to make her responsible for his crimes, and her sudden fears lying beneath his thinly veiled threat. He was not one to make idle warnings. She had to go to Vulcan as soon as she could. But she needed to make sure Maverick wasn't around. He couldn't know.

She had to save Mila.

TEN

Tala tossed her duffel onto the sofa in her unit. It surprised her how nice it felt to be back in The Village. Cara had never taken up much space, but it already felt emptier without her. Going to the bottom bunk, she took a seat, reaching for the pictures wedged between the side of the mattress and the wall. There was a tug inside her as she looked down at Mila and Ronin in her hands. She didn't feel it every day anymore, the dark holes left in the wake of her losses, but there were moments when it hit her all over again, the ache returning. She closed her eyes, pressing her rising emotion back down. If she wasn't going to be controlled by it, she would have to find a way to transmute it, to channel it into her drive and motivation. Quickly, she replaced the photos to their safe spot.

She glanced at the time on her palm pad. Dinner. She was looking forward to seeing Vi and Declan again, to introducing them to Maverick. As her permanent detail, they were going to be together, he'd have to get to know her friends. He would see an entirely new side of her with entirely new people in her life. Despite the caution she'd warned herself to proceed with, she couldn't help but be hopeful that their friendship would find a way to restore what had been lost. But she'd changed since then, and a part of her feared maybe he wouldn't want the same thing.

She took a deep breath, exhaling slowly. It was all out of her control. Time, she reminded herself again. It would take time, and she couldn't force anything. It would unfold how it was meant to. She left her unit and gave a quick knock on Maverick's door across the hall.

"Hey," he said in what looked like part surprise, part relief when it opened.

At the very sight of him, her hope surged, and she struggled to repress it. That hope frightened her. She reminded herself that she had him back, and for now, she had to let that be enough. He was dressed in a pair of jeans and a long-sleeve shirt rather than the fatigues she'd come used to seeing him in. This version of Maverick before her, casual, like he was simply going out with friends, was a crashing reminder of the one she'd once known.

"I'm going down for dinner. Want to come?" she asked. She hoped she didn't sound as awkward as she felt.

"Yeah, I do," he said with a half-smile. "I'm starving, plus you're the only one around here I know," he said with a small laugh. He looked relaxed, comfortable with her standing there, not appearing to share her nerves.

"I know what that feels like," she said, nodding. "Let's go." She waved her hand as she turned, heading down the hall. "I have people for you to meet."

The City Center was bursting with life, and Tala welcomed all of its noise and chaos, letting it swallow her up. There was something about it that was beginning to feel like home. She wound her way through the crowd to the table beside the koi stream that she'd come to know as hers. Both Vi and Declan looked up as she approached, and Vi was off her chair and on her feet in the blink of an eye. Tala felt joy in her friend's embrace. There was a time when her naïve self thought no life would be better than the one she had in Columbia City. She was wrong.

"I was just telling Dec at breakfast that I was dying to have you back," Vi said with excitement. Her gaze shifted to Maverick, a surprised look on her face. "You've brought a friend."

"Guys," Tala said with a glance over her shoulder at him, "this is Maverick. I've known him a long time," she said, not elaborating further. How could she ever explain all that had happened? She was still trying to grasp it herself.

"I'm Vi and this is Declan," she said. "A friend of Tala's is a friend of ours." She smiled as she moved to a seat beside Declan.

"I second that," Declan said with a nod. "Welcome to The Village. You'll come to learn we're the best ones here."

Tala let out a small laugh. True as it really was. "He's also my new security detail," she added. From across the room, she spotted Vulcan in conversation with a group of people she didn't know. All heads immediately around him seemed to turn in his direction.

"Get some food, then come join us," Declan said before he popped a carrot into his mouth.

"Surprisingly," she said, looking away, turning to Maverick, "the food line moves pretty quickly."

Ten minutes later, Tala and Maverick took seats at the table, their dinner plates full: chicken tenderloins, steamed carrots, rice, and a salad.

"This is far better than the food on base," Maverick said, digging in eagerly.

"Base? Like military base?" Vi asked, perking up. "My brother's Unified military."

"Same," he said, looking across the table at her.

"So, can you tell us where you were?" Declan asked, leaning in closer to Tala. "You were gone longer than we thought."

She caught Maverick's gaze, then looked back to Vi and Declan. "I can't elaborate. But I will say that I got to see the mountains," she said with a smile that she knew lit up her eyes.

"I've never seen mountains," Vi said with a shake of her head. "Some day I'm going to travel. I'm going to see all these places that I've only ever seen in books and on TV. The places I know the most random trivia about."

"Like where?" Maverick asked.

"The mountains, of course," she said with a grin. "And the beach. Somewhere warm."

"It's warm in here," Declan said.

"This is climate controlled. It's not the same," Vi said with an eye roll. "I want warmth from the sun. I want the breeze on my bare arms. I want the sound of ocean waves crashing into each other, the water creeping over my feet as the tide comes in," Vi said, a faraway look on her face.

"With a description like that, I think anybody would want to go to the beach," Maverick said with a chuckle.

"I want to go to the rainforest," she continued. "I want to see the Redwood forests in Pacifica, and I heard the Tahari coast is breathtaking. I want to sand surf in the desert and climb to the top of a cliff—"

"You're afraid of heights," Declan interrupted.

Vi turned toward him and gave him a small punch in the arm. "Stop ruining this for me."

Tala laughed as he feigned pain, gingerly rubbing his arm where she'd hit him.

"Those are just a few places I want to go," she said.

"An impressive bucket list," Tala said. "I wouldn't mind the beach either."

Maverick turned toward her. "You've been to the beach many times."

"No, I want the kind of beach Vi described," she said. "The beach in Columbia City isn't like that. It's always windy, and even in the summer the water is frigid."

"That's true," he conceded.

Tala's mind took her back to Kane, to the days they'd spent walking the deserted beaches of the city. She could almost smell the tinge of salt in the air, feel his warm hand in hers. Missing him hit her like a sudden wave, hard, feeling it resonate deep inside.

"Tal?" Declan said. "You okay?"

Tala jerked her head up, her eyes drifting between all of them, her cheeks filling with heat. "Sorry," she said.

"It's okay," Vi said, her gaze meeting Tala's. The look she gave her told Tala she knew what was on her mind. And for once, Tala didn't mind the gentle look. There was something about the way she understood her that was comforting.

"There's a small concert Saturday night in the club," Vi said, changing the subject quickly.

"I'd hardly call it a concert," Declan said with a laugh. "It's a small band from some nearby town up top."

"A band, playing music, to a crowd, in a club… kind of sounds like a concert to me," Vi said.

Tala smiled at their banter.

"I go where you go," Maverick said with a grin that told her he wouldn't mind going. She wondered how long it had been since he'd listened to a band. Maybe that was something they did in Camp Washington. Maybe it wasn't.

A part of her didn't want to be social outside the four of them. Her days at Camp Washington kept her busy, they'd been a good distraction. But now, she couldn't help but want to be alone with her thoughts. She wanted to keep Kane alive in her mind, in her heart, keep him real. If it weren't for the empty spot inside, she would have nothing to show for him. Some days, she was beginning to think he hadn't been there at all. And that thought broke her heart. Even if it hurt to think about him, it was better than not thinking about him.

"Yeah, sure," she said after a moment. She could hear the forced enthusiasm in her voice, but Vi seemed to be the only one to pick up on it, and she pressed her lips together, frowning.

"Okay," Maverick said as he tipped his head from side to side, stretching his neck. They stood in front of a hundred-pound punching bag at the back of the gym, past the stationary exercise machines, past the weight machines. "You need to stay sharp. You need to stay in shape, prepared. You may not be MF here, but you never know when your skills will be needed."

Now this, this was the Maverick she knew. Undoubtedly. When they'd first met, over six years earlier, she couldn't stand him. She thought him arrogant. He was better than his entire training class, and he knew it. And when it came to Tala, as a mentor, he was harder on her than anyone else. But it didn't take long back then for that dislike to mold into something different when she realized he was pushing her to make her better, bringing out of her what only he seemed to see.

Standing in the gym now, she had no doubt this would be similar.

Tala taped her hands and wrists to help prevent injury and provide support while she was on the bag. It also helped improve her punches. It had been so long since she'd done any physical training, and she knew he was right to insist on it. Being prepared wasn't just about firing a gun.

"Let's start out slow," he said, standing off to the side of the bag. "Just some light jabs."

Tala set her body up, her legs shoulder-width apart, her left foot turned toward the bag. She brought both hands up, put her chin down, her eyes up. Then with a loose hand, she extended her right arm, her knuckles lightly striking the bag. Two jabs with the right hand, one with the left. Two with the right, one with the left.

"Good," Maverick said as he began to circle around her, studying her body positioning.

It didn't take long for Tala to feel her heart rate quicken, her breaths deepen. She jabbed at the bag over and over as she warmed up her body.

"Okay, now some palm strikes," he said. "I want to see some of that force I know you've got."

Tala's mind zoned in on the bag before her as she resumed her stance, but rather than using a loose fist, she thrust her hand up hard, meeting the bag with the heel of her palm. Exhilaration pumped through her with the first hit. She hit again, alternating between hands.

"Higher on the bag," Maverick said. "You want your opponent's jaw, their nose. Remember height isn't on your side. You need to know your aim."

Beads of sweat gathered at her hairline as her breaths became rapid.

"Protect your face, keep that other hand up when it's not striking," he instructed. "Head down, eyes up."

Maverick's voice filled her ears, flooding her mind as she adjusted her body on command, her adrenaline pumping through her.

"Now throw in some hooks. I want to see this bag move under your power," he exclaimed.

Tala's arm swept around the side, the base of her palm meeting the side of the bag with force. With her opposite hand, she struck forward with an open palm, pulling her hand away as quickly as she'd delivered, then struck with another hook.

"Good!" Maverick called out. "Channel that energy. Sharp hits. Find the knockout point."

She struck the bag again, harder, her right arm finding the imagined point behind the ear of her opponent, then her left hand struck forward again. Hook, palm, hook, palm. Sweat ran down her neck, down her back. She felt it sting as it ran into her eyes, but she only blinked it away, keeping her focus ahead of her.

After working on her palm strikes, she moved to closed fist punches, working the bag under Maverick's careful critique. There was a power that rushed through her veins that she hadn't felt in a long time.

Maverick took his turn at the bag after Tala, his form pristine. All of his training was elite, and he thrived in it. He was a natural, striking the bag with force. Each one crisp, hitting exactly where he intended. When he was finished, they rounded out their workout with a brisk two-mile run, then stretched to cool and slow down their bodies.

Tala laid out on the mat, flat on her back. "I haven't done that in a while," she said, her breathing still not fully returned to normal.

He chuckled. "Then it's a good thing I'm here."

She turned, looking at him as he sat beside her. This was what forged their friendship in the beginning, maybe it could do it all over again.

"You were good today," he said, smiling. "Still got it."

Tala sat up, wiping at the sweat on her face. "Of course I do," she said, grinning as she elbowed him in the arm, and he laughed again.

"Tomorrow we'll do some endurance work, then the day after, I want to do some sparring. I'll get some punching mitts," he said.

She nodded, taking another deep breath. "You okay with this concert this weekend?" she asked.

"Yeah," he said with a nod. "Kind of looking forward to it. Want to tell me your hesitation?"

"I didn't hesitate," she said.

"You did. But you don't have to tell me. And we don't have to go," he said, his eyes meeting hers, small creases in the corners. She saw Mila in them.

He caught her off guard, and she found she wasn't quite sure what to say. "Maybe another time," she said quietly. "But yes, let's do the concert this weekend."

It had been a long week, and thanks to Maverick, a grueling one. Without question, her most strenuous day was when they sparred. Like always, he didn't go easy on her. He worked her hard, and while her body was sore, her mind was indebted to him for the mental diversion.

They'd spent the night before crammed in Vi's unit for game night, and Tala was impressed with Maverick's knowledge of random trivia. How he knew that a hashtag was actually an octothorpe or that the largest non-polar desert was the Sahara, she had no idea. Declan had been more than pleased to have him as an addition to his team, winning after too many consecutive losses.

Maverick stood in Tala's door wearing the same jeans from earlier in the day, but he now had on a navy V-neck shirt fitted just enough to show his toned body.

"You look nice," he said, and she glanced down at herself, a pair of jeans and a black one-shoulder tank top. She had put in little effort, though make-up could go a long way, and knew he was being kind.

"You know," he said, "we really don't have to go if you're not into it."

Either her feelings were etched more clearly across her face than she thought, or he could still read her better than she gave him credit for, picking up even the smallest nuances of her behavior. She was beginning to suspect it was the latter.

She shook her head. "Maybe not entirely, but we do need to go. I can't deprive you of a social life for the first time in five years," she said with a small laugh, hoping it sounded lighter than she felt.

He smiled. "I'd hardly say that, though you're right that I didn't get out a lot. We can leave whenever you want," he said genuinely, and she was grateful for that.

"Can I ask you a quick question before we go?" She was suddenly feeling bold.

"Of course," he said.

"You're UR. Which should mean you have ink somewhere. Do you?" she asked. It felt like asking Kane all over again. Like there was a secret in that ink.

"Technically, now I'm Unified military, but yes," he said, nodding. "I do."

She was quiet as she held his gaze. This felt so personal, testing the boundaries of their budding friendship.

Still standing in the door, he lifted his shirt, high enough to read the inked words above his heart. *One flag, one land.*

"The United States," she said quietly.

"It may not have land to stake claim to yet, but it's my country," he said, lowering his shirt again. He held her gaze for a moment. "I'd ask about yours," he said, cracking a smile, "but it's nowhere visible on you, even in a tank-top, so I won't."

She laughed. "Good. Now let's go."

Tala hadn't yet been to the club in The Village, which was just a large room with a stage on one side and a bar on the other. It was dim, lit by neon blue lights streaked across the walls, wrapping around the room, and colored lights like a laser grid on the ceiling, reflecting off a mirror ball that cast refracted light over the crowd below.

With Maverick behind her, she followed Vi and Declan who seemed to know exactly where to go, as they eased their way through the mass of people, closer to the stage, each of them with a drink in hand. In the dark and crowded club, Tala liked being just another body. It was easier to take her burdens off her shoulders, stepping outside of herself for just a while.

Outside the walls of the club, she was Thias's sister, she was the newest Revo against the Republic, she was supposedly a beacon of hope, her best friends were either dead or in a hospital, and she was a million and one miles away from the person she loved most. But inside the club, she was just a woman having fun with her friends, old and new. She felt the frenetic music pound in her chest, and she let it fill her up as she sighed in relief. She'd pick the weight of the world back up at the end of the night. But until then, she would seize the reprieve.

The music was loud, and her fingers had begun to tingle after her second drink. It was hot, the stagnate air stifling, strangers pushing up against her. And still, it all pulled her in. She let her hips sway with the beat of the music while she slowly sipped her third drink, laughing with Vi at Declan's terrible attempts to dance.

Twice, two different men tried to dance with Tala, but even in good fun, she wanted nothing to do with either of them, and Declan seemed to know just how to interject himself, sending each one away easily. Even Maverick, who slowly nursed a single beer throughout the night, seemed to enjoy the music, a smile on his face that made coming entirely worth it. She closed her eyes, letting the vibe around her soak into her skin, letting the energy consume her.

"Okay," Vi said, yelling above the noise, "it's not great music. But it's good music, and I say if it's good, then you dance!" She laughed as she lifted her arms high in the air and spun in a circle.

"I think it's the alcohol talking," Maverick said with a smirk, leaning in, "because this music isn't even good."

"It doesn't seem to bother you. I've seen your smile tonight," Tala said with a chuckle.

"Guilty," he said as he shrugged his shoulders.

"Roll out the purple carpet, the princess is here!" Wren yelled to no one in particular as she pushed her way through the crowd toward them.

Tala rolled her eyes at the sight of her. It figured that she couldn't go long without running into her again. With her, it felt more like being hunted than it did coincidence when they did meet.

"What do you want?" Tala hissed with impatience. Despite the music, her body stilled.

"I'd tell you I missed you while you were gone," Wren said with a sly smile. "But my father taught me never to tell lies."

"And would this be the father who's in prison?" Tala said, cocking her head to the side. Fight fire with fire, she told herself. If it was possible, Wren managed to get to her more than even Bishop did when she was MF. At least Bishop she knew how to handle.

"What did you say?" Wren snapped, her back straightening, her eyes narrowing. Something in her immediately darkened.

"You heard me," Tala said, lifting her chin, though she was still inches shorter.

"Do not speak to me about him," she said through gnashed teeth as she took a step closer to Tala, her hands clenching at her sides.

"You're the one who brought him up," Tala said. Vi stopped dancing, taking a step closer to her.

Even in the dark, Tala could see Wren's eyes were flooded with anger.

"Go ahead," Tala said tauntingly. "Hit me. I dare you." Wren may have stood half a head taller than her, but she knew she had nothing to fear.

"Tala," Maverick said, his voice low. But even with the music pounding through the room, she heard the warning.

Wren was quiet, her body stiff as she looked down at Tala with hatred.

"All talk and no moves," Tala said, her eyes holding Wren's gaze. "Now back the hell off." She seemed to bring out the worst in her, not recognizing this side of herself. But she wasn't going to back down. She wasn't a princess, and Tala was going to make sure Wren knew it. "Get out of my face," she spat as she turned away, taking the last swallow of her drink.

Vi stood with wide eyes, a smile on the corner of her mouth. Despite the people crashing around them, both Declan and Maverick stood unmoving.

"That's a nice shade of bitch you're wearing," Wren said quickly before turning on her heel. Pushing herself between people, she quickly disappeared, swallowed up by the crowd.

"That," Declan said with a laugh, "was the best thing I've seen all week."

"You should've just hit her," Vi said. "I'd never have the guts. Afraid she'd scratch my eyes out. But you've been trained for lethal force. You would've held your own just fine."

"Umm, no hitting people," Maverick said sternly. He wasn't wearing the same smile that Vi and Declan were. "Tals, what the hell was that?"

"That," she said with a nod in the direction Wren had run off in, "was me not taking any more shit. I'm tired of always having to play nice."

"She had it coming," Vi interjected in her defense, putting a hand on Tala's shoulder.

Maverick sighed, and while she knew he had more to say, he kept his mouth shut. But Tala could see it on his face, his disappointment.

The buzz of the evening quickly dissipated for Tala. And she could see plainly that Maverick was no longer enjoying himself.

"You okay?" Vi asked, her lips close to Tala's ear.

She glanced at Maverick as he stood watching the band, still holding the beer bottle that she knew was emptied long ago. Looking back at Vi, she nodded.

"Think I'm going to call it a night," she said, the fun time she'd been having deflated.

"You sure?" Vi asked, casting a sideways look at Maverick. "Really, she had it coming," she said encouragingly to Tala.

"I know," she said solemnly. "But my night's over." She reached out, pulling Vi into a hug, their skin sticky to the touch.

"You're leaving?" Declan asked, his shoulders falling.

"Yeah, but I'll see you tomorrow."

"Breakfast," he said, then leaned in closer. "And I don't care what he says," he added with a discrete nod toward Maverick. "But that was awesome."

Tala smiled. There was a small part of her that felt a little bad knowing exactly where to hit Wren. But mostly, she just didn't care.

Maverick was quiet as they took the stairs back to the fifth floor, and Tala could feel his seething disapproval.

"Be pissed all you want," she said when they reached the fourth floor and he still hadn't broken his silence. "But I don't regret what I said."

"Tala, you wanted her to hit you," he said, his eyes focused ahead. "She wouldn't have stood a chance against you in a fight."

"I knew she wasn't actually going to hit me," she said flatly. "But sometimes you just have to do what it takes to defend yourself. To put a stop to the bullshit."

Maverick came to a halt in the middle of the stairs and turned to her. "I don't know what you've been through. But I watched that video your brother made, and I know he cut you down hard. But Tals, you can't let him take the good from you. You can't let him leave you jaded."

"Are you kidding? Take the good from me?" She let out a mocking laugh. "He took the best from me. And you're right, you don't know what I've been through. Not even a little bit. Because you left," she snapped, then continued up the stairs, taking two at a time, leaving Maverick in her wake.

Tala woke to a soft rapping on her door, and she rolled over, reaching for her palm pad. She sat up slowly as she realized she'd slept through breakfast. She had a missed call and two missed messages from Vi. She set the palm pad back down, telling herself she'd read them later.

Another knock.

"I'm coming," she said, her mind still shaking away her sleepy fog as she pried herself out of bed. She opened the door, surprised to see Maverick on the other side. He held out his arms, two disposable cups in a holder in one hand, a small paper bag in the other.

"I've come with gifts for the sake of world peace," he said. His face was straight, and it took her a moment to realize his joke.

"Is that coffee?" she asked, her nose picking up its fresh aroma, her mouth beginning to salivate.

"Only if you forgive me for being an ass," he said, his face softening.

There was no way she was going to turn down coffee. She sighed in defeat. "Okay. I forgive you for being an ass."

"Good," he said as he handed her one of the coffees. "And a cheese bagel." Her eyes widened as he held out the bag, and she quickly snatched it from him. "I was hoping you still loved these, and I see that you do," he said with a chuckle as he stepped into her unit.

"We looked for you this morning in the City Center," he said as he crossed the room, taking a seat on her sofa. "But Vi said it's not unusual for you to sleep through breakfast."

"Not really. I don't always sleep well," she admitted, then took a sip of the coffee. It was hot on her tongue, but it tasted like a small piece of heaven. It was the wake-up call she needed.

"Your unit looks exactly like mine," he said a moment later. "And sort of like Vi's."

Tala nodded. "They all basically look like versions of each other." She took the seat on the other side of her couch, opening the bag in her hand. "No one in The Village is allowed to live alone," she said, then tore off a piece of bagel and popped it into her mouth.

"You mean, like how you and I have rooms that are just full of roommates?" he asked with a smirk.

"The fifth-floor units seem to be the exception to everything. It's the secured living quarters. Leadership live up here too, though don't ask me which rooms because I never see anyone coming or going," she said. "Everyone in the general population has at least one roommate. Vi said the largest units can sleep up to eight."

His eyes roamed the room while Tala took slow sips of her coffee and continued picking at the bagel.

"I knew the Revos had an underground compound, but this is far more extensive than I imagined."

She nodded. She'd felt the same way when she first arrived. "I'm still uncovering all of its little treasures."

"So," he said with a pause, his gaze settling on her. "I talked with Vi at breakfast."

Tala looked up, her eyes meeting his.

"She told me about Kane," he said gently.

She hated the look in his eyes, like she was something fragile, something breakable. She'd made it this far and was still mostly intact. The last thing she wanted was for him to feel sorry for her, even if he had the best of intentions.

"I had no idea," he said apologetically.

Tala swallowed hard. Even Vi didn't know all of it. "It isn't just Kane," she said, looking away. She hated the tears gathering in her eyes, and she blinked hard to keep them at bay. "It's my parents who it turns out were murdered. It's my partner that died in my arms. It's Mila still in the hospital." She felt him stiffen beside her at the mention of his sister. "And it's Kane. It was supposed to be just a couple days before the Revos could get him across the border. It's been over a month without a word. And I'm barely hanging on. Every day, I get up and I just try to do my best for that day."

"Do you want to talk about it?" he asked.

There seemed no point in continuously digging up her emotions, her pain. She was trying to bury it. She didn't want to feel it; she didn't want to think about it. But she also knew there was no escaping it. It lived deep inside her, a monster she couldn't slay. "What do you want to know?" she asked.

"What do you want me to know?"

She took a deep breath as she shrugged. "Maybe we could do this gradually. There's too much for one conversation."

"Okay, I can understand that," he said with a nod. "So today, let's do Kane."

She took a breath. "I didn't know you could love someone the way I love him," she said simply, her eyes meeting his. Others could judge her, even Maverick could, but it was the truth and she wasn't going to shy away from it. "Maybe that sounds trite, but it's true. On paper we were the least likely people to come together. But there are just certain things you can't stop once they're put in motion. With him, it was like destiny and the universe and all the galaxies shifted in one moment of time to bring us together. And I've never been the same since."

Maverick was quiet as he held her gaze. She wanted to know what he was thinking.

"I've never heard you talk about anyone like that," he finally said after a moment. "I didn't even know you believed in that kind of love."

"I didn't. Not until I felt it." She looked away, catching her breath, composing herself. "You want to know about Kane? I'll tell you about him," she said, turning back to him. And she did. She told him in loose detail how they met, how he'd become her friend, her ally, when she felt like she had no one. She told him how he'd changed her life from the very first night they met, and how he wouldn't let her leave the Republic without him. Not once did he ask for something from her that she didn't want to give willingly. He never tried to make her into his own version of Tala. And he'd gone down fighting… for her.

A small smile curled at the corner of his mouth, wrinkle lines spreading out from the corner of his eyes. "That's what you need to fight for, Tals, that kind of love. Not just for you and Kane, but for everyone else who knows something like that. And for everyone who deserves something like that. The world needs more love, more good. If that's what you fight for, how could destiny do anything other than conspire along with you?"

Despite the wound that came with talking about Kane, she smiled. There was something beautiful in that idea. Maybe it wasn't true, but maybe it was.

ELEVEN

It had been just over a week since Kane made it to Marina's farm, and he was growing more and more restless each day. More than once, he'd considered taking off on foot, but he knew that was just his desperation talking to him. It was over six hundred miles, and he'd be walking directly into the frigid temperatures of winter in the north. So he would have to continue to wait and hang on to the hope that something would come his way. He had to keep his mind focused; it had to be stronger than his emotions. He'd never get anywhere without a clear head.

Finally, after too many gloomy days to count, the sun had come out. It was warm on his skin as he did the morning chores. It was a quiet morning on the farm, and he was on his own. Gerrit had fallen ill the day before, most likely with the flu, but his condition had become concerning during the night when he'd take a turn. Unable to keep even liquids down, he was dehydrated and couldn't get out of bed, and had spiked a fever of over one hundred and three. Marina woke early, taking Iris and Burke with her into Edmond. Desperate to bring the fever down, she needed to go to the pharmacy and then get a few groceries as well. Burke went with her under the pretense of needing air filters for Marina's car, though Kane suspected she was fully capable of getting them herself. Burke seemed as restless as he was. So while Gerrit slept in the house, Kane was in the yard doing what had to be done.

He was finishing mucking his last cow stall when he heard the sound of crunching gravel below the tires of a car. He tossed the pitchfork to the side and pushed the wheelbarrow of shavings out of the barn to the dump pile in the back, but he came to an abrupt halt when he realized the car wasn't Marina's, but rather the same man who had stopped by days before. Bridger, Kane thought, wracking his brain for his name.

"Morning," he said as he walked around the front of his pickup toward Kane.

Kane clutched the wooden handles of the wheelbarrow harder. He tipped his head at the man. "Marina's not here," he said after a moment.

Bridger kept a good ten-yard space between them. "Ah," he said as he gave the yard a sweeping look around. "My wife baked a pie. Thought I'd drop it by. Just you out here?" he asked, his eyes settling on Kane.

"Yep," he said, trying to keep his voice calm, though his heart was racing. His natural inclination was always fight rather than flight. But in that moment, he didn't think fighting was his best option. The most important things he could do now were to not draw attention to himself and to not raise suspicion. "Marina ran into town." He set the wheelbarrow down, letting go of the wooden handles, sure he would break them if he clutched them any tighter.

"You're not one of her brothers," Bridger said as he hooked his thumb in one of his belt loops.

Kane wanted to roll his eyes. "And what gives that away? The fact that I'm about four shades darker than they are?" Despite himself, he heard the edge in his voice.

Bridger just chuckled from deep in his throat. "Thought you were just passing through."

This guy was observant, not missing a beat, and Kane knew he was failing at not drawing attention to himself. He stood out, and this guy wasn't missing him.

"I am," Kane said steadily. "Just getting some things in order first."

Bridger nodded and kicked loose a rock in the gravel.

"I'll let Marina know you stopped by," Kane said, hoping the guy would get the hint and just move on.

"Where're you from anyway?"

He sighed. He was definitely failing.

"The Republic? Maybe DeSoto like Marina and her brothers?" Bridger asked.

"I really don't think it matters where I'm from," Kane said.

"I think I've got an idea," he said with a nod, his eyes narrowing. "Well, hope you get that stuff in order. Hate for you to have to do farm chores longer than you need to."

Kane didn't react, just held his stare, his jaw set in a hard line.

"I'll grab that pie from my truck," he said, shifting on his feet. "Put it on the porch for whenever Marina gets back."

Kane didn't move but took a breath when Bridger finally turned away, retreating to his truck. A minute later, after putting the pie near the door, he got back into his truck. He gave Kane a quick nod, then headed back down the drive.

"Shit," Kane said under his breath. He had a feeling the time had come to move on. He'd waited long enough. Now all he needed was a plan. He dropped his head back, the sun bright in his eyes. He summoned Tala in his mind. She would fortify him for what was coming next. He'd been biding his time. But he wasn't going to waste one more second. He couldn't afford to.

Taking a breath, he lifted the wheelbarrow and headed for the back of the barn.

It was dark by the time they wrapped up the evening chores, and Kane waited patiently in the dark silence of the den for Burke to finish showering so he could go next. Gerrit's fever had finally dropped after being on an around-the-clock regimen of medicine, and he looked less lethargic after Marina had gotten him to eat an ice pop and keep down some water.

When they got back from town, Kane told them about his visitor, and he could see the alarm in Marina's eyes, though she tried her best to hide it. He understood her fear was well placed.

"Let us at least make some kind of plan for you, even if it's not much," she had insisted. "Money, food, some warmer clothing. You're walking into winter on the plains. If you're not prepared, you'll freeze to death. Gosh, what if you're caught in a blizzard?" She was anxious.

He'd tried to decline her offer for everything she wanted to give him, but the rational part of himself forced him to agree because he knew he'd need the provisions and money. Sheer force of will wasn't going to protect him from the elements or keep him fed. But he insisted on paying her back for all of it.

"Worry about that once you're safe," she'd said. He was grateful for her hospitality.

He had agreed to stay for two days while she prepared him for his journey. And everyone decided it was best to keep him indoors. If he thought he was restless then, he couldn't imagine what he'd feel like after two days locked inside. Even in Columbia City he'd never stayed contained in his bomb shelter for long.

Kane emerged from the bathroom, freshly shaven and in clean clothes as Marina handed him a basket of fresh laundry.

"You can fold it yourself," she said, but with less bite than usual.

He took the basket into the den and pulled his clean laundry from it, still warm in his hands from the dryer. He folded each piece sloppily, then tucked them in his duffel. He was trying to impress no one.

He and Marina and Burke ate a late, quiet dinner of breaded chicken, mashed potatoes, and green beans, and Marina was insistent he take multiple helpings.

"I've got thirty-six hours to fatten you up," she said, though her eyes didn't meet his.

He couldn't help but smile.

Marina explained that Bridger was her nearest neighbor, about a mile away. "He's a good man. I'm sure you're fine," she said, trying to convince herself more than anyone else. So while Kane and Burke washed and dried dishes after dinner, Marina decided to call Bridger. "At least to thank him for the pie," she said nervously.

Kane didn't even bother to try to listen, his mind was consumed with the details of his impending journey, of the dangers he posed for Marina and her family simply by being there. Mostly though, he was torn in different directions by fear. If he stayed, he put everyone at risk. If he left, there was a chance he'd never even make it to Tala. He promised her he'd find her again, and the thought of failing, of leaving her waiting for him twisted at his insides.

A sound caught in Kane's ears, and he straightened. A vehicle was coming up the drive. Just as soon as he realized it, Marina appeared in the doorway of the kitchen, her eyes wide.

"Someone's here," she said quietly as she ended the call on her palm pad, unanswered.

"Take the baby," Kane directed at Burke. "Bring her upstairs."

Marina didn't skip a beat as she headed for the pantry, emerging a moment later with a shotgun in hand.

"What the—"

"Firepower isn't just for men," she said, her eyes narrowing as she crossed the kitchen and headed into the living room, to the front door.

The lights were off in this part of the house, the white beams of headlights streaming in through the large picture window that looked out over the front yard.

Kane strained to listen. The squeal of a vehicle door opening, feet on the gravel. There was only one person, and they walked slowly as they approached the house. He could hear the easy, rhythmic beating of the stranger's heart, catching him by surprise. If someone had come for him, he expected a rapid heartbeat, an erratic heartbeat. Someone thrilled at the prospect of bringing him in. But this one was in control. It was steady. He wasn't sure what to make of that. Maybe it was no one, he thought to himself, though he was unconvinced. It was well after dark, too late for someone to casually drop by.

Burke eased down the staircase, leaving a sleeping Iris upstairs.

"Do we know who it is?" he asked in a whisper as Marina crept toward the window, her shotgun held firmly in her grasp. She leaned to the side, peering out the window, then quickly retreated, shaking her head.

A knock came at the door. The tension was thick, and Kane stood beside Marina and Burke just on the inside of the front door. While the stranger seemed calm and composed, Marina and Burke were anything but. And it only made Kane more anxious.

"Hello?" a man's voice called from outside.

"Who are you?" Marina asked with edge in her voice. "I don't know your vehicle. What're you doing on my farm?"

Kane had to hide his smile as he looked at her. She was small and unassuming, but she was feisty.

"I'm not here for you," the man said almost lazily, his voice rough.

"Then what'd you want?" she asked as she looked nervously at Burke.

"I'm not going to hurt any of you either," the stranger added.

"So then, what do you want?" she snapped impatiently.

"I have a message," he said.

Kane listened hard, the stranger's heartbeat was still the picture of calm, and by the sound of his voice, he seemed almost bored. Something wasn't adding up.

"A message? First, tell me who you are," she said.

"You can call me Sidewinder," he called through the closed door.

Marina shot another look at her brother, her brows furrowed. While they exchanged glances of confusion, realization was beginning to dawn on Kane.

"What the hell kind of name is that?" she yelled back.

"The only one I'm going to give you. Now, can you open up so I can give you the message? Or am I going to have to keep yelling?"

"I can hear you just fine through this door," Marina said firmly.

"Fine," the stranger said with a heavy sigh. "I'm here on orders from Vulcan with a message for Phoenix."

While Marina's breath hitched as she held Burke's gaze through the darkness, Kane felt his body relax, his shoulders falling under the release of their tension.

"It's time to fly north," Sidewinder said. "Bluebird's waiting."

"Am I supposed to know what that means?" Marina called out.

Kane stepped up to the door. "It's fine," he said calmly as he reached for the knob. "You don't need that gun."

"If you're opening that door, you better believe I'm going to be holding this gun," she said. "You know what the heck that crazy message means?"

Kane gave a solemn nod of his head. "I'm Phoenix."

Both Marina and Burke took a small step back as they looked at him with uncertainty.

"Someone going to open this damn door or are you going to keep me out here all night?" Sidewinder called out impatiently.

"It's fine. Really," Kane said. He switched the deadbolt and with a turn of the knob, he pulled the door open to reveal a man, older than Kane, and shorter, with broad shoulders and sinewy arms. The deep V-neck of his shirt revealed black ink along his collarbone and his left arm was covered from his wrist to the sleeve of his t-shirt in more colorful ink.

"Phoenix?" he asked at the sight of Kane.

"Sidewinder?" Kane said.

He seemed unfazed by Marina standing in the open doorway, still clutching the shotgun. He stretched his ink-covered arm out, then licked the thumb on his other hand. He swiped the wet thumb hard across his forearm, his way of showing the ink was real.

Kane turned, lifting his shirt to reveal the phoenix on his ribcage.

Sidewinder nodded. "Right then, get your stuff. You've got fifteen minutes. I'll wait out here," he said, then turned and ambled down the porch toward his truck.

Kane glanced at both Marina and Burke, bewildered looks on both their faces. "It's okay, guys. Promise," he said with an assuring nod as he passed them.

"This whole time," Marina said as she followed closely on Kane's heels.

"What? You're actually surprised?" Burke said, then turned and quickly headed back up the stairs.

"But Tala Alexander, she's a recent converter. I follow what's going on," she said with both bite and shock.

"I hid nothing from her," Kane said as he began tossing the rest of his things into his duffel.

"What if this guy is full of crap? What if he's really here to hurt you? Turn you into MF?" she asked, her voice laced with emotion that surprised Kane.

He turned to her, a small smile on his face. "Then I'm dead," he said. "But it won't come to that. He's for real."

"Because he knew a few code words? You don't even know his name!"

"He knows the right words. And I'd rather not know his real name. Or him mine," he said with a sigh. He turned toward her. "There aren't words for me to say that can show my appreciation for all you've done for me," he said softly. "I'll be just fine with this guy. You don't know what I'm capable of," he said with a smirk. "I've got to get back to Tala. Nothing else matters."

Marina was quiet as Burke came into the room with Kane's deodorant, toothbrush, and his dirty clothes from the bathroom hamper. "Sorry you've got to pack them with the rest of your stuff. They stink," he said with a low laugh under his breath.

Marina turned and walked briskly away.

"You think this guy's legit?" he asked Kane.

He nodded. "I do. This is my window. I've got to go."

"I understand," Burke said as he shifted on his feet. "Chances are I'll never see you again, so I've just got to say thanks. You helped Gerrit and me, and you pulled your weight around here."

"Listen," Kane said, lowering his voice. "I know people. And I don't want Marina to worry about it, but I'll have them take a look for Corban. They're the best. Hopefully, you can find out either way."

Burke nodded slowly. "I appreciate that."

Marina appeared a moment later, a plastic bag in her hand. "Here. Stick that dirty stuff in here. Tie it off. It's for diapers, so hopefully, it'll contain that smell well enough."

Kane took it, grateful, then quickly shoved his clothes in it. He tossed the last of his things into the duffel and zipped it up. He grabbed his worn leather jacket from off the chair, slung the bag over his shoulder, then turned, Marina's and Burke's faces sober.

"She's a lucky girl," Marina said after a moment, not trying to hide the emotion on her face. "And I hope you make it to her."

Kane pressed his lips together and offered a sad smile. He knew she was genuine, but he also knew that the loss of her husband was weighing on her in that moment. He was on his way to Tala while she was nowhere nearer finding out anything about Corban. He would do anything he could for her. He owed everything to her.

"Thanks," he said quietly. It wasn't enough, but he didn't know of anything else.

They stepped aside for him, and he walked past, leaving the den that he'd called home for far too long. Gerrit appeared in the doorway of the kitchen, his eyes sunken, his skin sallow.

"Hey man," he said weakly, then coughed to the side. "Heard your time's come."

"I think so," Kane said. He'd been through a lot with these guys, and to tell himself they didn't matter to him would be a lie.

"Thanks for everything, and good luck," Gerrit said as he reached out his arm.

Kane gave it a firm tap with his. "Same to you."

"Now back to bed," Marina said, shooing him with her hands.

Kane walked through the living room, then stepped outside, the night air cool on his skin. Sidewinder was sitting patiently behind the wheel in his truck.

He stepped off the porch, Burke and Marina right behind him, then turned toward them.

"Just stay alive, man," Burke said. "We didn't do all this for each other for things to go south for you now."

"Don't worry," Kane said, a smile curling at the corner of his mouth. "I didn't come this far to stop here."

Marina gave him a gentle pat on the shoulder. "You take care of yourself, you hear? I owe you thanks for helping get my brothers to me."

"I'd say that was a team effort," he said. "Good luck with Corban. I really hope he makes it back to you," he said, then cast a brief look at Burke who nodded knowingly. "Right," he said, then turned, making his way to the other side of the truck. He gave one last glance at Burke and Marina as they stood huddled together at the bottom of the porch, then tossing his bag onto the floor, he climbed into the truck, closing the door behind him. A moment later, Sidewinder shifted into drive, the truck lurching forward.

As he watched the farm disappear behind him, he breathed a sigh of relief.

"You've been a tough guy to find," Sidewinder said, his eyes focused on the road, the black pavement lit up by their bright headlights.

"Just trying to stay alive," Kane replied.

"We won't make many stops. About twelve hours straight through. Provided we don't hit any snow, which we might, based on radar. But I'm hoping to have you at The Village no later than noon tomorrow."

Kane turned his head, looking out the window, the world cloaked in obsidian darkness, the moon and the stars hidden behind heavy cloud cover. But he didn't care about the landscape. Nothing mattered anymore with one exception. He was on his way to Tala.

Tala took a drink of her coffee, which was now more tepid than hot, but she didn't care. Coffee was coffee. The breakfast crowd in the City Center had long since dispersed, and while there were still people lingering, there always were, most of the tables were now empty. The janitorial team was out in droves, cleaning the tables, the chairs, the floor.

"Have you heard anything from Vulcan since we got here?" Maverick asked, sitting back in his chair as he absentmindedly rotated his empty coffee cup around on the table.

Her anger flared at the mere mention of his name. "Nope, nothing," Tala said, biting back her emotion. That wasn't entirely true. While he hadn't sought her out since Camp Washington, she'd gone looking for him. The day after returning to The Village, she went to his office with Thias's warning.

"And what exactly would you like me to do? She's in a Republic hospital. My reach only goes so far. And she's not even one of us," he'd said coolly to her.

It wasn't necessarily his lack of options that had made her angry, it was his disregard for her that infuriated Tala. She wasn't asking much, Mila was just one person. She refused to believe there was nothing he could do, not someone who had as many connections as him. In the end, he said he'd do what he could. That was nearly a week ago.

But she couldn't tell any of this to Maverick. Mila was his sister. The five years he'd been gone didn't change that. She would check in with Vulcan in a day or two for an update. There was nothing she could do beyond that. Her helplessness only made her guilt claw harder at her. Thias would hurt Mila only to hurt Tala. Her best friend would be turned into a powerplay, and she was powerless to stop it.

"What do you make of him? Captain Vulcan?" Maverick asked, bringing Tala's mind back to the present.

No one had asked her that before. "I don't know," she said truthfully with a shrug as she straightened in her chair. "He gave the orders to get me out of the Republic. Not that it means he's some kind of saint."

"Smart, at least," Maverick said. "You and I both know his motivations behind having you at his side. Not that they're misplaced," he added quickly.

"I understand what you mean," she said, knowing it was true. "I guess I don't know exactly how I feel about him. But it's not about how much I like him or not. The people here, they all look to him, they respect him. So I have to think he's a good leader. On some level." She took a breath. "He's Kane's brother."

Maverick perked up in his chair, his forehead puckering. "Seriously?"

Tala nodded. "His real name's Addox. He's just over a year older than Kane."

"Didn't see that coming," he said.

"They're… estranged," she said. "They went different ways when they were younger. When we were trying to get out of Columbia City, out of the Republic, we had no idea it was him who was making it possible."

"But he just left him behind?" Maverick looked almost offended at the thought.

"Some saint, right?" she said.

Tala's pocket vibrated from her palm pad. "Want to bet that's him now?" she asked as she reached for it. Not many people messaged her during the day, and both Vi and Declan were working. She sighed as she read his message.

My office.

"Want me to come with?" Maverick asked. "I've got nothing else to do."

"No. I'll find you later. Go explore or something," she said, gesturing around them.

"Maybe I will," he said. "We'll train later today. Let me know when is good for you."

"Got it. See ya," she said as she passed by him, grabbing his empty coffee cup and tossing it into the trash along with hers as she made her way for the stairs.

Tala gave a small knock on the open door, Vulcan sitting at his desk. He looked up and waved her into the room.

"Take a seat," he said as he motioned to the chairs in front of his desk rather than his seating area.

Tala sat uneasily. She wasn't sure what to expect. Their last conversation hadn't gone like she wanted it to, but she also wanted something to do. A job. Maverick's pep talk from the other day stirred something in her.

"I've called you in here for two reasons," he said matter-of-factly, getting right to the point.

"Okay," she said, sitting up straighter.

"First, I want to give you an update on Mila."

"Mila? What about her?" she asked, instant tension in her neck and shoulders. She swallowed hard, suddenly unsure she wanted to know.

"She was released from the hospital yesterday," he said.

Tala didn't even know she was awake, but she could tell by the look in his eyes that there was more to it, that this wasn't a story of celebration.

"MF got to her before we did," he said calmly.

Tala's breath caught. "What does that mean? Is she okay?" she asked, her voice unsteady. Her mind immediately went to the worst-case scenario. "Is she alive?" she asked, nearly choking on the words.

Vulcan typed on his computer, then adjusted his holographic screen so that Tala was able to see it. She watched a silent video of a woman, of Mila, being escorted into Command, flanked by two MF.

"Thanks to some very skilled individuals, we have access to one of the surveillance cameras outside headquarters," he said.

"What happened to her?" Tala asked, her stomach in knots.

"They held her overnight, but she's alive. She left Command about an hour ago," he said soberly as he pulled up more surveillance footage, Mila stumbling out of the building. Even from the low-quality footage, Tala could see she was clearly disheveled. Her hair was in a messy ponytail, her shirt torn, and her arms clutched tightly around her body. A minute later, she disappeared into a public car.

"They hurt her," Tala said, answering her own question. Her heart fell at the thought of what they'd done to her while also being relieved to know she was alive.

"It looks that way. Though how, I'm not sure," he said. There was kindness in his voice somewhere. "They're looking for you. In the hospital, she was relatively safe because of the medical staff. Not to mention she was unconscious. MF didn't seem to be in any kind of hurry to have anything to do with her. It's possible Thias gave her no second thought in the beginning because he was confident he'd be able to locate you on his own. And I'm guessing MF likes to keep their interrogation techniques private. But they pounced on her within the same hour she was released."

Tala felt her anger surge. "I told you he threatened to harm her! She's his bargaining chip right now," she said, not even trying to hide her emotion.

"I understand that," he said steadily. "Which is why we need to act immediately and swiftly."

Tala swallowed, her brows furrowing. "What does that mean? Are you going to extract her?"

Vulcan nodded his head. "That's exactly what we're going to do."

Her relief palpable, she took a deep breath. "When? How?"

"Tonight. We've got a detail on her right now. No one is going to get to her before we do. And as for how, we're going to kidnap her," he said flatly, as though it were the obvious answer.

"What?" Tala gasped, sitting up even straighter in the chair. "You can't do that."

Vulcan folded his hands neatly in front of him, resting them comfortably on his desk.

"No! No, you can't do that," she said, slapping her hand on the desk. "She's been out of the hospital after nearly dying for less than a day. What do you think kidnapping her will do to her? How can that be the best option?"

Vulcan shrugged his shoulders, unaffected by her outburst. "It's not the best option, Tala, it's the only option. My people are aware of her injuries, her condition, excluding anything she sustained while in MF custody. She will be handled as gently as we can. But the kidnapping has to happen. If Avery showed up at her door and told her who he was, do you really think she'd willingly toss her belongings into a bag and hop in the car? Absolutely not," he said. "And I can't let my people risk having their identities blown over this. We make it look like a legit kidnapping, and we get MF off her tail. It'll keep her family safe too. MF will undoubtedly question them, but when they determine they know nothing, that they believe she was indeed kidnapped, they'll eventually leave them alone. It's not fair to them, I know. First Maverick, now their daughter. But I can't put a protective detail on everybody. This is the best way to protect them."

"If their grief doesn't kill them." Tala couldn't logically dispute Vulcan's argument. But the terror she knew Mila would experience made her heart hurt. After everything she'd gone through, and now she was about to go through this too.

"When she's out of the city, she'll be handed off to Freelancer—"

"Cara?"

He nodded. "Once she deems the situation safe enough, I've given her permission to disclose to Mila that she's being taken to you."

"But why would she believe her?" Tala asked. "Couldn't I just call her?"

He shook his head. "The Republic is interfering with in-country calls and data signals. And if they're monitoring for keywords, it could put us and the mission in a compromising position. And as for how Mila will believe Cara, well, that depends on you. I need details about something that only you and she would know. And I need a list from you, of any special items Avery should grab from your old pod. We don't have time for an endless list of things that are important to her. But a few things are good. We're not heartless monsters," he said with a smirk. "I can get a statement from you later today. So think about what you want to say."

Tala nodded. Maybe this really was the best way, but it didn't mean it was easy. She thought about Maverick and what this would mean to him. But she knew she couldn't say anything until Mila was in the clear.

"It won't be easy on your friend," Vulcan said. "But Boy Scout, Freelancer, they know what we're dealing with. I assure you they'll be… delicate."

Somehow, Tala didn't find this all too reassuring, good as Avery and Cara were.

"They'll grab her tonight. It's about thirteen hundred miles from Columbia City to here, and that doesn't include any stops or the handoff. We don't expect her here until the day after tomorrow. Sometime in the morning. Weather pending."

Tala took a breath. As hard as this was going to be for Mila, staying in the city would be worse. This kept her safe, this brought them together again, and after all these years, she would have her brother back.

"Thank you," she said after a moment. He'd kept his word. Even before she'd left the Republic, Avery agreed he would protect her, and that's exactly what they were doing.

Vulcan gave a slow nod of his head.

"You said you called me in here for two reasons. What else is there?" she asked.

Vulcan let out a heavy sigh. "It's Kane."

"Kane? What about him? Have you heard from him? Is he all right? Do you know where he is?" The barrage of questions was like word-vomit that she couldn't seem to stop.

"Tala."

It was a simple word. Just her name, spoken on an exhale that sent a shiver down her spine. She knew that voice like her own. It lived in her mind. It whispered to her in her heart.

She turned in her seat, her eyes finding his, dark and familiar, and she was on her feet in an instant, throwing herself into his arms. He was warm and strong and smelled of soap and leather, and in that moment, she thought her heart would burst from a surge of joy and relief and everything in between.

It was just like the very beginning, it was destiny and the universe and all the galaxies shifting in that very moment, bringing them together once again.

TWELVE

Tala couldn't fight the tears that welled in her eyes, nor did she try. She clung to Kane, her arms around him as he lifted her off the floor. Maybe she should've shown more restraint in front of Vulcan, but she didn't care. She'd dreamt of this moment, longed for it, and she wasn't going to let go.

His face buried in her hair, he breathed her in and only held her tighter. She knew that sometimes people built things up in their absence into something unrealistic. But having his arms around her was better than her heart could've imagined. She was home.

At some point, he set her back on her feet. It could've been two minutes, it could've been ten. She didn't entirely trust her knees, and she leaned into him to steady herself.

Gently, he kissed her forehead, then took her hand in his, his long fingers lacing through hers as they made their way to Vulcan's desk, taking a seat in the chairs beside each other. Even the couple feet between them felt like a vast distance.

"Where'd they find you? Why'd you leave Clara City?" she asked breathlessly, her voice thick with emotion. She couldn't take her eyes off him. He was beautiful and perfect, and her heart was full.

"He was already in the Colonies when we finally found him," Vulcan said.

Tala had to pull her eyes away from Kane as she turned toward Vulcan.

"One of my people in that area was contacted by a local farmer who suspected his identity," Vulcan said.

"What do you mean suspected his identity?" she asked, her eyes moving between both of them.

"I had to leave Clara City because I was named a person of interest in a Republic security alert. There was a bounty put out on me," Kane said.

Tala's eyes flared, and her brows furrowed. "But how did Thias even know about you?"

He shook his head, holding her gaze. "Not Thias."

"I don't under—" Her heart fell. "Vaughn," she said quietly. "It was Vaughn."

Kane nodded.

"How'd he get a photo of you?" She wasn't sure how much to ask in Vulcan's presence. Kane was already in the Republic's government database, she realized, because of his time spent in the research facility. But that had been over ten years earlier. She thought about Max. If Kane was found in the database, Max would likely be exposed too. Tala's mind began to swarm with all the new information.

"He didn't have one. It was a digitally created image. A damn good one too," Kane said. "I was cornered by two guys in a grocery store who recognized me right after the alert went out. I ended up hiding in a remote hunting cabin with them, both DeSoto nationals, about thirty miles north of Clara City. We were biding our time until an opportunity came up to get into the Colonies. With nowhere to go once I finally made it over the border, I ended up on their family's farm. Been there for the last week and a half."

Tala took a ragged breath, trying to imagine what he'd gone through to stay alive, to get to her. Her heart felt heavy. This was all because of her. Because she'd left him in that clearing.

"It's time to put this behind us. The point is that we found him, that he's here," Vulcan said. The indifference in his tone and expression took Tala by surprise. This was his brother. He seemed so cavalier about all of it. "I'm sure you'll have no problem sharing a unit? It'll take a day or two, but I can get you into one with a double bed rather than the bunks. Just please don't advertise this. Selene, at the desk outside my office, has your new palm pad programmed. It'll get you into the secured living quarters and your unit. It'll get you all your meals in the City Center, and there will also be funds available for any personal items that you need around The Village. Should you need more, please let Selene know. Take the next few days to relax and get comfortable around here. We'll discuss how to move forward afterward."

He was all business, and it irritated Tala. But Kane was with her now, so she didn't let Vulcan linger for even another second in her mind. He didn't matter.

Kane still held Tala's hand with a firm grasp as all three stood.

"Thanks, Addox," Kane said offhandedly, his apathy mirroring his brother's.

"I go by Vulcan here," he corrected him.

Kane cocked a brow. "Addox," he said again.

Tala felt a sudden tension fill the room. She had to remind herself that she wasn't the only one with an estranged sibling.

Together, she and Kane made their way to the administration desk down the hall. *Selene*. So that was her name. All this time and Tala hadn't realized that she didn't know it. And while she never smiled at Tala, she was smiling now at Kane as she handed him the palm pad. "It's all ready for you," she said sweetly.

"I've never had one of my own," he said quietly to Tala as they made their way toward the exit. He reached for her hand again, the touch of his skin warm against hers, sending a pulse of energy through her.

"We're not in the Republic anymore," she said, walking close enough to him that their arms brushed each other's. "You can be anyone you want to be here," she said as she glanced up at him.

"As long as whatever that is, I'm also yours," he said with a squeeze of her hand, a gentle smile on his face, and Tala felt her pulse quicken. Their time apart felt like an eternity, and with the blink of an eye, it was now over. It was behind them.

She led him to the living quarters, to her unit, her nerves buzzing as she pulled him along. Once inside, the door closed, she couldn't help but feel uncertain of herself. She hadn't been alone with him for so long, and she was still trying to convince herself that it was all real, that he was real. Standing beside him, the room felt impossibly small and shrinking by the second. All the regret that had consumed her seemed to be coming to a head. She swallowed hard, trying to force it back down.

"This is it," she said, hearing the nerves in her voice. "Cara was with me for the first few weeks. But I've been alone in here since. I sleep on the bottom bunk, and there's the bathroom," she added, motioning with her hand. "And my tiny living room space," she said with a small laugh. She was rambling now. She quickly turned away, unsure how to face him. Looking at him forced her to look at all the mistakes she'd made.

She inhaled a deep breath that shook as it filled her lungs. Her emotions were teetering on a precipice inside her, ready to spill over at any moment. As she stood there, she felt all of it. Her love for him, her regret for leaving him, the grief she had lived with since, the relief that he had made it back to her. She had been fighting her emotions for so long, and now they threatened to finally overtake her. People said that in the end, it was the choices they didn't make that they regretted. For her, it seemed to be every choice she did make. And it was eating away at her.

"Tala," he said, his voice low and deep and gentle.

She felt her tears well in her eyes, and she tried to blink them away.

He stepped behind her, his chest brushing against her back, his face in her hair. "Talk to me," he said, his mouth so close to her ear that she could feel the heat of his breath on her skin. As he slowly dragged the tips of his fingers down her bare arm, goosebumps raised across her body.

Her mind raced, filled with frantic thoughts, unsure of everything. But her heart, her body, they knew how to respond to him.

His hands grasped her shoulders, then he gently turned her toward him. She didn't fight it. He slipped his finger beneath her chin, lifting her face, her eyes meeting his. Those familiar dark, almost black, eyes with a tiny golden fleck glinting in the light. And just like they always had, they quieted her mind and settled her heart.

She blinked hard, and despite herself, a tear broke free, falling down her cheek. He gently brushed it away with his thumb and brought his forehead to hers, inhaling deeply, then slid his hands down her body. Tala closed her eyes as she let her senses take him in, the smell of him, his firm grasp on her hips, his steady and rhythmic breaths.

"Talk to me." His voice was a whisper between them. "We've never not talked to each other."

She was afraid to open her mouth, afraid she would fall apart. She'd been holding on to all the shattered pieces of her life for so long that she didn't know how to let go, how to let him in. But as she stood there, she reminded herself that this was Kane, that she was safe with him, that if there was anyone who would understand her, that would love her through everything, it was him.

"I don't know how you don't hate me," she said, her voice barely a whisper, though she knew he heard her. "I left you. I just… left you," she said, finding more of her voice.

"Tala, I could never hate you. You're an extension of me. It would be like hating myself," he said, pulling his head away from her forehead, his eyes finding hers again. "I wasn't giving you an option to stay."

She exhaled slowly, her body shaking. "But—"

"No buts," he said, cutting her off. He gave a firm shake of his head. "It was the right choice, and I don't regret it. I'm here now. We're together. And that's all that matters."

He leaned down, his lips brushing gently over hers, and she felt a tingle at his touch. He pulled back, his eyes moving over her. There was a radiance in them that pulled at something deep inside her, that woke her up.

She reached up, sliding her hands behind his neck, and pulled him to her. Her mouth crushed against his, her desperation overtaking her. His arms, strong and steady, slid around her, pulling her into him. She pressed her body against him, closing all the space between them, melting into him. Her hands dragged down his back, his muscles taut beneath her touch. She slipped her hands beneath his t-shirt and felt him tremble at her touch. She tugged at the soft fabric, lifting it up his body, revealing inch by inch the large black phoenix. He grabbed at the collar, pulling it up, over his shoulders and head. She took a small step back as she took him in. He was beautiful and sexy and perfect. But he was so much more than all of that. It was the way he moved, the way he spoke, the way his eyes met hers. He brought something to life inside her, and she knew that she was his and he was hers. It had always been that way, even before they knew each other, and it always would be.

In one swift move, sliding his hands under her, he lifted her body, and she wrapped her legs around his waist. He was strong, holding her with little effort as he made his way to her bed where he sat, letting her legs dangle on either side of him. Gently, he placed a hand on either side of her face. He brought his lips to her forehead, to her nose. Tala's eyes closed as he kissed her left cheek, then her right. His lips moved along her jawline and to her ear, exhilaration coursing through her veins.

She opened her eyes, meeting his gaze. The look he gave her was all she needed, and she brought her mouth to his, deepening her kiss each second that passed. His hands roamed her back, down her sides, his fingers slipping beneath the hem of her shirt, dragging across her back above the top of her jeans. Every kiss she gave him was a word she wasn't able to say. And she knew he understood.

She relaxed under his touch, under the feeling of his body pressed against hers, feeling herself release everything she'd been holding on to so tightly. There was something about losing herself in him that seemed to bring her back together.

Tala curled into Kane, his arm beneath her, holding her close. With the tip of his fingers, he traced the thin black lines of her ink, the phoenix on the side of her ribcage. Being with him, lying beside him, felt like the most comfortable, the most natural place in the world to be. These were the arms she always wanted to be wrapped in. And those dark eyes that arrested her with only a glance were the eyes she always wanted to get lost in.

They spoke in soft whispers, as if any other noise would break the spell and force them back into the world. He shared his story, his journey over the last month with her, and she shared hers. Their conversation was their worlds coming together, and she couldn't help but feel that by learning to be apart, it only made them stronger when they were together.

She wanted to bottle up their moment and keep it with her forever.

"I'm just trying to picture you on a farm," she giggled under her breath.

"It's the worst place to be with senses like mine, trust me. I mean, it was good to have something to do, but farming is never an option," he said, shaking his head.

"Good to know. No farming," she said. After a moment, she laughed again.

"What's so funny?"

"It's just, I keep having this image in my head. You with a hat, patched pants, maybe a twine belt," she said.

"You just described the scarecrow from *The Wizard of Oz*," he said flatly.

"I know! It's what comes to mind. And only you would ever get that reference."

"Okay, you do realize I was doing farm chores and not out standing in a field somewhere? There is a difference." He chuckled as he brushed a strand of hair off her bare shoulder.

She leaned in, pressing her lips against his. "I know," she whispered, then kissed him again.

"I watched your broadcast," he said.

"You mean my advoprop," she corrected, trying to sound professional and serious, this was her job now, but she couldn't hold a straight face with him. "And what did you think?"

"That you're hot," he said, his eyebrow cocked.

"No, really," she said, playfully punching his arm.

"Honestly? I thought you killed it. Seeing you like that, all fired up, I knew I made the right choice. You had to go on, to do what you did, what you're doing. And I was so proud of you."

She was quiet, her gaze holding his, and she felt her guilt return, gnawing inside her.

"And really though, I also thought you were hot," he said, grinning.

She kissed him once more.

"What about Max?" she asked. She had wanted to ask about him earlier, in Vulcan's office, but it seemed a more appropriate conversation for just the two of them. "I mean, if Vaughn can connect you with the research project, it seems only logical that he could connect you to Max. It wouldn't be a coincidence you were both from the same small town," she reasoned.

Kane gave a small shake of his head. "Max is an expert genius, and he hacked those records a long time ago," he said. There were no traces of worry or urgency in his voice. "He deleted all of my information. As far as anyone would know if they pulled those files is that there were twenty-three test subjects rather than twenty-four. Vaughn had no idea what pod we came from. He said so himself. There were hundreds of possibilities. I don't worry about Max. We had protocols in place. I know he's safe."

His certainty didn't do much to relieve the twisted knot in her stomach, but if he was sure he was safe, she'd have to find a way to let it go. She sighed and curled farther into him, running her thumb over the coarse hair along his jaw.

It was a beautiful thing, how easily they fit together. She thought of all he had traversed to find her. His was not a feeble heart, theirs was not a fair-weather love. They were built for hard times, they were built to endure the storm.

Reality found them when Tala's palm pad began vibrating. She sighed, and Kane pulled her closer, holding her tighter, then he kissed her, his lips lingering.

"I had to get one more in before you run off to save the world," he said with a lazy grin.

She gave him a peck on the mouth, then rolled over, reaching for her jeans on the floor. She had two missed messages from Vi, and now Maverick was looking for her, likely wanting to know when they'd be training. She looked up at Kane, his eyes on her, watching her carefully.

"The real world calls," she mumbled with a sigh as she pressed herself against him, not wanting to give him up. He slid his hand behind her head, his fingers tangling in her hair, and he kissed her deeply. Even her toes tingled at the touch of his lips.

She rolled off the bed, surprised they fit on it to begin with. Tala dressed quickly while Kane took his time, and she watched him, wanting to memorize everything about him. He looked up at her, his eyes catching hers, and he smiled. There was a natural pull toward him every time those eyes found hers. It was beyond her own understanding, but something she'd never question.

"There's someone I need you to meet," she said, looking over her shoulder at him. She couldn't help but repeat to herself it was all real.

"Okay," he said, his voice deep and rough as he looked up at her, stirring something in her all over again. She forced herself to take a breath and quickly looked away. She'd never leave her room if it were up to her.

Tala took Kane's hand as they left her unit, and together they made their way down the hall that was all too familiar to her. She was suddenly filled with hope that she'd no longer have a reason to wander it at night. They rounded the corner, the hall opening up to the lounge.

Maverick sat sunken into the cushions on a sofa, looking down at his palm pad. Tala gave Kane's hand a hard squeeze. Just touching him had a way of grounding her.

"There you are," Maverick said, looking up. "We still train…ing today?" he asked, his sentence falling away at the sight of Kane beside her. He stood, a curious eyebrow raised, the room suddenly quiet. His eyes flitted briefly to their hands and realization dawned on him. A smile curled at the corner of his mouth.

"You must be Kane," he said with a nod.

"I am," Kane replied with reticence, casting Tala a sideways glance.

"This was unexpected," she said, feeling his fingers flex in her hand, "but Kane, this is Maverick."

Kane was quiet as he studied him from across the room. Tala couldn't help but feel there was a shift in the air. Maybe she was the only one who felt it.

"I thought you were dead," he finally said.

"I was. Well, to the Republic I was. I still am," he said, slipping his hands into the pockets of his jeans.

"Did you know?" Kane asked, turning to her.

She shook her head fervently. "I just found out. I'm still trying to wrap my head around all of it," she admitted with a glance at Maverick. "He's my security detail."

Kane gave a slow nod as he looked between them. "Does your family know the truth? Mila?" he asked. Tala sucked in a breath and gave a small jerk of his hand, silently screaming at him to say nothing about Mila's extraction. That was a conversation she needed to have with Maverick, alone.

"No," Maverick said. "No one did. No one outside the UR does."

Having both Kane and Maverick in the same space felt surreal to Tala. It didn't seem that long ago that she had walked on the beach in Columbia City, sharing Maverick, her dead best friend, with him. And now they were together, meeting for the first time. Each of them, in entirely different ways, had irrevocably changed her from the person she was before them.

Maverick pushed her to her physical and mental limits in the academy. He taught her discipline and cultivated fortitude. He was the first person after her mother to really believe in her, to see someone other than just another Alexander, someone other than the princess of the Republic.

And then there was Kane. Were there even words to describe what he had brought to her life? He taught her what it was to love, the kind that was deep and strong and complex. The kind that filled a person up and seeped into the very marrow of their bones. He showed her that intimacy wasn't just physical, it was emotional, it was feeling safe to lay one's vulnerabilities bare. He took down her walls and helped her to see who she truly was. She didn't just love him with her heart, she loved him with her soul. She didn't believe in fairytales, but she did believe in the two of them. He lit her soul on fire.

She was sure she'd met neither of them by accident, both shaping who she was in that very moment. She was made of the pieces of all the places she'd been, the memories she had, the people she'd loved. It was a strange convergence of her old and new life, and she was desperate for those pieces, from vastly different puzzles, to somehow fit together.

Tala leaned into Kane, his body sturdy. "We're still navigating things," she said. "But it's important to me that you both know each other." She looked up, her eyes meeting his, and she saw the hint of hesitation in them. Then he gave her hand a gentle squeeze, and it was gone.

Tala's pocket vibrated, and she pulled her palm pad out to see a message from Vulcan. It was time for her to help with Mila's escape.

"It's Vulcan. I've got to go," she said, her eyes shifting between Kane and Maverick, and both nodded in understanding. It didn't seem the ideal moment to leave, but Mila needed her, and she wouldn't let her down. "Do you remember how to get back to the unit?" she asked Kane.

"I'll get him back if he doesn't," Maverick said, swaying on his feet.

She gave him a small smile, then turned back to Kane. Reaching up on her toes, she kissed his cheek, then reluctantly left the lounge.

The following afternoon, Kane sat at the table he'd eaten breakfast at that morning, the same table he'd eaten dinner at the night before, watching the orange and white koi swim back and forth in the stream. On his own while Tala was finally having the conversation with Maverick about Mila, he opted to wait for her in the City Center rather than in their unit.

He'd been told to relax, to take a break after the many grueling weeks he'd had. He'd gotten the best sleep he had since Columbia City, despite he and Tala being on only a twin-size bed together, but now he was already bored.

Kane couldn't help but think The Village was even more daunting than Columbia City had ever been. Too many things looked the same from one floor to the next. But he couldn't deny it was an accomplished feat of engineering, though, according to Addox, much of it had existed before the Revos took it over. Old nuclear shelters and missile silos expanded and converted into the small city deep underground.

He sat back, lifting the front legs of the chair, rocking it as he tipped his head up, gazing at the high ceiling above him. The ceiling, made up of panels of virtual windows that reflected an overcast sky, was supported by steel beams around the City Center that looked like leafless tree branches. The large atrium had glass elevator banks on all four sides, twelve in total, with stairs that wrapped around them. He wondered what the flow of foot traffic was like in the mornings and evenings as people came and went from their jobs.

He thought about Tala, wondering how her conversation with Maverick was going. It wasn't going to be an easy one to have, and she'd stressed about it all morning. In addition to already being anxious about Mila's extraction. Kane tried to reassure her that she was in good hands, that Cara was good at what she did. He couldn't deny the value of her skills when he and Tala were escaping. But his encouragements did little to assuage her nerves.

Despite her state of disquietude, he couldn't help but see that she was different here. There was something about being out of the city, out of the Republic, away from her name's notoriety, away from Thias, that seemed to bring something to life in her. He couldn't help but smile. This new life suited her. And with both new and old friends, her world was finally becoming what she deserved. Here, she was just Tala.

"Kane," a voice called out from behind him, and he turned to see Maverick headed toward him.

He nodded a hello as Maverick took a seat across the table from him. He sunk back in the chair, crossing his arms.

"Tala's with Vulcan. Said she'd be down soon," he said.

"Okay," Kane said. He couldn't help but glance up at the fifth-floor south wing, even though he knew she wouldn't be there.

"Amazing how much quieter this place is during the day, lunch aside," Maverick said, gesturing at the few people around them.

"Sure is," Kane agreed.

"I'm still getting used to it myself." Maverick looked at everything around him but Kane.

This was idle conversation. But he could play along. "Yeah, there's a lot to get used to."

"I assume you know about Mila," Maverick said. Kane looked at him, not sure what he was reading on his face. Sadness? Eagerness? Maybe a combination of both and everything in between. He was sure that his reunion with his sister wasn't going to be anything like his had been with Addox. He still didn't know what he thought of his brother. Though he conceded that he'd actually made something of his life. Even if it was as a revolutionary leader.

"It'll be an adjustment for both of you, I'm sure," Kane said. He didn't really have any better advice for him.

Kane could hear the quickening in Maverick's heartbeat. He was distressed.

"I understand you know what it's like," Maverick said.

Kane eyed him carefully. "Tala told you?" he asked in surprise. He didn't think Addox would've wanted it to get out that they were brothers. He wasn't sure he wanted it to.

"Just that you're brothers."

He nodded. Kane knew nothing about him, but it meant something to Tala that he did. "I can tell you from personal experience that family is complicated. Sometimes we never get over things. Sometimes we do. I think that as long as you give Mila the space and freedom to feel what she does when she sees you, then you stand the best chance for forgiveness. I mean, that's what you're looking for from her, right?"

Maverick was silent as he looked down at his hands in his lap.

"Just give it time. I'd say, don't force it."

"Tala told me what you had to do to get here," Maverick said, changing the subject. "I admire your fortitude." There was no mockery in his tone.

"It wasn't easy, but it was worth it," he said.

"You know," Maverick said, sitting up, resting his arms on the table, his eyes finally fully meeting Kane's, "I would imagine it caught you by surprise, Tala's dead friend suddenly emerging back in her life."

Here we go, Kane thought. He was finally getting to the point of their conversation.

"I need you to know three things." Maverick's voice was low and steady. "First, I know what you and Tala are to each other, and I respect it. Second, while Tala and I were close, she was my best friend, if that doesn't sound too feeble, friends are all we've ever been. I think the world of her. There isn't much I wouldn't do for her. But you never have to worry about my relationship with her," he paused for a moment. "And third, I would do anything to protect her."

His gaze didn't waver, and his heart now beat at a consistent rhythm. His body didn't twitch, he wasn't sweating. And Kane believed him.

"I appreciate your candor," he said. "Though I would always trust Tala."

Maverick nodded. "As you should. Tala said you're good at reading people. I want you to know you can trust me too."

It was true that Kane didn't know what to think about Maverick's sudden presence. Tala had been close with Ronin, and he never questioned that. But despite how close she had been with him, he knew that she and Maverick had something different. But he did trust Tala. He would always trust Tala. Now it was Maverick who had to prove himself. It didn't matter to Kane what he said, those were just words. He wanted to watch what he did. That would be the real measure of truth.

They were up before the sun, the halls still dark, lit with the faux moonlight. The virtual windows showed falling snow, coming down heavily, with strong winds whipping it around, limiting visibility. Tala gripped Kane's hand as they left the secured living quarters, making their way to the stairs. She knew he could feel her tension, but he was the picture of calm, and it helped to calm her.

The Village was still mostly asleep, though they did meet a handful of people on the first and second floors, and there was chatter and loud clanging coming from the kitchen. They made their way to the entrance foyer, a large space to the south of the City Center with sofas and chairs, as well as the secure elevator bank to the entrance above ground. An oversized desk along the wall was the information hub for The Village facility and community, the words *The Village* mounted behind the desk with soft lights glowing around them, making them stand out against the white stone wall. There was no one at the desk that early however.

Tala took a seat closest to the elevators. It was Vulcan who was in contact with Cara, and he'd given Tala an estimated time of arrival, but she wasn't exactly sure when Mila would finally come through the doors, and her anticipation was making her whole body shake.

"Take a breath," Kane whispered, though there was no one around to hear them. Vulcan made an exception, letting Kane escort her to the entrance rather than Maverick. Everyone had agreed that Mila's arrival wasn't the time for their reunion. That would happen later in the day, or possibly the next, after Mila had time to process what was happening to her, where she was, and hopefully get some rest.

"What if she resents me for all of it?" Tala asked, her voice thick.

Kane slipped his arm around her, pulling her closer, and she was glad it was him that was with her rather than Maverick. She needed Kane's emotional support. "I don't know her. So, I can't say anything definitively. But I'm pretty sure that she won't resent you for any of it."

Tala's heart hammered in her chest, and she stole a glance at Kane. "I'm sure you can hear my racing heart," she said.

"It's a little distracting," he said with a smirk.

Despite herself, Tala smiled, letting out a chuckle under her breath. She sometimes wondered what it was like for him to experience everything so much more vividly than anyone else. His hand slid across her back, and she dropped her head onto his shoulder. Just like always, there was something about his presence that divided her burdens. She closed her eyes, taking in slow, deep breaths.

Tala wasn't sure how long they had been waiting. It could've been thirty minutes, it could've been an hour. She had stopped watching the clock long ago. It was painful to check it, thinking it had been fifteen minutes only to find it had been five.

Eventually, The Village started to come to life, people gathering in the City Center for the early breakfast rush, others passing through the entrance foyer to the secure elevators, heading to their jobs above ground, some returning from overnight shifts. Every ding sent her heart to her throat, her breath hitching. But it was never Mila.

Tala watched mindlessly as the young man who worked the information desk arrived.

"Do you want me to get you anything?" Kane asked, his voice no longer a whisper. It would never be heard over the growing cacophony of the City Center.

She wanted a coffee. But The Bean was on the second floor, and she couldn't bear for him to leave her. Instead, she clutched his hand tightly and shook her head.

Dropping her head back onto his shoulder, she sighed. The sound from breakfast was loud enough to drown out the thoughts in her head, and she found comfort in the familiar scents of Kane.

The elevator doors dinged again, and with eagerness coursing through her, she once again turned at the sound. She watched as Mila suddenly appeared before her, Cara by her side. They both stepped through the open doors and into the foyer.

With her heart in her throat, Tala rose to her feet. From across the room, their gazes met, tears springing into Tala's eyes as she sucked in a sharp breath. One moment they were standing across the room from each other, then the next, their arms were wrapped tightly around one another.

Mila shook as she cried into Tala's hair. "They told me they were taking me to you, but I just didn't know! I didn't know!" she sobbed.

"You're safe," Tala assured her in a steady voice, though she felt anything but on the inside. When they pulled apart, she saw how disheveled Mila was, which was a rare thing for her. She practically woke up glamorous. Her brown hair was in a knotted, loose pony with long tendrils that had fallen free and hung around her face. One eye still wore most of its mascara, the other had none, and her new tears were running black down her cheek. Tala offered her a sad smile as she wiped at her tears, drying them on her jeans. She glanced at Cara as she stood unassuming behind them, holding a bag that Tala recognized as Mila's. Without making a sound, she mouthed a *thank you* at her. Cara smiled and gave a knowing nod.

Mila sniffled as she wiped at her eyes, peering briefly over her shoulder, then back to Tala. "I really didn't know if I'd ever see you again," she said, her voice leveling. "But she knew things. I mean, how else would she know that I loved cardinals in the winter, their bright red against the snow, and that they reminded me of Maverick because he taunted them when we were kids? But I just didn't know what had happened to you. I woke from a coma, and everything was wrong. It was all wrong. The things they said you did. I just… I didn't believe any of it."

Tala watched Kane as he made his way to Cara, and the two began a quiet conversation that was drown out by the bustling City Center.

"There will be time to talk about all of it. To tell you everything," Tala said as she brushed at a loose strand of hair out of Mila's face. "But let's get you a shower and maybe some sleep. I can't imagine you've slept much."

Mila let out a breathy sigh. "You have no idea."

Tala frowned. She'd been through so much. Kane and Cara slowly approached them from behind.

Mila turned over her shoulder. "I can't thank you enough," she said to Cara.

"For what? Kidnapping you? Keeping you tied up in my car for the better part of the drive?" Cara said with a laugh.

"To name a few," she said with a smile that Tala found comfort in. "But also, for keeping me safe. And keeping your word. For getting me here."

Cara nodded as she shoved her hands into her pockets. "Just doing my job. Tala, take care of her."

Mila seemed to notice Kane for the first time, her eyes lingering briefly on him as he stood nearby.

"This is Kane," Tala said, her heart swelling.

"Hey," he said with a somber expression. "Glad you made it safely. This one's been a wreck waiting for you," he said, gesturing toward Tala.

Mila pressed her lips together, then turned back to Tala. "I'm glad you're here. I'm supposed to meet someone named Vulcan?"

"A shower first," Tala said.

"Is that really his name?" she asked, her voice low and her eyes wide.

"Well, that's the one he goes by these days," Tala said, giving Kane a furtive glance. "You can come to my unit. Then we'll take you to Vulcan when you're ready," she said as she gently nudged her along toward the interior elevators.

"I'll catch you guys later," Cara said as she handed Kane Mila's bag, then strode off into the City Center.

"Your unit… this is where you live?" Mila asked, her eyes looking up at the high ceiling.

"It is," she said.

Mila came to an abrupt halt and turned, her eyes once again settling on Kane. She studied him for a moment, then took a breath. "You're him," she said with realization. "You're who Tala was seeing in Columbia City. You're who escaped the Republic with her."

Kane gave a slow nod of his head. "Yes."

Mila took a ragged breath as she walked toward him, then quickly threw her arms around him, wincing, a flash of pain on her face that Tala didn't miss. "Thank you," she said, her voice cracking. Kane gently lifted his hand, resting it on Mila's back, and Tala couldn't help but smile. "Thank you for keeping her safe."

"You'll learn that you can always count on me to do that," he said as she pulled away.

Tala urged Mila along again, guiding her with her hand on the small of her back. "We're up on the fifth floor," she said as they neared the glass elevators.

"Kane!" a voice yelled out above the noise of the City Center.

Tala turned quickly on her heel in the direction the shout had come from and watched as a head of wild, curly black hair rushed between tables. A moment later, a pair of arms threw themselves around Kane, and Tala's breath caught.

"Wren?" he said.

THIRTEEN

Tala stared, her mouth gaped, and completely speechless as Wren's arms wrapped tightly around Kane. Practically hanging off him. He didn't particularly embrace her, but he didn't push her away either.

After what felt like a small eternity, Kane stepped back, Wren falling back onto her feet. Still, Tala stood wide-eyed, watching them.

"What're you doing here?" she gasped. Wren didn't even seem to notice her standing there, only feet away from them.

"Uh, probably the same thing you are," he said, his voice deep. "I didn't know you left the city."

"Not sure that's what a girl wants to hear, that she hasn't been missed. So I'll pretend you didn't say that," Wren said with a laugh. "I left over a year ago. Dad wasn't going to be getting out any time soon, and I just couldn't stay any longer. Went west. Gage and Hunter are here too!"

Kane nodded. "So that's what happened to them."

"Come sit with us for breakfast. They'll be down here any minute," she said emphatically.

Tala rolled her eyes as she glanced at Mila whose confusion was written plainly across her face. Tala cleared her throat as loudly as she could while still trying to be conspicuous. Kane would be able to hear her even if she whispered, though suddenly she wasn't so sure that he really would.

He glanced over his shoulder at her, his eyes widening, like she had become a second thought and he was just realizing her presence.

That was when Wren, following Kane's shift of attention, turned toward her, her mouth twisting into a scowl. Tala couldn't help but roll her eyes again.

"Actually," he said as he shoved his hands into his pockets, "right now's not a good time. Maybe later. I'll find you guys later."

Her smile briefly fell. "I'll be in the kitchen all day, and Gage is on the janitorial team during the day. Hunter works above ground. So maybe tonight? Find us during dinner. If you get lucky, maybe you'll catch us for lunch," she said, perking up as she reached out and gave a small squeeze of his bicep.

Kane turned away from Wren, his eyes meeting Tala's, and she tried to hide her surge of emotion. She was shocked and completely irritated. Wren, of all people? And she had the distinct impression it hadn't been just a casual friendship, the quick wave as they passed on the street kind of friendship. Tala looked away quickly and without a word, headed for the elevators, Mila beside her.

There was a taut silence in the elevator as the three of them rode to the top floor. Tala was thankful for Mila's presence, though she knew she felt the tension between them too. *Wren?* She kept repeating it over in her head, her anger rising a little more each time. When the door dinged and opened, Tala released a breath that she hadn't realized she'd been holding. Quietly, she stepped out of the elevator, Mila behind her, Kane behind Mila.

She led the way through the secured living quarters to her unit and welcomed Mila as warmly as she could, though she was entirely on edge.

"This is where you live?" Mila asked as she gave a look around.

"I'm supposed to be moved in the next day or so," she said, careful not to look in Kane's direction, though she felt his eyes on her.

He put Mila's bag on the floor near the dresser, then cleared his throat. "I'll let you two talk," he said. "Tala, I'll be in the lounge." Without any further lingering, he left the room.

"Okay, what was that?" Mila asked after the door closed. "I mean, I know I'm new here, but that was obviously something."

Of course she noticed. With the exception of Kane, and possibly Maverick, Mila knew her better than anyone. Tala reached out, pulling Mila into another hug, and she felt her stiffen beneath her arms.

"You have no idea how happy and relieved I am to see you," Tala said. She didn't want to answer her question about Kane. She wasn't sure she even knew the answer. "How are you, *really*?"

Mila sighed, sadness filling her eyes. "I'm not exactly sure," she said, her face flushing. "I'd say it's been a rough couple of days, but the truth is that it's been a rough few weeks. First the hospital, then…" Her voice fell away, and Tala knew what she was thinking. Her interrogation by MF.

"Come sit," Tala said as she took a spot on the sofa.

Mila sat beside her, emotion all over her face, in her eyes. "You told me not to go," she said quietly. "But I thought… I don't know what I thought. You were being dramatic? Irrational? Strange?"

Tala swallowed as she recalled their conversation before the president's Annual Address.

"And then MF started questioning me about you. They said you had something to do with it all, and I realized that you must have known something or you wouldn't have told me to stay away. I was so confused because I didn't know how you could possibly be involved. The Tala I knew would never be part of something like that," Mila said, practically all in one breath.

Tala's shoulders slumped. "I did know about it," she admitted quietly. "But not because I was a part of it. I tried to stop it," she said, her voice wavering. "But I failed. I failed at everything. And then I had to get out of the city, the country, because they were going to come after me. They would kill me. I knew about their plan. I knew the truth."

"Whose plan?" Mila asked, her face screwed up.

Tala let out a ragged breath. This was so much for one person to take in all at once. But Mila deserved the truth. "The attack on the crowd. The assassination of Royer…"

Mila's eyes were wide with fear.

"It was Thias," she said sadly.

"Thias was going to kill you? Tals, that makes no sense," Mila said with a shake of her head.

"I know," she said. Sometimes she told herself it wasn't real, and saying it aloud made it sound wild.

"They thought I knew where you went," Mila said, her eyes welling with tears, her voice thick. "They took me from our pod. I had just gotten home from the hospital. I didn't even know you were gone. And…" she faltered over her words, a tremor in her voice, and was unable to make eye contact with Tala. "They put me in a room…" Her eyes shifted, shadows in her gaze like she was staring off into a nightmare.

Tala reached out, putting her hand on Mila's. It was cold to the touch. Tala's heart was heavy as she looked at her best friend beside her. "You don't have to tell me. You don't have to relive it."

Mila pulled at the cuffs of her long-sleeve shirt, slowly sliding them up to reveal dark blue and purple marks around her wrists, and Tala's breath hitched. The air in the room suddenly felt stagnant, and she didn't know how to breathe.

"They tied my wrists and hung me from the ceiling. My feet were still on the ground, but I couldn't sit. I had to just stand there, and after a while, my legs were so tired," she said quietly. "My strength is still so diminished after my hospital stay," she said, almost apologetically, like it was somehow her fault. "They blindfolded me. Whenever someone entered the room, I had no idea who they were. I had no idea what they'd do to me. Sometimes they just gave me water to drink." Mila's eyes met Tala's, then she reached for the hem of her shirt. Carefully, she lifted it, wincing as she pulled it higher. Tala reached out, helping her tug it off. Mila sat in her bra, goosebumps raised across her arms.

Tala wasn't sure what she saw first, the two wounds from where she'd been shot, the surgical scars, or the large, red welts, five of them, across her chest and abdomen. They were raw, recent. Mila hadn't been interrogated, she'd been tortured.

"Electric shock," Mila said in a hoarse whisper. "But there's something else. I can't be sure. It was just a voice. But I think it was Thias that was there. In the room. His voice was so familiar. I told myself I was wrong, but now, maybe it really was him."

Tala had to swallow the taste of bile in her mouth, but she refused to let herself look away. "This is all my fault," she said, tears springing to her eyes, clouding her vision.

"Don't ever say that," Mila said sternly. "Don't ever think that. Never."

Tala wiped at the tears that fell down her cheeks. She wasn't sure how *not* to think that. He did this to her to get information out of Mila. Information about her. She finally turned away, unable to look at the welts any longer. Those marks were her punishment, not Mila's, yet they were burned into Mila, not her. Thias knew what he was doing. He knew exactly how to reach her, even a thousand miles apart.

"Despite everything they told me," Mila said, her voice stronger, "I never believed what they were accusing you of. And I told myself I had to be strong, for you. And every time they shocked me or tugged on the rope I hung from, I told myself that I was strong enough, that I could be strong enough for both of us."

Tala felt her heart breaking, shattering into a million pieces.

"But Tala," she said, gently placing her hand on her cheek, guiding her face back to her, "I never knew how strong I could be. And not for myself, but because I needed to protect you."

Tala shuddered. She didn't know what to feel, what to think. But of one thing she was certain, they hadn't broken her, Mila. Somehow, she'd endured. It was in her eyes, her strength, her resolve. Tala now had another reason to fight. But she didn't want to just fight anymore, now she wanted to destroy. Her heart filled with a rage she'd never known before, and it was laced with anger that was so acidic she felt it burning in her veins. Her guilt was like a sudden vice gripping her chest. She wasn't going to let even one more person be hurt because of her.

"I can't shower," Mila said, her voice steady as she reached for her shirt. "But will you help me wash my hair?"

Tala nodded, pressing her hate aside, at least temporarily. "Of course. You also need a doctor."

"Cara said she would make sure I saw someone."

"Okay," Tala said, standing. "Let's wash your hair. Then we'll go to Vulcan."

They wound their way through the corridors of the fifth floor, Tala intentionally avoiding the lounge. She still hadn't talked to Kane. She didn't even know what she'd say to him. But in that moment, Mila was far more important, and she welcomed the distraction.

In the secured offices, they were permitted to go directly into Vulcan's office, and Tala was taken aback to see Gemini standing beside Vulcan. But as they looked at her, it was clear they both had been expecting them.

"How about we sit over here," Gemini said as she gestured to the seating area. In her sleeveless shirt, Tala could see all the fine detailed work of the lion ink on her arm. "Mila, I'm Gemini, and this is Vulcan. Welcome to The Village."

Tala watched Mila give a half-smile while she fidgeted with a thread on the hem of her shirt.

"Cara has apprised us of your condition," Gemini said gently, "and I think it's best you see a doctor."

"Yes," Tala said fervently with a nod.

"It's awful what you've been through," Gemini continued. "And you're welcome here until we can sort out a few matters."

"Like what?" Tala asked. She saw the confusion in Mila's eyes as well.

"Well, The Village is only home to those who are in alliance with the Revos, for one. And everyone here must be employed," she said. "But, like I said, that can all be sorted out at a later date. For now, what's important is to get you some medical attention and to let you rest."

"We have people you can talk to about what you've been through," Vulcan added, though his voice wasn't as gentle as Gemini's.

"Right now, I think I'm okay," Mila said.

"We've programmed a palm pad for you to use in the interim," he continued. "While you settle in, we thought we'd give you some privacy. You're on the fifth floor near Tala for now. We'll move you to a unit with a roommate in a few days. And of course, you'll be able to eat in the City Center for all your meals."

She nodded, though Tala didn't expect she even knew what the City Center was. She'd explained nothing to her.

"Tala," he said, his attention redirecting. "Your new unit is ready. You and Kane will have to move this afternoon. Your current one is scheduled for cleaning later today."

"Okay," she said with a forced grin, a tug in her chest at the mention of Kane. The image of Wren wrapped around him surfaced in her mind, and she felt her anger flare all over again.

"Mila, all the information you need you can find on your palm pad. You can get it on the way out from our assistant. Your unit information can be found on it as well. We'll have the doctor sent there. You can eat or sleep, or whatever you'd like after that. Tala can assist you throughout The Village," Vulcan said as he stood.

Tala couldn't help but get the impression he was eager to get rid of them.

"Tala," he said as she made her way to the door, "we need to speak with you later. I'll reach out."

She nodded, then left the office, Mila beside her.

Tala helped Mila find her unit and brought her things to her while the doctor examined her. After getting a pain-relieving salve and antibiotics to prevent infection, she was bandaged up and the doctor left.

What Tala wanted to do was tell Mila that Kane could heal her wounds, that with the touch of his hand, all those welts could be gone. Though she feared it was the marks they'd left on her mind that were going to be where the true healing needed to take place. The ones on her body were nothing.

"Are you hungry?" Tala asked.

She shook her head. "My shock and adrenaline are finally wearing off. Now I'm just tired."

"Then get some sleep. I'm programmed into your palm pad, so message me when you're up and we can get you fed. Spend some time together." Tala thought about Maverick, wondering when the best time to reintroduce him would be. Mila seemed both equally strong and fragile in her current condition.

Mila nodded as she made her way to the bottom bunk. She curled up tightly in the blankets, and Tala suspected she was nearly asleep before she'd even slipped out of the room.

Tala quietly made her way down the hall, her heart heavy. She'd been gone so long that she wasn't sure she'd even find Kane in the lounge anymore. But to her surprise, there he sat, sunk back on a sofa, watching something on one of the TVs mounted on the wall.

He sat up at the sight of her, turning off what he'd been watching.

Tala sat on a different sofa than him, wanting some distance between them. She couldn't explain it, didn't understand it, but her heart felt like it needed some protection.

"How is she?" he asked. He leaned forward, his elbows on his thighs.

"She's been through a lot. And all because of me," she said, looking away.

"You know that's not true," he said. "She's been through a lot because of Thias."

She blinked away the tears as they pricked the back of her eyes. "Maybe," she whispered. She didn't want to have this conversation anymore. She took a heavy breath and steeling herself, she looked at him, their gazes meeting.

"How do you know Wren?" she asked, spitting it out before she lost her nerve.

"From Columbia City," he said, and she saw the tic in his jaw.

"That's pretty obvious." She heard the bite in her voice. "Just be straight with me. I've been through a lot in the last two hours. I don't want to be placated. I don't want you trying to manage my emotions."

If he was taken aback, he didn't show it. "Okay, we were sort of friends."

Tala crossed her arms over her chest and leaned back into the sofa. She refused to fill in the blanks for him. She wanted to hear him say what she already knew.

"And yes, we were together a few times."

She had known it was coming, but she still felt it in her chest. It was completely irrational, she told herself. Kane wasn't the only person she'd ever been with. But none of them were around, none of them were running up to her and throwing their arms around her. Vaughn suddenly appeared in her mind. She shuddered at the very thought of him, his hands on her. But she'd never been with him in that way.

"We didn't date or anything," he said. "I never did relationships. Until you," he added, and she saw his eyes soften. "Why does it even matter?

That's all long over, and it'll never happen again. Not only am I not remotely interested in her, but I'd never do that to you."

She knew all of that in her head, but it was her heart that seemed to be running things at that moment, and it wasn't convinced after seeing his and Wren's dramatic reunion.

"She's an awful person and has been riding me ever since I got here. That's why it matters," she said. She didn't even try to hide her anger. Though that anger went deeper than just Wren.

It was pointless to even try to explain the animosity between her and Wren without sounding petty. She was twenty-six years old. Secondary school ended a long time ago. She thought about her dig the last time she'd seen her, at the club. Wren wasn't the only one who'd been nasty. Though, she reasoned with herself, she wouldn't have given her the time of day had she not sought her out in the first place.

"I'm sure she doesn't mean it," he said. "She hasn't had it easy—"

"And what, this is a competition?" she said, cutting him off. "I haven't had it easy either. Or maybe my privileged upbringing just negates all that. I wouldn't understand, right?" she said sharply.

"That's not what I meant," he said, tension in his voice. "No one's had it easy. We all just handle it differently."

She knew it wasn't what he meant, but that's how she'd taken it regardless. Everyone seemed to think the *princess of the Republic* never understood hard times, never understood hard work. But at fifteen, she'd lost both of her parents. No special schools or fancy clothes and upscale restaurants took away that loss. When she was in the academy, she had pushed herself harder than everyone around her, determined to prove that she belonged there. Determined to prove that even though she was a woman, that even though she was an Alexander, she deserved her spot with the Militia Forces. That she'd earned it.

Tala rubbed her temples, her head beginning to pound.

"Hey," he said, getting up from his place on the sofa and moving to hers, taking a seat beside her, their legs pressed against each other. Tala's body straightened. "I'll have nothing to do with her if that's what you want. She's nothing to me anyway," he said gently, his hand slipping behind her.

Her eyes were fixed absently somewhere in front of her. Her brain was overwhelmed, her thoughts fragmented and scattered into a jumbled mess.

"This isn't just about Wren, is it?" he said.

With that, her tears returned, and she didn't have the energy to stop them as they ran down her cheeks. She took a deep, ragged breath, her body quaking.

"Talk to me," he said, his voice deep but soft.

She closed her eyes, the image of those welts on Mila in her mind, and her stomach twisted into knots. The sudden urge to be sick came over her.

He exhaled, his arm slipping all the way around her, and pulled her to him.

She curled into him, in the spot that only she fit in, but when she opened her mouth, nothing came out. She wanted to tell him, but she couldn't do it. She couldn't say what she'd seen, what she knew happened. Her anger was alive inside her, but she wasn't sure if it was anger toward Thias or anger toward herself. She had failed over and over again. They told her she was brave, that she was strong. But the truth was there was nothing heroic about her. Ronin was dead, Mila had been tortured. Even Kane had given up everything to be with her, leaving behind any semblance of a life in the city. All she'd done was stand in front of a camera and record some scripted words. In the Republic, terrible things were happening. But there were people there doing far more than she was, like bombing the shipping hub in Michigan City. And what did she do? She ran.

She hung her head; her shame was at her. It had been lurking in the shadows, and now it had its icy grip clasped around her heart. And it began to squeeze.

That afternoon, after Mila had rested and eaten, she seemed renewed which helped ease some of Tala's anxiety. Though not entirely. Her burdens were still heavy on her shoulders. Kane could see it. It was in his eyes every time they looked at each other. But she still couldn't bring herself to tell him. Saying the words would somehow make it all the more real.

Declan hadn't been able to slip away from work for lunch, but Vi was more than welcoming of Mila, as Tala knew she would be. Just like when she'd introduced Kane to them.

"This place is incredible," Mila said, her eyes wandering the City Center with its vaulted ceiling, the glass elevators, the small pond and koi stream that could be traversed by two bridges. Tala had felt the same when she'd arrived.

"Kane!" two deep voices called out in unison, and he sat up quickly. A smile spread across his face as two men approached them. Tala recognized them as the same men she'd seen lingering with Wren. Gage and Hunter.

"Hey!" one said with a large grin. He was tall and thin, with an angular face and faint freckles. His head full of wavy hair bobbed as he walked, hanging across his forehead.

With a wide smile, Kane stood and the two tapped forearms as the second one caught up, tapping his to Kane's as well.

"I couldn't believe it when Wren said you were here," the second exclaimed. He was shorter than Kane, though not by much, and his skin was darker. Tala could just make out the faint lines of ink crawling out from the collar of his shirt and up his neck.

Kane turned to Tala, his smile going all the way to his eyes. "Guys, this is—"

"Tala Alexander," the second finished for him with a nod and a pleased grin.

"Uh, yeah," Kane said, seemingly caught off guard.

That was it? *Uh, yeah?*

"This is Gage," he said, pointing with his thumb to the taller of the two. "And Hunter," he said, tipping his head toward the other. "They're friends from my old neighborhood," Kane said, glancing at the rest of the table. "Mila and Vi," he said, pointing at each of them.

"So man, tell us why you're here. When did you get here? I heard it's impossible to get out of the Republic these days," Gage said.

"That's a long story," Kane said, sighing as he ran his hand across his shaven head.

Tala sat quietly in her chair at the table, studying the three of them. It occurred to her that other than Max, she'd never met any of his friends in the Republic. Maybe Avery, but they never addressed each other like this. This was smiles and laughter. She gave a quick peek at Mila and Vi who seemed to be watching the three of them just as closely. Tala shifted in her chair, unable to pinpoint her unsettlement. Maybe it was simply how he'd introduced her. Wasn't she more than just *Tala Alexander* to him? Her palm pad vibrated in her pocket, and she pulled it out to see the all too familiar message from Vulcan.

My office.

"I've got to go," she said to Mila and Vi with relief to have an excuse to leave.

"Don't worry about Mila," Vi said. "She can stay with me until you're done."

Tala looked between them. "You sure? What about work?"

"I'll be fine," she said with a shrug.

Mila gave her an encouraging smile. "I'll be okay. Promise."

Tala offered both of them a half-hearted smile as she stood. She realized then that Kane had gotten a message too.

"Hey, I've got to get going," he said, his shoulders falling. "But we'll catch up later."

"The tavern at eight tonight?" Hunter asked.

"Yeah, sure. I'll have to find it," Kane said with a low chuckle. "But I'll be there."

Tala passed him quickly while they were saying goodbye, dumped her tray, and hustled to the stairs.

"Wait up," he called after her. He was on her heels in no time. "What's wrong?" he asked as he fell in stride beside her.

"Nothing," she said coolly, keeping her eyes ahead. In a matter of only a few hours, she'd discovered an entirely different side of Kane. And it wasn't that it was a bad thing, but it was unexpected.

They climbed the stairs to the fifth floor in silence, and she wondered what he was thinking. Her heart was pounding hard in her chest and it had nothing to do with all the stairs. It was tension, and maybe something more, though she wasn't sure what.

When they stepped into Vulcan's office, they were met by Vulcan, Gemini, and Maverick, Tala's eyes flicking between the three of them.

"Come on in," Gemini said. Tala had seen the other Revo leaders so little since she'd gotten to The Village that it took her by surprise to see her again. "Take a seat," she said, motioning toward the seating area.

Kane and Tala took chairs beside each other while Maverick and Gemini sat across from them, Vulcan lingering behind Gemini. Tala could see the blowing snow from the virtual windows behind him, and it sent a chill through her body.

"We've been discussing your role here in The Village," Vulcan said, looking at Kane. He put his hands on the back of Gemini's chair and rocked on his feet. "Everyone here over eighteen has a job. We all have a role to fill. That's how we earn our place in The Village, that's how our society functions. Everyone over eighteen must also pledge to the Revos to live here. That means ink. Which I hear isn't a problem for you," he said, his long dreads falling forward, his nose ring briefly catching the light.

"Maverick made a suggestion that we think could be a good fit for you," Gemini said as she crossed her legs. Though she now wore a black blazer over her t-shirt, lending her a more sophisticated look, she wore casual, blue leather boots over her fitted jeans. "But of course," she said, "it would have to be a good fit for you too. All three of you."

Kane and Tala exchanged a furtive glance, then she looked across at Maverick whose expression seemed impassive.

"We'd like you to be a second security detail for Tala," Vulcan said. "We don't think it's necessary for her to have a detail during the day, we have plenty of security, but for after dark and if she were to go above ground, whether that's Hatfolk or anywhere else. She would always have at least one of you. Both if the situation warrants it."

"And that wouldn't be a conflict of interest?" Tala asked and then cringed inside. She didn't want to give anyone the impression she didn't want Kane as one of her details. Her gaze caught Maverick's, and he gave her a strange look.

"That's exactly why we think he'd be the perfect person for the job," Gemini said. "We assigned you Maverick because who two have a history. We need people who are invested in you. Who would go above and beyond to keep you safe."

Tala couldn't argue with their reasoning. It seemed a logical idea. And if there was someone she felt completely safe with, it was Kane.

"This would also meet our criteria for a job for you," Vulcan added to Kane.

"I'm in," he said without hesitation.

A pleased grin curled on the corner of Maverick's mouth.

"Next order of business," Vulcan said. "We need to release another advoprop for the people in the Republic."

"We're going to hijack the National Statement again?" Tala asked.

"Nope. We'll record a video, then when transmission interference is down for the next National Statement, we'll distribute it to Revo leaders within the Republic. From there, it will be forwarded to the next level, who will forward it to the next level, and so on. The goal is to get our message to as many people without the government knowing about it. For as long as possible," he said as he walked to the digital wall. He unlocked it with his hand, and with a tap and a few swipes of his finger, a map of the Republic appeared before them, four red X marks across central Republic of Columbia territory.

"What you're looking at here are the locations of the third, fourth, and fifth largest steel mills, and the largest foundry in the Republic. All of which had their blast furnaces destroyed in a coordinated bombing just a few days ago," Vulcan said.

Gemini brushed the longer strands of hair on the left side of her face away from her eye. "Over seventy-five percent of the steel produced in North America is done so in the Republic. The Great Lakes Federation produces the second largest amount. This attack is a significant blow to the Republic. It cripples one of their largest export industries, but unfortunately, it simultaneously has created a rapid decline in personal liberties and human welfare for the people," she said with a grim expression on her face.

"Did anyone claim responsibility for the bombings?" Kane asked as he sat up straighter in his chair.

"We did," Gemini said, her frown turning into a pleased smile. "Ash released a statement to the Republic's government, though it never went public."

Tala exchanged glances with Kane. "This is where I come in," she said. She knew exactly where this was going.

Gemini nodded. "The success of these bombings will be the content of your message."

"The risks of being a Rebel in the Republic have never been higher," Vulcan said. "But people have been inspired. The days of simply acquiescing to the demands of the government are over. We want to continue to incite the rebellion, and to do that, we need to remind those within the borders that our mission aligns with theirs, that their action is supported. That it's encouraged."

"You said there's a decline in human welfare. How so?" Maverick asked.

"There's an increased presence of MF in all larger cities. Anyone suspected of dissenting is arrested on the spot. Some have been executed, an example being made of them, others are put in labor camps," Vulcan said. His jaw was set in a hard line. It was when he resembled his brother the most.

"But," Gemini said, perking up, "the Pacifica and Tahari armed forces have intervened on behalf of DeSoto. Joint military action there is holding off MF troops along the coast."

"Thias Alexander has some tough choices to make," Vulcan said. "Although Militia Forces is great in numbers, he doesn't have the manpower to divide and conquer on both ends. It's either the Rebels or it's DeSoto."

Satisfaction spread through Tala as she imagined her brother scrambling. He was losing control, and that thought sent a thrill of excitement coursing through her.

"Tala," Gemini said, squaring herself to her, "Jasper will oversee your advoprop. He'll be here this evening. I'll send your script to your palm pad. Review it. Learn it. We'll reach out later."

Tala nodded.

"That's all for now," Vulcan said as he closed the map on the screen, and with the swipe of his hand, he locked the terminal.

It occurred to Tala as she left Vulcan's office that she'd never asked about casualties from the bombings. The thought of innocent lives tugged at her heart, it really did. But she also couldn't help but reason that this was war. That nothing would be easy. That there would always be casualties. And even she wasn't exempt from it.

♦♦♦

Tala and Kane packed up their belongings and moved four doors down the hall, right beside the unit Mila was temporarily in. They unpacked their clothes, each taking two drawers in the dresser, each taking half of the cabinet in the bathroom. Tala carefully tucked her photos of Mila and Ronin in her drawer beside her shirts, then looked at the double bed. She'd never lived with a man. Not one that she was dating anyway. And even though it was Kane, she still felt both excited and nervous.

Kane's palm pad vibrated, and when he pulled it from his pocket, his eyes lingered on it for a minute, then he looked up at Tala.

"If you're going to be doing an advoprop, would you mind if I met Gage and Hunter at the tavern later?" he asked.

Tala wasn't sure why he was asking permission or if it was just a courtesy, and she noticed he didn't mention Wren. She didn't know if it was intentional or if she really wasn't going to be there. A part of her didn't think she wanted to know. He'd said he would have nothing to do with her, and she had no reason to doubt him.

"First night on the job and already you want time off," she joked, though the smile on her face felt forced.

"I don't have to go," he said.

"No, it's fine. You should go. I'll get Maverick," she said with a nod as she crossed the room and took a seat on the sofa. This one was softer, cushier than the one in her previous unit.

"You want to tell me what's on your mind?" he asked, his voice deep but soft as he sat beside her. "You might be good at hiding your emotions from other people, but you can't hide them from me."

Tala was quiet, avoiding eye contact. Instead, she stared at the tips of her shoes. "I don't know what you mean." She winced at her lie. It tasted bitter. There were a million things on her mind.

"Your heart is beating faster, you won't look at me, you're fidgeting with your sleeve, your cheeks are flushed," he said. "Would you like me to go on?"

She turned, finally meeting his eyes. "That's not fair. You're a human lie detector."

"I'd still know something was off," he said.

"I'm fine," she asserted.

He exhaled loudly with obvious frustration, then stood. "Fine," he said curtly. "I'm going for a walk."

"I've got a script to memorize," she said as calmly as she could, though she knew she was fooling neither of them.

A minute later, he was gone.

It was infuriating that she wouldn't talk to him. Somehow, they'd gone from elation at being together after weeks of uncertainty and separation to hardly being able to look at each other when they were in the same room in just a matter of days. He didn't know when or how it started. And he didn't know how to fix it.

He'd left Tala in the capable hands of Mila and Vi, who were helping her prep for her advoprop. He didn't know who Jasper was, and he really didn't care. They'd spent the late afternoon apart and ate a dinner that was monopolized with conversation by Vi. Not that he minded. He found he had little to contribute anyway. He tried to catch Tala's attention a few times, if only to give her a half-smile, but she had avoided him throughout the meal.

He found the tavern easily, without the use of the map on his palm pad. Despite the similitude on every floor, he was beginning to get comfortable with his surroundings.

Gage and Hunter were already at the bar when Kane walked in, and he took the empty seat beside Hunter.

"I still can't believe you're here," Hunter said as he waved the bartender down to them. "What do you want? Your first one's on me."

"Whiskey and water," Kane said. The bartender nodded, then quickly filled a glass and put it in front of him.

"How'd you manage to get out of the Republic? Are things as bad as they're saying?" Hunter asked between swallows of beer.

"That's a long story." One he didn't want to get into. "Not sure what you've all heard, but yeah, things are pretty bad." He recalled his meeting that afternoon. While Addox and Gemini had been pretty vague, he still got the hint. He thought about Max. Maybe it was time to make contact with him. He knew their protocol, but he still couldn't help but worry about him. He was the only real family he had left. He and Tala.

"Tell me," Kane said after a sip of his drink, wanting a change in conversation, "what've you two been up to? How'd you end up here? You guys were just suddenly gone."

"About a year and a half ago, Wren said she was leaving. With her pops in prison, she said she couldn't stay in the Republic. And we were up for an adventure, nothing keeping us in Columbia City, so we thought, what the hell?" Hunter said with a chuckle. "Roamed around Lakewood Colony for a little while, then met some Revos. Seemed like a good idea at the time."

"Been here over a year now," Gage added. "I mean, my job kind of sucks. I'm a damn janitor. But at least it's a job. The Village ain't too bad to live in. Better than the city ever was for us."

"I'm the one who lucked out," Hunter said. "I work above ground. I'm in the admin offices in St. Grace Hospital in Hatfolk. I get the real sun. Well, not really." He laughed. "I'm indoors all day. But the walk to and from gives me real fresh air and some real vitamin D."

Kane nodded and took another drink. It wasn't good whiskey, but after a couple of drinks, he knew he wouldn't even notice. Not that he was all that familiar with top-shelf whiskey, but at least higher grade than what he was drinking now.

"You got a job yet?" Gage asked.

"Security detail for Tala," he said. He felt an ache just mentioning her name.

"Ah, how'd you land that job? That's way better than mopping floors," Gage said, his shoulders slumping forward.

"I think I'd ask her out," Hunter said flatly.

"Tala?" Kane asked, caught off guard.

"No, no, no. She's way out of your league," Gage scoffed. "Besides, Wren would have your head." He elbowed Hunter in the shoulder as he was taking a drink, his beer spilling down his chin.

"Watch it!" Hunter chided as he wiped at his face and the collar of his shirt.

Kane wasn't sure if this was his moment to tell them about him and Tala or not.

"Wren can't stand her. But she'd have to get over it. It's Tala-freaking-Alexander," Hunter said emphatically with a smirk. "Enough said."

Kane was silent. Yes, Tala-freaking-Alexander. He took another drink of his whiskey, draining it, then waved the bartender back down.

"Same thing?" he asked, and Kane nodded.

"Julian," Gage said as he poured Kane's glass, "I'll have another beer." He turned back to Kane. "Max didn't come with you, did he?"

His window to tell them about Tala had just closed. "Nah. He's got stuff to do in the city still. Kind of strange to be without him though," he admitted.

Gage's pocket chimed, and he pulled out his palm pad, his face falling, a frown on his mouth. "Damn it."

"Work?" Hunter asked knowingly as Julian put Kane's whiskey in front of him.

"I'm on-call. Apparently some big mess in the kitchen," he said. He grabbed his fresh beer and took several long pulls. "Kane, man, we'll finish catching up another time." He tipped his head back and finished the beer in record time.

"Good luck with that mess," Kane said with a chuckle under his breath.

"So, you talked to Wren at all?" Hunter asked after Gage was gone.

"Nothing beyond hello," he said and took a large drink.

"You guys were good together. Back in the day," he said.

Kane cringed. "We were never together," he said firmly.

"Ah, you know what I mean. She was just always happy when you were around."

This was definitely a conversation he didn't want to have. "Tell me what else you do around here," he said.

"Just living the dream," he said with a deep laugh as he raised his beer bottle in the air, then took a drink. "It's really just my job and friends. That's about it. Single," he said with an eye roll. "I've asked out Vi, who you know, like half a dozen times. She shoots me down every time. Wren doesn't like her much either. Don't quite know why," he shrugged.

"Yeah, I know Vi. A little bit," Kane said. "She's definitely out of your league." He smirked and took another large swallow, then waved the bartender down for a third.

"Now you sound like Gage," he said. "But I always say, aim high. Oh hey! Her ears must've been burning. Look who's come to join us."

Kane turned over his shoulder as Wren made her way across the tavern, a bounce in her step and a wide smile across her face. Her eyes met Kane's even from across the room as she headed for them, and he sighed.

"Heyyyy," she said, dragging out the word. She took the open seat on the other side of Kane. "Heard a rumor you were here. Thought I'd come say hi for myself," she said and gave him a sly smile, a gleam in her eyes.

Kane felt the sudden tension in his shoulders and neck.

"I told you this was guys only," Hunter said in annoyance.

She shrugged. "Sorry. I've never been good at following orders. Julian, I'll take a gin and tonic," she said to the bartender. "So, Kane," she said with a grin as she dragged her hand across his forearm. Quickly, he pulled it away, setting his hand in his lap. "Tell me what've you been up to. Why'd you leave the big city for underground life?"

She hadn't changed one bit from the Wren he used to know. There was a time he liked her forward and flirtatious attitude. Now he had a feeling it was only going to mean trouble for him. Maybe Tala's judge of character wasn't so far off.

"Only been here a few days and already snagged a security position," Hunter said with feigned irritation. "He's protecting your very favorite person," he said with an antagonizing laugh.

"Ugh," Wren said, her distaste obvious. "I don't want to talk about her. Although, I will say that her other detail is pretty dreamy. How she lucked out with both of you, I'll never know. The princess always seems to get what she wants no matter where she is." She grinned as she looked at Kane. "Oh, but you don't need to be jealous of her other detail," she said, leaning closer to him.

"I'm not," he said, avoiding her eye contact, his irritation flaring inside. This wasn't how he was going to talk about Tala. He shifted his body, though sitting between Wren and Hunter gave him little room to move. With every giggle out of Wren's mouth, she seemed to only inch closer to him, and it was putting him on edge. Tala's enmity was becoming clearer and clearer.

"Is it true," she said, "what they're saying about things in the Republic?"

"Don't know what you've all heard," Kane said coolly, keeping his attention forward.

Wren shrugged as she reached for Kane's drink. "What've you got here?" she asked, then took a large swallow. "Whoa, I forgot you like that strong stuff," she said with a smile as she set it down, then put her hand on his thigh, hidden beneath the bar.

Kane grabbed her by the wrist and set her hand on her own leg, then took another drink of his whiskey. What he wanted now was to simply walk away, but Julian was on the opposite side of the bar, mixing drinks for someone else, and the last thing he could do was walk out without paying. He was right about one thing though, now that he'd had a few drinks, the taste of the whiskey wasn't so bad.

"Let me get you another," Wren said as she waved wildly down to the bartender. "Julian! Julian," she yelled, then pointed at Kane and Hunter.

"No, I'm good after this," Kane said, but only a minute later, a new one was put in front of him.

"Oh, you're not going to turn down my drink, are you?" she said with sad eyes and a pouty lip, then let out another giggle, sliding her hand over his arm again.

"Don't," he said sharply as he pulled it away. He'd told Tala he would have nothing to do with her, and now he was pinned in beside her as she was all but throwing herself at him. In a large swallow, he finished his drink, then took a swig of the next one. "This is my last," he said, turning away from Wren toward Hunter. The alcohol was beginning to hit him, and he felt warm all over.

"So, do you know people?" Hunter asked between sips of his beer. "I mean, you must if you got such a high-level job."

"A few," he said. It was safer with his back turned to Wren.

"Could you be any more vague?" she asked, nudging him.

"Nope," he said flatly.

"Well, I see you haven't lost your strong-silent-type personality," she said, then took a drink from her own glass. She slipped her hand below the bar again, resting it on Kane's thigh.

Grabbing her by the wrist, he forcibly moved her hand away. "I'm not kidding," he said sternly as he looked at her.

She looked taken aback, her eyes wide with surprise. A scowl formed on her mouth as she straightened, then looked at Hunter. "Where'd Gage go? I thought he was meeting you guys too," she said, irritation in her voice now.

"Some janitorial crisis," Hunter said with a shrug.

"I can't even imagine the things he has to deal with every day," she said, her face relaxing as she readjusted on her chair, pressing the side of her leg to Kane's.

"Wren," he said through a clenched jaw as he moved away from her, closer to Hunter. He took a large swallow of his whiskey as he heard a palm pad begin to vibrate. He tapped his pocket instinctively, though he knew it wasn't his.

"Hey, I've gotta take this," Hunter said, looking down at his palm pad. "I'll be right back."

As soon as his seat was vacated, Kane slid over, putting a stool between him and Wren, though he knew if she had her way, it wouldn't stay empty for long.

"I'm leaving," he said sternly, waving down the bar at Julian, who nodded to acknowledge him.

"What?" she gasped emphatically. "It's so early yet. And we've only had one drink together. Well, I'm still working on mine. You seemed to have drunk yours in record time."

"One was more than enough," he said and took one last swallow, finishing the whiskey, feeling it burn in his chest. He pulled out his palm pad, ready to pay as soon as Julian got to him.

"Okay," Wren said, her smile falling, the happiness in her voice draining. She reached for his face, taking it in her hands, holding it firmly as she looked at him. "I've been flirting with you this entire time, and all you do is push me away. You've never been like this in the past, so what is it? Are you just not interested, do you have a girlfriend?"

"Yep," he said and pursed his lips, shoving her hands off his face.

"Yep, what? You're not interested or the girlfriend?"

"Both," he said. He should've said it right in the beginning. It seemed like a slap to Tala and what she meant to him that he didn't.

"Oh," Wren said, looking stricken. "Since when do you have girlfriends? I mean, I tried that route with you. You were very clear about it. Kane doesn't do relationships." There was mockery in her voice.

"Not girlfriends. Just one. Things can change when you meet the right person," he said, satisfied that Wren looked completely deflated. Julian appeared, taking Kane's palm pad.

"Is she here… in The Village? I mean, because if she's not—"

"She's here," he said, the corner of his mouth curling in pleasurable anticipation.

"Do I know her?" she asked, her brows furrowed.

"You certainly know of her," he said as he stood. "But no, you don't actually know her. Though I get the impression you don't particularly like her."

Wren's face was blank for a moment, then her eyes grew wide. "Nooooo! Tala Alexander?"

At the mention of Tala's name, he couldn't help but smile.

"Kane, no! You've got to be kidding me. This, this is all wrong," she said. "Miss I'm-an-Alexander, Miss Privileged, Miss Preferred, Miss Princess of the Republic?"

Kane flexed his right hand, his irritation rising to the surface. "You don't have a clue."

"*I* don't have a clue? I think it's you who's lost his mind. You forget I waited on her and her pompous brother when I was a server at Chez Casimir in Stoughbour. Until my father was imprisoned, that is. Because then they fired me from my job because I was a supposed security risk," she spat.

Her resentment was palpable, and he sighed. "You're being dramatic. Tala had nothing to do with any of that."

"Kane, you're a Nameless, she's a Preferred. Whatever she gets out of your relationship will inevitably dry up and lose its appeal, and then you'll be just another Nameless to her."

This was his breaking point, and he lost his resolve. "You're way out of bounds, Wren." He struggled to keep his voice low, though heads had begun to turn in their direction. "You don't know the first thing about her outside your own judgments and prejudices. Those citizenship classes were just labels, and they were irrelevant for us. Besides, last I checked, we aren't in the Republic. Here we're just Kane and Tala," he said sharply, snatching his palm pad off the bar, then headed quickly toward the exit.

"Sorry, Hunter," he said as he passed him coming back inside. "My night's over. I'll see you around."

"Umm… okay," he said in confusion. "See ya!" he called as Kane turned down the hall.

Kane used his walk to the fifth floor to calm his nerves, feeling suddenly sober. One hug between him and Wren was all it took for Tala to see right through her, and he wondered how he could've been so foolish. He'd been worried about Maverick, and for what? He'd been completely true to his word. And Kane, able to easily pick up on any physiological responses, had no reason to doubt him.

He wasn't sure how he was going to tell Tala about his night knowing it would only frustrate her, upset her. But he knew he couldn't keep it from her either. There seemed to be so much between them suddenly, and he couldn't let this be one more thing to divide them.

When he stepped into their unit, he was surprised to see Tala dressed in her pajamas, gray cotton pants that tapered at the ankle and a loose t-shirt, her long, blond hair cascading over her shoulders, her eyes as blue as the sky on a cloudless day, and he smiled, taken aback. She was beautiful all the way to her soul. Wren was wrong about Tala in every way. He knew that even with whatever it was that was between them, he would only ever want Tala. For the rest of his life. It would always be her.

She gave him a sad smile as he approached, their eyes holding each other's gaze. One moment they were standing there, an unfamiliar distance between them, then she was suddenly in his arms, her body against his, her face buried in the crook of his neck.

"I love you," she whispered on a breath, and all he could do was hold her tighter.

"And I love you," he said, taking her in. He closed his eyes, letting everything about her consume him. She pulled away, holding his gaze for a brief moment, then pressed her mouth against his. She kissed him long and she kissed him hard, and suddenly everything felt right again.

FOURTEEN

Tala looked around the familiar living room, the room she'd called home for five years, her pod in Columbia City. The sun was setting in the distance, casting a soft orange glow all around her as she sat on the large sectional sofa. She heard a noise, a small thud from down the hall, and assumed Mila was home. A moment later, there was a hand on her shoulder. Startled, her body jolted, and she craned her neck to see Vaughn sitting beside her. He smiled, perfect white teeth, the dimple in his right cheek. But his smile didn't meet his eyes. There was something else reflecting in them. Hunger.

His fingers dug into her shoulder, and she tried to pull away, but he was stronger than her, holding her firmly in place. She knew right away she was in danger. It was the way his smile twisted into something menacing, the way his eyes narrowed as they fixed on her.

She tried again to pull away, but his other hand reached for her wrist, his cold fingers wrapping all the way around it. She tried to jerk her hand away, but he seemed only to grow stronger the more she resisted.

He pressed his mouth to her neck, his breath hot, leaving a moist trail behind as his lips roamed across her jaw.

"Vaughn," she said, hearing the fear in her voice. "Vaughn," she repeated louder.

He had no reaction to the sound of her voice. Letting go of her shoulder, he slid his arm around her, pulling her body into him, and once again, she struggled against his grasp.

He pulled his mouth away, his eyes meeting hers. "You cheated on me. You lied to me," he said. It was the voice she always remembered, but distant and flat, automatic. With a hard push, he had her on her back, and he swiftly positioned his body over her. There was something feral that flashed in his eyes. Fear was rising quickly in her, the hairs on the back of her neck standing on end. She began to writhe beneath him, which only seemed to bring him more pleasure. Her eyes widened with panic as he pressed his mouth to hers. Hastily, she jerked her knee up, hitting him in the groin. His body lurched forward as he yelled out. For a brief moment, his grasp slackened, and she struggled free, shoving him to the floor. Standing quickly, she began to run toward the door of her pod. She could see it just ahead of her, but with every step, she seemed to be no closer to it than before. It kept moving farther away from her.

"Stop fighting," a loud voice commanded.

She came to an instant halt, her stomach dropping, and turned. Vaughn was gone, and now she stood face to face with Thias. His jaw was set, a deep crevice between his furrowed brows, his blue eyes looking cold and severe.

"Stop fighting me," he said, his voice deep and sharp. "Look what you have done," he said, turning his head.

Tala followed his gaze to find Ronin standing to her right. Mila beside him. She swallowed hard as she looked back at Thias.

"You did this to them," he said, a deadly grin on his face.

Tala turned back to her friends. Ronin was now covered in blood from a bullet wound to his chest. He coughed, his breath labored, blood seeping from his mouth. He coughed again.

She looked to Mila, now on her knees, her wrists bound tightly. She had tears on her cheeks, red welts across her exposed chest, and her eyes were filled with terror.

Tala struggled for breath, the air in her lungs turning solid. She tried to run to them, but her feet were cemented in place.

"You did this," Thias repeated. "You."

Tala gasped for air as she sat up. She looked around, her mind coming back together as her nightmare drifted away. She was enshrouded in darkness, Kane sleeping beside her. Her heart racing, she brought her hand to her head, her forehead damp. She knew it was just a dream, but she could still feel it, Vaughn's hands on her. She saw the fury in Thias's eyes, the helplessness in Ronin and Mila. Her body shook and she swallowed hard. She'd had this dream before.

There was a time when a pair of dark eyes haunted her, a person who had pulled her from the fire all those years ago. Those dreams were gone, replaced by something darker, something that bled into the depths of her.

She was flooded with regret. Her shame contaminated her heart and held her prisoner inside her own body. The only way to be set free was to destroy Thias. She had to kill him.

Kane stirred beside her. He reached for her, finding her empty pillow. His hand fumbled through the darkness until he found her.

"You okay?" he mumbled groggily.

She turned to him, looking down at his shadowed face. He was the only one left untouched by Thias. And she would make sure he never had the chance to hurt him, ever.

"I'm okay," she said quietly, unsure he heard her in his sleepy stupor.

Tala lay back down, curling into him, his arm wrapping around her, pulling her close. He rolled toward her and lightly kissed her neck behind her ear. A moment later, he was back asleep. Tala let out a slow exhale. His chest rising and falling against her, she closed her eyes and matched her breathing to his. Maybe by holding her, he'd be able to keep her nightmares at bay.

❖

Kane waited in an uncomfortable chair in a small waiting area, Selene sitting at the administrative desk, casting him sideways glances from behind her glasses. Tala was with Mila and Maverick, overseeing their long-time-coming reunion, and Kane saw it as an opportunity to talk with Addox, one on one.

He glanced frequently at the time on his palm pad, watching the minutes tick by slowly. It was excruciating, the waiting. But what he had to say was important, and so he stayed. He'd wait as long as it took.

Tala was listless during breakfast that morning, her mind seeming to be far away. He remembered her being awake during the night. He heard her racing heart, felt her body shake in his arms, and he knew she was having nightmares. He saw it when he looked at her. She was trying to carry the weight of the world on her shoulders. Although he'd always hated Thias, he resented him now more than ever. He knew exactly where to stick the knife into her, and exactly how to twist it and turn it for maximum pain. Even after everything, he was still the puppeteer.

Kane knew she would hate him if she knew he was coming to Addox, but he refused to let her lose herself, to lose what was good in her.

"You can go in," Selene finally said in a sweet voice.

Kane didn't give her a second glance as he passed, heading toward Addox's office. Inside, he found him sitting at his desk, a hologram screen before him and papers scattered across the desktop. He was surprised to see the distress on his face when he walked in.

"Wasn't expecting you," Addox said in a low voice that sounded tired.

Kane took a seat opposite his brother and leaned forward, his elbows on his knees.

"What's up?" Addox asked.

"I'm here about Tala," Kane said, his voice steady.

"What about her?"

"I'm worried you're putting too much on her. She's personalizing everything. I see it in her, and she's going to break," Kane said, getting right to the point. He didn't want to have to linger any longer than he needed to.

"I disagree," Addox said, rubbing his hand along his jaw. "She's stronger than you're giving her credit for."

"Are you kidding me?" Kane snapped. He took a slow breath and reminded himself to keep his emotions in check. "She's one of the strongest people I know. But everyone has a breaking point. She's taking all of this on like it's her responsibility to save the world. Part of what makes her good is her loyalty to her people. But Thias is using that against her, and you're letting him."

"Her people, those you say she's loyal to, need to be inspired, they need to be encouraged. Fanning the flame of a rebellion is complex and it's long-term. And her role is vital," Addox said sternly, the tired look in his eyes now gone.

Kane sighed audibly. "I don't think you understand how deep Thias's betrayal, how deep her hurt goes. To her, he's not just some power-hungry, cruel dictator, he's her brother, and that brings with it a whole different level of complication," he said.

"Is this really about her family's betrayal, or is it more? Is it yours?" Addox asked, his eyes narrowing.

"Damn it, Addox," he said, his fist slamming down on the desk. "That has nothing to do with this. I've put all that bullshit behind me a long time ago."

"I killed him for you," Addox said, his voice rising.

Kane knew immediately he meant their father. He'd been shot, then his house burned down.

"And I looked for you. For years," he said.

Kane willed himself to breathe, deep and steady. "I don't care what you did or didn't do for me. This is about Tala. I won't let you destroy the best parts of her."

Addox was quiet for a moment, holding Kane's gaze. "Do you know why we appointed you to her security detail?"

Kane's brows furrowed, unsure how this had anything to do with what he'd come for.

"Maverick completely suffices when it comes to her physical protection. But you, your protection runs much deeper. Which is why you're sitting in my office right now," he said coolly. "I see the connection you two have, and if there's anyone who can help support her emotionally while she carries this mountain, it's you."

Kane ran his hand over his head, feeling the stubble of his hair growing in. "You don't get it. I don't want her to carry this mountain. Victory comes when she climbs it. Don't put the burdens of your cause, of your vision, on her shoulders."

"So help her carry it," Addox said. "Tala has never been forced to do anything for us. She's been a willing participant in everything."

"You're as bad as Thias. You all know exactly how to manipulate her and make it look like it was her choice to begin with."

"Tell her to walk away then," Addox said with a shrug.

Kane was silent.

"You know she won't. She's too invested. Which is why you're here having this conversation with me rather than her," Addox said, pushing a dread away from his face.

"Believe me when I tell you that if you jeopardize her life in any way, I will come after you."

"Then I certainly hope that never happens because we both know that I wouldn't stand a chance against you," he said, his lips pressed together.

Kane saw something flash in his eyes, there one moment and gone the next. He took a deep breath and rose to his feet. "As for Ismet, I don't care how he died. He was a mean son of a bitch and a poor excuse for a father. If you thought that killing him would somehow engender trust between us because we're brothers, you were dead wrong. You all died to me the day I was taken away. Now I have Tala, and that is exactly why I'll fight you for her." He turned on his heel and headed for the door.

"How's she doing?" Maverick asked, his sad eyes meeting Tala's as she put two guns and ammo on the small counter in her bay at the shooting range.

Mila appeared at Tala's door that afternoon after she and Maverick were reunited, her eyes red and swollen, her cheeks stained with tears. All she wanted to do was curl up on Tala's sofa and cry. And then she eventually fell asleep.

"She just needs time," Tala said. "She's in shock. And you can't blame her for that."

He nodded solemnly. "I thought dying was hard. Turns out this is ten times worse."

Tala reached out, putting her hand on his shoulder. She knew there were no words to help him. To help Mila either. They both had to process.

"Will you tell me what MF did to her?" he asked with hesitation.

Though his were more hazel, there was a hint of brown in his eyes that was the same as Mila's. She gave a slow shake of her head. "That's her story to tell," she said, frowning. That was going to break his heart; it wasn't something she wanted to do.

He sighed and nodded, like he was expecting her answer. "Let's shoot," he said after a moment. "It's why we came. It'll distract me."

"Okay," she said, turning toward her target at the end of the lane. She had two guns: one standard-size handgun, the other a much smaller, more compact handgun, weighing less than a pound, no more than six inches long and four inches high. It fit perfectly in the palm of her hand. It was Jasper who'd suggested it to her, to learn how to shoot a smaller gun, one that would fit in a concealed ankle holster.

"We'll start with the standard," Maverick said as he approached Tala from behind. He had suddenly shifted into soldier and trainer mode. "This is different than shooting a plasma gun."

"I've practiced some," she said, thankful Vi had shown her a few things. Maverick would never judge her, but she didn't want to look incompetent either.

"Okay then, show me what you've got," he said, stepping aside and putting his muff over his ears.

Tala focused on her hands, the gun in her grip. It didn't feel as heavy as it had in the past. She moved her body into position, Vi's voice telling her to lean forward ringing in her brain. She took aim, finding her target in the rear and front sights of the gun, then pressed the trigger.

The bullet hole in the target down the lane was too high, missing the silhouetted human's head.

She repeated what she knew in her head, then fired. Once again, the bullet went high. Engaging the safety, she set the gun down and removed her muff, then turned to Maverick.

"I did it before," she said defensively.

"You've got good positioning," he said as he picked up her gun. "The more you lean into it, the better control you'll have over the recoil. That's your problem. Your aim is good. You know how to do that. But plasma guns don't recoil. So you've got to learn to manage it with this one." He didn't lecture, his voice staying even. "Cam your elbows in. You've got good grip, which you need for rapid-fire, but your arms are breaking with the shot, and then the gun cants, which is why you're high." He showed her the position with his own body, then set the gun back down. "Again."

She felt the tension in her body as she resumed her pose, shoulders and head thrusted forward, her left leg kicked back to keep her body forward. Like Maverick had instructed, she rotated her elbows slightly. Taking aim, she fired. Though her shot hit the target, it wasn't where she was aiming. She sighed and set the gun back down.

"You have too much shot anticipation," he said as he approached again. "You know what to expect, and you're responding before it even happens." He picked up the gun as she stepped back. He took aim at her target. "Watch the muzzle," he called loudly over his shoulder. A second later, he fired the gun, the bullet hitting high, near hers.

"Tell me what you saw," he said.

"It dipped," she said. "Just before you fired, then went high."

"Exactly," he said with a nod. "You're anticipating the recoil, pushing against the gun, and as a result, you're dropping the gun right before you fire so that when you do press the trigger, the shot breaks and you actually have greater recoil. Trust your biomechanics and let the shot happen.

"Now watch again when I don't push against it in anticipation," he said. He took aim and fired three shots in rapid succession, hitting the target squarely in the chest each time.

"See the difference?" he asked, setting the gun down. He backed up to make room for her.

"This is nothing like a plasma gun," she said, feeling her stress.

"Well, you weren't great with those in the beginning either," he said with a smirk. "You'll get there. You always do."

Tala sighed as she stepped into the bay. Her mind took her through all the steps, the grip, her body positioning, her aim. *Let the shot happen,* she repeated. Sucking in a breath, she fired, hitting the target squarely in the chest. She stepped back, a grin on her face.

"See," Maverick said with a laugh. "You already know how to shoot. It's just a matter of making some adjustments. The rest you know how to do."

Tala nodded, then turned back to the target. She took shot after shot, each time, her mind played through all the steps. She was far from consistent but was making progress. And Maverick was right, she hadn't been good with the plasma in the beginning either.

"There's so much to remember," she said after she'd emptied her third magazine. "I swear I'm the slowest shooter on the planet."

He smiled. "Not even close. It just takes practice. Repetition. Rapid-fire will be easier the more comfortable you get. Now," he said, stepping past her and reaching for the smaller handgun. "If you thought recoil was a challenge with that gun," he said with a nod at the standard, "this one will prove to be an even bigger one because it's smaller."

"That makes no sense," she said with a frustrated sigh. Once she'd figured out the plasma gun, marksmanship wasn't an issue for her. Until now. None of these guns seemed practical in comparison.

"Think of it like this," he said, still holding the gun. It looked even smaller in his hands. "There's momentum in both the gun and the bullet, which is why they go in opposite directions. To absorb the same momentum in a smaller gun, it has to move faster. The force applied to it is greater than with the standard gun. Everything you learned about managing recoil still applies. If you keep technique in mind, you should be able to leverage against it. It just takes practice. Watch," he said, turning away from her.

Tala stepped back, carefully watching his body positioning, his grip on the gun, which practically disappeared when he had both hands on it. He fired, the bullet hitting squarely in the target again.

"There's greater recoil," he said, setting it down, "but it also lasts for a shorter time. So once you learn to manage that kickback, you'll be able to re-aim quicker."

Maverick stepped aside, and Tala picked up the gun. She sighed, looking at it, already overwhelmed before even firing it. Taking a deep breath, she imitated Maverick's stance, holding the gun as he had, and took aim. Pressing the trigger, the force the shot broke with caught her by surprise, her bullet missing the target completely. She turned to Maverick to see a grin on his face.

"Why was that funny to you?" she snapped.

"Don't be so hard on yourself," he said with a chuckle. "If there's anyone who can master a gun, it's you. I trained you, I trained with you. I know what you've got in you. Try again."

Tala exhaled, her shoulders dropping as she turned toward her target.

"Stop, stop, stop," he said.

She looked back at him in confusion. "I did something wrong already?"

"Yeah, you did. You're acting all defeated just because a gun recoiled. Get over it," he said, his voice stern but not harsh. "You need a fighter mindset, Tals, not this pathetic one you've got right now. This is not the Tala I trained with six years ago. You either reframe things and get your mind right, or we may as well leave."

She sighed. He was right, and she knew it.

"What pisses you off?" he asked as he folded his arms across his chest.

"Everything," she said with an eye roll.

He let out a small laugh. "I mean *really* pisses you off?"

"My brother," she said. The thought of him sent a surge of anger through her, her fingers and toes tingling. The image of him from her dream surfaced in her mind.

"Yeah, me too," he said, his grin falling away. "Think of him. Think of all the bullshit. Channel it. Your mind is a battlefield, Tals. And you are the commander."

She stared at him for a moment, a rush of familiarity coming over her. Not because of who they were in that moment, but because of who they'd been years earlier. He'd helped build her up, he'd helped her harness the fighter she was inside. She'd forgotten about that, about the fire that once burned in her when she was determined to show anyone who doubted her what she was made of. She was being doubted again. Thias would always underestimate her, and that was his weakness. It was time to tap back into that fighter. Back then, it had been to show the world. Now, it was to show herself.

Tala turned, walking through the steps in her mind. She brought her left foot behind her, thrust her shoulders forward, cammed her elbows. She checked her grip and double-checked the cant of the muzzle. She took a breath, Maverick's voice in the back of her head telling her to hold back her shot anticipation, and on the exhale, she fired.

It wasn't until she brought her hands down that she realized her heart was racing, and she looked down the lane to see where the bullet had hit. It still missed the target but was only an inch above the left shoulder of the silhouetted body. She turned, catching Maverick's approving nod, and she relaxed.

"There she is, the Tala I used to know," he said, a pleased smirk on his face. "We'll get you there. I have no doubt about it."

Tala followed Kane into the hallway as they left their unit, her stomach growling with hunger. As she turned to make her way down the hall, she heard her name in a faint whisper. She looked over her shoulder, surprised to see Mila coming out of her unit. She was dressed in jeans and a fitted top, and both her hair and makeup were done. Beautiful as ever, though she approached Tala with a sadness etched across her face.

"Can I join you all for dinner?" she asked quietly, tugging at her sleeves at her wrists, pulling them lower to hide what was left of her bruises. "I know Mav will be there."

"Of course," Tala said as she slipped her arm around her. "Just know, it's not easy for him either."

She nodded. "I know. And I feel better, really. I'm just trying to make sense of it all. There's a lot to wrap my head around."

"It won't happen over night," Tala said. "But things like dinner, they're baby steps."

"I mean, I'm lucky, right? Who gets a second chance with someone they thought was dead?" Mila asked with a smile filled with both sadness and hope.

"That's right," she said, understanding where her heart was at.

They wound their way through the crowded City Center, alive and loud for dinner, and took their seat at their usual table, which now had a second pushed against it to accommodate their growing group.

"About time," Vi said as she and Declan sat waiting for them. "I was about to send out a search party for all of you."

"You know all too well what happens when this one gets hungry," Declan said as he pointed his thumb at Vi. He caught Mila's eyes as she sat across from him, giving her a grin that Tala didn't miss.

When Maverick arrived a few minutes later, he took a seat beside Kane as he and Mila exchanged a silent glance. When she finally gave him a small smile, Tala saw the tension in his shoulders release.

Though she didn't love chicken potpie, Tala was ravenous, and carefully picked around the peas in the saucy center of the flaky crust. She glanced around the table, Mila and Declan leaned in closely, deep in a quiet conversation while Vi engaged lively with Maverick about shooting technique, Kane speaking up every now and then.

It was the melding of the old and the new and the new again. She was so far from the city, far from everything she knew, but there was something about all of it in that moment that felt right. These people weren't with her out of any sense of obligation. Each one had chosen her. And she had chosen each of them. This was her home and these people were her family. She had to protect all of it, all of them. She felt a seed of darkness taking root inside her. She would not let Thias take anymore from her.

"You're quiet," Kane said, studying her.

"Just thinking," she said with a shrug. She knew she was keeping him at a distance by not telling him about the momentum her anger was gaining. But she didn't know how to explain it, how to put it into words.

"Jeez, Tal," Vi said. "If looks could kill, you'd be dead on the spot right now." She nodded in a direction behind Tala.

She turned, catching Wren's glaring eye as she walked across a bridge over the koi stream.

"Something happen?" Vi asked with an amused chuckle.

"She got put in her place," Kane said flatly.

Tala exchanged an uncertain look with Vi, and a moment later, Kane leaned into her, pressing his mouth to the side of her face near her ear, kissing her. His hand slid across her cheek, his skin soft on hers, then he pressed his lips lightly to hers. She felt the eyes of the table on her, but in the moment, she didn't care.

"I think," he said quietly, brushing a strand of hair out of her face, "we should blow off this group. Go upstairs early." His breath was hot on her face, and she felt herself flush.

Tala watched Wren's face screw up with anger and irritation, her eyes narrowing on her.

"I know what you're doing," Tala said with a laugh under her breath as she looked at Kane. The look in his dark eyes sent goosebumps down her back and across her arms.

He smiled as he leaned in closer, then kissed the corner of her mouth.

"Am I a terrible person to admit I like it?" she asked, pressing her forehead to his.

"Not even a little bit," he said, his voice hushed. "But for the record, that's not the appeal of my proposal."

Tala could hear Wren's emphatic grunt from several tables away, a scowl on her face. Looking away, Tala smiled as she gave Kane a quick peck on the lips. "Let's go," she said, standing, pulling him up beside her. A moment later, after dumping their trays, he slipped his arm around her, and they headed for the stairs.

FIFTEEN

The weeks were beginning to tick by, slowly, quietly, with not so much as a whisper from Addox or the Revos' leadership. There were rumors that floated around The Village about what was happening in the Republic, but no one knew for sure what was true. It left Kane on edge. Living in The Village sometimes made it feel like the real world wasn't out there, that his life underground was a normal one. He had to remind himself that it wasn't; he couldn't afford to think otherwise. It was dangerous to do so. Those thoughts would make him complacent, and they would inevitably lower his guard.

Between the gym and the shooting range, Tala spent most of her days training with Maverick. Kane joined them from time to time, finding that he enjoyed learning to shoot a gun. He was more of a natural at it than he thought he'd be. When she wasn't training, Tala sometimes spent time with Mila and Vi, though Mila was quickly becoming scarce as she spent more and more time with Declan. Every now and again, Kane would spot Addox around The Village, though neither of them spoke to the other. They simply nodded in acknowledgment of each other, then went their own way. Kane seemed to divide most of his time between the gym which was more of a distraction than anything else, and books as he rediscovered his affinity for reading. Like when he'd been younger, he gravitated toward non-fiction, toward history, things that had really happened. In the thick of his boredom one afternoon, he decided to get another tattoo. Unlike in the Republic, where he had to conceal his ink, in The Village, it didn't matter. He chose the ancient Greek key meander, wrapped like a band around his forearm, for no particular reason other than he liked it.

Tala was having nightmares nearly every night. She tossed and turned, she mumbled incoherently, she would wake up in a sweat. Sometimes she even left the room for a while, though he never followed her. In the beginning, he asked about them, but she shut him out, always telling him she was fine. Sometimes she told him she didn't remember them. They both knew she was lying. But it was clear to him that she wasn't ready to talk, so he finally stopped asking about them and pretended to sleep while she sat awake in the dark room beside him.

She would smile throughout her days, but it was her eyes that gave her away. She was battling things that she never said aloud. Slowly, she was putting up walls around herself, keeping even her friends at a distance. Whatever she was harboring went deep. He hated that he didn't know how to bring those walls down. He hated that he couldn't fix things for her. He hated that she didn't give him the chance to try. He didn't know how to reach her, and it made his heart heavy. Eventually, after she'd calm herself following a nightmare, or returned to their room, she would curl into his arms, and he'd hold her tight.

There were times though, when she would look at him like she used to, and he'd feel that tug inside himself, that pull he'd felt from the very beginning with her. And every time, he gave in to her because having her in his arms was better than anything else in the world.

He didn't know what she needed, he wasn't sure if she knew. But what he did know was that he was going to be there when she was finally ready to let him in. He was sure of her, and that would never waver.

◆◆◆

Kane took a drink of the bottom-shelf whiskey and water the tavern served. He sat alone at the bar waiting for Gage and Hunter. It was still early in the evening, the tavern nearly empty, but Gage was working the night shift and didn't have much time. With Tala at game night at Vi's which he hadn't been eager to go to, he was thankful to have something else to do.

His friends strode into the bar with smiles that he envied, taking a seat on either side of him. They waved to Julian who gave them each a familiar nod, knowing exactly what they wanted.

"Haven't seen you much," Hunter said as he took his cold beer.

"Been busy," Kane said with a shrug, not meeting their gazes. Busy was the last thing he'd been. But he was trying to avoid Wren, which also meant keeping his distance from them.

"I've been thinking," Hunter said between drinks, "you're friends with Vi. Any way you could put in a good word for me? Pretty sure she keeps rejecting me because of Wren. But if a *friend* of Vi's had good things to say about me, then maybe she could overlook Wren?"

Kane let out a breathy laugh. "I can," he said. "But I'm not sure it would do much."

"That's what I told him," Gage said. "She's said no probably five times. She even turned down that Oliver guy that works at the bank, and I'm pretty sure most women around here don't say no to him."

"She's got standards, can't blame a girl for that," Kane said. Really, the thought of Hunter and Vi made him laugh inside. Vi was strong-willed and independent and needed someone with those qualities. Hunter was a good guy but rarely stood on his own two feet. When it came to Hunter and Gage, Wren ran the show.

As he worked on his second whiskey, its bitter bite was beginning to dissipate. He sat in silence, content to listen to them ramble about nothing important, Gage telling horror stories of his janitorial work. Kane had decided to meet with them so that he could think about something other than Tala for once. And it wasn't working. His mind always wandered back to her. And while she was on his mind, he wondered if she might be thinking of him too, even in the middle of trivia night.

"You're quiet," Gage said, waving his hand in Kane's face, bringing his mind back.

"Yeah, sorry," he said as he straightened on the barstool.

"You look like you're not all here. Not used to seeing you like this. Maybe you need Max," Hunter said. "You guys were tight."

He hadn't thought about that. Max had been a constant in his life. He had no regrets about leaving the city with Tala, but he could no doubt benefit from seeing him again. But simply up and leaving the Republic wasn't an easy thing. It wasn't like he could hop a plane to the Colonies for a weekend vacation. Both Max and Tala felt equally far away in that moment. He sighed in defeat and reached for his third whiskey.

"Just tired," he finally said.

"Thought I'd find you guys here," an airy voice said, and Kane looked up to see Wren approaching. She wore a smile as wide as her shirt was tight which he suspected was the point.

"I had a feeling you would show up," Hunter said as she took the seat beside him.

Wren was the last person he wanted to see in that moment. He didn't want to hear anything she had to say, but there was at least a person between them now, and he simply didn't have the energy to leave. Besides, he told himself, he couldn't run from her forever.

"That awful whiskey again?" she asked with a nod at the drink in his hand.

"It's not bad once you get used to it," he said.

"I don't know about that. Tasted a little like nail polish remover when I tried yours before."

"That's why I stick with beer," Hunter said.

Wren ordered a gin and tonic, then took a huge swallow of it after it was put in front of her. "Whoa!" she said, a grimace on her face. "That's strong."

"Then slow the hell down," Gage said with a laugh.

"I've got to catch up to you three," she said with a giggle, then took another large drink, wincing again.

"Well," Gage said after he drained the last of his second beer. "I've got to get going. My job beckons." He paid his bill quickly. "Don't have too much fun without me," he said, giving them each a nod goodbye, then turned and left.

"Another one?" Hunter asked Kane, nudging him with his elbow.

Kane looked down at his drink, maybe three or four swallows left. "Nah. Think this will be my last." His body was already feeling warm from the alcohol.

"You said that last time right after I sat down," Wren said as she got up, drink in hand, and walked around Hunter and Kane, taking the stool beside him that Gage had just vacated.

Kane tensed with her so near him. "Not my fault you come at the end of the night."

"It's not even nine," she lamented. "You're almost thirty. I didn't realize you had a curfew." She flagged Julian down, ordering the three of them another drink.

He sighed, quickly finished his drink, then pushed his glass away. A fourth was going to give him a full buzz. But as soon as the next one was set in front of him, he reached for it, taking a large swallow. This one, he told himself, would definitely be his last.

"That's better," she said with a satisfied smile.

Kane gave her a sideways glance. She was thin and curvy, taller than Tala, though not as strong. She had the darkest eyes he'd seen in anyone other than himself, and her hair was wild and curly and bounced with every movement of her head. There was a time when he looked at her and wanted her. She was always up for some fun, just like anyone he'd been with. But it was always the same, never more than that. Until Tala. Looking at Wren now, he felt nothing but irritation at the sight of her.

"You look sad," she said as she put her hand on his arm.

He shook it off. "Watch it," he warned and turned away from her.

"He's been in a slump all night," Hunter said.

There was a brief silence among them.

"Hunter, can you give us a minute?" Wren asked. Kane heard it in her voice, she wasn't giving him a choice.

"Sure," he said, reaching for his beer, then sliding off his stool, he turned and walked across the tavern.

"Want to talk about it?" she asked quietly after Hunter was out of earshot.

Finally, there was someone who wanted to hear what was on his mind, though Wren was the last person he was going to tell anything to.

"There's nothing to talk about," he said irritably. He looked down into his glass, the amber liquid calling to him.

"You know," she said, "I watch you two together. You don't know it, but I do. And I can see you're not happy."

"You don't know anything," he said. Reaching into his pocket, he pulled out his palm pad and set it on the bar. "Julian, I'm ready," he said as he gestured to it.

"Maybe you two are more divided than you think. Maybe it's really not possible for people so far on opposite sides of the spectrum to work out," she said, her hand sliding onto his arm again. "I know you, Kane. Maybe not your story, but I know what your life was like in the city. The Republic didn't give you a chance."

"Wren, you don't have a clue. About any of it. Jeez, you don't even know my last name," he said, pushing her hand away.

"That's because you never let me in. You never let anyone in," she said, though she looked more sad than defensive.

Kane pushed his unfinished drink aside and reached for his palm pad after Julian set it back down, then rose to his feet.

"Just tell me one thing," she said, grabbing him hard by the arm.

He stopped and turned to her.

"What was her first reaction to you when she found out you were a Nameless? That you had no citizenship? Maybe you grew on her, but her first reaction, that was how she truly felt," she said sharply. "Those are her true colors. And I'll be here for you, whenever you're ready. When you finally figure things out."

"Know this," he said curtly, his eyes narrowing, "I will never seek you out." He jerked his arm from her grasp, then turned and made his way to the exit.

Outside the tavern, he took a breath. He felt his anger seething. It had started out small, just a flicker, but now he was raging, and he didn't know exactly where it was coming from. Was it Tala? Was it Wren? Was it himself? With a grunt, he turned and headed toward the stairs, his mind racing.

Standing outside his unit, he took slow, deep breaths as he tried to steady his breathing. He didn't even remember getting to the fifth floor. One minute he'd been outside the tavern, then the next, he was at his door.

When it opened, he saw Tala on the sofa, her palm pad in her hands, and she looked up in surprise at the sight of him.

"I didn't expect you back so soon. Vi sent me pictures of the latest clothes she's designing. She wants me to wear them in my next advoprop. If I ever get one," she said with a sigh. "Are you okay?"

His heart hammered as he looked at her, and at first, he didn't know what to say to her. There was so much between them that went unsaid. He felt warm, his head thick from the whiskey as he stood there.

"I have to ask you something," he said. Unable to suppress the accusation in his voice, he spoke harsher than he'd intended. But he had to know.

Tala rose to her feet, her brows furrowed in concern. "Okay," she said slowly.

"The night we first met, that warehouse near the docks—"

"I remember," she said. "How could I forget?" she asked with a small smile.

"It occurred to me that you never asked about my citizenship with the Republic. I distinctly remember you asking about Max's because you weren't sure you should trust working with him. And once I told you he was a Preferred, you seemed to relax. But you never once asked about mine. And I can't figure out why that is. I mean, did you take one look at me and assume I was a Nameless? What was it about me that screamed I had no value?" The words were out of his mouth before he could stop himself.

"Are you kidding me?" she asked, looking instantly stricken. "Where is this coming from? This is Wren. She was at the tavern too. This is her talking." She folded her arms across her chest.

He cringed, knowing she was right. This was Wren. But she'd had a point, one he couldn't overlook. "That doesn't answer my question," he said.

Her face flushed. "I never asked," she said, angry, "because even from the very beginning, it never mattered to me. Maybe you're right and knowing Max was a Preferred put me at ease that one night, and yeah, the people in my life were Standards or Preferreds, but it never mattered to me what you were. Never," she said sharply. "And I can't believe after everything we've been through you would doubt me." Her eyes filled with tears as she grabbed her palm pad off the sofa and made her way across the room. At the door, she gave him one last glance over her shoulder, and with that one look, he saw her heart in her eyes, and it was shattering. She'd been carrying everything on her shoulders, feeling responsible for everyone, hanging on by a thread, and he knew right then that he finally broke her.

And then she was gone.

It was like a punch to the gut, the wind knocked out of him. He'd gone too far. He'd let Wren get inside his head. He'd let her create doubt where there was none. He wanted to take it all back. His regret was palpable, and all he wanted in that moment was to unsay it all. Because he never believed it. He knew that from the very beginning, she truly saw him. She'd only ever looked at him like he mattered, like he had worth. She'd seen the darkest parts of him, and her love for him had never wavered.

He collapsed onto the sofa, still warm where she had been sitting, and dropped his head into his hands.

Around midnight, Tala was still not back, and without so much as a whisper from her, Kane set out to find her. After all, he reasoned, he was her security detail, and she wasn't permitted to be alone in The Village after dark.

He started with Maverick, just down the hall. And when he opened his door, the look on his face told him she'd talked to him. Though he knew right away she wasn't in his unit. He was alone. Of that, he was sure.

"Do you know where she is?" he asked, dropping all pretenses.

"I do," he said with a nod, and Kane realized he wasn't going to elaborate. "Look, I don't want to get involved, but she asked me not to say anything. Wants some time to herself."

"I'm her security detail, don't you think I should know?" Kane argued.

"I'm her security detail too, and I know exactly where she is. She's just fine for now."

"Fine. I'll find her on my own," he said, his jaw clenching as he turned away.

He made his way down to the third floor to Mila's new unit, now that she'd been moved out of the secure quarters and into the general population. He knocked twice, and her roommate answered. He couldn't remember her name, having only met her once before, and gave her a forced smile which was the best he could do at the moment. Like he had when he went to Maverick's unit, he knew Tala wasn't there.

"I'm looking for Mila," he said. His voice seemed loud in the quiet corridor.

"She went up top with Declan a couple of hours ago. I think to a movie or something. Haven't seen her since," she said.

"Thanks," he said with a nod. Turning, he headed toward the stairs again, shoving his hands deep into the pockets of his jeans. Vi was his last option. He wouldn't know where to look for her after that.

Arriving at her door, he knocked once, then heard a couple of small thuds on the other side of the door.

"Who is it?" a female voice called out. He recognized it immediately as Vi's.

"Kane," he said in a gruff voice.

There was silence for a few seconds, then the door opened, Vi filling the doorway. He heard it instantly, her heartbeat, the one he knew so well he could pick it out in any crowd. She was there.

"I'm here to talk to Tala," he said, trying to keep his voice soft. There were no more traces of anger, which had since been wholly replaced with regret.

"I haven't seen her," Vi said coolly.

Behind her, he could see Vi's mom and brother on the sofa, the TV muted, all of them with their eyes on him.

"Really?" he asked, his brow cocking.

"Really," she said firmly. Vi had all the physiological signs of lying, but he wasn't going to push it. Tala, he knew, would come back when she was ready.

He took a breath, his hand rubbing the tension at the back of his neck. "Fine. If you see her, can you give her a message?"

She nodded. "If I see her."

He knew Tala could hear him from wherever she was in the unit. There weren't many places to hide, the bunks or the bathroom. "Tell her I was an ass. I was stupid and said things I didn't mean, things I never should've said. If I could take it all back, I would. I just want to talk to her, to give her the apology she deserves, to make things right." His words sounded feeble to his own ears.

"You're an ass, you were stupid, you're sorry. Got it," Vi said, tucking her hair behind her ear.

He lingered for another moment, just to hear the beating of Tala's heart. Then, with a nod of his head, he turned and walked away.

It was late when Tala finally slipped into their unit. He'd been doing nothing but tossing and turning as he tried to sleep. He debated pretending he was asleep when she came in, but at the last second, he sat up, though he said nothing.

She looked at him, and even in the darkness, their eyes found each other. Neither said a word, the silence building a physical space between them that was louder than any spoken words ever could be.

He opened his mouth to say something, but she turned away. Going to the dresser, she grabbed her pajamas, then stepped into the bathroom. He sighed, falling back onto his pillow.

When she emerged a few minutes later, she quietly crawled onto her side of the bed, pulling the blankets up to her chin, then she rolled to her side, her back to him.

"I've never doubted you, not then, not now," he whispered. "I didn't mean anything that I said. I was stupid, and I'm sorry." His breath shuddered. "Tala, I love you."

The silence returned, and he could hear nothing but the sound of her beating heart. It was faster than normal as her body lay tense beside him.

"I got your message," she said, her voice clipped. "I love you too," she whispered after another minute, her voice barely audible. But he heard her as clearly as if she shouted it.

Their table at breakfast was quiet more than it was anything else. Tala was speaking to him again, but there was sadness in everything she said. There was tension between him and Vi, as well as him and Maverick. He didn't know exactly what they knew, but they knew enough for him to feel foolish. The only conversation that seemed to float comfortably around was between Mila and Declan, in their own world at the end of the table. How he envied them.

Tala, he noticed, hardly touched anything on her plate. Her pancake and fruit had only small nibbles taken out of it, even her orange juice went untouched.

"Not hungry?" Vi asked.

Tala looked up, her face ashen, and she shook her head. "Not really. I feel a little off," she said.

Kane turned to her, and she met his gaze.

"My head is pounding," she said. "I'll be fine."

He knew it was because of him. Because of everything that was happening between them that not even he understood. He was only compounding her stress.

A minute later, Tala stood, reaching for her plate. "I'm going to go lie down."

Everyone nodded quietly as she turned and went to dump her food. Even her gait was different, sad, her shoulders slumped forward, her pace sluggish. With a heavy heart, he watched her walk away from him.

"Kane," an all too familiar voice said from behind, and he turned to see Wren approaching. His anger spiked at the sight of her.

"Don't," he said harshly, his jaw set, "speak to me again." He felt everyone's eyes on him as he rose to his feet. Having lost his appetite in an instant, he picked up his plate. "Never," he said with a caustic glare as he sidestepped her and went to dump the rest of his breakfast, then headed for the fifth floor.

"Tala," he said as he stepped into their unit. She was lying across the sofa, wrapped in a blanket, and she looked up as the door closed behind him. He moved to the sofa, taking a seat on the edge. He reached out, his fingers sliding through her long hair, and he felt emotion building in his chest.

"I know you're sorry," she said with a quiet voice. "I just don't want to compete with her."

"Who, Wren? Tala, she's not even in the same galaxy as you. No one is," he said, and he saw the tears spring to life in her eyes. He slid off the sofa, onto his knees, his head close to hers. "In a million lifetimes, it will only ever be you. I'll choose you every time."

Her eyes met his as she reached up, her thumb brushing along his jaw, over his chin, over his lips. He felt himself come alive. She slid her hand behind his head, the warmth of her skin on the back of his neck raising goosebumps across his arms and down his back. She pulled him to her and kissed him gently, her lips soft to the touch.

"And I choose you," she said. "Every time."

Kane's heart leapt in his chest. There was still a ways to go between them, a distance that needed to be traversed, but they could do it. He would never doubt her, never doubt them again.

It was mid-afternoon when Kane got a message on his palm pad from Addox saying he was needed in his office immediately, and he let out a low sigh, not eager to see his brother.

Leaving the gym, he made his way to the fifth floor where he met Maverick in the waiting area of the secured offices.

"You too?" Maverick asked.

Kane nodded. So, he realized, this wasn't a personal call. There was work to be done, which brought with it its own tension. Not so much for his sake, but because he still worried about Tala.

He and Maverick sat in the uncomfortable chairs outside the office, Selene keeping busy at her desk, though she still made furtive glances in Kane's direction.

"Wonder what this is about," Maverick said as he readjusted his body in the chair, his foot bouncing absentmindedly on the floor.

Kane shrugged. "Not a clue."

"Maybe there's finally something to do rather than waiting around every day," Maverick said with a sigh.

A moment later, Kane looked up at the sound of approaching footsteps to see Tala walking toward him. She'd been sleeping since breakfast, and the color seemed to have returned in her face, a small smile on the corner of her mouth as she took the seat beside him.

"You look like you're feeling better," he said.

She reached for his hand, lacing her fingers through his, and he felt a tingle at her touch.

"Much," she said.

"You know what this is about?" Maverick asked.

She shook her head. "I haven't talked to anyone in weeks."

"You can all go back," Selene said. "The last conference room on the left."

Kane exchanged a curious glance with Tala, then Maverick who shrugged. The three of them made their way down the corridor to the last door, to a large room that looked like a lounge rather than a conference room, with sofas and chairs filling it. They were greeted by four faces, two he was familiar with, Addox and Gemini, and two he wasn't.

"Thanks for coming," said a small woman with hair a blended combination of black and aqua-blue. "Have a seat."

Still holding his hand, Tala pulled Kane into the room, and they took a seat beside each other on an empty sofa. Maverick took a chair nearby.

"I realize that Tala is the only one who knows all four of us," the woman said. "I'm Ash and this is Jasper," she said, motioning with her hand to a man who sat across the room from them. Kane was familiar with only his name because he had worked with Tala on her last advoprop.

"The four of us," Jasper said, "make up UR leadership."

Kane's eyes wandered the room. If all four of their leaders were meeting with the three of them, it was about more than just another advoprop.

"Someone want to tell us what we're doing here?" Maverick asked with impatience that mirrored Kane's. He seemed just as tired of being kept in the dark.

"This isn't about an advoprop," Kane said.

"Not entirely," Ash said. "We have a mission."

"A mission?" Maverick asked.

"A real advoprop. We're going to put Tala into play," she said, her eyes bright.

Kane's chest tightened. This conversation wasn't leading down a good road. He exchanged a glance with Maverick, seeing the same uncertainty in his expression.

"We need to rally our people," Addox said, standing, towering above everyone as they sat, all eyes on him. "We want Tala to speak directly to her people. It'll be at an undisclosed location, everyone who attends will be highly vetted, and we'll livestream it. We're sending her back to the Republic."

"No way," Kane said loudly as he shot to his feet, his hand dropping from Tala's. "You're not putting her back in there. Her life is at stake there. There's a bounty on her there."

"Sorry to be the one to tell you that you don't make these decisions. We do. And it's already been decided," Addox said as he folded his arms across his chest. He was challenging him, and Kane knew he'd never back down in front of all the people in the room.

"I agree with Kane," Maverick said as he stood up beside him, though his voice stayed level. "She's a high-risk target there."

"It'll demonstrate her commitment to both the cause and her people," Ash asserted.

"Security will be tight," Jasper said. "And she'll have both of you."

"Your entire job is to keep her safe. Are you telling me that we can't count on you?" Addox asked. Kane wanted to lunge across the room, to strangle the very arrogance out of his brother.

"She's not the only one with a price tag on their forehead. Kane has one too," Maverick argued.

"Kane, I have no doubt, can defend himself just fine," Addox said, his eyes narrowing on him. "We'll have other security, of course," he said, looking away. "But both of you have a unique skillset that will keep Tala safe. Which I know you will. She's our best asset."

"If she's your best asset, why the hell are you willing to risk her life like this?" Kane snapped, his voice rising again.

"We have a plan to safely get her in and out, and we're confident we can mitigate the risks at the rally," Jasper said.

"Where are you planning to send her?" Maverick asked, and Kane could hear the increasing edge in his voice.

"Michigan City," Addox said coolly.

"Where that huge bombing was? The fuck you are, Addox!" Kane yelled, his tension taking over him like rigor mortis.

Tala rose to her feet, tugging hard at his arm.

"That's the second biggest city in the country and it's crawling with MF," he spat.

"Kane," Tala said under her breath.

"You either do the job you were hired for, or we'll fire you. And then you can find yourself kicked out of The Village," Addox said. "And it's Vulcan to you," he said with fury in his eyes, his jaw taut. "Have you stopped to consider what Tala thinks about this?"

Kane turned to her, his eyes meeting hers, and he saw her resolution. He knew she hadn't even considered otherwise, and it suddenly dawned on him what it was that she hadn't been saying in all these weeks. She was so filled with regret and shame and vitriol, and it was poisoning her. In one look, he saw the dark desperation that had been brewing inside her. She was losing herself to her hate.

"I can't believe you're going to do this," he said, his voice booming through the room that had fallen silent. "Risking your life isn't going to bring Ronin back, it's not going to undo what happened to Mila." His anger was seething, and now he was the one who was desperate, desperate to reach her, desperate to save her from herself.

"Those people wake up every day, oppressed by the fist of the Republic, of my brother," she argued, her face hardening. "If they can be brave enough to stand up in the face of injustice, I can be brave enough to look them in the eyes, to help fortify them, to make a difference."

"This is a mistake," he said, looking around the room. He saw it in Maverick, that he agreed with him, but he managed himself differently. It was Kane who stood to lose the most if something happened to Tala. They said she was valued, an important part of their cause, but the reality was that she was disposable. And even if she died, they'd still use her, just as a martyr instead of a rallying cry.

"None of you really care," he said. "You say you do, but every single one of you is willing to risk her life, risk ruining her just so you all can get a little further ahead in your goddamn cause. She's just a cog in your machine, and you're all manipulating her the way Thias has. Tala," he said, turning to her, his eyes finding hers, "don't let yourself be used like this."

"I'm sorry, Kane. But I have to do this," she said, her voice eerily calm. His heart fell.

"I think you should take a walk," Addox said.

The very sound of his voice made his skin crawl, and as he scanned the room, the agreement of every one of them was written across their faces.

"Fine," he spat. He caught one last glimpse of Tala, then turned and left the room.

SIXTEEN

Kane wasn't sure where he was going until he'd arrived. He stepped into the small, dimly lit tavern, giving it a sweeping glance around. It was late afternoon, and the only other patrons sat in a corner banquet, not bothering to look up at him. Declan, he was sure, was somewhere in the back, but he didn't come to socialize.

Kane took a seat at the bar and ordered a whiskey. This time though, he skipped the water. A moment later, the bartender, someone other than Julian for a change, placed his drink in front of him, and he quickly took two large swallows, the alcohol burning in his chest. In another two swallows, the drink was empty, and he set the glass down for a refill.

"Something tells me you're having a bad day," a soft voice said, startling him, and he turned to see Mila standing behind him. Her eyes were so similar to her brother's, and they studied him carefully.

"What gives that away?" he said with a glower as he turned away and took a drink from his refilled glass.

"I'll have what he's having," she said to the bartender as she took the stool beside him.

"You drink straight whiskey?" he asked, raising a skeptical brow to her as a drink was put in front of her.

"Is that what this is?" she asked, peering into the glass. She took a whiff and winced, her face recoiling. "It smells like fuel."

"That's why you drink it, not smell it," he said, still watching her.

Without hesitation, Mila took a large swallow. Her eyes flared, and she coughed. "Tastes like fuel too! That's awful," she said as she looked at him.

"Yeah, it is," he said with a nod. "So, why are you drinking it then?"

"So that you can't finish the bottle all on your own," she said. Reaching for the glass, she sucked in a breath, then took another swallow, her face grimacing.

Kane couldn't help himself and let out a small laugh, then took a drink from his own glass. "It really is awful," he said.

"I'd say anyone who willingly drinks this poison is feeling pretty desperate," Mila said with a shrug.

He watched her brace herself for a third drink.

"You don't have to drink it," he said. "There're lots of other options." He motioned to the back of the bar which was lined with bottle after bottle of every kind of alcohol.

"I'm good with this," she said.

He wasn't quite sure what to say and couldn't argue that she wasn't at least comical to watch while she tried to drink it.

"Just out of curiosity, how much of this do we have to drink before I can ask what's wrong?" she asked, her eyes catching his. "I mean, with girls, you just open the wine. But I don't think it works like that with guys."

"At least until this one is gone," he said, half-joking, but then she nodded and took another drink, and he decided not to refute her. They sat in silence, Kane finishing his second while watching Mila painfully choke down her first.

"We'll both have a refill," she said, waving to the bartender.

Kane thought about trying to argue with her, but he knew it would be pointless, so he kept his mouth shut until his glass was refilled.

"Okay," she said, turning her body, squaring herself to him. "We've had our drink. Now it's time to talk."

He looked at her with narrowed eyes as he thought about his meeting less than thirty minutes earlier, anger flaring all over again.

"Do we need one more drink?" she asked seriously as she held his gaze.

"What do you want to know?" he finally said. One look at her and he knew she wasn't about to leave any time soon.

"Let's start with where you're coming from," she said, then took another drink. She still grimaced, but less so with each drink.

"A meeting with leadership," he grumbled.

"Then I assume Tala was there," she said, then took another drink.

"Yeah," he said, turning away. "She was there."

"And what happened?"

He couldn't help but feel like a ten-year-old again, sitting in the principal's office because he'd gotten into a fight during recess. Then he reminded himself that Mila was a teacher.

"They're making a mistake. I don't even know how much I'm allowed to say. But at this point, I don't even care. They want to bring her to the Republic, for some kind of rally," he said. He felt Mila tense up beside him. She took slow deep breaths as she averted her gaze.

"I could see how that would piss you off," she said after a minute, her voice cracking slightly.

"It's an unnecessary risk. She's being reckless with her life all because she thinks she's got something to prove. She's on the warpath for revenge," he said, hearing the anger in his voice.

"I agree. She's a different Tala these days," Mila said quietly. "But she's been through a lot."

He nodded. "I get that. And I'm not saying she doesn't have a reason to feel that way, but I don't want it to cost her the best parts of who she is."

Mila's head bobbed, and she sighed. "That's incredibly admirable of you."

He turned, looking at her.

"I don't mean that ironically. I meant that genuinely," she added quickly.

"I just… I just want to fix this for her," he said with frustration.

"I want to too. But we can't," she said. "The only way to fix her is to love her. Let her be who she is, let her feel the way she feels, let her make her own mistakes. Our job is to just be there for her, to support her. We can't carry her torch. And then we have to be there to either celebrate her victories or help her pick up the pieces of her mistakes."

His shoulders fell forward, and he ran his hand over his head. "I don't want her to lose herself," he said quietly, his voice unsteady.

"And this is probably the hardest part, but you have to let go of your expectations and believe in her to do the best she can. Even if that means going back into the Republic. Have faith that she'll find a way back. Do you believe in her?" she asked.

Kane looked up, his eyes meeting hers. They were soft and kind and full of compassion, and he understood why she was Tala's best friend. "Of course I believe in her."

"Make sure she knows that. We have to show her we believe in her, that we love her, to remind her who she is, to give her something to come back for."

He wasn't sure why none of this had occurred to him, but he knew Mila was right about all of it. Suddenly, he began to question if he'd really been that supportive of her or if he just thought he had been. Did she know he believed in her, as Mila said? Did she know he'd love her no matter what?

"How're you so smart?" he asked.

"It's the whiskey talking," she said with a smile, then finished her drink.

Despite himself, he smiled.

"You know, back in Columbia City, I caught her off guard when she came home one morning after being with you all night," she said as she waved the bartender down for a refill.

Kane quickly finished the last of his drink, and his glass was refilled along with hers.

"I busted her like a kid stealing candy," she said with a nostalgic smile. "What I remember most is the look on her face. She'd never looked like that before. It seems so cliché to say it, but she just glowed. Naturally, she didn't give me even a breadcrumb about you, but I knew even then that whoever you were, you were different than the others before you.

"And then when I was in the back of Cara's car on my way here, she said something I'll never forget," she said, her eyes holding his gaze. "I was a complete mess, so confused about what was happening to me, where I was going, who I was with. And then she told me she was taking me to Tala. Long story short, there was a moment when she told me that she was the one who'd gotten you both across the country. And I was confused because who would she be with? And then it dawned on me, and I knew it was you, her mystery-man. I asked Cara what you were like, I asked her if you were good to her. Because that's what I wanted most, for whoever you were to be good to Tala.

"And Cara looked at me through the rearview mirror with a funny smile and said to me, 'If only we could all be so lucky to have someone in our life who looks at us the way he looks at her.'" Mila had a mixture of happiness and sadness in her eyes.

Kane felt a tug deep inside his chest.

"I love the way you love her. And just like Cara saw it in you when you look at Tala, I also see it in her when she looks at you. Just be there for her, and I know she'll come back to you," she said, her lips pursed, her mouth curving into a half-smile.

This, he thought to himself, was the most honest conversation he'd had in weeks, and he suddenly knew what he needed to do.

"That's my advice," Mila said, perking up. She reached for her drink and took a large swallow. "Wow!" she said, her mouth opening and closing. "That's really got some kick to it."

"You don't have to finish it," he said with a smile. "It's pretty awful."

Mila laughed. "And that's exactly why I'm going to," she said, then took another drink. "So tell me, did I talk you off the bottle or do I need to have another one of these? I mean this one is already making my fingers tingle."

"Yes, the bottle, the ledge, all of it."

She nodded, satisfied. "Now, just tell me one more thing."

He squared his shoulders to her. "Okay?"

"If they bring her back into the Republic, do you swear to me you'll bring her back safely?" she asked, her face serious.

"I swear on my life that I would die before I let anything happen to her," he said. And that was the truth.

Mila seemed appeased and gave him a sad smile. He knew she didn't want Tala to go just as much as he didn't, and he couldn't help but think how much stronger Mila was than him. She didn't want her to go, but she trusted Tala. And she trusted him to keep her safe. All that mattered to him now was that he kept his promise, not for Mila's sake, but for Tala's.

"Let's finish these so we can move on with our lives," she said with a smirk. "I've got a bottle of turpentine in my unit with our names on it."

"Anything's got to be better than this," he said and smiled.

Tala braced herself as she opened the door to their unit, not knowing if Kane would be there or not. She wasn't sure where he'd stormed off to. The Village wasn't that big, he'd only have so many places to go, and she wouldn't put it past him to go up top either. But as she stepped inside, the door quickly closing behind her, he was coming out of the bathroom, his body wet from a shower. Her eyes went to the new ink on his arm. She felt a thrill at seeing him standing there in just a towel.

But this wasn't the time for that.

She was mad at him.

He gave her a half-smile, sadness in his eyes.

His outburst had been both embarrassing and infuriating, but standing in front of him now, she couldn't help but remember every reason why she loved him. But it broke her heart that he didn't seem to have the same faith in her that everyone else did. She couldn't understand how he didn't see why she had to do this. Why she had to go back to the Republic.

Without a word, he dressed, his t-shirt clinging to his chest where his skin was still damp, and he made his way to the sofa. Tala crossed the room, taking only a few strides in their small unit, and took a seat beside him, though she kept a small space between them.

"I feel like I'm saying this a lot lately," he said, his voice low and gruff. "But I'm sorry."

Tala pursed her lips as she looked at him, meeting his eyes, those dark eyes with their tiny fleck of gold in his irises.

"I was completely out of bounds back there," he said.

"I feel like you're the only person who doesn't think I can do this," she said as she struggled to keep her voice even. She was torn between so many emotions.

"I can see how you'd feel that way," he said with a nod. "But the anger and hatred you're carrying around with you scares me a little. I worry that your need for revenge compromises your objectivity."

"It's not revenge that I want," though she knew that wasn't entirely true, "it's justice. Justice for the people Thias hurt, for the people he oppresses. Justice for you. I know it wasn't Thias who did all those experiments on you, but it was a corrupt Republic, and I can't live with that. If there's something I can do to bring about change, don't you think that it's my responsibility to do it? No matter how hard it is?"

"It's not your job to fight everyone's fight—"

"But I'm not. I'm just a part of the catalyst," she said, stiffness in her voice.

"Desperation can lead even the strongest people into some pretty dark places, and I don't want that for you. The truth?" he asked. She could tell he was trying to keep his emotions in check. "I'm terrified of losing you. You… you're my whole world."

She took a slow, deep breath, her anger ebbing. "I understand your fear. It's mine too," she said, her voice cracking. "But I don't feel like I can rely on you, and that's about the worst feeling in the world because you have always been the person who holds me together. I know you want the old Tala back, the person I was before everything was turned upside down, but I'm not her anymore. I never will be again."

He looked at her with a pained expression etched across his face, and she felt her heart break all over again.

"It's true, I want her back," he said quietly. "And you're right, she's gone. But also, she's not. Everything I love about you, the good in you, your drive, how deeply you care, that's all at the core of you, and I see that still. I will love you no matter who you are, in all your forms. I support you. I know we can't go back to who we were. So all I want now is for us to be even stronger as we move forward."

"We've been through troubled waters," she said, her voice thick, and she had to bite the inside of her cheek to fight the tears that were threatening her. "But I promise I've never lost sight of you. Not once."

Silence settled between them, and he reached out, taking her hand in his. His thumb brushed softly over the inside of her wrist. Tala leaned into him, pressing her forehead to his, and closed her eyes. For weeks, the tension had been building between them, and she didn't know how to talk to him. But she felt her walls coming down.

She took a breath, their faces so close they were breathing the same air. "Just because everything else has gone wrong doesn't mean we have to," she whispered, and despite herself, her tears welled in her eyes. "If I have you, I know I won't break."

"And you have me," he said quietly as he ran his fingers through her hair and down her back.

"You don't have to do this mission," she said without spite as she pulled away, her eyes meeting his.

"Are you kidding? I am absolutely doing this mission. Nobody wants to keep you safer than I do."

A small smile curled on her mouth. "I was hoping you'd say that. I told Vulcan... Addox," she corrected herself knowing Kane refused to call him by that name, "that you'd be there. No matter what."

Sliding his hand around the back of her head, he pulled her to him, his mouth against hers in an instant. All it took was one touch, and she felt herself wake up, come to life. She wrapped her arms around him and kissed him with all the fervor of every emotion simmering inside her.

With each passing second, their kiss deepened, and she felt him in her soul. Nothing was right in the world. But in that moment, his lips and his hands on her, they were right.

Tala was awake before the sun, her anticipation and nerves getting the best of her, leaving a gnawing sensation in her stomach and a throbbing in her temples. She looked over at Kane, asleep beside her. His mouth slackened, his breaths slow and steady. Quietly, she eased out of bed and made her way to the bathroom where she slipped into the shower, letting the hot water run over her body, leaving her skin pink and tender. She felt her tension relaxing in her shoulders. It was going to be a big day, and she needed to focus.

Two hours later, after Tala attempted a breakfast she had no appetite for, she stood beside Kane, his hand in hers, as they took the secured elevator up to ground level. They were leaving The Village for the first time in two months. She looked up at Kane, a flutter low in her belly, and despite the limited space in the elevator, she hardly noticed Maverick, Ash, and Jasper riding with them.

Since Jasper and Ash were the leaders who maintained the public image of the Revos, it made the most sense that they would be the ones to take point on their mission.

At the first burst of fresh air, Tala sucked in a deep breath, letting it fill her lungs. There was something refreshing, rejuvenating about the winter air, the sun, the real sun, on her skin.

They took a car a few miles outside of Hatfolk to a small airport where Elias Barrington's private jet waited for them near a solo hanger, which looked mostly like a large pole barn with three bays for small aircraft.

Elias, Lakewood Colony governor, maintained an amicable relationship with the Republic of Columbia's government, specifically with Vaughn as he was the Chancellor of International Affairs. They were flying into Michigan City under the guise of negotiating joint use of a major shipping port in the colony along Lake Superior. The destruction of Michigan City's intermodal shipping hub was proving to have a devasting impact on the distribution and transit of both imports and exports for the Republic. Elias, Tala learned, often used his diplomatic immunity to aid the Revos. He was just one more cog in the complex machine of the rebellion.

The five of them made their way across the apron to the jet, Tala seeing her breath in the cold air with every exhale. Kane reached for her hand. She knew he could hear her racing heart, and she glanced up at him with a nervous smile. The look in his eyes seemed to match the anxiety she felt inside, and it did nothing to calm her.

Ascending a small staircase up to the door, they stepped into the jet, a luxurious cabin rather than row after row after row of seats in commercial planes. Though she'd never actually flown in one. Until now, the only aircraft she'd ever been in was a military jet for an incentive flight with Militia Forces Air Guard years ago. On the left side of the plane were large, tan leather seats. Two seats facing another two seats with a table between them. Behind those, were another four seats facing each other, a table between, and behind those was the same, making up twelve seats in total.

On the right side of the plane were two long sofas with dark blue throw pillows as well as a minibar, the bottles secured in canisters, and the glasses hanging in neat rows above. At the back of the plane, two attendants spoke in low voices, then smiled when they saw Tala making her way down the aisle.

Tala cast a sideways glance at Kane who looked as impressed by it all as she was.

"Sit wherever," Ash called from behind them.

Tala made her way to the last row, taking a seat beside a round window that looked out over the runway and an empty field covered in snow beyond that. Kane sat beside her, and Maverick took a seat across from them.

"Never traveled like this," Maverick said with a quiet chuckle.

Ten minutes after they had settled, Elias boarded the plane, accompanied by two men and two women dressed in olive green military uniforms, guns holstered at their waist. Colony soldiers. The Colonies' National Guard being just one of the branches of the Unified military. Two of the soldiers were there for Elias, she knew. The other two would be going with Tala to the rally.

The four soldiers took the first four seats while Elias took a seat opposite Ash and Jasper in the middle. Less than five minutes later, the plane began to move, taxiing toward the runway.

Tala reached for Kane's hand, gripping it hard as they picked up speed, careening down the runway.

"You're terrified," Maverick said with a smirk.

"Maybe a little," she said, her voice tight.

"Statistics show you're two thousand times more likely to die in a car accident than a plane crash," he said matter-of-factly.

"Did you swallow a textbook? Your useless information isn't helping right now," she said. She sucked in her breath as the wheels lifted from the runway, and she stole a glance out the window, watching as they pulled away from the ground, her heart in her throat.

"Breathe," Kane whispered as he leaned toward her.

"I'm not sure I can," she said, her voice shaking.

He reached out, gently taking hold of her chin and turning her face to meet his, then he kissed her. When she tried to pull away, he only kissed her harder. After a moment, she felt her shoulders drop, her hammering heart beginning to slow.

When he pulled away, she felt her anxiety cut in half, and she gave him a small smile. "Thank you," she whispered. She was also relieved to see it was only Maverick who'd seen her panic.

Kane grinned, kissed her forehead, then sat back in his chair.

After they reached cruising altitude, the attendants made their way through the cabin, offering drinks and food to everyone. Tala took a glass of water and a turkey sandwich, but feeling both out of sorts and anxious, she had no appetite, her stomach flipping at the sight of it.

"Not hungry?" Maverick asked between bites of melon from a fruit cup. "It's going to be a crazy day, you should eat."

Tala knew he was right and pulled off a small corner of the sandwich, more bread than meat and cheese, and reluctantly popped it into her mouth.

A moment later, Elias appeared before her, taking a seat in the empty chair beside Maverick. Tala swallowed hard. He was a stern-looking man that she wasn't able to read, which made her nervous in his presence.

"Welcome aboard," he said kindly, though he didn't smile.

"Thanks for this. Taking us to do this," she said, straightening in her seat. She didn't want to look small to this man.

He nodded. "There's not a lot of traffic going in and out of the Republic right now. Even for me. But this bombing and the fallout from it gives me an in. They want something from us. And I always do what I can for the cause."

"Can I ask why? I imagine it's a huge risk for you every time you go in and out of the Republic," she said. "Even with immunity. I don't see the Republic honoring that if they were to discover your duplicity."

He pressed his lips together as he nodded his head. "That's true," he said calmly, his voice deep.

"Does it ever scare you?" she asked, her moxie surprising her. She felt Kane's and Maverick's eyes on her.

Elias shrugged, his head tipping to the side. "In the beginning. Maybe still a little now. But the way I see it is that fear, uncertainty, doubt, they're all just feelings. Brave is action. And the future relies on those who can be brave in the present. We all have a role to play."

A role to play. That's what Victoria had said to her.

Tala nodded in understanding.

"Be brave today, Tala," he said. He quietly rose from the chair, then retreated to his seat.

Tala's eyes flitted between Maverick's and Kane's, but neither of them said a word. She picked up the sandwich again, picked off two more bites, then set it aside. She drank half the water in her glass, then curled up against the window. She reached for Kane's hand, resting it on her leg so that she could feel a part of him beside her, then closed her eyes.

"Quick introductions," Jasper said, standing, commanding the attention of everyone on the flight. "We'll be landing shortly. Specialists Griffin and Hales will be escorting us to our destination." He nodded at two of the soldiers who had changed out of their guard uniforms and into civilian clothes.

Specialist Griffin wasn't a very tall woman, but she had broad shoulders, her dark hair slicked back into a tight bun at the base of her neck. Hales, on the other hand, was tall, his hair buzzed short, his skin a deep, russet brown. They both looked equally capable.

"Kane, Maverick," Jasper continued, "your weapons." He nodded as a flight attendant approached, handing each of them a handgun and a holster for inside the waistband of their jeans. "There's a van waiting for us on the ground that will take us to our location. Move swiftly from the plane to it after we land. Eyes on alert at all times," Jasper said, giving a sweeping look around the cabin. "Good," he said, satisfied, then returned to his seat.

When their plane landed, Tala was given a hat to tuck her hair up into while they exited the plane. As Jasper had said, a van with dark tinted windows was waiting nearby, and Tala climbed in the far back with Maverick and Kane on either side of her. Griffin and Hales were in the middle with Ash, and Jasper was in front with their driver.

Tala's heart was in her throat as they drove with ease through Michigan City, their van in autonomous mode despite having a driver. The skyscrapers were like man-made mountains of steel, the sidewalks swollen with people, reminding her of Columbia City. Many of the buildings looked like those in the modern Stoughbour borough, including blocks of vertical villages like where she had lived. She felt an unexpected pull in her chest at the thought of her old city. It had been her whole life up until a few months ago.

Winding through the avenues, they crossed a river, heading deeper and deeper into the city. No one spoke a word the entire drive. The farther they drove, the more Militia Forces Tala spotted along the way, their armored prowlers driving through the city, passing them in both directions. They also had a heavy presence on the streets, patrolling intersections on foot. For every one she saw, Tala knew that somewhere there was another one in plain clothes. More than once, when they were stopped at a traffic light, an agent would appear, sometimes only yards away from them, and Tala would instinctively reach for Kane. She willed her breathing to keep steady, her racing heart to calm.

One minute they were deep in the city, swallowed up by the dense metropolis, then suddenly, the high-rises fell away, replaced by a breathtaking view of Lake Michigan, its end disappearing far beyond the horizon, meeting the blue sky above. The lake was an icy, snowy tundra as far as her eyes could see. Where there was no snow, the sun reflected off its frozen sheet of ice.

Tala peeled her eyes away from the view to glance at Kane. He had grown up on the shores of Lake Michigan, though not in the city, and she wondered what was going through his head. Maybe it meant nothing to him to see it again, maybe it meant everything. His face gave nothing away, but he gave her a small squeeze of her hand. He didn't have great memories from his childhood, but Lake Michigan was where he knew his mom. Maybe he was thinking of her.

The van turned at the lake and went northwest, anticipation building inside Tala. They drove for nearly half an hour, the minutes ticking by slowly on the clock on the digital dashboard. The city now behind them, their driver took their van into a residential area, large, sleek houses of glass and steel flanking the streets, snow piled high around sidewalks and driveways, yards blanketed in endless white. It reminded her vaguely of the one she grew up in.

Slowly, they left the affluent neighborhood, disappearing into a more modest area with small to medium single-family homes, ordinary, with brick and stone facades and wooden siding. As they rounded a corner, an old, brown brick building came into view, the dilapidated sign reading John C. Elementary. They pulled into the parking lot, two medical vans parked near the school's entrance, and made their way around the back where they parked near a black, windowless door nearly hidden in a recess of the building.

Tala's breath hitched as an MF agent emerged from the building, his face obscured by a balaclava. She glanced at Kane knowing there was terror in her eyes. He wore a hardened expression, and she watched as his hand moved to the gun at his waist.

"Relax," Jasper said calmly over his shoulder as if reading her thoughts. "Barber's one of ours. You really think we wouldn't have people on the inside?" he said with a small laugh.

They opened the van doors, and Tala was caught by the cold, a sharp wind blowing. If it was somehow possible, it was even colder than it had been high in the mountains. She shoved her hands into the pockets of her jacket, tucking her chin into her collar.

"This way," Barber said with a wave of his hand as he led them toward the door.

Tala couldn't take her eyes off his plasma gun. She wondered who she might have worked with at Command that had been loyal to the Rebels. She tried to imagine Captain Kole's reaction if any of them had been discovered. Surely, there was at least one that she had worked with.

They stepped inside the building, which wasn't much warmer than it was outside, though there was no longer the bite from the wind.

"People are still coming in. You're a little early," Barber said to Jasper and Ash, and they both nodded.

"We're operating today under the guise of a blood donation drive. Registered with the city even. Appointment only, of course," Ash said as she looked at Tala. "We've been vetting people for days, and they all have scheduled times to arrive on site."

"We attract less attention than if there was a mass of people all trying to get in at once. Some people have been here for hours," Jasper said.

"You can wait in the room down the hall," Barber said as he slid off his balaclava, revealing a full head of blond hair, just as light as hers. "There's a space heater in there."

Tala followed behind Ash and Jasper who seemed familiar with the building, down a narrow corridor lit only by cracks of light streaming in through the dirty, half-boarded windows.

Both Maverick and Kane followed in silence closely behind her. She swallowed hard, the unsettled feeling in her stomach returning, accompanied by hunger.

The room they stepped into was much warmer than the hallway, and Tala sighed, letting the heat relax her tension. Both Kane and Maverick stayed close to her, and she felt safe beside them.

"Right," Barber said once they were all in the small room, "I've got a post to keep. About fifteen more minutes."

While Ash, Jasper, Griffin, and Hales took seats on metal folding chairs, Tala stood quietly in the corner of the room. She suddenly realized that everyone, including Ash and Jasper, all carried a gun, while she had nothing, which irritated her.

"Do you remember what you're going to say?" Jasper asked her from across the room.

"Of course," she said with a nod as she removed the hat, her hair falling over her shoulders. She had read through her agenda late into the night, committing all the points she was supposed to hit to memory. What they wanted most from her was authenticity.

Standing near the heater, Tala quickly warmed and unzipped her heavy jacket.

"Tala," Ash said while looking at her palm pad. She looked up, her eyes fixing on her. "Come with me. I want to show you something. I only need one of you," she said, looking at Kane and Maverick.

Tala glanced between them.

"I'll go," Maverick said, stepping away from the heater.

Tala watched Kane study Ash as she made her way to the door. Then he looked at Tala, giving her an assuring smile.

With Maverick on her heels, Tala followed Ash back into the hallway. They turned down three separate corridors, Tala quickly losing track of where she was coming from and how to get back. The deeper they went, the more windows they lost and the darker it got. And then she heard it. It was small at first, then began to grow.

It was the animated clamor of an excited crowd. Energy sprang to life inside her at the sound of all the people who had come to see her, and she looked up at Maverick with wide eyes.

"They're here for you. It's a capacity crowd," Ash said. "In a few minutes, we'll get started. You're the fire, Tala. So light 'em up."

Tala's nervousness was ebbing, replaced with adrenaline pumping through her veins. She turned at the sound of approaching footsteps, Jasper and Hales making their way toward them.

"Where's Kane?" she asked, trying to look around them down the hall.

"Assisting Barber and Griffin. Ash, could you head down and help them out?" Jasper asked. "Two guys trying to get in the back door. No IDs on them. You're always good with these."

Ash rolled her eyes. "Always someone," she said, turning on her heel and heading back down the hall.

Tala took a deep breath, her chest rising and falling, and bounced on the balls of her feet with nervous anticipation.

"Showtime," Jasper said a few minutes later. "Tala, I'll call you out after my short introduction. Maverick, you can stand just off the side of the stage."

Tala nodded as he turned, disappearing around a corner. The crowd erupted in yelling and cheering, the sound taking over her, filling her up. Never in her life had she had a voice for herself. She'd obeyed her parents, had cowed to Thias, and taken orders from Kole. No one ever wanted to hear what she had to say. Not until now. There was an entire crowd that had gathered to hear her, and she was determined to make every word count.

Tala hadn't heard a word Jasper said until suddenly her name was called out over the roaring applause and whistling. A fire burned through her as she rounded the corner, Maverick beside her, and just before stepping onto the stage, he grabbed her by the arm, pulling her back.

"I just want to say I'm rooting for you," he said with pride in his eyes. He tipped his head at her, then released her arm.

Tala gave him a grin of appreciation, then turned and took the steps up onto the stage, the noise of the crowd deafening at the sight of her. It was an entire gymnasium filled with people. Everyday people, normal people, husbands and wives, brothers and sisters, young and old, all of them there so they could build a better tomorrow.

Their energy was like a thrill pulsing through her, igniting a spark inside. She made her way to the center of the stage beside Jasper, and turned to the crowd, smiling, waving.

It was then that a deep electrical blast rose above the sound of the crowd. Tala looked in confusion over everyone's heads. Then she heard it again. The raucous cheers of the crowd morphed into instant screams of terror. Before she could process anything, Jasper grabbed her by the arm, pulling her abruptly to the floor. Stretching his body over hers, he pinned her down. The blasts continued as realization dawned on her. It was a sound she knew well, the sound of a plasma gun. It was the sound of many plasma guns.

Chaos broke out throughout the gymnasium as people dropped to the ground, as people fled in every direction with no real clue where to go.

Panic flooded Tala as she watched Maverick, his gun drawn, race across the open stage, firing four times, though she didn't look to see where he was shooting. The sound of the plasma charges seemed to surround them. From the corner of her eye, looking beneath Jasper's arm as he lay sprawled atop her, she watched as MF stormed the gym at the entrances opposite her.

"Get her to the van!" Jasper yelled above the cacophony as he rolled off of Tala.

In an instant, Maverick pulled her to her feet, nearly dragging her across the stage as they ran for cover, Jasper pulling his gun, shooting cover shots while Tala fled.

Hales met them just off the stage, his gun drawn. "Go!" he yelled loudly in a deep voice as he took off in a sprint.

Maverick pulled Tala along as they twisted and turned down each dark corridor. While she had lost all sense of where she was, he seemed sure of himself, and she fought to stay on his heels. The back door of the school appeared before them as they rounded their last corner, and together they burst into the cold, winter air.

Barber was no longer at his post, and Hales ran to the van, nearly tearing the side door off as he pulled it open. Maverick all but threw Tala inside. Ash suddenly jumped in after, followed by Hales and Maverick as Griffin climbed into the driver seat, starting the van.

Jasper emerged running from the building, a gash above his eye bleeding as he yanked the front door open and hurled himself inside.

"That's all of us!" Ash yelled as she pulled the side door shut with one hand, the other clutching her gun.

"No!" Tala screamed. "We need Kane!"

Griffin wasted no time, slamming her foot on the gas, bypassing autonomous mode, the van taking off with a lurch, its tires squealing against the pavement.

"Kane!" Tala yelled again as she reached for the van door, pulling it open. A pair of arms wrapped around her, pulling her backward.

Griffin paid her no attention as they fled the parking lot, the sound of sirens wailing in the distance.

"Kane!" Tala screamed again as she wriggled in the grasp of a pair of unknown arms.

"He's gone!" Ash yelled as she pulled the door closed again, though her voice was no match for Tala's screams. "They've got him. I watched it. Barber's dead. Our driver's dead."

"No!" Tala screamed again, her body thrashing. She threw her head back, hitting someone, and they cried out. "No!" she screamed again.

"Get her coat off," Jasper yelled from the front seat.

The pair of arms that clutched her suddenly released her, and she felt multiple hands on her as they pulled her jacket from her flailing body. She dove for the door again, but someone behind her was faster, pulling her back.

She kicked her legs wildly as she screamed Kane's name, desperate to break the hold on her.

"Hold her still," a voice said.

There was a sharp pain in her arm, and she turned to see Hales with a syringe in his hand. Tala took a breath and kicked again, her voice going hoarse as she yelled Kane's name.

In only seconds, Tala's body suddenly began to feel heavy, every movement she made becoming sluggish, a weight settling into her legs and arms. Her vision blurred, and dark spots formed in her periphery. She tried to yell again, but all she heard was a weak grunting noise escape her mouth.

Her chest felt leaden, and her body, too heavy to move, slackened. She felt tired, so tired. She tried to blink it away, tried to scream again, but nothing came out, and a moment later, against all her willpower, everything went dark.

SEVENTEEN

Tala's eyes fluttered open, then closed. Her body was heavy, and her mind was groggy. She was vaguely aware that she was on her back, the silhouette of someone hovering over her. *Kane.* She tried to reach out, but her hand was clumsy, and it fell away.

"Tala."

She heard her name from somewhere far away.

"Tala. Open your eyes."

Those words were familiar to her, she'd heard them before. The hard pavement below her. The cold, damp air, the gentle sound of lapping water in the distance.

No, she thought. That wasn't right. That was something else, that was another time.

"Tala."

She heard it again, the voice stronger, closer. It wasn't Kane.

"Open your eyes," it repeated gently.

She felt fingers sliding through her hair, and her eyes fluttered open again. The overhead light was bright, and she winced. She blinked, trying to bring the world into focus. Her leaden body was exhausted.

Maverick, she realized.

"Mav," she whispered on a breath.

"I'm here," he said, his voice strong. With every blink, her surroundings came more and more into focus. She was on a sofa, her body sunken into the supple leather. Familiar faces looked down on her from behind Maverick. Ash. Jasper. Elias Barrington.

Her eyes roamed over each of them as though she were in a dream and couldn't understand what they were all looking at, why they were standing there.

"Tala," Maverick said. There was something in his tone that brought her attention to him, the fog in her mind still clearing. "Do you know where you are?"

She gave a sweeping look around her. "An airplane," she said. Her voice was strained and hoarse, her throat sore.

"Good," he said. "Tell me what you remember." His voice was gentle, but there was trepidation in it.

Tala's mind tried to go backward. There was a rally, she was in the Republic. She could remember standing on the stage, all those people, their cheers ringing in her ears. Then suddenly they weren't cheers. They were screams. The blasts. Plasma guns.

Kane.

He shot through her mind like a bullet from a pistol, and her breath caught. She wrenched her body up, her world starting to spin, making her woozy. She fumbled to her feet as she scanned the plane. Maverick. Jasper. Ash. She swallowed hard, her panic rising. Elias. Griffin. Hales. And two uniformed soldiers she didn't know. Where was Kane?

She tried to take a step and stumbled, falling to her knees. Maverick was at her in an instant, his arm slipping around her.

Then she remembered. Kicking and screaming as they drove away. Tears sprang to her eyes as she turned, meeting Maverick's gaze. There was a pained expression in his eyes.

"Where is he?" she asked, her voice thick, scratchy.

"I...I..." he stammered.

"Where is he?" she snapped.

"Militia Forces got him," he said, his voice falling.

The world seemed to come to a complete stop, halting on its axis. Her body was paralyzed, the air in her lungs frozen. *Militia Forces got him.* She heard the words. They repeated in her mind. But they weren't real. They were a mistake. Her mind couldn't process. Where was Kane?

"Tala?" Maverick said softly.

She gave the room another glance. He wasn't there. There was a void where he should be, and reality dawned on her, it crashed through her like an unmanned freight train, and she collapsed into Maverick's arms. He was strong and pulled her to him. Tears escaped her eyes, and she looked up at him with blurry vision.

Somewhere in the distance, she could hear crying, choking, screaming. They were the sounds of terror, of devastation, of heartbreak.

She took a breath, her body shuddering, and she realized she was hearing herself.

"She's in shock," someone said.

"She needs a sedative," someone said.

"She needs some water," someone said.

Maverick lowered his body to the floor and wrapped his arms fully around her. She curled into him, feeling small. She sobbed, her tears pouring from her eyes like a heart bleeding out.

"Tala, take this," Ash said kindly as she crouched down beside her. She held her hand out, a small, purple pill in her palm, a bottle of water in her other hand. "It'll help you sleep."

Tala's eyes met hers. They were an unexpected combination of brown and hazel and gold. They were thin and narrow. Striking. And there was a look of sorrow in them.

"I don't want it," Tala said with a raspy voice as she pushed the pill away.

"It's here if you need it," she said, then stood, stepping back, giving her room.

"Tala," a deep voice said, and it took her a moment to realize it was Elias. "Come sit."

It wasn't until that moment that she realized she was on the floor, curled up in Maverick's arms. She crawled out of his grasp, and Maverick stood, then pulled her up beside him. She stumbled, unsteady, as she tried to find her feet. She glanced over her shoulder to the seat that had been Kane's on the way to Michigan City. She knew it was empty, but the sight of it brought tears back to her eyes.

Maverick guided Tala into a seat in the middle of the plane, her body sinking into the cushion, and Ash spread a blanket across her lap. Tala looked around, her head pounding, and she saw the sadness in everyone's eyes as they watched her. The pity in every one of them.

"Tell me what happened," she said, her voice so hoarse she didn't recognize it.

Elias, Jasper, and Ash filled the seats around her while Maverick stayed on one knee beside her.

"We're still trying to piece things together." The voice seemed to ring in Tala's ears, echoing in her brain. She looked up into the brown eyes of Griffin as she stood behind Jasper. "Kane and I were asked to assist Barber," she said. "Two men without IDs were trying to enter the school from the back door. They were giving Kane a hard time. Then one stepped away for a minute on his palm pad. When Ash arrived, we said we'd take them around front where they could be handled by our security," she paused like she was searching for her next words.

Tala noticed for the first time that Griffin's arm was bandaged, wrapped in thick, white gauze. Jasper had a cut above his eyebrow. Ash's lip was busted open, and there were deep shades of purple spreading across Hales's face, under his eyes, with a thin tape over the bridge of his nose. She knew immediately that she'd done that to him, though she felt no guilt over it, no remorse. She was simply numb.

"It all happened so fast," Ash said. "We got less than ten yards away when an unmarked white van came tearing around the building, and at the same time, the two men pulled out plasma guns. One of them shot Barber before I even realized what was happening." She swallowed, then took a breath. "They shot our driver standing beside our van. I knew both were dead immediately."

"One of them shot me," Griffin said, motioning toward her arm. "It's superficial. That's when Ash killed him. Then we heard all the screams from inside the building. Two MF jumped from the white van. One of them shot Kane with darts. In the neck, in the thighs, over and over, and the other tased him. Brought him to his knees."

Tala's breath hitched, her tears welling in her eyes again. The airplane seemed to be contracting around her.

"Do you want us to stop?" Ash asked gently.

Tala shook her head, not trusting her voice. She had to know. Maverick reached for her hands, and she realized then that she was shaking.

"Ash was fighting with the man we'd been escorting around the building, and I tried to shoot at the two MF from the van as they went for Kane. But with my arm, I couldn't get off a good shot," Griffin said, her shoulders slumped forward. Dejection and regret were etched across her face.

"I shot him in the head," Ash said solemnly. Tala knew she meant the man she'd been fighting. "I turned just in time to see Kane pulled into that MF van as it peeled out. We tried to shoot it, but it was armored. Our bullets did nothing, and it got away."

"That's when we saw you all running from the building," Griffin said. "All I could think was that we had to get you out of there. I ran to our van and jumped into the driver's seat while you all piled in."

The rest Tala remembered. Arms around her, holding her down while she screamed for Kane. She felt the color in her face drain, the urge to vomit coming over her, and she swallowed hard the taste of rising bile.

"Get her some more water," Elias said quickly.

She took slow sips from a bottle, feeling the cold on her teeth, then breathed deeply. It hurt in her lungs as her head fell back in the chair, closing her eyes.

"Sorry we had to tranq you," Jasper said. "But you were about to throw yourself out the van. We've got people everywhere looking for him, for that white van."

"There's a bounty on him," Tala said quietly.

Tala recalled Vulcan's warning before her escape from the Republic. *"Someone would sell you out for so much as a hot meal."*

Is that what had happened to Kane?

"The security alert issued on him wanted him alive," Jasper said. "We've got to believe that whoever wanted him wants him alive for a reason. They didn't shoot him, so we're operating under the assumption that he's not dead."

Tala's chest tightened. "It's not *whoever* wants him. It's Vaughn Adams who wants him."

She watched as Jasper and Maverick exchanged a furtive glance. The silence that fell among them was deafening, and Tala felt a weight settle on her chest.

"I think Tala's right," Elias said. "The chancellor was abruptly pulled away from our meeting. It wouldn't be a stretch that he's connected to this. I've already put out some calls to his office to find out whatever I can."

Her mind raced, confused how anyone was able to overpower Kane, but she couldn't say this to anyone. She cringed at the thought of what was in those darts he was shot with. If it was Vaughn who had him, it likely meant he knew about the experiments. He'd seen what he could do, and it meant that he had a plan for Kane, that he had been prepared for him.

"Nothing changes," Ash said, her voice strong and commanding. "We still proceed with the search mission. We explore every lead until he's found."

"It might be easier to find him if we know we're looking for the chancellor as well," Jasper said.

"We just need time now," Ash said. "We have as many people as we can on this. People are reviewing any security footage they can access, they're getting witness statements, and they're conducting a grid search. But things were chaotic, they still are. We just need time."

"Max," Tala said, straightening. "I need Max."

"Who's Max?" Jasper asked.

"Merlin," she said, remembering his codename. "He's Kane's closest friend. He's a complete genius with technology. We need Merlin."

Max knew about Kane, about the super-soldier program. He knew what he was capable of, and he would understand how dire their situation was, more than anyone.

His voice filled her brain as she recalled what he'd said to her in the very beginning. *"One thing you should know about me is that if there's a computer involved, there's not much I can't do."* It was time to put that to the test. And she hoped like hell he was right.

Numb and with Maverick at her side, Tala was welcomed back to The Village with Mila, Vi, and Declan waiting in the lobby. Maverick had called ahead to warn them they were coming, to tell them what had happened so Tala wouldn't have to relive it. They sprang to their feet at the sight of her as Maverick ushered her along. It was late, the City Center quiet, its lights dim, the hallway lights casting their moonlit glow around.

She knew she was walking, she could feel it in her legs, but couldn't remember moving her feet until she arrived at her unit. She stood immobile outside the door, her friends surrounding her. She couldn't do it, open the door. One glance inside her unit would show its vacancy and Kane's void would be all the more real.

"Maybe she can sleep in my unit. So she doesn't have to be alone," Vi said quietly, as though reading Tala's mind. "There's an extra bed with my brother gone."

"Tals," Mila said, her hand sliding down Tala's back. "You hear that? You can sleep with Vi. You don't even have to go in there."

But this was hers and his, this was their home. If there was a place in The Village where she'd feel him, it would be here. As hard as it would be to feel his physical absence, it would be even harder not to feel him at all.

She shook her head and reached out, using her palm pad to open her door. The unit was dark when she stepped inside. The virtual window on the wall showed it was snowing outside. She couldn't remember walking from the plane to the car, the car to The Village's secure entrance. Was it snowing then?

The sound of the door closing made her jump.

"Tals," Mila said, "do you want someone to stay with you?"

She turned, looking at her friends, their eyes all filled with sorrow, with compassion, and she felt her emotion rising. She wanted only to be alone. She shook her head, afraid to speak, afraid her tears would come pouring out of her all over again. She wondered how much a person could cry. There seemed to be no end for her.

"Okay," Vi said, her voice cracking just enough for Tala to catch it. "We're all just a quick call, a quick message away."

Tala nodded as she turned away. Mila pressed herself against Tala, her arms wrapping around her from behind.

"I love you, friend," she said quietly into her hair.

As Mila stepped away, Vi approached her, gently pressing her forehead to the back of Tala's neck. She took a slow breath. "I'm here for you," she said, her voice thick.

"We all are," Declan said as he reached for her hand, giving it a firm, reassuring squeeze. "Whatever you need."

Maverick was the last to reach out, and he smoothed his hands over her shoulders. "We'll find him," he said, his voice strong. "I won't rest until we do."

She heard the conviction in his voice and loved him for it. But it tugged at her because she knew there was no way for him to guarantee his promise. She wiped at her eyes before her tears could fall, her hands wet, and she dried them on her jeans. Her friends all lingered for another moment, then they were gone, and Tala was alone.

She was alone, and she felt it in her bones. She slipped out of her heavy jacket, letting it fall to the floor where she stood, then kicked off her shoes. She went to her bed, but instead of crawling in on the left side, on her side, she pulled back the blankets on Kane's, slipping in between the cold sheets. Her head fell onto his pillow, and she took a breath, inhaling him, the smell of soap and leather and a subtle hint that was unique only to him. She rolled to her side and pulled her knees to her chest. She felt dizzy, her head pounded, and her stomach churned with worry.

"Where are you?" she asked aloud. Though she was only met with silence. She felt her tears fall, and she sniffled, her body quivering. Drawing in a deep breath, she closed her eyes, desperate to just fall asleep. It would be the only reprieve she would get from the ache she felt all the way into her soul.

When Tala woke, she had no idea the time. She wasn't entirely sure she'd actually fallen asleep, but a glance at her palm pad showed she had, getting at least a couple hours. She didn't know what woke her until she heard the soft knock on her door.

She rolled to the side, her feet hitting the floor. She rose, unsteady, taking a moment to orient herself. Her body was exhausted, sluggish. Slowly, she made her way to the door. Opening it, she found Mila standing before her, a frown on her face, a coffee in one hand, a paper baggy in the other. Without a word, Tala stepped aside to let her in.

"Maverick let me through security. I wasn't sure if you'd be up to eating, but breakfast is finished downstairs, so I brought you a waffle just in case. Though I have no syrup," she said, waving the baggy. "And here, I know coffee goes a long way for you," she said, handing Tala the disposable cup.

She took it, feeling it hot in her hand, then crossed the unit to her sofa, Mila taking a seat beside her.

"I won't ask how you're doing," she said gently but timidly. Tala could hear it in her voice, she didn't know what to say. Were there really words to explain how Tala felt? Were there really words that could comfort her?

"Mav said that when you're ready, you're supposed to go to Vulcan's office," she said.

Tala nodded, then took a drink of the coffee. It was warm in her chest, and she hoped the caffeine would help shake her body from its funk. Nothing would help her mind or her heart, but maybe it would help her to not feel like she had just run a marathon.

"Say something. Please?" Mila pleaded with sadness.

It was then that Tala realized she hadn't spoken since Mila got there, not a word.

"I'm not sure what to say," she finally choked out. Her voice was still hoarse from screaming the day before. Her throat was dry and sore.

"Anything. Cry, scream, throw something. This catatonic state you're in makes me nervous."

"It's all my fault," she whispered. "I was the eager one. I insisted on going to the rally. He thought it was a terrible idea, but he went because of me, because he wanted to protect me. If I had only listened." Her eyes welled with tears. She took another drink of the coffee but had suddenly lost her appetite even for that, so she set it aside.

"No. This was absolutely no one's fault. Well, not yours anyway. He knew the risks and went anyway," Mila asserted, her voice strong.

"I knew the risks too. And I disregarded all of them," she argued. "He was worried about me, about my motives. He thought I was doing it for all the wrong reasons, and he was right," she admitted, though now it was too late. A tear slipped down her face, and she didn't bother to wipe it away. More tears were likely to fall, it would be futile.

Mila reached for Tala's hand, her skin warm against hers, and Tala looked at her through clouded eyes.

"Right now, we need to focus on finding him. If ever there was a fighter, I know it's him," Mila said as she blinked away her own tears.

Of course this was true. He was a fighter, more than anyone. She suddenly thought about Vulcan. She needed to see him immediately. Maybe he had information.

She stood quickly. "I've got to see Vulcan. I've got to see what he knows," she said hurriedly as she went to her dresser. She threw on the first pair of jeans she saw and grabbed a shirt that she was sure needed to be laundered, but she couldn't care less. "Come with me," she said, waving Mila along.

Tala walked as fast as her weak legs would carry her and was let into the secured offices without delay. She bypassed Selene altogether and went straight for Vulcan's office where she found him, along with Jasper and Ash, standing at the digital wall in his seating area. An image of the empty parking lot Kane had been taken from was blown up on the screen.

They all turned when she entered, and she saw the pity in their eyes. Everyone's except Vulcan's. Tala couldn't read him.

"Tala," Jasper said, "we were just discussing you. Discussing the situation."

"Please tell me you have information," she said with desperation.

"Not yet," Ash said. "But we're still combing the area, and we have people going through all the security footage they're able to access in the immediate vicinity to see if we can pick them up. The problem is the lack of city surveillance in the area. It's partially why that location was chosen. Our other challenge is there are so many white vans. Who would've thought? And we have no license plate, so it's kind of a needle in a haystack at this time."

"What about Max? I told you, we need him. He's the best," Tala asserted.

"Avery made contact with him late last night, and we've made an extraction plan. He should've left Columbia City a few hours ago," Jasper said. "But getting out of the Republic, getting across the country takes time. It's almost thirteen-hundred miles from the city to here."

Tala swallowed hard. He wouldn't be there until at least tomorrow morning. What if Kane didn't have that much time?

"How did this even happen? You told me it was safe!" she snapped, her emotion rising. "You told me you had measures to mitigate the risk."

"They didn't even try for you," Jasper said. "We don't think they knew you were there."

"So then, how Kane?"

"Someone likely spotted him," Vulcan said. "They recognized him and cashed out by reporting him. The chances of any of this happening were so small. It was a fluke."

"A fluke?" she gasped. "I don't even know if he's still alive, and you're calling it something so cavalier as a *fluke*? He's your bother!"

"Tala, we're doing everything we can," Ash said. "Just give us time. Hold it together a little longer."

Tala's eyes met hers, and she saw the affirmation in them. There was no other option but to wait, but to hold it together. She had wanted Kane to believe in her, now she had to believe in him. Believe that he was strong enough to endure until they could find him.

"Since you're here, Mila," Vulcan said, redirecting his attention, "there's something else that needs to be addressed. It should've been discussed a while ago, but things have been, well, hectic around here."

Tala glanced over her shoulder at Mila, feeling as confused as she looked.

"You've been in The Village for several weeks now," he said. "And we have rules about living here."

Tala's heart fell.

"Vulcan," Jasper said curtly. "This isn't the time for this."

"It's overdue," he said as he cast Jasper a sideways glance. "All of our residents have committed to our cause. That's one of the stipulations of living here. And I'm sorry to say that you're no exception to this," he said.

"Vulcan," Ash said sharply. She was a small woman, shorter than Tala even when she wore her chunky heels, but her bite was harsh. "Not now."

"It's time you make a decision," he said, ignoring the others. "I certainly don't want to force your hand just to stay. And if you decide not to commit, we can make arrangements for you above ground in Hatfolk." He crossed his arms, a show that he would not budge on the issue.

"You're not trying to force her hand?" Tala retorted. "That's exactly what you're doing."

"You can't seriously kick her out while Tala is going through this," Jasper argued.

"She knew the precepts of staying here since the beginning," Vulcan asserted.

"Mila," Ash said, "what was your career in Columbia City?"

"I was a teacher. A private primary school," she said, speaking for the first time.

"Our children in The Village attend school above ground. I'm confident I can get you a job. They're always looking for staff at the school," Ash said.

Tala understood what she was doing. While Vulcan showed no heart, Ash was showing as much heart as she could.

"But that doesn't solve the entire problem," Vulcan said, sounding impatient.

"You want me inked," Mila said flatly. While Tala's anger was raging inside, Mila appeared the picture of calm. "You're right," she said, straightening and taking a step closer to Vulcan. "I did know the precepts."

"So? What'll it be?" he said.

"I'll do it," she said without hesitation.

Tala's head snapped in Mila's direction. Mila was hardly a rebel in life, and now she was about to pledge to the actual Rebels. She felt her jaw slacken.

"But not because I necessarily believe in the Revos' cause." She folded her arms across her chest, mirroring Vulcan. "But because I believe in Tala. She's going to be the one to make a difference. And you know it too. Or you'd never have put so much on her shoulders. You'd never have set such high expectations of her unless you thought you could do it without her. So I'll do it. I'll get ink. And I'll do whatever I can to help my friend."

The room fell silent, the tension thick. Mila and Vulcan stared at each other. She was not backing down to him.

"Okay then," he said, his voice tight.

Tala caught Jasper's face, a faint smile in his eyes.

"Should I escort you to the tattoo parlor?" Vulcan asked.

"I can find my way," she said.

"Mila, give me a day or so to get things settled with the school," Ash said. She, too, had a pleased look on her face. "I'll get in contact with you."

"Is that all?" Tala asked.

"For now," Vulcan said. "I'll let you know when Merlin arrives," he said coolly.

Tala turned to leave, Mila in stride beside her.

"Your codename is Bluebird, right?" Mila asked as they took the stairs to the third floor.

Tala nodded. "Yeah. Why?"

"Just making sure."

"You impressed me back there," Tala said. "How you wouldn't back down to Addox." Kane always refused to call him Vulcan, and she decided he didn't deserve the eminence of his moniker.

"That's his real name?" Mila asked, glancing at Tala. "And he's Kane's brother?"

"His older brother," she said. "They were estranged for many years. I'd say that they still are," Tala said. Once they reached the third floor, they turned, heading toward the south wing.

"I mean, you'd never know at a first look. But I can see it. In their face, in their bone structure. And they sure know how to glare with enough severity to set anyone on edge," she said with a small laugh.

Tala nodded, a sad smile on her face as she thought about Kane's eyes. So dark and intense, yet deep, arresting. They were her safe place.

"Well, I think he's an ass," Mila said as they arrived at the tattoo parlor.

They stepped into the small shop. It immediately reminded her of the room in the safehouse back in Columbia City where she'd gotten her ink. A phoenix. Like Kane's. Theirs looked nothing alike, but there was something about sharing that connection with him. And what it symbolized was the epitome of her life, of his life. Reborn of the ashes.

While Tala's eyes wandered the seemingly endless options on the walls, Mila described to the artist exactly what she wanted. He listened carefully as he sketched her vision, though Tala mostly tuned them out. In only minutes, he had astutely brought Mila's creation to life, and when she was pleased, he put her in a reclined chair.

"Here," she said, holding out the inside of her left wrist, and he nodded.

"Good place. Minimal pain," he said in a gruff voice.

Tala took a seat in a nearby chair and watched in silence as he carefully began the outline with the tattoo gun, the small needle leaving behind soft blue lines in the indelible ink.

While she sat there, Tala's mind wandered back to Kane. Not that he ever left. He filled her brain, and as she closed her eyes, his face appeared before her. The gnawing of so many emotions was felt deep inside, and her stomach churned as her head throbbed, feeling it in her temples. He'd been through hell before, when he was just a teenager, when all those horrible experiments had been done on him. He'd died on the table during the final one, resuscitated as he was now. He was strong. His will was indomitable, and he would not give up. She found a glimmer of peace in that knowledge. No matter what was happening to him, he would not go out without a fight. What scared her most was how extreme any treatment used on him could be. He wasn't easy to overpower. What did Vaughn know that they never had?

"What do you think?" the tattoo artist asked as he finished and pulled away. Tala was brought back to the present, and she stood to see Mila's ink, a bluebird in flight, its wings open and strong, covering the inside of her wrist, its baby blue shading done with a watercolor effect.

"It's beautiful," Tala said, and she felt a flutter in her chest. Mila believed in her so much that she was willing to permanently mark herself after her. This was not the time to fall apart. Kane needed her to be strong. He needed her to fight as much as she needed him to. She felt it deep inside her, that single thought fortifying her. She would find him.

Tala couldn't spend another night alone in her unit. It was too quiet, Kane's absence too large, so Mila agreed to stay with her.

Although she was grateful to have someone beside her, her soft snoring kept Tala awake. Or maybe it was her own heavy heart. Breathing in the heady scent from Kane's pillow created a dichotomy of emotion in her. Both comfort and sadness. Despite her resolve to not fall apart, for his sake, her stress was palpable, and it was manifesting physically. She couldn't eat her waffle from breakfast, she'd missed lunch because she was with Mila getting her ink, and she'd forced down a slice of pizza at dinner. Nothing was appetizing to her, and her stomach stirred with unease.

Its constant roiling distracted her mind from Kane as she lay in the darkness. She felt car sick, like she had going through the mountain passes to Camp Washington. She eased out of bed, stumbling in the dark, and made her way to the bathroom. Making it to the toilet, the bile inside her rose with the force of a volcano.

Over and over again, she threw up. Her body hunched over the toilet bowl as she heaved, her body shaking. She took slow, deep breaths through her mouth so she wouldn't smell the vomit, which only made her throw up more.

When she was confident she had nothing left to come up, she slumped back, her body propped up against the tub behind her, and she saw Mila standing in the doorway, a groggy look of concern on her face.

Mila lowered herself to the cold tile floor, closed the lid of the toilet, then flushed it.

"You're so stressed you're making yourself sick," she said. "Tals, you can't do this to yourself."

Tala's head pounded, and she rubbed her temples. "I don't know how to do this," she admitted slowly, the taste of bile lingering in her mouth. "I don't know how to be strong for him when I feel so broken."

"Let's take a walk," Mila said. "Get you out of the room."

Tala thought back to her first few weeks in The Village, before Kane made it back to her. She wandered the corridor every night, always finding the single lounge in the secured living quarters. Somehow, she found peace in that space. It was worth it to try again.

She turned to Mila and nodded. "Okay."

Tala woke to the buzzing of her palm pad. Groggy, half unaware she was moving at all, she reached for the device to see a message from Addox. She read it, her body bolting upright as soon as the words registered, the sleepy fog in her brain clearing instantly. She looked back down at her screen, her emotions running rampant in her heart, tears welling in her eyes as she stared at those three simple words.

Merlin is here.

EIGHTEEN

Tala threw herself into Max's arms with a fury, knocking him backward. Thankfully, he was able to stay on his feet but just barely. When she stepped back, she saw the same worry in his eyes that she felt inside.

Unlike with everyone else, they didn't feel the need to say anything to each other. One look and they just knew. She knew he wouldn't stop until he found him, he knew she wasn't about to give up hope. There was comfort in finding someone who just… understood.

Max had given Addox an extensive list of the technology and software he needed on a computer, and Tala was surprised by his swift response. Maybe somewhere deep inside, he really was concerned for his brother.

Tala helped Max settle into a guest room, and while they waited for his computer to be set up, she took him to the City Center for lunch.

The mood at their table was morose, no one brave enough to even say Kane's name, but everyone was kind to Max. She could see it on their faces when they looked at him, this unassuming man: short, round in the midsection, glasses, combed back hair, a high-pitched voice, they were putting all their hope in him. Tala included. The Revos were looking for Kane, and she didn't doubt their efforts, but Max was better than all of them. He knew Kane, and he understood the added element of danger he was in.

"This place is crazy," Max said as he gazed up at the high ceiling. "And it's completely fortified?" he asked.

Leave it to him to be the one to ask.

"That's what we're told. That's what we hope," Declan said. He and Mila no longer sat across from each other, and though they tried to stay inconspicuous, Tala noticed them holding hands beneath the table. She was slightly surprised by the longevity of Mila's interest in him, though she couldn't deny he was good for her. In the Republic, the old Mila committed to no one, and Tala couldn't help but like the change in her.

Tala stared at the grilled chicken on her plate, the few carrots she'd taken, and the small bowl of fruit. She knew Mila and Vi were scrutinizing her, watching her closely, so despite her non-existent appetite, she nibbled on her food.

"How was it trying to get across the border?" Maverick asked after the table had fallen silent for so long that it had begun to feel awkward.

"Surprisingly uneventful," Max said. "We took a boat across the Mississippi, somewhere into Ozark Colony. Had to have people that were breaking up the thin ice so we could get across, but it was a narrow part and didn't take long. No MF. I think they're being stretched too thin. They can't monitor the whole western and southern borders. Not with all the unrest internally and the ground they're trying to maintain in the south. Though they don't advertise any of that."

"They don't tell us much here," Vi said. "People talk, of course, but no one seems to know anything with any certainty."

Thinking about the MF, the unrest Max was referring to, the conflict with DeSoto, Tala lost what little appetite she did have and instantly felt the unsettled feeling in her stomach return. The world was at war. It was too much to process, and she already felt like she was hanging on by a thread. She pushed her plate aside, ignoring the glance Mila and Vi exchanged.

Realizing she was finished with her lunch, Max leaned close to her. "Think we could chat in private?" he whispered discreetly.

Grateful she had an excuse to leave, she nodded. As she headed toward the garbage with her uneaten lunch, she spotted Wren a few tables away who was glaring at her with daggers coming from her eyes. Anger instantly flooded Tala's veins at the sight of her. She wanted to throw the remains of her lunch at her. She wanted to slap her across the face. She knew her anger was misplaced, most of it anyway, but Wren would be the perfect person to let it all out on.

"Tala," Max said, snapping her from her trance. She turned away from Wren and quickly dumped her food, then led Max to the fifth-floor lounge. They walked in silence beside each other, and she was relieved for once to not be expected to talk. She knew everyone was trying to be kind, to be comforting, but none of it was working. It was exhausting to try to explain herself, to talk through her emotions and the thoughts in her head.

When she was sure they were alone, Max and Tala took seats in chairs near each other, and he got right to the point.

"I've been apprised of the situation. All the details," he said, talking low and with caution.

Tala nodded, thankful she didn't need to repeat the story. She didn't think her mind could handle going through it again.

"Aside from worrying whether he's dead or alive, my biggest concern is that I have no idea how they've got him constrained," he said with a shake of his head. "I can't imagine handcuffs would go far. He'd have to be restrained with something strong, and anything they could put in him to subdue him his body would quickly burn off. He can't even keep cold medicine in his system long enough to help when he's sick."

Tala swallowed hard. Max's concern did nothing for her internal unrest. There was so little that they understood about Kane's abilities. Max was brilliant with computer science, not biology.

"I was so limited on what I could study about him. I feared the wrong kind of search would flag me and alert the government, and it's not like I could ask around. The only things I learned came from the data I hacked from the lab which wasn't much. Most of it had been destroyed, most likely after those kids escaped and the whole thing was compromised. I did manage to purge everything that remained that connected Kane," Max said. He looked tired, his eyelids sagging, his mouth turned down. He removed his glasses and pinched the bridge of his nose. Maybe all of this was giving him the same throbbing headache it was giving her.

"Max," she said quietly, "I've never been this scared in my whole life." It was the first time she admitted that even to herself.

He nodded, understanding. "Me too."

They stared at each other in silence. Having him there helped her to not feel so alone. No one knew Kane better than them, and it brought her comfort that they could be there for each other.

A buzzing from Max's palm pad interrupted the quiet, and he let out a heavy sigh of relief as he read the message aloud.

"My computer is ready," he said, looking up.

She envied him, having something to do, having an active role in the search. Tala had nothing to contribute. She had fighting skills and could fire a gun, but those did nothing to help the current situation. She wanted to scream. She wanted to hit something. All of her emotion was pent up inside her with nowhere to go. At any given time, she wasn't sure if she was going to break down or throw up. Then she thought of Kane and was reminded that he needed her to be strong for him. Holding herself together for him was the only thing keeping her from falling apart.

Max rose to his feet, reaching for Tala's hand. She stood, unsteady, their eyes meeting. They were complete opposites from each other, but in that moment, they shared the greatest commonality. They were the two people in the whole world to love Kane the most.

"We'll get through this, right? You'll find him?" she asked, her voice uneven.

"I won't rest until I do," he said, his face solemn but determined.

Tala watched him as he walked away, her heart in her throat, her emotions threatening to burst from her chest. Turning, she found her way back to her unit. It was quiet, and turning off the lights, she let the darkness swallow her up. She wanted nothing more than to just disappear.

She crawled into bed on Kane's side, breathing him in, her face buried in his pillow. Her heart ached, the air in her lungs burned, and her stomach churned. She closed her eyes, taking slow breaths through her nose, fighting the tears that prickled the back of her eyes.

Her mind was swarming with thoughts. From remembering her last moments with Kane to when she found out he was taken to the night they first met to when they had separated to get out of the Republic. Then there was all the conflict, the world crumbling around her, and she decided then that she wouldn't go on with any of it without him. She would simply walk away from all of it and let herself dissolve into the background of life. Maybe she should've done that already. If she had, he never would've gone missing.

Pushing her thoughts away, she summoned Kane in her mind, like she had done every night they were apart. She inhaled deeply, the scent of him on his pillow taking over, and just like that, she could almost feel him beside her.

Tala woke to the buzzing of her palm pad. She reached for it, blinking to focus her eyes, and saw a message from Vi.

Where are you? Sent so many messages. Getting worried.

She sighed, sitting up. She had three messages from Vi, four from Mila, and two from Maverick, all of them checking in and looking for her, and she felt a pang of guilt. She hadn't intended to worry anyone. But she'd managed to sleep. There had to be something in that.

Crawling out of bed, she quickly sent a message back to each of them, then looked at the time. She had slept through dinner. She thought about

Max and wondered if he'd made any progress. She was sure she would've heard if he had.

Tala made her way down to the second floor, the lingering smell of dinner in the air, the City Center quiet, and turned down the west wing as she headed for Vi's unit. She barely knocked before the door opened, Vi and Mila both wide-eyed with relief at the sight of her.

"Really," Tala said pre-emptively, "I'm sorry. I fell asleep. I didn't mean to worry anyone."

"We were just concerned," Mila said gently. "And I'm relieved you got some sleep. Feeling better?" she asked, scooting over on the sofa to make room for her.

"Some," she lied. Tala took a seat, curling her legs up beneath her.

"Any updates?" Vi asked.

She shook her head. She wasn't entirely sure she wanted any updates. If they hadn't found him, she just didn't want to know. She didn't think she could handle any more bad news.

"Are you hungry?" Mila asked. "Dinner is over, but we could go to the café."

Tala hadn't tried either of the restaurants in The Village, but she wasn't hungry. Her stress had a way of making all food unappetizing. It had been like this when her parents died too, though she didn't remember the headaches. She shook her head.

"Tal, you've got to eat," Vi said seriously. "If they came to you tonight and said they found Kane and needed you on a rescue team, you wouldn't even be able to stand up, let alone go on some high-risk mission to save him."

Tala considered this. Food or not, would they even let her try to extract him? She didn't think Addox would care either way. It was Ash or Jasper she'd have to appeal to.

"Maybe later," she said, mostly just to appease them.

They both looked at her grimly, though they didn't push the issue.

"Mila was giving me details about her and Declan," Vi said with a hopeful smile. "Maybe a change in topic? A distraction?"

"I'd love details," Tala said with more enthusiasm than she felt. She hated that she really didn't care. She wanted to be there for her friends. They were certainly there for her, and it wasn't fair to them, but nothing in life seemed to be fair.

She quietly half-listened as Mila told stories about Declan taking her to the movies, on late-night walks through The Village, to restaurants in Hatfolk, including a park near the main entrance to The Village that had a beautiful fountain resembling dandelions puffs.

"Oh," Mila said, perking up as she turned to Tala. "I forgot to tell you. Ash reached out to me. There's a position at the elementary school for an art teacher," she said with a wide grin.

Tala pressed her lips together in a smile as she reached for her hand, giving it a squeeze. "Boyfriend, ink, new job, it's like a whole new you," she said.

"Speaking of ink," Vi said. "Just curious. Why a bluebird?"

"It's Tala's codename. I didn't necessarily want to pledge myself to the Revos, not that their cause isn't admirable, but I had to pledge to something. And I decided to pledge to Tala," she said with a shrug, though Tala knew it ran deeper than that.

"I support the Revos, of course," Vi said. "And I know how to shoot a gun if it ever came to that. But it's not like I'm going to pick up arms and forge into battle. It's more what they represent that I support. A life with democracy and the freedom to make our own choices. To build a life of my own."

Isn't that what Tala had been trying to do? Promote that very message? Look where it had gotten her. Her head began pounding again.

"I think I'm going to go to bed. Try to sleep some more," Tala said as she pulled out her palm pad to message Maverick. It was late, which meant she needed him to be out in The Village. "Where's your family?" Tala asked as she glanced around. It hadn't occurred to her until just then that they weren't around.

"Dinner and a movie in Hatfolk," Vi said. "They like to get their heads above ground now and again."

When Maverick arrived, Mila left with them, and together they walked in silence back to the fifth floor. She saw the worry on Maverick's face when he looked at her, so she kept her eyes averted. She was losing patience with all the pity. She knew she was a mess, she didn't need to be reminded of it every time she looked at everyone.

Tala put on her pajamas and slipped into bed, the sheets cold, and she pulled the blanket up to her chin as Mila crawled in beside her.

"I'm worried about you," Mila said quietly, interrupting the silence that had fallen between them. "I know you don't want to hear that, but I am."

"I'm trying," is all she could manage. And it was the truth. She was trying.

Mila reached out, finding Tala's hand. "Just remember that we're all here for you."

Tala took an uneven breath, feeling her tears again. A moment later, Mila rolled to her side, and within only a few minutes, she was asleep.

Lying in the dark, Tala willed her mind to shut down. To remember the good. But her thoughts were far from the good ones. And they were loud and frantic and kept her awake. It wasn't even Mila's soft snoring anymore. She simply couldn't turn off her brain.

She closed her eyes, her headache only intensifying. She knew she had a pain reliever somewhere, but the thought of moving only made it worse. Then the nausea returned. She tried slow breaths until it passed, but the threat of her rising bile brought her to the bathroom in a hurry. She made it only just in time before she vomited, over and over again. Her body heaved and her chest hurt as tears ran down her face.

She looked up as Mila stepped into the bathroom, taking the same spot on the floor beside her that she had the night before.

Tala collapsed against the tub behind her and sighed, wiping at her tears. "I'm sorry I woke you," she choked out. "I tried to be quiet."

Mila let out a breathy chuckle. "I don't think anyone throws up quietly."

"I don't know how to do this," she said quietly. It was the same answer she'd given the night before. "I don't remember the last time I told him I loved him. We got separated at the rally and I didn't say goodbye. I should've hugged him."

"Tala, you had no reason to suspect any danger," Mila reasoned. "I understand why these thoughts are running rampant in your mind, but you can't do this to yourself. I promise he knew you loved him. Without a doubt in his mind."

Tala took a deep breath. All that time they'd spent arguing, the walls she'd put up around herself out of anger. She wanted to take it all back. She wanted to go back and do everything all over again. She would make so many different choices.

"Tala," Mila said gently, her voice soft, "you've been throwing up, you haven't been eating, you're sluggish, you've complained of headaches—"

"I know, I know," she protested. "I need to get a grip. I'm making myself sick. I need to relax. I need to trust that everyone is doing all they can. I know all of this," she said, harsher than she'd intended.

"But it isn't just since Kane disappeared that this has been going on," Mila said.

Tala looked at her, her brows furrowed. "What?"

"Before you left for Michigan City, you said you weren't feeling well."

Tala shrugged. "So? People get sick."

Mila gave a slow shake of her head. "That's not what I'm getting at."

"Then what?" Tala asked with impatience.

"When was the last time you had your period?"

"What?" she gasped. "You think I'm pregnant?"

Mila was quiet for a moment as she held Tala's gaze. "I think you might be, yes."

Tala was stunned into silence. There was no way. Just no way. She shook her head fervently. "Not possible."

Mila let out a small laugh. "Pretty sure it's possible."

Tala started counting the days in her head. There was so much that had happened, and she couldn't remember the last time she'd cycled. Time seemed to blur together. Was Mila right? Was all of this more than just stress? And then her heart fell. How could she have a baby without him? She felt sick again, her body lurching forward for the toilet as she vomited.

She wasn't sure how long she'd sat hunched over the toilet, but at some point, she felt herself doze off. When she woke, she was sprawled across the cold tile, her head on a folded towel, a blanket from her bed lying across her. She called out to Mila, but there was nothing but silence. She sat up, rubbing her eyes, her head still pounding, and slowly, her conversation with Mila came back to her. She slid her hands across her stomach, staring down at it in disbelief.

Was she?

Only minutes later, Tala heard the click of her unit door, then Mila appeared in the bathroom doorway, a cloth bag in her hand.

"Where'd you go?" Tala asked, her throat scratchy and dry.

"To the market. As soon as it opened. I stole your palm pad to get in and out of your unit. I got some things for you," Mila said as she sat down beside Tala. "Ginger ale," she said, pulling a bottle from the bag. "Soda crackers, dried fruit. And," she paused with a grin as she eyed Tala, "a pregnancy test."

Tala's body went still as she stared at the box in Mila's hand.

"You don't have to take it. But maybe it's better to find out either way?" Mila said.

Her mind raced. This was the last thing she'd expected. She reached out, grabbing the purple and white box. Holding it, it felt foreign. Never in her life had she taken one. But Mila was right, and she sighed. "A little privacy," she said as she stood on shaky legs.

Mila hurried out of the bathroom, and Tala carefully followed the directions on the box. Once she was finished, all that was left was to wait. She opened the door to the bathroom, then resumed her spot between the toilet and the tub.

"How long do we wait?" Mila asked as she sat beside her.

"Two minutes and forty-two seconds," Tala said, glancing at the timer on her palm pad.

"So, basically a lifetime," Mila said with a nod.

That's exactly what it felt like. They sat in silence, neither of them knowing what to say as the seconds ticked by. Tala was flooded with emotions she couldn't pinpoint, that she couldn't process. Mostly, she couldn't decide what she wanted. Did she want the test to be positive? Did she want it to be negative? Was there even a right answer?

Her fingers tingled and goosebumps were raised across her arms. She pulled the blanket around herself, picking up the scent of Kane on even that. But this time, it didn't make her want to cry. This time, it made him feel near.

When the timer chimed, Tala and Mila both jumped, then glanced nervously at each other.

"Want me to read it?" Mila offered.

Tala gazed up at the white stick that sat on her vanity counter. Was she brave enough to look for herself? Her eyes moved back to Mila, and she nodded.

Mila reached for it quickly, taking it in her hands, and Tala tried to overlook the fact that she'd peed on it.

"Well?" Tala asked, her anticipation running rampant inside her.

Mila looked up, a funny smile on her face. "It's positive, Tals."

A noise that Tala had never heard before bubbled up from somewhere inside her, a strange combination of laughter and coughing and gasping and crying. Her eyes welled with tears as she reached for the test from Mila, looking at the small word glaring back at her: Positive.

She took a deep breath, falling back against the tub.

"Looks like these late-night vomit sessions might go on for a while," Mila said with a wave of her hand. "Maybe we should invest in some furniture for in here. A sofa would be good. Beats the cold floor," she joked.

Despite herself, Tala laughed. For the first time in days. Her eyes swimming with tears, she reached for Mila, pulling her into a hug. How, she wondered, had she gone from unsure about all of it to suddenly loving something no larger than a pinto bean deep inside her?

Mila hugged her tightly, and Tala could hear her sniffles from the tears she knew she was crying, and she let out another laugh.

"Not a word. To anyone. Under any circumstances," Tala said when they pulled apart.

"Got it. State secret." There was a gleam in Mila's eyes as she looked across the small space between them, then she smiled, big and wide and full of teeth. "This is a good thing, Tals. I know that things aren't good right now, but this is a good thing."

Tala swallowed hard and nodded.

Her palm pad started buzzing on the tile floor beside her just as a banging came at her door, and her body tensed. Mila was on her feet quickly, sprinting to the door as Tala crawled across the floor, craning to see who it was. She watched as it opened, Maverick standing on the other side, his eyes big and wild.

"Max found Kane."

NINETEEN

Tala had never moved faster in her life as she ran from her unit to the secured offices, Maverick on her heels. She was met at the door by Ash who led them to an office Tala had never seen before. Like in Addox's office, the room had a digital wall, and on it was an image of the school parking lot Kane had been taken from. It was large and empty, houses with giant icicles and large snowbanks lined the street beyond it, cars parked along the curbs.

Max looked up with a mixed expression of elation and fear, and Tala wasn't sure how to read that.

"Show me what you have," she said with urgency.

"As soon as the search mission was issued, everyone began looking for the van Kane had been taken in. But with shoddy surveillance, we were never able to locate it. And because there were dozens and dozens of vans that met its description," Max said. "At first, I tried to take this approach too. But it quickly proved to be futile. So I had to step back and re-evaluate, look at what was there that hadn't been considered. And then it occurred to me, the parked cars around the school where the rally was. The answer had been staring me in the face from the beginning."

Tala raised a brow in confusion as she glanced at Maverick. For the first time since coming into the room, she noticed Jasper and Addox.

"All autonomous cars are equipped with exterior surveillance," Max explained. "It's how they can detect other cars or people in their way. Likewise, they're activated by motion. So even when they're parked, they're still able to record video of what's happening in close proximity around them if they pick up the motion.

"Using this image," he said with an edge of confidence as he nodded at the large screen, "and through each of the license plates of the cars on the street, then the cars they passed on the road, I was able to identify them, then hacked their video memory. All video is automatically saved for thirty days."

"Every car that van passed?" Addox asked with skepticism. "Every one of those vehicles has its own individual security measures. That sounds complicated."

"It is," Max said flatly as he nudged his glasses, then turned away.

Tala felt her excitement building, and for the first time in days, she didn't feel the unease in her stomach.

"Using the timeline from Griffin and Ash when the van drove off with Kane, I found this," he said, tapping at the keyboard on the desk. A new image appeared on the wall, the backside of a white, unassuming van. "If I zoom in," he said, the image expanding, "you can make out these small dents along the back fender. They're bullet marks."

Tala's heart was racing so fast that she feared it would burst from her chest.

"They left behind a digital breadcrumb with every autonomous car they passed," Max continued. "Hacking every one of those vehicles, I was able to map their route. And this is where they ended up. It's about an hour north of Michigan City. In an industrial park."

A new image of a warehouse appeared on the screen.

"This is the last image I have," Max said, the edge in his voice giving way to something sober.

The elusive van was parked near the warehouse's adjacent office building with three men outside the van carrying a fourth, limp body in their arms.

Kane.

Tala's stomach lurched, and for a moment, she thought she was going to vomit again. She braced herself with the desk, taking slow breaths. After a few seconds, the nausea subsided, and she righted herself.

"Tala and I are taking this mission," Maverick said.

"I don't think so," Addox said. "We have people who are qualified for this kind of thing."

"She and I are qualified. I'm a soldier, Tala is a trained MF agent. This mission is going to no one but us," he said forcefully, folding his arms across his chest and straightening his back. He stood taller than Addox and made sure he knew it. He wasn't going to back down.

"I think it should be their mission too," Jasper said.

"I agree," Ash said with a nod.

Addox looked around the room in obvious defeat, then sighed. "Then you go at your own risk."

"Fine, if that's how you want to do this," Maverick said with the tip of his head, his eyes narrowing.

Tala wasn't sure if she wanted to jump, scream, or throw up.

"We're not sure how much time we have, we've no clue what they're doing to him. We can't waste another second. We need a plan," Jasper said, his eyes catching Tala's, and she saw the determination in them.

Their mission was to be executed after dark for both the cover of night and because a presence around the industrial park would be limited. First was a plane ride to Elliott, a small town that bordered the Republic. From there, they would take a specialized military chopper to a wooded park along the shore of Lake Michigan, approximately a mile from the warehouse they believed Kane was being held in.

The day progressed slowly, painfully, but Tala was able to keep her focus on the mission as they tried to account for every detail. Records showed it was a food distribution center. They could only assume that a part of it doubled as a government black site. Max's hacking abilities were unparalleled, even the computer techs in The Village couldn't deny his skills. With little complication, he found the builder of the warehouse, then obtained the floorplan of the building for Tala and Maverick to memorize. With the help of a small team, he recreated a bug like the one she'd used on Thias's security system for the system in the warehouse. They simply had to plant it, and he'd be able to access the system, guiding them through the building by using their internal security surveillance. Tala and Maverick also studied the layout of the industrial park, memorizing their routes in and out of the complex.

Tala made a point of eating, even if her stomach didn't want to cooperate. She drank the ginger ale Mila bought, nibbled on soda crackers, and ate some buttered toast and a bowl of fruit. Then before it was time to leave, she ate a sandwich and drank a protein shake. To her surprise, she found that despite the lingering unsettlement in her stomach, she did feel better.

When it was finally time to leave, Tala waited beside Maverick and an escort guard at the secure elevators, a concerned Mila standing nearby. They were armed and dressed in military fatigues, and to Tala, it felt like the old days. There was something about finally having something to do that excited her, that empowered her. She hadn't realized how bored she'd been since arriving at The Village. As she wasn't Revo security or a soldier, she'd technically been retired from the field. But this is what she'd been trained to do. She had purpose again, and she knew that in all the years she had been an agent, it all boiled down to this. This would be the most important mission she'd ever carried out.

And then she'd be done. She was going to walk away, let someone else fight the fight. She'd given up too much, sacrificed too much. Kane and their baby were all that mattered now. And she wouldn't lose sight of that.

"Do you really think you should be doing this?" Mila asked quietly. Though she knew no details, she could assume enough, and her worry was written plainly across her face.

"I'm going to be just fine. We both are. I've got to do this," Tala said. Even if Mila didn't understand, Tala was sure of herself. "Remember—"

"Not a word," Mila said. "I got it." There was sadness in her eyes.

The elevator door chimed, and Tala gave Mila a quick hug. "I promise. We'll be safe." Though deep down, she knew that was a promise she couldn't make. But it was all she could give, and it was better than nothing.

Another thirty minutes and she and Maverick were flying high above the clouds in a small prop plane that was so loud they had to wear ear protection. Her stomach was jumbled and unsettled, but not with nausea. This was her nerves. She'd been on more missions than she could begin to count throughout her five years with MF, but the stakes had never been higher than they were in that moment. This was the culmination of all her training. She wasn't about to fail Kane now.

Maverick reached out and took her hand. She glanced up at him, and he smiled. The conviction in his eyes grounded her, it fortified her. There was no one else she would've chosen for this mission. He was capable, and she trusted him.

They rode their hour and a half flight in silence, Tala using the quiet before the storm to get her mind right. Yes, she was emotionally connected, but she couldn't let that interfere with what she knew she had to do. And first things first, she had to be focused. Her physical execution of the plan depended on her mental preparedness. Everything happens at a mental level before a physical level.

After landing in Elliott, they exited the plane quickly, stepping into the dark of night, the wind harsh and biting, the air so cold in her lungs it made it difficult to breathe. Her breath plumed in front of her face with every step. They trekked across the packed snow on the small apron of the tiny airport toward a black helicopter near the hangar. Had it not been lit from behind by the airport lights, she was sure she wouldn't have noticed it at all. Which, she knew, was the point.

The state-of-the-art chopper was designed with stealth capabilities. Though it wasn't silent, its custom-engineered blades managed its blade-vortex interaction, allowing it to fly through the sky at a three-decibel whisper. Even quieter than the sound of rustling leaves. It was also designed with countermeasures for radar, infrared, and sonar through shape, radiation absorbent materials, and specialized chemical treatments.

The flight through the Republic, though just over half an hour long, passed quickly. Tala was energized, adrenaline coursing through her. She was ready. She wanted more than anything to tell Kane she was coming, to hold on. She wouldn't let her mind consider any alternatives.

Though she was eager, she was equally terrified. But her fear had no place in her mission, and she tucked it away. She was only going to be as good as her mindset. She would not waver with Kane's life hanging in the balance.

With the city in view in the distance, its bright lights shining in the darkness, Tala and Maverick put their comms in their ears, a small bead with a thin wire tucked just inside the ear canal. They were patched in with both their driver on the ground and Max back in The Village who was standing by once they bugged the security system.

Their chopper landed easily in a vacancy surrounded by trees in the park near the lake, a black van waiting nearby for them. One brief flicker of its headlights signaled them. She and Maverick swiftly crossed the dark park, their boots sinking into the snow that glittered under the light of the moon as they approached the vehicle, their guns drawn.

"Bluebird. Lancer," the woman in the driver's seat said through the open passenger window. "Raptor," she said, identifying herself, her face heavily shadowed in the darkness. "Operation Phoenix…"

"Rebirth," Tala finished as part of their coded message to each other.

Maverick pulled the side door open, and they jumped inside, the van taking off even before they slid the door closed.

"I'll be two blocks away," Raptor called over her shoulder. "Waiting on your mark."

"Got it," Maverick said.

As they came to a stop at their drop-zone, Maverick and Tala exited the van, then took cover in the shadow of a nearby warehouse, snow and ice in frozen chunks on the ground. Their guns out, they jogged lightly along the perimeter of the building, carefully sidestepping icy patches. They approached the edge of it cautiously, and Tala used a small mirror on a telescoping handle to peer around the corner. Tala's senses were in overdrive, her mind sharp, and she no longer felt the cold. When they were sure it was clear, they continued around the building toward the next. Following the same protocol, staying in the shadows, they made their way from building to building until finally, the warehouse office of their target location came into view.

Tala brought her arm up, her hand in a fist, to halt Maverick, then used the small mirror to look around the corner of the building, the entrance to the office less than thirty yards away. Confident they were alone, she silently signaled to Maverick, and while he took off toward the building, she remained back in the shadows with her gun ready to cover him if he encountered anyone.

Maverick cautiously approached the office door, and Tala watched from the glow of the nearby lamppost as he placed Max's bug onto the digital security panel, then quickly stepped aside, clear of the door. "Merlin," he said, his voice in her ear along with Max's, "bug is in place."

"Got it," Max said on a long breath. "Accessing the system now."

There was a moment of silence, then Max spoke again, "Lancer, you're good. New password is 5263."

A moment later, his gun still drawn, he signaled to Tala to come. She stepped out of the shadow of the building, light on her feet as she swiftly crossed the distance to the building. As Tala made it to the door, she took a breath, then entered the new password. The door unlocked, and grabbing the handle, she opened it to an empty hallway. They both slipped inside, careful not to let the door slam behind them, then they stepped into a recessed doorway to hide themselves from view.

"I'm still sweeping the building, looking for him," Max said into their comms. Tala's heart was racing in her chest, a thrill of energy pumping through her, making her fingers tingle. This was the high she always felt in the field.

"I think I got him. Bluebird, Lancer," Max said, "proceed down the hallway. Once you round the corner, go three doors down to the south corridor, then first door on the right. He's alone in the room."

"Can you tell his condition?" Tala asked as Maverick peered around the corner.

"Surveillance quality is terrible. Looks like he's on a table. I can't tell if he's restrained."

Tala took a deep breath as Maverick waved a flat hand in the air, signaling to proceed behind him. She was tight on his heels as they eased down the hall as directed, then rounded the corner.

"You've got company coming your way," Max said loudly in their ears.

Maverick brought a fist in the air to halt them. With a glance over his shoulder, he nodded toward another recessed doorway, both stepping into it as voices echoed down the corridor. They exchanged a glance as Tala clutched her gun firmly, but a moment later, they heard a door open then close, the voices quickly dissipating.

Tala peered around the corner, down the vacant hall. With a wave of her hand, she and Maverick continued at a brisk pace until reaching the third door. Maverick reached for the handle, his eyes catching hers. She nodded, and he pulled the door open, another empty hallway.

Stepping into the hall, the first door on the right staring at her, Tala felt a lump in her chest. She was so close now.

"Merlin," she said, "we've got a security panel on this door."

"Okay. Give me a second," Max said in her ear.

The sound of distant conversation carried down the hallway, and Tala felt the muscles in her shoulders tense.

"Security is overridden," Max said a few seconds later. "Same code. 5263."

Tala entered it quickly, her hand steady. With a nod at Maverick, she swiftly pulled the door open.

And then she saw him.

Kane lay on a metal table in a windowless room, his body limp, his eyes closed.

"Kane," she gasped. The room clear, she ran to his side. Setting her gun on the table, she went to him, shaking him, but he was unresponsive.

Tala pressed two fingers to his neck. "He has a pulse," she said with a breath. This was a Kane she hardly recognized. His face had deep, purple bruises around his eyes, and his bottom lip was swollen and cracked open in the corner. He was bare-chested, with red welts and lacerations cut along the width of his chest and abdomen, dried blood crusted on his skin.

On his head and temples were small nodes with wires that fed into a digital control panel beside the table. Three IVs, one in the inside of his elbow, one in his wrist, and one in the top of his hand, led to the same control panel.

The same nodes were on his chest and the sides of his abdomen. Wires came out from beneath the cuffs of his pants, all leading into the panel as well. His feet were bare, his toes tinted blue.

"What is this?" Maverick asked as he approached, looking at the control panel that seemed to be monitoring his vitals.

Tala watched the up and down zig-zag line on the panel that she assumed was his heart rate.

She caught Maverick's gaze, her eyes wide. She turned back to Kane, tapping firmly on his cheek, cold and clammy to the touch. "Kane," she said. She leaned over him, feeling his breath on her cheek, his breathing slow and shallow.

"Kane," she repeated louder as she shook his shoulders. She reached for his head, turning it toward her. "You need to wake up!" Her emotion was suddenly rising.

"We need to unhook him," Maverick said, his voice steady as he went to the control panel.

"Guys!" Max yelled in their ears. "I think you've been made. I was just kicked out of the system."

Tala turned quickly to Maverick, then back to Kane. She didn't know what to begin removing from him.

"Don't. Touch. Him," a cold voice said from behind as a door slammed.

Tala grabbed her gun and turned on her heel. Her breath caught as her eyes found Vaughn. Having entered from a second door, he stood across the room from her, a plasma gun in his left hand and something small and black in his right.

"Vaughn," she gasped, both hers and Maverick's guns aimed at him.

"I thought I might see you. Eventually," he said coolly with a tip of his head. "I don't know who this guy is though," he said as his gaze moved to Maverick. "Don't really care either."

"Tala," Maverick said, his voice calm and steady. "Unhook Kane."

Tala took a small step backward, closer to the table Kane's flaccid body was sprawled across.

"You don't want to do that," Vaughn snapped sternly, his left hand shaking, the plasma gun moving unsteadily up and down. "You see this?" he asked, holding up the black device in his right hand.

Tala could now see that it was a remote.

"This handy little thing," Vaughn said, waving it in the air, "allows me to control everything on that control panel. So if I decided to electroshock him, I just press this button on the right. If I want to send a surge of lithium through him, which for the record, would kill him, I just press this button on the left."

"Lithium?" Tala asked. Her body felt heavy. She wanted to look at Kane but knew she couldn't look away from Vaughn.

"At first, I didn't have a clue how your boyfriend could do what I saw him do," he said. His voice was calm to the point that it was eerie. "It was Thias who pointed me in the right direction. And then I found it, Project Magnar. I never did find a record connecting him to it, revealing his identity, but I suddenly understood what he could do and why. Well, enough of it anyway."

"What did you do to him?" she asked sharply.

"I couldn't put a hit out on him until I knew how to control him," Vaughn continued casually. "Lithium was my answer. Enough of it suppresses brain function which limited his physicality. Meaning he was suddenly on my level." A diabolical smile curled at the corner of his mouth.

She already knew there was nothing good about Vaughn, aside from a pretty face, but she'd never expected him to be so depraved.

"Put your guns down, both of you, or I press this button and a surge of lithium will go through him faster than you can shoot."

Tala swallowed as she caught Maverick's eyes. Both hesitated for a moment, Tala's mind racing as she searched for an out. The last time she'd been in this position, Ronin died in her arms and Thias had escaped her.

"Now!" Vaughn yelled with angry impatience.

"All right," Maverick said, the first to withdraw his gun, though his eyes were fixed on Tala. Slowly, he bent down, setting it on the floor.

"Now, Tala!" Vaughn yelled. "Or your boyfriend gets it."

"Okay," she said, turning back to Vaughn. She set the gun on the floor near her feet.

"Kick them to the side," Vaughn said, waving the plasma gun at them.

They both kicked their guns out of reach, then Tala took a slow step closer to Vaughn. "Why're you doing this?" she asked, keeping her voice even, holding his attention.

"Why? *Why?*" he asked, his eyes wild. "Because you chose him over me!" His voice boomed through the room. "Him… a monster. No one should be able to do what he can do. He's an abomination. He should've been terminated with the others."

Tala swallowed hard as she took another small step forward. "Your issue is with me. Let him go and you can have me," she said.

"No, Tala," Maverick said. He was no longer in her peripheral.

Vaughn shook his head. "I would've given you everything. But you chose a nobody," he sneered. "I loved you, you know." The barrel of the plasma gun shook unsteadily.

"You loved your ego," she said, taking another step forward. "Not me. And having me on your arm only fed that ego."

"There might be some truth to that," he conceded with a smirk.

"This is between us," she said calmly, holding his eyes as she continued to inch forward. With every step she took, her heart raced faster.

"I hate him! And he's going to die." Anger flashed in his eyes, and he let out a hysterical laugh that made the hair on the back of her neck stand.

Tala eyed the plasma gun, not seeming to be aimed at either her or Maverick.

"The kicker is I didn't even get much out of him. Not even a name which evidently is Kane. Your brother got nothing out of him either," he spat.

"Even incapacitated, overloaded with drugs and tortured, he still didn't give me what I wanted."

Tala felt a tug in her chest at the word torture. What had they done to him?

"Just tell me, Tala, tell me… why? Why him and not me?"

Tala pursed her lips together, still sliding her feet closer and closer to him. Her eyes flitted between the remote and the gun, then back to him. She swallowed hard. With another step forward, time seemed to suddenly stand still, everything happening around her at half-time.

"He's a freak!" Vaughn yelled, but she barely heard him.

Tala sucked in a sharp breath and swung her leg through the air, kicking Vaughn's right hand, the remote sailing through the air behind him. He yelled as the plasma gun fired, the blast pulsing just past her as Maverick yelled out her name.

As Vaughn struggled to grip the plasma gun in both hands, Tala lunged at him, knocking him backward, the gun falling from his grasp. She quickly kicked it away as he punched her in the jaw, sending her spinning.

She stumbled backward. "Unhook him!" she yelled to Maverick as she oriented herself. Vaughn turned for the remote lying on the floor near the door, and in a rush, she launched herself at him, knocking them both to the floor. With his body beneath hers, she punched him, her fist crashing into his nose, instant blood running down his face.

He struck his elbow into the side of her head, knocking her onto her back on the floor. Dizziness came over her, and she took a breath to steady herself.

Vaughn crawled over her, his hands clasping around her neck. She struggled to take a breath as he squeezed her windpipe closed. She clawed at him, scratching the skin on his forearms and hands raw. His cheeks were bright red, his teeth gnashed as he stared down into her eyes.

She thrust her knee into his groin, and instantly his grip slackened. She coughed, the air burning in her lungs as she scrambled to her feet while he struggled onto his knees, his shoulders slouched as he groaned. She screamed out as she kicked him hard in the side of the ribcage, his body lurching, but not falling.

"Bitch!" he spat breathlessly.

As she turned for the gun, his body crashed into hers, both of them careening across the room, colliding into the wall, then falling to the floor, and she cried out in pain. The room was spinning as she tried to separate her body from his.

"I'm going to kill him!" he yelled in a fury as he stood.

Tala felt the trickle of blood run down the side of her face, and her body floundered as she rose to her feet. Vaughn charged at her again, his fist swinging. She jerked her head to the side, his knuckles only grazing her eyebrow, and she jabbed him in the throat. He staggered backward, gasping and making a gurgling sound.

She looked up to see Maverick pulling out the last IV from Kane's arm just as Vaughn kicked her in the legs. Her knees buckling, she fell to the floor, her head slamming against the tile. Black spots formed in her periphery, and she blinked hard, pushing them away. She rolled onto her back, bringing her hand to the side of her head. As her fingers grazed her contusion, she winced, and there was an instant pounding in her skull.

Grunting, she pushed her body up, putting her knees beneath her just as he bare-knuckled her in the fleshy part of her side. She screamed out, her body falling back to the floor. From the corner of her eye, she saw him stagger away, his body unsteady as he struggled to keep on his feet. Then she saw the small remote. While she was at least fifteen feet from it, he was only a few.

She took a breath and fumbled at her pants, then pushed her body up.

"Hey, Vaughn," she called out, her voice rough but firm.

As he reached for the remote, he turned toward her, and she fired. Once. Twice. Three times. His body stiffened, the remote falling from his grasp as he dropped to the floor with a thud, his blood soaking through the front of his shirt in three places.

She shook from pain, from adrenaline, from relief. Quickly, Tala holstered the small gun at her ankle, then pushed herself to her feet. Her body reeling, she struggled to keep her balance for a moment. The pain in her head was excruciating, and she recoiled when she brought her fingers to it.

Breathlessly, she went to Vaughn, kicking the remote away from his hand as he faded away. She hurried across the room as Maverick removed the last of the nodes on Kane's head.

"Kane," she gasped, instant tears mixing with the blood running down the side of her face.

"Tala, it's bad," Maverick said gravely as he placed his fingers on the inside of Kane's wrist.

She reached for him, slapping at his cheeks. "Wake up. Open your eyes!"

His breathing was weak, and a groan escaped his mouth as his head fell to the side.

"Kane, stay with me," she said, her tears running down her face. She held his head in her hands as she leaned over him. "You have to stay with me," she cried.

His eyes fluttered, and he opened his mouth, as if to speak, another groan, low and frail escaping his lips.

"It's me, you've got to stay with me," she called loudly, choking on her tears as she held his head.

His eyes continued to flutter, open and closed.

"You can't leave me. You can't leave us!" She took a breath, her body shuddering with emotion and pain. "You hear that? You can't leave us. That's right, *us*. You're going to be a father," she sobbed. She felt Maverick still beside her for a moment.

"Stay with me," she said, her tears running over her lips.

"We've got to get him out of here before anyone else shows up," Maverick said, his voice stern and steady. "Help me get him on my back."

They pulled Kane upright, and while Tala supported his weight against her body, Maverick turned his back to him, then reached for his arms as Tala put one over each of Maverick's shoulders. She noticed the bruised bands around his wrists.

Maverick crossed Kane's arms over his own chest, gripping him at the wrists with both hands while he hoisted him onto his back, supporting his weight under his own hips.

Once he was secured, Tala grabbed Maverick's gun, holstering it at his waist, then did the same with hers. Quickly, she grabbed Vaughn's plasma gun from off the floor.

"Raptor," Tala said through her comm, calling out to their driver. "We're on our way out."

She ran to the door, easing it open slowly, peering down the empty corridor. She silently waved Maverick past her while she propped the door open.

They shuffled down the hallway and through the door to the second corridor. When Tala was sure the coast was clear, she waved him on again.

Tala followed behind with the familiar plasma gun in her hands as Maverick hurried down the long hallway. It was then that she saw the burns on Kane's back and her breath hitched.

Finally rounding the corner, the exit came into sight, and Maverick grunted as he picked up speed. Tala heard the low echo of voices coming toward them, and she peered briefly over her shoulder, relieved to see no one.

Reaching the door, she pushed it open, an alarm instantly blaring in their ears.

"Go," she urged Maverick, pushing the door open wide enough for him and Kane to slip through.

She followed after them into the cold night, her head on a swivel, Maverick breathing heavily as he hurried across the parking lot to the shadows of the nearby building.

Once the warehouse was out of sight, Tala called out through her comm. "Raptor, we need extraction. I don't think we'll make our pickup."

Her heart hammered in her chest as they eased along the side of one warehouse and then the next, once again sticking to the shadows.

"Bluebird, what's your location?" Raptor asked.

"Building thirteen," she said, her breath visible in the cold. "West side."

"On my way. Two minutes out," she said.

"Help me set him down," Maverick said breathlessly.

Tala helped slide Kane off Maverick's back and supported him, nearly buckling under his weight, until Maverick was able to grab him. Together, they lowered him onto the icy ground. He was in only a pair of jeans in the frigid cold, his feet bare. Tala shifted and winced from the pain in her side, her head pounding. She smoothed her hand over Kane's cold cheek, his head lolled to one side.

"Kane," she whispered as she leaned over him, pressing her forehead to his.

His breathing was steadier, stronger.

"I'm here," she said, tears stinging in her eyes.

His eyes fluttered in the darkness. "Ta…" he mumbled weakly. "Ta…"

"Yeah, I'm here," she said, a small smile pulled at her mouth, a mixture of happy and sad, of relief and fear.

A moment later, their van appeared in the darkness, giving one quick flash of its headlights.

"That's Raptor," Maverick said, slipping his shoulder under Kane's arm and around his back. Tala, though much smaller, did the same from the other side, sucking in a breath as she supported his weight with hers.

She and Maverick walked, struggling, Kane's limp feet dragging on the asphalt as they carried him along. Once at the van, Tala crawled inside, then took Kane under the arms and pulled him in, Maverick quickly jumping in after her.

With their headlights off, Raptor wound the van through the industrial complex and out onto the road. In only minutes, they were back at their landing zone at the park, their helicopter coming into view. Its blades began to rotate as their pilot located them, slowly at first, then quickly picking up speed.

"Guys," Max said, breaking his silence in Tala's ear. "I've spotted MF on a surveillance camera, about five minutes out."

"Well, in five minutes we'll be flying above ground, so good luck to them," Maverick said as their van came to a halt. He jumped out, then reached for Kane, pulling him hard out of the van. Tala jumped out after, the wind from the chopper blade whipping her hair as Maverick dragged Kane through the snow from under his arms.

Reaching the chopper, Tala climbed quickly inside, and Maverick hoisted Kane up. She pulled him inside the small cabin, his body heavy on hers as she fell backward. Maverick jumped in, pulling the door closed behind him in a swift movement.

Seconds later, the helicopter left the ground. Quickly climbing higher with every passing second, Tala felt herself relax. She readjusted her body, cradling Kane's head in her lap.

"Merlin," Maverick said into his comm, "we're going to need immediate medical attention when we get to Elliott."

TWENTY

It took just over half an hour to get from Michigan City, across the border, and into Elliott in Ozark Colony. Once there, they were met by a medic crew that took Kane, then boarded him onto a private jet. Tala and Maverick, having hardly spoken a word, climbed on board, along with the medical team, and they were back in the air in less than fifteen minutes.

She had been instructed to sit across the plane while one of the medics put in a central line in Kane's subclavian vein and began pumping a clear solution into him. A second medic put him on oxygen, checked his heart rate, blood pressure, temperature, and pupil dilation, and the third took note of his injuries, reporting them to someone over a palm pad, presumably to the hospital they were bound for.

"Bruising of the face, along with a mouth laceration suggesting blunt-force trauma," he said matter-of-factly. "Four incised wounds across the abdomen and chest. All are approximately five inches long and seem to be shallow. No current hemorrhaging. Burn lesions present on the scalp, temples, the chest, near the kidneys, and on the shins, consistent with electroshock. Bottoms of both feet are severely burned, presence of blistering."

Tala felt like she was going to vomit as she listened to the medic report Kane's condition. She pulled her knees to her chest as tears pooled in her eyes. She was too late. She had been too late.

It took all three medics to roll Kane to the side, his body limp.

"Patient has abrasions and lacerations on his back, as well as several large welts consistent with blunt-force trauma."

Kane was gently rolled onto his back once again as the medic picked up his hands. "Ligature marks present around both wrists."

The room began to spin for Tala as she sat helplessly in her seat. Then she jumped to her feet, rushing to the bathroom and making it just as she began to vomit.

A few minutes later, Maverick appeared in the doorway. "Going to be okay?" he asked patiently.

Taking slow, deep breaths, she nodded.

"We've been cleared for landing," he said. "Let me help you back to your seat." He reached for her as she stood, unsteady and weak in the knees, then made her way back to her seat.

The only movement that came from Kane was the rising and falling of his chest with every breath. Once again, Tala felt tears stinging in her eyes.

"He's going to pull through," Maverick said, leaning in. "I know it, Tals."

When they landed in Des Plain, they were met by a caravan. Kane was rushed by ambulance while Tala and Maverick followed in another vehicle to the hospital where they were met by three nurses and a doctor. Kane was immediately whisked into the emergency room, Tala running after him.

"Where're you taking him?" she called out, her voice thick.

No one responded to her as they hurried him down a long hallway, past a nurse's station and around a corner.

"Where're you taking him?" she repeated, nearly choking on her emotion.

"Miss," a woman said loudly. "Miss," she said as she jogged after Tala. She reached for her, grabbing Tala by the arm and pulling her back. "You can't go back there."

"But…" she said as her eyes welled with tears. "I can't leave him."

"Let them do their job. I promise he's in good hands," she said, her voice steady, reassuring.

Tala felt Maverick's hand settle on her shoulder as she gave one last fleeting glance at Kane before he disappeared behind two secure doors.

"You need medical attention," the woman said to Tala.

"No, I'm fine," she protested, still watching the double doors as if he would suddenly reappear, though she knew he wouldn't.

"You need medical attention," the woman repeated. "He's in good hands. I promise," she said gently as she tugged at Tala's arm. "Come with me."

"I'll stay with you, Tala," Maverick said.

She looked up at him as a tear rolled down her cheek. She turned toward the woman, a nurse who still had a hold on her arm. She was blond, her hair pulled into a short ponytail, and was dressed in navy pants and a bright top that looked like sunshine.

"Come with me," she said with a tug.

Defeated, Tala nodded.

The nurse let go of her arm, then turned, leading the way down the hall in a direction opposite of Kane, and Tala felt an ache in her chest. She was brought into a small exam room with a narrow, reclined bed, and a small desktop.

"Take a seat." The nurse gestured, then she pulled a large curtain around them for privacy.

Tala eased onto the bed, another tear falling down her face, and she quickly wiped it away.

"I'm Georgia," the nurse said as she approached Tala with purple gloves over her hands. She prodded at the side of Tala's head where Vaughn had hit her, then parted her hair where the blood congealed along her scalp from the contusion after smashing her head on the floor.

Tala winced at her touch, her body recoiling.

Delicately, Georgia pressed her fingers along the bruises on her neck, and Tala sucked in a sharp breath.

"Some swelling and bruising. I'll let the doctor evaluate that. You'll need a couple of stitches in that head wound. But I think we can do it without cutting away the hair," Georgia said. "And just suture strips on the side of your face. I'll grab the doctor." She turned toward Maverick. "Make sure she stays put," she said firmly.

He nodded solemnly.

"How're you doing?" he asked quietly when Georgia left the small room.

"Think I'm about to fall apart," she said, her voice cracking.

"Not yet. Keep it together for a little while longer. He still needs you," he said.

"You saw him, Mav! What if he's past help?" she gasped, her voice loud.

He shook his head fervently. "You can't think that way. He's in good hands. And they'll do everything they can."

"Knock, knock," a voice called out as another woman appeared beside Georgia. "I'm Dr. Woods. I hear we need some stitches," she said with a kind smile.

Georgia pushed a small cart with her into the room as Dr. Woods approached Tala, carefully pulling her hair apart.

"Looks like you've been through a lot tonight," she said in a voice that wasn't patronizing. "Doesn't look serious. But stitches would be best. Just a few."

Tala nodded.

"Can you tell me your name?" Dr. Woods asked.

She took a slow breath. "Tala Alexander."

"Well, hello, Tala. We're going to get you cleaned up, and then we'll see what information we can get on the man you came in with," she said.

Tala felt a small leap in her chest. "Kane Ryan," she said. "His name is Kane Ryan."

Dr. Woods nodded. "We had a heads up that you were all coming in. His doctor is very good," she said confidently.

Georgia pinned Tala's hair to the side while Dr. Woods reached for a small syringe from the cart. "A little numbing agent," she said.

Tala flinched as she felt the sharp prick of the needle go into the tender flesh of her wound. The sting making her eyes water.

"Give this just a few minutes to set in," Dr. Woods said, then she gently pressed the tips of her fingers to Tala's neck. She stiffened at her touch. "Looks like you were in quite the scuffle," she said.

"It looks worse than it is," Tala insisted. The numbing agent in her head wound was already taking the edge off.

"Zone two neck trauma," Dr. Woods said as she looked at Georgia who typed on a tablet. Using her stethoscope, she listened to Tala's breathing from her chest and back, instructing deep breaths. "Some swelling and definite bruising in that neck. Is your throat sore?" she asked Tala.

"Just a little."

"Does your tongue hurt when you move it? Any difficulty breathing?"

"No," Tala said as she shook her head.

"Your voice seems to sound fine when you talk," Dr. Woods continued. "But I'm not the best judge of this. Do you hear any changes in her voice?" she asked, now looking at Maverick.

"A little scratchy, but seems mostly normal to me," he said.

The doctor nodded. "Any stiffness or pain when you move your head?"

"No, nothing," Tala said, which wasn't entirely true, but she had been through worse.

She turned back to Georgia. "Minor laryngeal trauma present. Nothing to indicate tracheal damage." She turned back to Tala. "Okay. I want you to keep an eye on it. If you do start to have pain when you move your neck or a persistent headache, you need to be re-evaluated," she said.

"Got it," Tala said.

"Now, back to this laceration." Dr. Woods clamped the needle driver over the threaded needle, then reached for the small forceps. "The numbing agent will take the edge off, but you'll still feel some pain," she cautioned.

Tala sucked in a breath as Dr. Woods, one by one, threaded each suture, then tied them off. Just as she said, Tala felt the bite with every tug, and she clutched the edge of the bed she sat on, keeping her eyes averted.

"All done," she finally said after a few minutes. "Eight stitches. Should heal up well. Now," she said, placing the needle driver back on the cart beside the forceps. "I see there's some bruising on your chin. Looks minimal. Anywhere else need to be looked at?"

Tala thought of the injury on her side but decided against mentioning it. Even if, worst-case scenario, she broke a rib, there was nothing that could be done about it. She wasn't knowledgeable of all the things to avoid during pregnancy, but x-ray machines, she knew, were on that list.

"I'm good," she said.

Maverick eyed her carefully from across the room.

"Anything for the pain?" Dr. Woods asked.

A pain reliever sounded too good to be true, but again she shook her head. Most pain meds were also on that list. "I'll be fine."

"You're one tough cookie," Dr. Woods said with a smile. "Let me go see what I can find out about Mr. Ryan. Georgia will finish cleaning you up and bandaging the side of your face."

Tala gave the doctor a half-smile of gratitude, and then she was gone.

"This might sting a bit while I clean up this wound and your hair," Georgia said. But unlike the stitches, this burn was nothing. Her mind was only on Kane.

"Okay," Georgia said when she was finished. "You're all patched up."

"Miss Alexander," Dr. Woods said, reappearing in the opening in the curtain. "Mr. Ryan's in a private room on the other side of the emergency room. If you follow me, I can take you to him. His doctor is expecting you."

Tala hopped quickly off the bed.

"I'll be in the waiting room," Maverick said, and Tala nodded, then quickly followed after the doctor, winding through the labyrinth of hallways. They came to a stop at a closed door, a large window beside it that had blinds drawn shut.

"Here you are," Dr. Woods said with the same kind smile she met Tala with. "Good luck." She nodded, then turned on her heel and walked back in the direction they had come.

Tala gave a small knock on the door, then opened it slowly. Her eyes went immediately to Kane as he lay on a hospital bed similar to the one she'd just been on. He was covered in a blanket, his eyes closed and an oxygen mask over his mouth and nose. Her heart fell at the sight of him.

"Come in, come in," a voice said.

It was then that Tala realized there were other people in the room. A tall man in black scrubs and a lab coat that hung open in front approached her. He had a full head of thick, silver hair, cut short, receding just slightly in the front. Then Tala spotted Addox standing inconspicuously in the corner of the room, his arms folded across his chest.

"What're you doing here?" she asked sharply.

"He's my brother," he said sternly.

Tala wanted to lurch across the room and strangle him. When had he ever really cared about Kane as a brother?

"I'm Dr. Smithing," the doctor said as he closed the door behind Tala. "I'm going to be overseeing Kane's treatment and recovery."

Tala turned toward him, her back to Addox. She was at a loss of words, not knowing what to say. She knew Kane needed medical attention, badly. But how could she ever explain what he was capable of? They would find out. And then what?

"I understand that you're concerned," Dr. Smithing said. "But I assure you that my team and I will take good care of him."

She nodded, meeting his eyes.

"You should also know that I am familiar with Kane's condition," he said. "His unique abilities. Which is why I was called in."

Tala's brows furrowed. "Wha… what do you mean?" she stammered, caught off guard.

"We know, Tala," Addox said, stepping out of the corner.

Her eyes darted between the doctor and Addox. Now she was really at a loss for words.

"You can drop the pretenses," Addox said.

Tala took a breath, turning away from him and back to the doctor.

"Over the years," Dr. Smithing said gently, "I have worked with three others who were also in the same study as Kane. I'm familiar with the experiments as well as what he's capable of."

"And you knew? All this time?" she snapped, her head jerking as she looked at Addox.

"I didn't know with any certainty. But I suspected it. I looked for him for a long time," he said, his eyes narrowed.

"Well then," she said, "if you know everything, tell me why his body isn't healing itself."

"Kane was administered incredibly high levels of lithium, his toxicity level is so high that it would be lethal for you or me," Dr. Smithing said.

"Vaughn said that was how he was able to subdue him," she said.

He nodded. "That's correct. Lithium acts on the central nervous system, the brain and spinal cord. He's suffering right now from neuronal atrophy that is resulting in a decrease in the functions of certain areas of his brain. And despite how it looks, his lack of cognizance at the moment, he is doing better as we speak than he was when he arrived. His body is burning off the lithium, just at a much slower rate because of the suppressed functionality.

"This," he continued, "is why we have a central line in him. He is currently going through rigorous intravenous detoxification. Meaning we are helping flush his body and supplementing with amino acids, vitamins, minerals, and such to help facilitate the process."

Tala's anxiety was ebbing as she listened to Dr. Smithing. She couldn't deny that he did seem well versed on Kane's situation and needs.

"We've also given him an anticonvulsant to reduce the risk of seizure, and we'll monitor his kidney function while he goes through this. But I have no reason to think he won't pull through and return to his former self without any long-term effects."

She nodded, wrapping her arms around her body, then winced from the pain and let them fall loosely to her sides. "What can I do in the meantime?"

"I'll give you a few minutes with him, and then I suggest you rest. It looks like you've been through a lot yourself. All he needs now is time. I'm estimating he won't regain normal consciousness for another twenty-four hours or so," Dr. Smithing said.

"I've booked rooms for both you and Maverick at the motel across the street," Addox said. "Both are under your callsigns."

Tala glanced at him, not understanding the two sides of him. One moment, he was detached and cold, then the next, he had hopped a plane to see his brother in the hospital. She struggled to reconcile the two versions of him.

"I've been given your contact information and will reach out to you as soon as he wakes up. In the meantime, use that motel room and sleep," Dr. Smithing said. "Do you have any questions?"

Tala looked at Kane across the room. He looked peaceful, yet his body was in complete turmoil.

"Actually, may I have a private word with you?" she asked, then glanced at Addox.

"Of course."

"That's clearly my cue," Addox said. "You know how to reach me." He gave a single nod of his head, then turned for the door. A moment later, he was gone.

"What can I do for you?" Dr. Smithing asked. There was something soothing about his voice, her worry lightening.

She took a deep breath and looked at him nervously. "I'm wondering how someone like Kane, with his condition," she said, using his word, "how it would impact a child."

"You mean, should he conceive?" he asked.

She nodded.

"Am I to take it this isn't a hypothetical situation?"

"No, it's not hypothetical," she said.

He gave her a smile that, although was small, still met his eyes. "Does Kane know?"

"I told him after we rescued him. But he was barely conscious," she said.

"Well, I think this is a conversation we can all have once Kane has regained his strength. But in the meantime, I can assure you that you have no reason to think you won't have a healthy baby where things are concerned with Kane's role in it."

"Okay," she said, and despite his vague response, she still couldn't help but feel comforted.

"Take a few minutes with him." He reached out, putting a comforting hand on Tala's arm for a moment, then he turned and left.

The room was quiet, like she was alone, though she wasn't. She turned toward Kane, approaching him on the bed. Her tears stung in her eyes as she looked down at him, his face partially obstructed by the oxygen mask, discolored and darkened bruises under his eyes. She ran her hand over his head, careful to avoid the lesions on his scalp, and felt the prickle of new hair coming in. Then she leaned over him, pressing her lips to his forehead. Unlike before, his skin was now warm and dry to the touch.

"Come back to me," she whispered. "We're going to have such a good life." A tear fell down her cheek, and she wiped at it. Reaching for his hand, she gave it a small squeeze, then kissed his forehead one more time. She wanted only to stay with him and had to peel herself from him, but somehow, she found that, one step after another, she was able to leave his room.

Seeing a sign in the hallway that pointed to the waiting room, she turned and walked away.

Stepping through the double doors and into the large and empty waiting room, Tala felt herself take a breath she hadn't realized she was holding. It was hard to see him like that, but it was heartening to feel confident that he was in good hands. That while it didn't immediately look like it, he was improving. She spotted Maverick across the room, standing at the sight of her.

"You look… rough," he said.

"Yeah, well, better than the other guy," she said with a sigh. Though it was meant as a joke, she couldn't bring herself to even smile.

She crossed the room toward him, and he reached out, pulling her into a hug.

"How is he?" he asked.

"Not great," she said as she pulled away and looked up at him. "But better." She took a seat in a nearby chair as he took the one beside her.

Silence settled between them, and Tala suddenly felt wracked with exhaustion. She glanced at the clock on the wall, seeing that it was well after three in the morning. Her mind was so full, her heart divided in so many directions. She knew she should message Mila or Vi, or both, since she wasn't going to be back anytime soon, but the thought of even reaching for her palm pad in the side cargo pocket of her pants seemed too large a feat.

She let her head fall against the wall and closed her eyes. Despite the motel room she could go rest in, she knew she wasn't going to leave the waiting room.

"Why didn't you tell me you're pregnant?" Maverick asked, his voice quiet but clipped.

She opened her eyes and straightened, looking at him. "Because I knew you wouldn't let me come. And I had to come," she said.

He took a breath, and she could tell by the look on his face that he was trying to choose his words carefully.

"What if something happened? You took a beating back there," he said.

She had nothing to say to that. How could she explain that she did what she did for herself, Kane, and their baby? She knew it would make no sense, though in her heart, it made perfect sense.

"I'm sorry for not telling you," she said. There wasn't anything else to say.

"Can I ask you about something else?" he said with hesitation.

She nodded, meeting his eyes. They were shadowed in the dimly lit waiting room.

"What was Vaughn talking about back there? Kane, an abomination, a freak, able to do things he shouldn't? He mentioned some project and how he should've been terminated, treating him with lithium. What's that all about?" he asked.

Tala was quiet for a moment, looking away.

"You don't have to tell me," he said softly. "But I can't help but feel there's so much more going on here than just a jealous ex-boyfriend. I risked my life tonight to save him."

"The thing is," she said, glad they were alone in the room, "it's not really my story to tell." She turned back to him and felt a tug in her chest. It was true, he risked his life and only had a fraction of the facts. "If I tell you… it's going to sound insane," she said. "And you could never tell a soul."

"Tals, after all this time, I hope you know you can trust me."

"With my life," she said with a half-smile. "People have died over this information. But you know enough now, so you may as well know the rest," she said, swallowing hard, hoping she wasn't making a mistake.

"Kane spent his teenage years in a medical facility run by the government," she said, keeping her voice low.

"In the Republic?" he asked.

She nodded. "His father sold him. Took his money and sent Kane away. He was there with twenty-three other kids, all around the same age, and they did experiments on them."

"Project Magnar?" he asked.

She vaguely recalled Vaughn calling it that. "I didn't realize it had a name," she said. "It was a super-soldier program. The Republic's effort to make an unstoppable army. It was the last experiment. He said it was the worst pain he'd ever experienced. Kane died during that procedure. And when he was resuscitated, he was what he is now."

"Which is what? What does a super-soldier mean?"

"His senses are heightened, drastically. He could hear a pin drop from across the room. His speed and agility are unparalleled. He can move so fast that he just blurs. He's strong. His body can heal itself. And he can heal others," she said.

"Heal others?" Maverick asked, disbelief in his voice.

"I've seen it. He did it to me," she said. "The first night we met. I had been in a fight, got my ass kicked. I was so beat up that I couldn't even stand. And somehow, he repaired all my injuries, my broken bones."

His jaw was slack as he looked at her, an incredulous look on his face.

"I told you it sounds insane. And if I hadn't experienced all this for myself, I wouldn't believe it either, but it's all true," she said.

"How does that even work?"

Tala shrugged. "Not even he knows the science behind any of it. It's not exactly public information. He's lived all these years in hiding."

"So, how'd he get out of this facility?" he asked, leaning forward, his elbows on his thighs.

"My mom," she said.

"What?" he gasped, his brows raising as he inclined his head.

"I had no idea either. I only learned the truth several months ago. She was a part of it all though. They decided to terminate the project. They weren't able to control any of the children. One night, she tried to help them escape. Some got away, some didn't. And then in response to her betrayal, the Republic drugged us and lit my house on fire."

Even in that moment, all these years later, she could bring herself back, feel herself moving through the house, carried by someone she didn't know, the flames licking the walls, smoke filling the house.

"Assassination?"

She nodded slowly. "And Thias was part of all of it." It was all she could bring herself to say.

"Kane's been living his life in the shadows, all these years," Maverick said.

"I'd do anything to keep him safe." She looked down at the floor, a strand of hair falling forward, and she grimaced as she tried to tuck it behind her ear, grazing the contusion on the side of her head.

"I'd say the Republic has cost us all a lot of things in our lives," he said sadly. He knew just as well as anyone. "But we need to wear our scars proudly. Not to show we've been broken, but to show we've survived. I agree with Kane that the Revos are using you just like Thias had. Even if they have better intentions, it doesn't make it right. You've got a real opportunity with your life here, you and Kane, and the family you're building. At the end of the day, nothing will matter more than any of that. You're going to have to live the rest of your life with the choices you've made, trust me, so make sure you make them for yourself. Don't let people like your brother or Vulcan steer you where they want you. Make your own way."

The ache in her chest returned as she looked up at him through blurry eyes. It was like he was giving her permission to walk away. Even more than that, he was encouraging it. One of the things she loved most about Kane was that he never tried to make her decisions for her. He'd let her change and grow and evolve all the while being there for her in every form. She wasn't going to let him be her sacrifice.

She knew she had a great capacity for love, it was what had always motivated her into action for her people. But there was something in the idea of choosing herself for once that made her feel like the shackles were finally cut free.

"I just think that it'll be difficult to step into this new phase in your life while still holding on to all this other stuff. It's only bringing you down," he said.

"People are going to hate me," she said with a smirk, though suddenly she was okay with that. Her choice to walk away wouldn't matter to those who truly mattered. And she found comfort in that.

"There's always going to be someone," he said, shaking his head. Sitting back in his chair he reached his arm around her. "Get some sleep, it's going to be a long night. We need you on your A-game when Kane wakes up."

"Oh, you have a motel room across the street," she said. "We both do. But I'm going to stay here."

"I figured. Who needs a motel room when you've got a cushy waiting room like this? I'm a trained soldier. I've slept in much worse places. Besides, who would look out for you?"

"I don't know," she said with a shrug, "I think I'm pretty scrappy."

"I watched you kick ass tonight. I'd say you're more than scrappy," he said with a deep laugh. "Though I am still technically your security detail. But maybe I also just want to keep you company."

She looked up at him and smiled. "Thanks. For all of it. Especially with Kane tonight. I never could've done it without you."

"Which reminds me," he said, sitting up straighter, pulling his arm back. "Did you really think kicking the remote out of Vaughn's hand was the better option than the gun? That blast sailed right by my head."

"Sorry about that," she said with a sheepish grin. "But yes, I did think it was the better option. See, he's right-handed. And not trained to use a gun. So his chances of shooting with his left hand and actually hitting a target were slim. I took a chance."

There was a gleam in his eyes as he looked down at her.

"What I can't figure out is why we were never pursued when that alarm went off," she said. "They knew we were there. Vaughn was clearly notified. So why no security? Why no MF? We just walked out of there with their prisoner."

"That's been on my mind too," he said. "And I don't have an answer."

"A problem for another day," she said with a sigh.

"Hey, Tals," he said.

She turned toward him. He looked as exhausted as she felt.

"Congratulations."

A smile curled at the corners of her mouth as her hands moved to her stomach. She tipped her head against the wall as she closed her eyes and felt a sense of peace come over her, settling into her chest. Kane, she knew, would be okay. She could feel it. And they had a whole new adventure in store. That thought was enough to help carry her mind away as she drifted off.

When Tala opened her eyes, it took her a moment to get her bearings as she glanced around the room. She looked up at the clock on the wall, it was half past ten. She couldn't believe she'd been able to sleep at all. Maverick wasn't beside her anymore, and she pulled out her palm pad to see if she had any messages with updates on Kane.

Her shoulders dropped when she saw she had none from the hospital, but she did have two others. One from Mila, another from Vi. She quickly sent them back a response, assuring them she was okay. Kane too, in time. Then left it at that.

She stood, her body sore and stiff. Her side was tender to the touch, as was the side of her face and her head, and the unsettled feeling in her stomach returned. Food, she decided. She needed food. It had been over twelve hours since she'd eaten. And though she had no appetite, quite the opposite, she couldn't deny she'd likely feel better once she ate. Maverick was right, she needed to be on her A-game for when Kane woke up.

Making her way through the hospital hallways, she followed the signs to the cafeteria, a large room filled with tables and a minimal crowd. She grabbed several packets of crackers, a fruit cup, a yogurt, and a ginger ale, then quickly paid. Balancing it all in her hands, she made her way back to the waiting room where she found Maverick in the same seat as before.

"Ah, I was wondering when you'd wake up," he said, picking up a disposable cup from the floor beside his feet. "I got you a coffee."

That, of all the things in her hands, sounded the most appealing.

Tala nibbled her way through her breakfast and sipped on the hot coffee that seemed to surge in her veins, waking her up. Afterward, she sat back and watched the show that played on the TV screen mounted on the wall. She had no idea what it was, but it was something to hold her attention while the time ticked by.

By mid-afternoon, with an anxious energy making her restless, Tala took a walk. The hospital was surprisingly small, and she'd found herself back in the waiting room far too soon.

When the time eventually ticked into the evening hours and there was still no word on Kane, Tala's stomach growled once again with hunger. With every passing hour throughout the day, she had grown more and more fidgety, and she was beginning to think she would burst from pent-up energy.

She stood, bouncing slightly on the balls of her feet and shaking her arms just for the sake of moving her body. "I think I'm going to wander down to the cafeteria," she said to Maverick.

"I'll join you. I'm not sure I can sit here any longer," he said, standing and stretching his body with a loud yawn.

They crossed the room and stepped into the hallway. Having wandered the hospital so much, they knew exactly where they were going. Then Tala's pocket buzzed. She reached for her palm pad, and her heart leapt when she saw it was a message from the hospital.

"Kane's awake," she read aloud.

"Go," Maverick said before she even looked up from her palm pad.

She spun on her heel so fast, running through the waiting room, then past the double doors. She didn't need to be reminded where to go, her feet knew the way, as if by instinct. A moment later, she found herself at his room. Her heart in her throat, she paused for a moment, then pushed through the door.

Tala drew in a breath at the sight of him. He looked tired, lying in a slighting reclined position, the central line still near his neck, a blood pressure cuff around his arm. From across the room, their eyes met and everything in the world fell away. She ran to him, her body collapsing across his as she wrapped her arms around him. She swore she'd never let go.

Her tears welled in her eyes and ran down her cheeks, and she struggled for breath, overcome with relief.

"It's okay," he said, though his voice sounded weak.

Tala sobbed into him as he ran his fingers through her hair and down her back.

"It's okay," he said again as he clung to her. "I'm okay."

Reluctantly, she pulled away, looking down at him through the pools in her eyes. She sniffled as she wiped at her cheeks, then smiled. Despite everything, it was happiness that filled her now.

"You were here awfully quickly," an unexpected voice said from behind.

Tala spun around to see Dr. Smithing standing nearby with a smile, and she wasn't sure if he'd been there the whole time or not. She didn't care.

"I have a feeling you didn't take my advice," he said knowingly.

"I got some rest. Just in the waiting room rather than the motel," she said, wiping at her cheeks again.

"You've been here this whole time?" Kane asked as he reached for her hand. Even his grip was laxer than usual.

She turned back to Kane with a guilty smile.

"I'd expect nothing else from you," he said with a tired chuckle.

"I'll let you two catch up in a moment, but first, an update," Dr. Smithing said as he approached the bed, standing near Kane's feet.

Looking at him, the bruising on his face was faint, and the burns on his head were no longer red and raw. His hospital gown covered his chest, but she was hopeful those injuries, along with the ones on his back, were improving as well.

"He's progressing very well. We didn't see any of the anticipated reactions from the lithium toxicity, such as seizures, tremors, hyperthermia, low kidney function, and so on. Kane, your body is still in overdrive as it purges the drug and repairs itself. Though I expect your progress will really take off from here. But you can still expect to feel fatigued, maybe even some muscle weakness over the next several days. You need to take it slow. And unfortunately, you still need to be bedridden until the bottoms of your feet are healed. Give it some time. We'll see how tonight goes, and hopefully, I can discharge you tomorrow," he said, his voice equally stern and gentle. "Tala, let me know when you're ready to talk. They can locate me at the nurse's station," he said with a nod, then turned and slipped out of the room, closing the door behind him.

"What's that about?" Kane asked.

"Oh, nothing," she said with a wave of her hand. "I've been a wreck waiting for you to pull through."

He gave her a sad smile. "I'm sorry."

"Are you kidding? After everything you've just been through—"

"It'll take more than that to bring me down," he said with a small smile.

"Vaughn, my brother, the things they did to you," she said, her emotion rising.

"Tala, I'm okay. I'm going to be okay," he said reassuringly.

She lurched toward him again, wrapping her arms around him, though more careful around his central line near his clavicle. She felt the sting of her tears again, and she blinked hard to keep them at bay.

"Your face," he said quietly after she pulled away. He tugged at her hand, pulling her closer to him. Reaching up, his fingers trailed lightly down the side of her face, over the suture strips. He turned her head slightly for a better look at the contusion on her scalp, and she was relieved he didn't touch it.

His hands roamed over her bruised jaw, then down her neck. She was thankful he couldn't see the bruise on the fleshy part of her side which was now dark purple and bluish.

"I'm fine," she said to dismiss his concerns because, really, she was fine. She would heal.

"If I had it in me right now, I would take every one of those marks off your body," he said sadly.

"I don't know," she said with a shrug and a small smile. "I kind of like them. Besides, I'm alive and he's not. That's all that matters."

"Vaughn did this to you?" Kane's expression looked pained.

"He was no match," she said, her smile falling away.

Kane was quiet as he ran his hand across her arm, goosebumps rising on her skin at his touch.

"Can I ask you an odd question?" he said, his face softening, his thumb brushing along the inside of her wrist.

"Anything," she said.

"Over the past few days, I have these flashes, moments of clarity in my mind, but I don't know if they're real or not," he said with a pause. "Like, I kind of remember being in an airplane."

"That's right," she said, nodding. "We got out of the Republic by helicopter, then took a plane here."

He nodded slowly. "When they had me really incapacitated, I have foggy recollections of things Vaughn asked me. Thias too. More than that, I have flashes of memory of resisting them. Vaughn was angry. Thias was impatient but more controlled."

"He said that even after he had you drugged, you still wouldn't give him what he wanted," she said with a sad smile. Of course he was able to resist. He'd been through horrors like that before.

"I remember you," he said, his face sober. "More your voice than anything. Crying. Telling me that you were there."

Tala saw where this was going, and her heart began to race in her chest. She swallowed as she nodded.

"I guess," he said with a pause, "I don't really know how to say it, but did you tell me we're going to have a baby?"

Tala pressed her lips together, a grin forming on her mouth, and she nodded. "Yes, I did say that. We're having a baby."

Kane's eyes brightened as they welled with tears. Tugging on her arm, he pulled her to him and slid his arms around her. He took a breath, his body quaking beneath her. "I love you more than you'll ever know," he whispered into her hair, then pulled her even closer.

TWENTY-ONE

Tala sent Maverick to the motel while she stayed for a second night in the hospital, this time with Kane. An orderly brought a small reclining chair into his room for her. With her bruised side, it was hard to find a comfortable position in the already uncomfortable chair. And then she'd been awake for two hours, between two and four, sick once again. Kane insisted his feet were healed enough to get out of bed to help her, but she refused him. He seemed to be better with every passing hour, his lesions continuing to improve, his bruising fading, and there was strength in his voice again. But Tala was adamant that he explicitly follow Dr. Smithing's orders. By late morning the next day, his central line was removed, and he had finally been cleared to walk again.

Now they sat side-by-side in an exam room on the second floor of the hospital. Tala's foot bounced nervously, her boot squeaking on the polished floor while she fidgeted with the ends of her hair. Kane reached out, resting his hand on her thigh.

Her leg stilled as she turned toward him, then took his hand in hers, lacing her fingers between his. "Aren't you nervous?" she asked.

"Of course. Actually, a little terrified," he said with a grin. "But it's going to be okay."

She swallowed hard, then let her head fall onto his shoulder. She was tired, exhausted, and her body was sore.

"Do you get sick every night?" he asked. His voice seemed to echo in the small room.

She nodded. "Yes. Every night. I've slept on the floor of our bathroom in The Village more than once."

"I hate that you've been alone, going through this," he said, squeezing her hand.

"I wasn't alone. Mila was with me," she said. "And don't do that, bring yourself down for not being there. We need to put all that past us."

He nodded slowly and brought his other hand up, running his fingers through her hair, careful to avoid the stitches in her scalp.

"Ah," Dr. Smithing said as he pushed the door open, stepping into the room. "My apologies for the delay. I don't work at this hospital, so things have been a little hectic," he said with a chuckle.

"This isn't your hospital?" Tala asked, sitting up in her chair.

"No, no," he said. "I'm in Santa Monica in Pacifica. Vulcan brought me in to handle your case. I tend to go where my patients are."

Tala cast a sideways glance at Kane as he shrugged. She hadn't seen Addox since they first arrived at the hospital. Kane either.

"Now," Dr. Smithing said as he took a seat opposite them. "I've looked through the questionnaire you filled out. Calculations show you're six weeks, six days along. Which is great because that means we can try to listen for a heartbeat today." He smiled brightly.

"But before we get to that, I know you're eager to discuss how Kane's condition influences the situation. And I can tell you simply that it doesn't," Dr. Smithing said as he crossed his legs, then rested his arm across his lap.

"I don't understand," Kane said. "How could it not? I mean, isn't it my DNA that was affected by my transition?"

"Actually, it isn't," he said.

Kane's jaw slackened, his brows furrowing.

"Since my first patient came to me seven years ago, I've spent a lot of time researching what happened to all of you. Enhanced human biological abilities. It's equally tragic and fascinating. We've retrieved as much data from the lab as we could. Much of it was destroyed, but we've also had some very skilled people who've managed to recover lost and deleted files. And then there was my first patient who wanted answers badly enough that she let us run extensive tests. For years, all of you in the facility underwent many experiments, including repeated injections of varying viruses, some with antidotes to treat them, some untreatable," he said.

Kane nodded while Tala listened to the horrible details. It wasn't something he spoke of much.

"They did all of that to create and perfect their final virus, which is what created your current condition," he continued.

"Super-soldiers," Kane said as he leaned forward. "The Republic wanted an unstoppable army."

"Yes. And sadly, they're not the only ones throughout history to ever try it," Dr. Smithing said. "It was called Project Magnar. So how does this affect you without being transferred to any offspring? What's unique about your transformation is that it was a virus that affected your RNA, ribonucleic acid, rather than your DNA. Let me explain. And please, let me know if I lose you," he said with a kind smile.

Tala liked him. He was both intelligent and kind, and he had a way of comforting her just by speaking.

"Your DNA stores your genetic information, the codes for your inherited traits. The DNA is then copied by the RNA, which acts as a messenger, giving instructions on how to create proteins. And proteins are the building blocks for everything in the body. Project Magnar introduced a virus to your system that mutated your RNA, which then corrupted the messages it sent on how to create your proteins.

"The mutation rates in RNA viruses are drastically faster than viruses impacting the DNA. They're rapidly evolving, making many of them drug resistant. And their mutations are genetically diverse which make them almost impossible to vaccinate against. This is why there isn't a cure for your transformation. It's your DNA that is passed to your baby, not your RNA," he said as he unfolded his legs and then crossed his arms. "There are other viruses that affect the RNA and not the DNA, viruses that can't be passed on genetically, such as those as extreme as Ebola or HIV, or as minor as the flu or a cold."

"I never knew any of this," Kane said with a shake of his head, his bewilderment etched across his face. "I didn't know what I was and just assumed my DNA had been corrupted."

"A reasonable assumption," Dr. Smithing said. "All those viruses they experimented with were trial and error for their ultimate virus. When they lost control of their subjects, you for example," he said, gesturing toward Kane, "and they weren't able to fight the mutation, their answer was to terminate all of you."

"So how is it that I can heal someone else when the mutation is inside me?" Kane asked as he ran his hand over his head, a dark shadow where his hair was beginning to grow in.

"That part is complicated and still murky, despite all my research. The best understanding and explanation I've been able to come up with is cell regeneration related to kinetic energy. Every human begins from two cells that evolve into the fifty to seventy million cells that make up who we are today. Our cells naturally respond to our bodies when there's an injury," he explained. "If I were to cut my finger, my cells would take over to heal my cut, first by stopping the bleeding, then by scabbing, and finally restoring skin. Our skin, in general, is constantly being renewed and repaired.

"Your cells shift into overdrive in response to an injury and that creates energy which is possessed because your cells are rapidly moving for the sake of regeneration. So when you touch someone else where they're injured, the energy that you can create within your body is then expended through you. It's not contained and it stimulates their cells and creates energy in their body, which rapidly regenerates their cells to expedite the natural healing process in them.

"But like I said, incredibly complicated. The science behind it is so advanced and unparalleled to anything I've come up against," he said at the dazed looks of both Tala and Kane. "And it's all still something I'm trying to understand myself."

"Complicated is one word for it," Kane said. He turned to Tala, and she could see the still confused expression on his face, a look that said he was trying to digest all the information that had just been thrown at him.

She was mostly at a loss, understanding only half of it.

"Now," Dr. Smithing said, straightening, smiling. "Let's take a look at this little one in the making. Tala, hop up on the table, and I'll send the technician in to do your sonogram. Kane, I'd like to go through a few last checks before I discharge you. I'll find you back in your room."

"Thank you," Kane said as he stood in unison with the doctor, reaching out to shake his hand.

"Of course," he said, then quickly slipped out of the room.

Tala looked at Kane with a wide smile, unable to hide her anticipation. She sat on the exam table, and glancing down at herself, still in her fatigues, though she ditched the jacket in Kane's room, she frowned.

"What?" Kane asked, seeing her displeasure.

"I just need a shower and change of clothes," she said, her shoulders falling.

"Hopefully, we'll be back in The Village by tonight." He gave her an encouraging smile.

There was a soft knock on the door, and a young woman peered around the corner.

"Come in," Tala said, perking back up.

"I'm Sydney, I'm going to do your ultrasound," she said, stepping into the room. She was a small woman, with long black hair that sashayed as she walked across the exam room. "Tala, if you'll just lie back and unbutton your pants."

Tala did as she was instructed. Sydney tugged her pants lower and slipped a towel over the top, then lifted the hem of Tala's shirt, pushing it higher on her stomach.

"That's quite the bruise," she said, Tala's side now exposed.

She stole a nervous glance at Kane as he eyed her carefully, though he said nothing.

"Just a little jelly," Sydney said as she squirted a warm gel low on Tala's abdomen, oblivious to their exchange. "Okay," she said as she put a probe onto her stomach. Sliding it around, a sepia-toned image appeared on a digital screen near her head.

"How do you even know what you're looking at?" Tala asked as she peered up at it.

"Lots of training," Sydney said with a side-grin.

Kane moved closer to Tala, taking her hand in his, his thumb brushing along the side of her finger.

"This dark oval you see here," Sydney said, pointing at the screen, "that's your gestational sac. It's a cavity of fluid around your baby. And this little thing here," she said, pointing to a little, light brown, 3D oval that moved in and out of clarity on the screen, "is your baby. He or she is about the size of a blueberry right now."

Kane leaned in closer as Tala propped aherself up higher. Slipping her elbows beneath her as she craned her neck to see the little bean-shape that was her baby on the screen, making out the round shape of the head, the curve of its back, two stubs where arms were growing, two for legs, all folded up together. Her breath hitched, never knowing something so small and obscure could captivate her so much. She couldn't peel her eyes away. Her baby looked like a tiny blip on the screen, but deep down, it was so much more.

She looked at Kane in the silence that had settled throughout the room, a smile of joy on his face and a look of wonder in his eyes, and she smiled. This baby was theirs, a creation only they could make. Suddenly, she wondered if he would have his eyes, or if she would have his lips. There was a world of wonder growing inside her.

"And this," Sydney said excitedly as she slid the probe around. Suddenly a soft, rhythmic lub-lub-lub-lub filled Tala's ears, "is your baby's heartbeat."

Kane tightened his grasp as Tala's eyes welled with tears listening to the beats, strong and steady and fast, that played like music to her own heart. Kane leaned down, pressing his mouth to the top of Tala's head, running his other hand gently down her arm.

"That's incredible," he said a moment later into her hair, then kissed Tala's head.

She had never realized that love had an on switch. That one moment there was nothing, and the next there was so much love it was spilling over the edges of her heart. She'd thought love was a gradual thing, something that happened slowly. But this was instant. As soon as she saw that tiny speck on the screen and heard that steady thumping, she knew her life was no longer hers. It was about this tiny life growing and thriving inside her, and she had to do everything she could to keep it safe, to nurture it, to bring it into the world.

They arrived back at The Village sometime after nightfall. Addox had never reappeared during the rest of Kane's stay at the hospital, and neither Tala nor Kane knew what to make of it. But of all the things on their minds, that mattered least of all.

The three of them were met with eager anticipation by their friends, and Tala had never before been happier to be *home*. They gathered as a group in the fifth-floor lounge, Kane and Max reuniting like the lost brothers that they were, warming Tala. Looking around, she couldn't help but begin to spot the small moments of good in their chaotic lives which only reinforced her decision to walk away.

When they shared with them the news of the baby, the happiness that bubbled up in the room was like sunshine ebbing out the darkness. Kane had always had a way of dividing her burdens, but in that moment, it was all of it, him, the baby, their friends, that multiplied her joy.

There was so much she'd do differently if she had the chance, but since she couldn't go back and change the beginning, she would seize what she could in that moment. She would reclaim her life and lay the first bricks of the road to something beautiful.

It didn't take long for the many sleepless nights to catch up to Tala, her exhaustion hitting her like a wall. She saw it in Kane too, in his eyes. She shuddered to think of what he'd been through, then quickly swallowed those thoughts and pushed them away.

"Tala, you're beat," Maverick said, the first to stand. "You too, Kane. You guys should get some rest."

Tala was thankful for his nudge, the others nodding in understanding.

"I've never designed maternity clothes," Vi said jovially as she pulled Tala in for a hug. "I'm so excited for you. And you," she said as she turned to Mila, "I can't believe you knew this and never said anything. I was hoping for some kind of slip of the tongue."

"I was under strict orders," Mila said as she slipped her hand into Declan's.

"I suddenly feel like such a grown-up," Declan said with a pensive nod. "I don't have any other friends with kids."

"That's because you don't have other friends," Vi said with a laugh as she elbowed him in the rib cage.

"Really, though, it's the best news," he said. "And I'm glad you're both safe."

"Get some rest," Mila said. "Three AM comes early enough." She gave Tala a knowing look. "Maybe have a pillow and blanket ready and waiting in the bathroom for you."

"I got her," Kane said as he slipped his arm around her.

"Yes, I believe you do," she said with a smile.

He turned toward Tala. "I'm going to sit with Max for a little bit. I won't be long."

She looked at Max, feeling so profoundly indebted to him. It was because of him that she had Kane back. "Take all the time you want," she said, her eyes finding Kane's. She reached up on the tips of her toes and lightly kissed his cheek, then turned around to a now nearly empty lounge and headed for their unit.

Tala stepped into a hot shower, the steam rising from the water cascading over her, and felt her body finally relax, her tension falling away. Her hands found her stomach, settling on the fleshy part below her naval. It was surreal to think about a life budding inside, and she felt that joy again, continuing to edge out the darkness.

She wasn't sure how long she stayed in the shower. Time seemed to both blur and stand still at the same time, but eventually, she reached out and turned it off, goosebumps raising instantly on her skin from the cool air. She wrapped herself in a towel, dried quickly, then slipped into her pajamas. As she headed for the bed, the door opened, and Kane stepped inside their unit.

Their eyes met, and instantly, they were at each other, their arms wrapped firmly around the other. They held each other in silence, and Tala wanted to live in his arms forever. He was her safe harbor, the place her heart could reside without all the madness of the world.

But too soon, they pulled apart. While Kane took a shower, Tala crawled in bed, on her side for the first time in days, the sheets cool on her bare arms, and she shivered. She pulled the blankets high, just under her chin, and closed her eyes, letting the sound of the shower fill her ears.

Just as she drifted off, the shower stopped, and her eyes opened. A few minutes later, smelling of fresh soap, Kane crawled into bed beside her. He slipped his arms around her. They were warm and comforting, and despite everything, they were strong as he pulled her close, drowning the space between them.

"The best things in my life, I never saw coming," he whispered into the darkness that enshrouded them. "First you, you took me by storm. And now a baby. I'm literally holding my whole world in my arms," he said, his voice deep and thick.

"I didn't know I wanted this," she admitted. "And it surprises me to know I do. But I do want this, I want this badly."

He tipped his head closer, his forehead touching hers. "I learned today, seeing that ultrasound, that unplanned doesn't mean unwanted, it doesn't mean unloved. Just unexpected," he said.

Tala looked at him, shadows covering his face. But she knew him perfectly, the dark obscuring nothing. "Let's move to the beach," she said.

"The beach?" he asked, taken aback.

She nodded. "Not like the beach in Columbia City. I mean somewhere warm, where our house overlooks the ocean, and all I need to do to feel the sand in my toes is step off my patio. Let's leave all of this behind, just disappear from the rest of the world and live in one we make ourselves."

"Sounds idyllic," he said.

"I can't do it anymore, being someone for everyone and nothing for myself," she said, emotion rising in her voice. "I want to walk away from everything. I just want to be yours, no one else's."

"What about our friends? Everyone that's a part of our lives is here," he said, his mouth so close to hers she could feel his hot breath on her face.

"They can come with," she said with a hopeful chuckle. "Or they can stay. They can do whatever they need to for their lives."

"Okay," he said, his voice strong. "You want to leave, let's go. We'll get things in order, make a plan, then we'll walk away from all of this. I'd love nothing more."

She leaned into him. "Really?" she asked, her lips grazing lightly across his.

"Yeah, really." He pressed his lips to hers, softly and gently at first, then pulled her harder against him and kissed her deeper.

Tala's eyes fluttered open lazily, and she rolled over, reaching across the bed for Kane only to find it empty. She was alone. She rolled back over and glanced at the time. She was surprised to see that it was mid-morning. She'd slept through breakfast like she always seemed to, though her stomach didn't seem to mind. For once, it felt content. Though she was still so exhausted. Like she had been for the last week, she was up in the middle of the night, miserably hunched over the toilet. But this time, Kane was beside her on the floor, holding her hair back, running his hand tenderly over her back to comfort her. Mila had been there for her, making sure she wasn't alone, but there was something about his presence, her partner, that was reassuring, that was heartening, in ways it never had been with her.

The door clicked, opening a moment later, and Kane came quietly into the room. She sat up, blinking the fog of sleep away.

"You're awake," he said with a smile. The bruises on his face were now gone, and the burn lesions were so faint they weren't noticeable unless someone knew to look for them. He went to her side of the bed, then kissed her forehead. "How're you feeling?"

She gave a half-shrug. "Fine, I guess. Better."

There was something about the way he looked at her, and she knew he wasn't entirely convinced. "Am I right to assume you're not hungry? I hear you aren't a huge eater these days."

She looked at him sheepishly. "Where were you?" she asked, changing the subject.

"With Max. He was supposed to go with Governor Barrington back to the Republic tonight, but evidently, that's been canceled. So now he doesn't know when or how he's getting back," he said as he ran his hand over his head, and she noticed he'd shaved, his face trimmed too.

"Did you tell him we're leaving?" she asked.

He shook his head. "I figured we wouldn't mention anything until we had a plan."

"Probably best," she said. She reached her arms into the air, her body stretching, aching, as she let out a yawn. "Although I don't know how I'll tell any of them."

"They'll understand," he said softly.

"Doesn't make it easy."

He was quiet, his gaze holding hers.

Tala's palm pad buzzed from beside the bed, and a moment later, Kane's buzzed from inside the back pocket of his jeans. They looked at them, knowing they were both seeing the same message, then looked at each other, neither saying a word.

They were needed immediately in the leadership offices. But this message didn't come from Addox. This was from Ash.

Tala pushed the blankets off, then made her way to the dresser. In less than fifteen minutes, they left their unit, making the short walk through the corridors to the offices in silence. There was something unsettling about their message, and they both seemed to feel it. While Kane gave nothing away with his face, she saw it in his eyes, she felt it in his silence.

"The last room on the left," Selene said with a sullen nod, and Tala stole a glance up at Kane, though he kept his eyes averted.

They stepped into the lounge-style office, met by the familiar faces of the Revos' leaders and Maverick. But it was Victoria's presence that caught Tala by surprise. She instantly reached for Kane's hand, gripping it firmly as he stood beside her.

"Thank you for responding so quickly," Ash said. The blue tips of her hair seemed brighter.

"Please sit," Victoria said. While everyone found a chair or sofa, she remained standing at the front of the room. There was something in her voice, in the way she looked over them all that sent a chill down Tala's spine. She cast a sideways glance at Maverick who gave her a discreet shake of his head.

"While most of you are aware of the current situation with the Republic of Columbia," Victoria said, her eyes leveling on Tala and Kane, "some of you are not." She spoke with gravity in her voice, and Tala squeezed Kane's hand tighter.

"First," she continued, "I am pleased to announce there has been great progress along the front in DeSoto. Our Unified military and coalition troops with DeSoto and Mazanada have been able to not only hold the Republic Militia Forces but have pushed them back to the border."

Tala knew this was a victory, but she also understood by the looks around the room that this was not why this meeting had been called.

"There have been retaliatory airstrikes in the Republic," Victoria said. Her mouth pursed into a tight line.

"Retaliatory?" Maverick asked. "By whom?"

"The Republic," Victoria said, folding her hands together.

"You mean the Republic bombed itself?" Kane asked, his voice low and deep.

"Yes. The central cities of Alexandria and Harrison, Weston Port along Lake Erie, and Augustana in the northeast. All of which have a large Rebel presence," she said. "At this time, we do not have accurate casualty counts, but they are estimated to be into the thousands."

Tala's body went cold as her blood drained from her face. Kane's grip on her hand was so tight it was beginning to hurt, though she didn't let go.

"I don't understand," Tala said, hearing the faint quiver in her voice. "Thias bombed his own people?"

"Because of our troops, he's lost his progress in DeSoto, and the unrest within the borders is at an all-time high, drastically complicating things within the country—"

"When did this happen?" Kane asked, interrupting her.

"It began two days ago. There were airstrikes yesterday and this morning still," Victoria said. "We don't know if there are additional strikes planned or if there will be a reprieve."

Tala's eyes caught Addox's for the first time; they were hardened, cold. She now understood why he'd disappeared from the hospital.

"What does this have to do with us?" Maverick asked.

Tala knew exactly what it had to do with them. What it had to do with her. "I'm not going back into the Republic," she said, her voice firm.

Victoria shook her head. "No, that proved to be too risky and completely futile. A poor judgment call," she said, casting a sideways look at Addox.

"You want another advoprop," Kane said.

"Yes, we do," Victoria said.

Tala shook her head. "I can't do that. I can't pretend to be their hero anymore," she said, her voice rising.

"Then who's it going to be?" Addox shot at her. "They know you, they trust you. It's just a video. You won't even be leaving The Village."

"Unless you've had a change of heart," Victoria said calmly, though sternly, her eyes fixing on her.

Tala readjusted in her seat, her leg pressed against Kane. "This beacon of hope you wanted me to be," she said, trying to keep her voice level, "it has cost me almost everything I have. I won't risk it anymore."

"Then you're a coward," Addox said.

"What?" Kane shot to his feet, dropping Tala's hand. "A coward? And what the hell is it that you do exactly?" His hands balled into fists. "She's done everything you've asked of her. You chose her specifically to send your message. If the people rallied, it was because of her and nothing you did. So who's the real coward?"

"That's enough," Victoria said loudly, her voice echoing through the room.

Tala reached for Kane's hand, tugging him back into the seat beside her.

"Tala, you're at no risk of any kind to do this," Victoria said, taking a step closer. "And you're right, you put a lot on the line and stood to lose it all had it not been for some brave action. The only difference is that it's your people who stand to lose it all now. There are many out there who had nothing to do with the rebellion and their lives have been destroyed. We need someone to acknowledge their loss, their suffering, then bring them together and unify them so that they may, in turn, mirror the same bravery you exhibited in saving Kane's life. Bravery to keep going, bravery to not stand down. They trust you, and if you show them your heart, you will be giving them hope."

The room fell quiet, and Tala swallowed hard. She cast furtive glances between Maverick and Kane. There was never going to be an end. No matter how hard she tried to walk away, no matter how far she'd go, she'd always be found. Her life would never be hers.

Her shoulders slumped forward, and tears gathered in her eyes. She blinked and bit hard at the inside of her cheek. This wasn't the time for an emotional display.

"Can I talk to Tala in the hall?" Maverick asked, his voice loud in the silence.

"Of course," Victoria said.

Tala rose to her feet, Maverick nodding for Kane as he passed them.

Once in the hall, he closed the door to the room, then turned to Tala with a serious expression on his face. "You don't have to do this."

"I agree," Kane said.

"It would just be one more advoprop," she said, more to herself than to either of them.

"We have no idea how long this could go on for. There will always be just *one more*," Maverick asserted.

Tala looked at Kane, meeting his eyes. She wanted to disappear, to get lost in them. She wanted to be just about anywhere other than where she was.

"I saw it in you," Maverick continued. "You want to walk away. I saw it in you, and I know that's what you're thinking."

She turned to him, her lips pursed.

"So just walk away," he said, as though it was that easy.

"Don't you get it? It's going to follow me wherever I go!"

"In North America, maybe. We could go overseas. South America," Kane said. "But this is entirely your call to make."

"This is it," she said, raising her chin. "After this, it's up to all of them."

Maverick and Kane were quiet as they studied her.

"I mean it. This last one," she said.

"Okay," Maverick said after a moment, then reached for the door. "Like Kane said, it's your call."

Tala was the last to step back into the room, everyone's eyes on her. For a brief moment, she wanted to shrink down, let her grief and exhaustion make her small. But then she straightened her back, bringing herself as tall as she could. She would do it, this last advoprop, it was the last thing she had left to give her people. And then she was done. She would walk away.

"Fine," she said. "I'll do the advoprop. Just tell me what you want me to say."

"I understand you know some personal things about me," Kane said without preamble as he stood in Addox's office, the door closed behind him. He refused to sit in front of him. "Why didn't you say anything, all this time?"

"I only suspected it," Addox said, sinking back into his chair, pushing his long dreads away from his face. "Besides, would you really have admitted it to me if I had?"

They both knew the answer to that.

"I don't understand why you were at the hospital at all," Kane said.

"Why?" Addox asked, his face screwed up. "You're my brother. Not that you like me or we're friends. But at the end of the day, we're still brothers. I was there to make sure you were okay. And I brought Dr. Smithing."

"Well, they tell me I'm going to be fine. So, don't sweat it," Kane said.

Addox took a deep breath, casting a glance to the other side of his office, to the virtual windows that showed a sunny day, then back to Kane. "Tala's done, isn't she?" Addox said, the muscles in his face tight. "It's a mistake. You can't let her do it, leave all her people hanging."

"All she's ever done has been with her people in mind," Kane argued as he folded his arms across his chest. "I will support whatever decision she makes."

"So she is, walking away."

"I'll let Tala discuss her own plans with you," he said.

Addox gave a knowing nod of his head, then sighed loudly. "I'm sorry, you know," he paused. "For never trying when we were kids. For letting our father just give you away like he did. I looked for you. For years."

Kane looked at him with surprise. "Ismet was what he was. No amount of regret will change anything. I've moved on with my life."

"Yeah…" Addox said, his voice falling away.

Kane's eyes lingered on him for a moment, then he turned to leave. Just before the door, he stopped himself and turned back to Addox.

"I'm going to ask Tala to marry me," he said.

Addox rose to his feet behind his desk.

"I don't know why I told you that really. I haven't told anyone," he said. "But I guess you're right. We're not friends. And I doubt that'll change. But we are brothers."

Addox was silent, a look on his face he couldn't read, then dropped to his knees, all of him but his head hidden from view by his desk. Kane heard a drawer open, a little shuffling around. Then Addox stood, placing a lacquered, wooden box with intricate carvings on the desk.

Kane's breath caught in his throat at the sight of it. He recognized it immediately. It had belonged to their mother. "Where'd you get this?" he asked, taking a step nearer the desk.

Addox shrugged. "You don't really think I'd torch the place without taking the few valuable things we had with me, did you?"

Kane was silent, his eyes meeting Addox's. They stood that way, unsure who was going to make the first move. Addox was certainly no longer the tall, skinny boy who was always quiet, always obedient.

Addox looked away and opened the box. He grabbed a handful of photographs, tossing them onto his desk.

Kane reached for them. On top was a baby photo, though whether it was him or Addox, he didn't know. He slid the picture to the back of the small pile, and his breath hitched.

It had been so long since he'd seen her familiar face, round and smooth with milky white skin, eyes as blue as the sky, and a head full of blond curls, ringlets hanging past her shoulders. His mother. She was sitting on their front porch step, her arm tightly around a young Kane, a laugh on both their faces. He wondered what had been so funny to crack the both of them up, and Kane couldn't help but smile now. He often looked back on his childhood with disappointment and anger, but looking at his mother after so many years reminded him there had been good too. She had been the happiness in his life.

"You should keep it," Addox said, his voice disrupting Kane's thoughts.

He nodded quietly.

"After mom died, I hid this from Ismet. To keep him from pawning it. And," Addox said, pulling out a small, black velvet bag that was closed tightly by a drawstring, "I think you should have it."

Kane took it in his hand, then loosened the string. Turning it upside down, a small rose gold ring fell into the palm of his hand. He picked it up, pinching it between his fingers, knowing exactly where it had come from. It was his mother's.

It was a simple band, two thin threads twisted around each other, one with the tiniest of diamonds strung along it, just enough to catch the light and glisten in his grasp. He wanted nothing that reminded him of his father, but this reminded him of his mother, and his heart warmed. This was exactly what he would put on Tala's finger.

TWENTY-TWO

Kane sat at the familiar bar in the dimly lit pub that was nearly full that Friday evening, Max beside him. Like usual, he drank his terrible whiskey and water while Max had a rum and cola. He wasn't much of a drinker, but it was always his default choice when he was with Kane.

"Well," Max said as he nudged his glasses, pushing them higher up the bridge of his nose, "that explains why my return to the Republic was canceled. But they're going to start asking questions at my job."

Word had finally gotten out about the bombings inside the Republic, and The Village had become a frenzy. People knew people in the Republic, people had family and friends there. Tala made her advoprop late that afternoon, and it was scheduled to be sent out that evening during the Republic's weekly National Statement. Kane waited with his palm pad on the bar for when it would start.

Wanting to be nowhere public when it went live, she was hiding away in their unit with Mila and Vi. And had insisted he spend the time with Max which he wasn't going to protest. He knew she was in good hands.

"I saw that Wren, Hunter, and Gage are here. Talked to them for a bit," Max said. "I didn't even realize they'd left."

"I didn't either," Kane said. "She's been nothing but a complication for me here."

"Let me guess, she doesn't like the word *no*," he said with a chuckle. "I could've told you that. She always looked at you like you were hers. It was always pretty pathetic in my opinion."

"If that's how you felt, why didn't you say something?" Kane asked, raising a brow. "Would've saved me a headache."

Max shrugged. "You wouldn't have listened. Just like you never listened when it came to Tala. Man, I told you to stay as far away from her as possible. But you disregarded all my warnings. And now look," he said with a jesting smirk.

Kane smiled, then took a drink of his whiskey. "Speaking of Tala," he said as he reached into his pocket and pulled out the velvet pouch. Glancing over his shoulder to make sure no one was paying them any attention, he took the small ring from the bag, then held it out for Max.

"It was my mother's," Kane said, keeping his voice low. "Just about the only nice thing we ever owned. I'm going to ask Tala to marry me." Just the thought of it brought a smile to his face.

Max grinned, his eyes lighting up behind his glasses. "Husband, father… those are two roles I never imagined for you. But I have a feeling you'll be great at both," he said with a nod.

"Believe me, I never thought so either."

Max said nothing, though the dopy smile on his face was enough.

"Know how you're going to do it?" Max asked after a drink.

"Not completely, I'm taking her out for dinner. Really though, I've got things so backward. I'm living with my girlfriend, who's pregnant, and I'm about to take her on, technically, our first date so I can ask her to marry me," Kane said.

Max laughed loudly, a few heads turning briefly in their direction. "You've never been one to be conventional."

"So, I've got to ask," Kane said when the others looked away, "think you'd be my best man? I'm going to need you there beside me."

"Are you kidding? There's nowhere else I'd be."

Kane's palm pad began to buzz, louder against the hard bar surface than it ever was in his pocket. He grabbed it quickly, as did everyone else in the tavern as theirs buzzed to life, just as Tala appeared on the screen. They'd superimposed her on a background of still smoking rubble, as though she stood on the very ground of the bombings, and it was a devasting sight to see. With Vi's influence, she looked the part of a Rebel, the black jeans, the thigh holster that held her gun, and an olive short-sleeved shirt that showed the defined lines of muscle in her arms. While she was small, she stood tall, strong, and that was never more evident than in that moment.

"People of the Republic of Columbia, this message is for all of you. Every single one of you. I stand before you with a heavy, heavy heart," she said, a grim look on her face, but a fury in her eyes that he knew wouldn't be overlooked by anyone watching. "If you don't already know, your government, your President Thias Alexander, is exterminating you, bombing the very citizens of the Republic. I am calling this an outrage!" her voice boomed, laced with anger, her fist clenching at her side.

"Your grief is very real, and it runs deep. You have been used and abused, under-valued, and doubted. You have been oppressed for too long! These bombings are meant to weaken your spirit, break your heart, and instill fear in you. Grieve, yes, but allow yourselves to do it together to divide your pain. Let the power of your unity make you stronger in the broken places.

"Your fight is not over, and you do not have to do it alone," she said with a firm shake of her head. Her voice was tight, and there was an intensity in her expression. Kane felt her gaze as though she was looking directly at him, addressing him personally. "It has never been more vital to keep going, to make sure those you lost didn't die in vain. You are stronger than you know, all of you, which is why you were targeted and attacked by your own leaders who are nothing more than cruel dictators. They fear what you are capable of when you come together under one purpose, one vision. Defy them! Show the indomitable spirit that lives inside you, rise above and fight. Be the change you want to see. Do not let them break you.

"Do not just endure and survive. Use what you have inside you to oppose this regime that has set out to cripple you. Step out of the box of conformity. The life that lies before you, the world you build for tomorrow, for the next generation, is more important than whatever you leave behind. Don't let the past hold you back, break those chains, and set yourselves free." She took a slow breath.

"I believe in you, every one of you. You are my people, the ones I've sworn to defend and protect. A renowned leader long ago once said, 'The only thing necessary for evil to triumph is for good men to do nothing.' We may stumble and fall and break, but we will also heal and rise, and we will overcome." She lifted her chin a little higher. "This is your call to action. Take back your power. Be braver than your fears!" There was more than just a spark in her eyes now, there was an inferno inside them that sent a chill down Kane's spine. He felt her anger, but he also felt her compassion, her devotion, and all he could do then was hope the people felt it too.

He gazed around the tavern that had gone silent, the expression on people's faces seeming to mirror what he felt inside. This was to be her last advoprop, and he couldn't help but be filled with pride in all that she had done.

That night, they lay awake in the darkness of their unit, Tala propped up on one elbow as she lay on her side, facing him.

"I don't even know what I would do, this future version of myself," Kane said, his fingers tracing along the side of her face. He'd been thinking about it since she first told him she wanted to leave The Village. "I'm trained for nothing," he said with a chuckle, though it was true. The only real work he'd ever done in his life was fish. Which he knew he didn't want to do. "Maybe a truck driver. Like armored vehicles or something."

"Even though they're autonomous, you're still going to have to know how to drive. Which you don't," she teased. "You could do pretty well in some kind of security job. It's what you do now. And you're stronger than anyone who would come up against you."

"I don't want a career putting my life at risk. Not when I have a family. I'm good, but not infallible," he said, reaching out, his thumb brushing over her lips. They were soft and supple. Even the simplest touch of her brought him to life. "What about you, what would you do?"

"Gosh," she said with a sigh. "I don't know either. All I'm trained for is security, an agent, a soldier. But you're right, I don't want that when I have a family. The point of walking away is to do something different, not fall into the same patterns somewhere else."

"We could find some small island in the Mediterranean in Europe and open our own restaurant," he said.

"That's a great idea. Because we're both such amazing cooks," she said sarcastically with a quiet laugh.

It was true. He could make toast, scrambled eggs, and spaghetti if the sauce came in a jar and all that had to be done was boil noodles.

"I'm grasping," he said with a smirk, sweeping a strand of hair off her shoulder.

"I don't want to talk about this anymore," she said as she leaned forward, her lips skimming across his.

"Did you have something else in mind?" he asked as he slid his fingers through her hair, smooth and silky to the touch.

"I absolutely do," she said with a playful smile, her eyes bright, even in the darkness. He could hear her beating heart, his matching its rhythm. Without hesitation, she pressed her mouth to his, electrifying him, his body tingling.

He slid his hand around the back of her head as he pulled her down on top of him.

Tala had been in the bathroom for nearly forty-five minutes, forbidding him to see her until she was ready, and as he sat on the sofa, he was growing restless, his eagerness only making him anxious. He had not a single doubt about their relationship. But he was still nervous, the ring in his pocket nearly burning into him. She was his future. It was because of her and the life they stood on the precipice of that he understood he hadn't been born to simply exist. His life was about to be so much more than he ever imagined.

"Okay," she called through the closed door. "Ready?"

He sprang to his feet, straightening the tie he'd bought just for this very night. He hadn't worn a tie since his mother's funeral sixteen years ago. The knob turned, and the door opened, Tala appearing before him. His breath caught, and he swallowed hard, unable to look away. The blond waves of her hair framed her face, her lashes dark and long, her lips punctuated with red. The baby blue dress she wore brought out the blue of her eyes, hugging her body, perfectly highlighting her curves. She took the very breath from his lungs.

He looked at her and just knew… she was worth everything.

She smiled as she approached him, reaching for his tie and adjusting it slightly at the neck. "I didn't even know you owned a tie," she said with a coy smile.

"I didn't." He laughed. "Please tell me I can kiss you right now." There was a glinting brightness in her eyes that made him feel unsteady in the knees.

"Absolutely."

He pulled her body against his and pressed his mouth to hers, his nerves falling away.

"We really should go, before my resolve breaks and I forget all of our plans," he said.

She giggled. She knew exactly what she did to him. She went to the bed, grabbing a navy, wool coat with oversized buttons down the front.

"When'd you get that?" he asked, watching her carefully as she slipped it on.

"I didn't. It's Vi's, which is weird because she never leaves The Village. She's letting me borrow it."

He smiled. "Some things never change," he said, remembering all the times she'd borrowed Mila's. That felt like another lifetime. It was another lifetime.

"Where're we going?" she asked. He could see the skepticism in her expression. "We're obviously overdressed for The Village. And I certainly wouldn't need a coat."

"Into Hatfolk. Declan gave a recommendation."

"You mean, I'm really allowed to leave this underground commune?"

"You are tonight," he said as he offered his arm to her. He leaned in, giving her a small kiss on her cheek, then they headed for the door.

They ate at the small Italian restaurant, Miseria E Nobilta', that Declan had insisted was the best. And Kane had to agree. He didn't make it to restaurants much, hardly ever, mostly never, but it was possibly the best food he'd ever eaten. And Tala seemed to be just as pleased.

More than once, he found himself just staring, his mind forgetting how to function as he gazed across the small table at her. She was always beautiful, always made his breath catch, but in that moment, everything went deeper, from the curl on her red lips when she smiled to the gleam in her blue eyes when she laughed. He had fallen for her quick and hard, but as he couldn't peel his eyes away from her, he knew he'd never loved her more than he did right then. His life had been mediocre, at best. But Tala, what he felt for her ran deep, bleeding into the fibers of his DNA. She was the extraordinary in his life.

"I saw the photo on the dresser," she said between bites of pasta, long noodles swimming in a rich, white sauce. "Your mom?"

Kane nodded. "Addox had it. He gave it to me yesterday."

"Really?" she asked with surprise.

"I know. I didn't take him as the sentimental kind either."

"Do you remember when it was taken?"

"No," he said, shaking his head. "I wish I did. We looked happy in it."

"I don't have photos of my parents. But these," she said, pushing her hair behind her ear, exposing the pearl earrings "were my mother's. They were found in the safe. At least something survived the fire."

There was a look on her face that was both happy and sad. Though he wanted to remember his mother, he wanted her to remember her family, their conversation was taking a turn down a more melancholic road than he wanted.

"Well, you're gorgeous in them," he said with a smile.

"This feels so weird," she said after a moment, her emotion passing from her eyes.

"What does?" he asked.

"Us, being out. In public." She gestured around them to the crowded dining room. "Dinner in a restaurant is such a normal thing to do, for normal people."

"And we're not normal?" he asked with a smirk.

"You know we're not." She laughed under her breath. "Do you realize this is our first date?"

He nodded. "I know. Trust me, I didn't overlook that. Not really winning in the boyfriend department, am I?" He smiled.

"Not like we didn't have special circumstances or anything," she said.

Her smile was arresting, and for a second, he felt his mind wander, distracted by it.

"So why the exception for tonight?" she asked as she sipped her water. Never in his life had he been to a restaurant where water was served in stemmed glasses.

He shrugged, though he felt heat rising in his face. "Because why not?" he said, his voice steady, a complete contrast to how he felt.

She pressed her lips together as she grinned. "Well, everything's perfect."

"It's good to know I can pull off a good first date," he said.

"Not good. Great," she said emphatically.

He laughed. "Even better."

After they finished their dinner, Kane paid, and together they made their way to the entrance, now full with a throng of people waiting to be seated. They collected Tala's coat, then stepped into the crisp night, the lights of Hatfolk illuminating the streets.

"There's a park near the front entrance of The Village that Mila told me about," she said. "I'm told there's the most beautiful fountain there that looks like dandelions in the summer. Think we could wander that way?"

Having caught a glimpse of it on their way out of The Village, he knew immediately what she was talking about. "Of course." He could never turn her down. A walk through the park, a beautiful fountain, what could be a better place to ask her than there?

He slipped his hand in hers, his thumb brushing the inside of her wrist. Although there was still a chill in the air, the cold didn't bite anymore. He looked at Tala in her dress that hung to just above her knees. "Are you cold?" he asked as they wound their way down the street, traffic whizzing by.

"No," she said, leaning in closer to him. "I'm from the northeast. I can handle a little chill."

"But just a little," he said, eyeing her with a smirk.

They passed people on the sidewalk as they walked through town, most offering polite hellos and kind smiles, but stepping into the park, they were alone. They wound their way down a curved path, lit by the pale glow of the lamp posts and the silver moon high above reflecting off the partially melted snow across the lawn. As he thought about the ring in his pocket, his growing anticipation set his nerves into motion. He wasn't sure exactly when he would do it, but he was sure he would recognize the moment once it was upon them.

Up ahead, they spotted the fountain. It was a large pool with a polished stone ring around it. And Tala was right, the water flowed into it from what looked like three dandelion puffs. Surrounding the entire fountain were large stone columns, deep grooves cut into them, with a ledge supported along the tops that was draped in bare vines. He wondered what it looked like in the summer when they were lush and green.

Tala slipped off her heels, then stepped onto the ledge of the pool, a wide smile on her face. She was happy, truly happy, and that warmed his heart more than anything.

"What're you doing?" he asked with a laugh. He wasn't sure the last time she had been this carefree.

"Enjoying my night of freedom," she said with a devious smile as she walked along the edge, clutching her shoes in one hand, her arms outstretched to balance herself.

She laughed a little more with each step as she made her way around the pool. He reached into his pocket, feeling the cold ring with the tips of his fingers. His excitement was coursing through his veins as he watched her. This, this was where he'd do it.

Her laughter was like music in his ears. From somewhere in the distance, he picked up the sound of a faint whistle. He glanced over his shoulder trying to pinpoint it, then looked back to Tala, her joyful smile still on her face from across the fountain.

The whistling grew louder, and by the time he realized what it was, the world around him exploded with a bright flash, sending him careening through the air with an unstoppable force. Concrete and trees and buildings and vehicles were upended, fragmented pieces of the world, large and small, hurling through the air as an inferno of fire spread to anything it could burn. The loud booming in his ears he also felt in his chest as explosion after explosion erupted around him.

Kane pushed himself up off the ground. He stumbled to his feet, his shirt torn and a large gash down his forearm, a warm trickle of blood running down the side of his face. A loud ringing and sharp pain lingered in his ears, disorienting him. Looking across the fountain, his heart fell when he didn't see Tala. In the flash of a moment, he blurred to where he'd last seen her, looking frantically for her, the fountain shattered, rushing water flooding across the sidewalk, saturating the lawn. Explosions continued around him, but in that moment, the world seemed to stand still, his heart in his throat.

A siren went off, wailing in his ears, the high pitch reverberating in his head. He spun desperately in circles, screaming for her, though his voice was drowned out by the thunderous bombing that echoed around him. There was the overpowering smell of fire burning, and heavy smoke billowed into the air. Then he spotted her, a baby blue flash, her unmoving body lying amid a mass of concrete rubble, and he was at her in the time it took to take a breath.

Her arm was bent at an impossible angle at the elbow, her face bloodied, more blood running down her leg from a deep laceration on the side of her calf. He quickly pressed his fingers to her neck to check for a pulse, the sound of her heartbeat muted by the cacophony of continued explosions. Relief flooded him when he found one, though it was faint.

"Tala," he cried, his words caught in the back of his throat. He pushed away the concrete she was partially buried beneath, then scooped her into his arms, her body warm to the touch. Across the large park, he could make out the main entrance to The Village and set off as fast as his body would move.

A shower of dirt, rock, and glass fell around them, ash carrying through the air like snowflakes. Reaching The Village entrance, he found the reinforced security doors sealed and latched. A protocol from the airstrike. He set Tala down, sliding her into the corner of the doorway for the smallest amount of protection.

"Tala, stay with me," he yelled as he tapped her cheek, trying to bring her back to consciousness.

He took a ragged breath, his body shaking as he turned to the doors. He hit them hard with his fists, leaving behind two faint dents but nothing more. The doors were several feet thick, and he knew he'd never get through them.

He reached into his pocket and pulled out his palm pad, the screen shattered. He hollered out as he threw the device against the doors that wouldn't open. It broke into pieces as it fell to the ground. He stepped in front of the security camera in the corner and waved his hands furiously as he yelled for help. But deep down, he knew no one was coming. They wouldn't open the doors until the strike was over.

Kane went to Tala, coughing on the thick ash in the air which burned his lungs. The thunder of the bombs was growing fainter as they moved farther away, though not relenting. He knelt down, looking at her. He felt for her pulse again, then pressed his ear to her chest, listening to her slow, shallow breaths. His eyes found her arm, her elbow dislocated. Hopping to his feet, he went to the security camera, ripping it off the wall, then returned to Tala's side. He eased her out of the wool coat, her bare arm exposed in the cold. He carefully took it in his hands, then quickly wrenched it back into place, feeling a pop in his hand. She didn't react, her eyes not so much as fluttering. He wrapped both of his hands around her elbow, then closed his eyes.

He felt his hands heat up as he focused his mind, pushing away the blaring siren, silencing the explosions in the distance. His heart began to race, his hands shaking as he gripped her harder. Less than a minute later, he pulled away, his hands falling to his sides. He moved to her leg, the gash deep, still bleeding, and he feared it went to the bone. He pressed his hands firmly over the wound, her blood warm to the touch in the cold air, then closed his eyes, repeating the process.

Afterward, he pulled the coat tightly around her. She had small cuts and scrapes across her face, but they were minor, superficial, and didn't matter at that moment. He slid his arms under her body, lifting her high enough to ease himself beneath her, then rested her back down in his lap. Slipping his hand out from beneath her, his breath caught at the sight of blood soaking his sleeve and hand. He rolled her body to the side, his eyes immediately fixing on the large stain of blood on the back of the dress, just below her bottom, and his heart fell. He rolled her back toward him, clutching her tightly to his chest. Tears sprang to his eyes, and he tried to blink them away, but despite himself, they fell, running down his cheeks, wetting his face.

He closed his eyes, his tears still falling, and brought his head to hers. Pressing his cheek to the side of her face, he reminded himself to breathe.

"I love you," he whispered, his voice hardly audible. "I love you," he repeated. "I love you."

TWENTY-THREE

Tala's eyes blinked open, then closed again. Her eyelids were heavy, leaden. Her mind was clouded and foggy. It didn't smell like her unit. It was familiar to her but she couldn't pinpoint it. She could pick up the subtle hint of Kane. She tried to lift an arm. It, too, felt heavy, and there was a flash of pain that spread through her chest, an instant pulsing in her head. Her eyes fluttered open again, and despite the strong pull of sleep, she forced them to stay open.

Her vision coming into focus, her eyes were drawn to the only light in the room. To her left, a soft glow flooded in through a window looking into a hallway. A steady beeping sound caught in her ears, and her head turned from side to side, her eyes wandering the room in the darkness. It was a hospital room.

Then she saw Kane. He sat in a chair beside her, slumped over and sleeping, his head on the bed near her hip. Even in his sleep, he held her hand. She watched the steady rise and fall of his shoulders. He seemed so peaceful.

She looked down at her body, draped in a white blanket. Every movement, even the smallest shift in her body, sent pain through her chest. She pushed against the throbbing in her head as she realized that she was the patient. Why was she in the hospital?

With a thick head, she closed her eyes, taking herself back to the last memory she had. She saw Kane, his eyes on her, smiling. Even from across the fountain, she could see the wrinkles in the corners of his eyes. Or maybe she just knew they were there. They always were when he smiled like that.

The fountain. They had been above ground, out of The Village. Her mind began to swarm as images came back to her in a rush. But none of them explained why she was in the hospital, why it hurt to even breathe.

She glanced at Kane and resisted the urge to run her free hand over his smooth, bare head. She didn't want to disturb him, and she also knew it would be incredibly painful to reach her arm across her body. She kept as still as possible, the only thing to keep her pain at bay, moving only her head as she looked around.

Why couldn't she remember?

A thought suddenly came to her, flooding her and filling her brain. The baby. Her body shuddered as she took a sharp breath, the movement just enough for Kane. He stirred beside her, his head lifting slowly, blinking. Then his eyes caught hers and were instantly awake. He was on his feet in only a moment.

"You're awake," he said on a breath. It was then that she realized how disheveled he was. There was blood soaked on his torn shirt, on his loosened tie. But one look at his expression and all that fell away. There was fear, at least worry, on his face. And there was something more. He had pain in his eyes, heartbreak.

"Wha.. wha…" she stammered, her throat scratchy. "Where am I?" she managed to ask.

"The Village medical center. They needed somewhere secure for you," he said. His voice was low, quiet. But it was more than that. It was sad. "Do you remember what happened?"

She shook her head, harder than she'd intended, and pain riddled her chest, and she let out a gasp.

"The doctors said you have fractured ribs along your sternum," he said. "I can fix it for you. When we're somewhere private."

"I don't understand," she said, finding her voice. Her mind was swimming.

"Tala, there was a bombing. In Hatfolk, hours ago. We were caught in it." His voice was taut.

"Are you hurt?" she asked.

He briefly looked down at himself. "No… not really. My body did what it does."

There was something else. A bombing was horrible, terrible, tragic, but there was something devastating in his eyes, something personal.

"You're not telling me everything," she said, her voice quiet. Maybe she didn't want to know. Maybe she wanted to live in ignorance for just a minute longer. "Tell me."

He reached for her hand, taking it with both of his, gripping her tightly. "We uh…" His agony was almost tangible. "We lost the baby."

Tala's body went still, rigid. And for the flash of a moment, she felt nothing. It wasn't real.

But it was the look he gave her that told her it was.

We lost the baby.

The words expanded around her, suffocating her, stealing the breath from her lungs. This had to be a mistake.

"They called it a trauma-induced placental abruption," he said.

"No," she cried out. Tears welled in her eyes and fell down her face. She shook her head and brought her free hand to her stomach, pressing against her soft flesh. It wasn't that she'd been able to physically feel something before, but now it was just… empty.

"No, that's not true," she said, sputtering over her words.

"I'm sorry," he said, his voice thick as he leaned closer, bringing her hand to his cheek.

His face was wet, and she turned her head toward him. Her brain couldn't process, couldn't string the pieces of reality together. But her heart felt it, she saw it on Kane's face, and she felt the sudden ache deep in her chest.

She rolled onto her side, toward Kane, the pain in her chest excruciating, taking her breath away. It made her eyes water, and she bit hard at her cheek to keep from crying out. But it had nothing on the pain that was taking hold inside her heart. Her tears rolled onto the pillow beneath her, soaking it in only seconds.

He reached for her other hand and tightened his hold, reminding her that he understood her heartbreak, that he felt it too.

She pulled him to her, pressing her forehead to his, and her body shook. She was suddenly cold, though no amount of blankets would be able to warm her. She thought about that little bean she'd seen on the ultrasound. One moment, it was alive and thriving, growing into creation, and the next, there was nothing there. But the truth was that there was something there. There was pain and hurt and devastation, and though they weren't tangible like that little babe had been, they were still very real, and Tala felt all of it.

It was a goodbye she didn't want to make, one she wasn't ready for. But the longer she and Kane held each other, the more her mind put the pieces together, the more her reality became clearer, and it grew heavier with every passing second.

That tiny baby, that strong lub, lub, lub heartbeat had changed everything, and now the loss of it changed everything all over again. In the blink of an eye, it was over, that beautiful time of loving someone so deeply that she'd never met but already knew. She took an unsteady breath as she felt herself move from one world into another, from one of anticipation and happiness to one of heartbreak and loss.

"Kane," she whispered, her voice cracking.

"I'm here," he said, his voice soft, broken.

"Will you hold me?"

He pulled his head away, and though his eyes were dry, she could see the wet stains on his cheeks glistening in the soft light coming in through the window. He dropped his hold on her hands, then walked around the foot of the bed. He lowered the guard rail, then carefully eased into the open space behind her, pressing his body against her. He was delicate as he draped his arms over her hips, but she still winced from the pain that shot through her like a bullet. There wasn't much room for the two of them, so in that moment, they became one, and not just to fit in the bed, but to fortify each other, to grieve together, to complete each other so that there was a way their broken hearts could endure.

Tala had fallen asleep, Kane too, and woke to the sound of someone in her room. She tried to lift her head, the simple movement sending pain coursing through her, and she let out a small groan through gnashed teeth.

"You're awake," the nurse said quietly as she came around the side of the bed and into Tala's line of vision. Kane's arm was still draped over her, and his slow, heavy breathing told her he was still asleep.

"How are you feeling?" the nurse asked in a hushed voice.

With that one simple question, reality came crashing through her, ripping her apart, and she felt all her heartache return. A pain far greater than that in her physical body. She swallowed hard, choking back her rising emotion. She didn't know what to say. Was there really an answer? Were there even words?

"Are you in pain?" the nurse asked.

Yes! She wanted to scream. Though she knew that wasn't what she was asking about. Slowly, Tala nodded. "Yes," she said in a hoarse voice. How was it that crying could wreak so much havoc on one's voice when tears came from the eyes?

The nurse nodded. "I'll get you something for that," she said kindly. "I'll let the doctor know you're awake. He's up at St. Grace Hospital in Hatfolk.

Lots of people needing a doctor right now. He'll come down as soon as he can. But let me first get you something for your pain. I'll be right back."

Tala nodded, wincing again, regretting the movement. A thin layer of tears clouded her eyes, so she closed them and took a shallow breath.

The nurse returned in only minutes with a small syringe, and she reached for the IV line that Tala hadn't noticed until then. She eased the clear liquid into the tube of the line, pressing down the plunger, and it didn't take long for Tala to feel the effects of the pain meds as her body warmed. She felt it circle around in her head, and almost instantly, her chest felt better. If only there was something for her heart.

"That should help take the edge off," the nurse said, and Tala nodded. It was taking more than just the edge off. "Okay, press this button if you need anything," she said, motioning toward a panel near her head.

The nurse left, and Tala closed her eyes again, though she knew she wouldn't fall asleep. In Kane's arms was the only place she wanted to be. Those arms were holding her together. She knew his mind was somewhere far away as he slept, in a place of comfort and peace, where reality's harsh winds didn't blow. She envied him, though she knew that the ache inside only meant the love in her heart had been real. Was still real.

Her mind went back to the ultrasound, the tiny bean that, for a short time, had been her dream. It had been their dream. It was a loss she knew she'd carry with her through the rest of her life.

There was a time during the night when Kane thought he might just lose it all. He knew they lost the baby, and while the doctor assured him Tala would wake and be okay, an irrational part deep inside, the one already reeling over one loss, couldn't help but fear the possibility of the other loss.

But Tala woke up like they said she would. And then the next hardest thing happened. He had to tell her the truth.

They told him they could do it for him, but that was never an option. And as much as it broke his heart to tell her, he never could've let someone else. This was their loss together. There was joy that left her eyes in that moment, a million dreams of *what-ifs* dying before them, and he felt her devastation. He felt hers, and he felt his own, and he hated that there was nothing he could do to minimize any of it. He was powerless.

How, he wondered, do you look at someone you love, knowing their grief and loss, and tell them it's going to be okay? It wasn't okay, not for him and not for her. So, if you couldn't say that, what was there to say?

Nothing.

So he'd held her. He couldn't fix it, couldn't take away any of the heartbreak. He held her for her, and he held her for himself.

Like partners, like two sides of a coin, standing beside his sorrow was his anger. At first, it had just been his sorrow. But his anger had now planted itself like a seed deep inside him, and with every passing hour, it grew.

When she was finally released from the medical center the following afternoon, Tala disappeared into their unit. In the privacy of their room, he healed her fractured ribs, wishing he could take away the rest of the pain. Then she just wanted to sleep, and he understood that.

He sat with their group at their usual table in the City Center, his untouched dinner on a plate in front of him that he had no appetite for. He didn't participate in any of the idle conversation. He had nothing to contribute. There was already the proverbial elephant lingering in the corner and talking would only draw attention to it. Everyone was empathetic, everyone was kind, but they didn't understand. And when there's really nothing to be said, it can be easier to say nothing at all. And he was okay with that.

The one exception was Max. He was also quiet, but Kane knew he was studying him, watching him. Next to Tala, he knew more about him than anyone. He missed nothing. So when the group thinned, Max stayed behind until it was just the two of them.

For several minutes, neither of them spoke. Kane sunk back into his chair, feeling drained. The flicker of life inside him was extinguished. It was shocking to him how much emotional exhaustion impacted the physical body.

"How're you doing? Seriously. No BS," Max finally said. He kept his voice low, but Kane could easily hear him over the thrum of the large atrium. The Village was on edge, the tension throughout taut as anxiety ran high. No one knew what to expect. They had all been safe from the bombing in Hatfolk, their reinforced bunker-city protecting them, but there were casualties above ground. The last count was in the hundreds, though he stopped paying attention. His mind was far away, focused on his own personal loss.

He could be real with Max. Kane had known him almost his entire life; he would see through anything other than the truth. And he was the last person who would judge him. He let out a frustrated groan.

"For three days, I thought I was going to be a father. A dad. It was the last thing I'd expected, and then in the blink of an eye, became everything I wanted. For three days. And now in another blink of an eye, that's all over. You wouldn't think that three days could change something so much. Could change someone so much. But they did." At least if he could be honest with Max and get it out, he could be strong for Tala. "It kills me to watch her hurt like she does. And the truth is," he said, his voice growing louder, though he didn't care who heard, "I'm fucking pissed. This was Thias. And I want to just—" He didn't know how to finish that sentence as he flexed his jaw.

Max was quiet as he nodded his head.

"He's ruined too much, taken too much. And not just from me. He needs to be stopped," Kane said. His mind was swimming in a state of limbo between grief and fury.

He wanted to make Thias suffer the way he was. He wanted him destroyed. And he wanted to be the one to do it. His hatred tasted bitter, but it also burned alive in his veins.

"I get why you're angry," Max said in a nonpatronizing way as he leaned in across the table and adjusted his glasses. "You've been changed by this. Both in good and bad ways. You'll never get back what you lost. Just because it was only three days doesn't lessen what it was to you."

There was truth in that, and validation too. Three days or a lifetime, it still mattered.

Kane perked up as he heard his name called through the noise, and he turned to see Addox approaching him. He always wore a hardened expression, but this one was more so. Straightening in his chair, Kane sighed, steeling himself for whatever was about to come.

"Since you don't have a palm pad anymore, I decided I'd come look for you myself," Addox said. "Maverick said you might be here."

Heads turned in their direction like they always did at the sight of Addox, but he seemed indifferent.

"What's up?" Kane asked. His voice sounded hoarse, thick.

"We need to talk," he said, giving nothing away.

Kane turned back to Max, his shoulders falling. "I'll find you later."

Max nodded as Kane stood, then followed after Addox as he wound his way between the tables to the elevators. While he preferred the stairs, he took the elevator with his brother, the two riding in silence to the fifth floor.

Kane was surprised to find that Tala wasn't waiting in Addox's office. He'd expected that whatever he needed from Kane, he'd likely need from her too.

"Take a seat," Addox said, and as Kane was about to take a chair in front of his desk, he realized he had gestured to his seating area.

Kane looked at him suspiciously as he crossed the room. While Addox's heart seemed to beat a little quicker than usual, he was still composed and difficult to read.

"You going to tell me what's up?" Kane asked as he sat, Addox taking the chair across from him.

"How's Tala doing?" he asked.

Kane cocked his head, surprised. There seemed to be something genuine in the way he asked about her. "Last I saw her, she was sleeping," he said.

Addox nodded. "So, I wanted to talk to you because I received a message. Well, it's meant for Tala, not me, but it was relayed to me."

Kane didn't respond, his brows furrowing.

"The thing is," he continued, "I'm not entirely sure she should see it."

There was more to it. "Why not? I'm assuming it's from Thias. That's what you're not saying," Kane said sternly.

He nodded. "Yes, that's right."

Kane's anger flared. Thias's was the last name he wanted to hear. "Why don't you think she should see it?"

"I'm concerned that considering everything that's happened recently, it wouldn't be good for her psyche," Addox said.

Kane was taken aback by his sudden compassion. "What's the message?"

"You can watch it for yourself," Addox said as he rose to his feet and walked toward the digital wall. He woke it up with his hand, and with a few taps and swipes, a video appeared, then he pressed play.

Thias appeared before Kane's eyes, sunk back in a deep chair, his hands together in a steeple. In an instant, Kane's blood was boiling. This man had cost him too much.

"Tala, Tala, Tala," Thias said as he brushed his hand along his jaw. "Tsk, tsk. I'm disappointed in you. I'm disappointed that you chose the Rebels over me, and I'm disappointed you didn't walk away from this fight when you had the chance." His voice was clipped, and there was something menacing in his eyes.

"I saw your last broadcast that you once again hijacked my communication system for. I was really hoping that by giving you your boyfriend back that you'd walk away. I mean, did you really think it was a coincidence that you were able to just walk out of that black site you rescued him from? How he survived was a miracle, in my opinion, and I really hoped getting him back would be what'd finally make you walk away.

"I've had to come to terms with the fact that maybe I didn't know you, my own sister, quite as well as I thought," he said. His voice was cold and distant. He was detached, even while addressing his own sister. He played on the idea of familial connection, but it was just another way to manipulate the situation. He was incapable of genuine connection. How he could have a family was baffling to Kane. "I didn't even know you had a boyfriend, or whatever you call him." He laughed as he rose to his feet. "You're more deceitful than I ever gave you credit for," he said, shaking a finger at the camera.

Kane was seething, and he balled his fists at his sides as he fought to stay in the chair, to keep from attacking even the digital version of Thias before his eyes.

He didn't just hate him. He loathed him.

"Your choices have come at a price, though, haven't they? You stirred angst within my people. You made them believe that they knew better than me. And the fallout from all of it, well, that's on you. There are always consequences, Tala. You really forced my hand. You left me no choice as soon as I figured out where your transmission was originating from. I mean, the first time you did this, you caught me off guard. But I was waiting for you for this last one," he said with a sardonic grin.

Kane gave a sideways glance at Addox, who sat stiffly, his arms folded, watching the video message in silence.

"I have a proposal for you, Tala," Thias said as he slipped his hands into the pockets of his slacks. "I want to discuss an armistice. But I will only, and I repeat only, talk with you. And you will come to me," he said, then he clenched his jaw, a small tic in his neck. "I'll let you into the city. If you want to stop the bloodshed, and I know you do, you will do this," he paused for a moment. "See you soon, little sister." Thias fell silent, but the video continued, his icy, steel blue eyes staring intensely into the camera. Then finally it ended, and the screen turned black.

Kane's knuckles were white, and there was an ache in his jaw from clenching so hard. Even though Thias's face was no longer filling the large screen, he struggled to keep his anger at bay. If he had something to throw in the moment, he would. He looked across at Addox, their eyes meeting.

"I'm sure you can understand my reticence. If you thought she was taking things personally before, she will undoubtedly do so after watching this," Addox said.

"The airstrike," Kane said as he stood, "was a tantrum. If Thias knew about The Village and that it's where Tala was, then he'd have known he couldn't hurt her here. He wouldn't have known she was above ground when he hit Hatfolk. He didn't want to hurt her, he wanted to make a point. He's trying to *force* her back into Columbia City." Kane paced between the chairs.

"That's the last place she'd be safe, and it's exactly where he'll have all the control. Everything would be to his advantage there. This is why we can't show it to her," Addox argued.

"I don't get you." Kane sighed, turning toward him. "One minute you're telling her she's a coward, and now you don't want her to act at all."

Addox was quiet for a moment. "Making an advoprop isn't even on the same page as going back into the city. And that's exactly what she's going to want to do."

"Things are personal now," Kane said, his voice low. He took a slow, deep breath. "Tala was pregnant. And she miscarried when we were caught in the bombing." He swallowed his rising emotion. Even saying the words made his chest tighten.

Addox's mouth slackened, his arms falling to his sides. "I… I had no idea."

"Well, it's not exactly public knowledge," he said. "Show her the video."

"What?" Addox said, his eyes widening. "You just said—"

"I know what I said. But she gets to make this decision for herself," he asserted.

"Kane, let our leaders negotiate this," Addox said.

"He's not going to stop any of this, and the more control he loses, the worse things are going to get. He'll burn everything to the ground before he gives up. You heard him, he won't work with anyone else. She's the only one who's a real match for him," he said. He could feel the tension in his muscles, across his shoulder blades and into his neck.

"And then what? What happens when they come face to face, huh? Does she shoot him? I know you're not delusional enough to think he'd just surrender to her," Addox said, his hands gesticulating through the air. "Is that what you want? For her to point-blank shoot him? Is that how this ends? And what's left of Tala after killing her own brother?"

Of course that wasn't what he wanted for her. But he now understood that walking away was never going to be an option for her. Their dream of a quiet life and a house on the beach was just that, a dream, and it always would be as long as Thias had a hold on her. Kane shuddered at the thought of how much worse things could get. But Tala was strong and smart, and she was the only one who could face him head-on.

"Show her the video," he said sternly, then he turned and made his way toward the door. "I mean it," he said with a brief look over his shoulder. And then he left.

◆◆◆

With a new palm pad that Selene had given him on his way out of Addox's office, Kane returned to his unit. He tried to enter quietly and was surprised to find Tala and Vi on the sofa when he walked in. Tala's eyes were red and puffy, and he knew she'd been crying, but they were dry now. She looked as tired as he felt.

"Oh," he said at the sight of them. "I can come back."

"No, no," Vi said with a shake of her head as she stood. "I need to find Declan." She reached for Tala and gave her a small squeeze of her shoulder. "Message me if you need anything."

Tala nodded and gave her a half-smile. Her eyes met his as Vi left, and silence settled between them. He crossed the small room and sat beside her, taking her hand in his.

"I'm okay," she said. They both knew it wasn't true, and it wasn't that she was trying to appease him, she was trying to convince herself. He understood because he'd been trying to do the same all day.

"This will always be with us," she said, her voice quiet. "Won't it?"

He nodded slowly. "Yes."

"I hate that I wasn't able to protect it. I wasn't able to keep it safe until it was ready to make its way into the world," she said. Her shoulders hung, crestfallen.

"You can't think like that," he said, his thumb brushing along her hand. "Sometimes we can do everything right and things will still go wrong. That's life. It always has been, it always will be. And that's no one's fault. Least of all yours."

"Vi said something, and I'm trying to find comfort in it. That even though there will always be the loss, there will also always be the love," she said, looking away. She took a deep breath.

There was truth in that.

She took a slow breath. "Where've you been?" she asked, composing herself, turning back to him.

"With Addox."

"Oh," she said, her eyes wide with surprise.

"He got a message from your brother. He doesn't think you should see it, but I disagree," he said. "But not until you're ready."

"It's about the airstrike," she said knowingly.

"Some of it," he said with a nod.

"Tomorrow. I'll be stronger tomorrow. I'll watch it then," she said, her voice steady, her resolve firm. It was exactly what he admired about her. He knew she felt broken. But he saw something else. Yes, she was cracked and fractured, but she was far from broken. She stumbled, but she would get back up because that's who she was.

Tala was awake before dawn, the virtual window in her unit showing the ebbing night, and she shook Kane awake.

"Kane," she said quietly.

"You okay?" he mumbled, half asleep. Though he reached out for her, his eyes never opened.

"I want you to take me up top," she said as she leaned over him, whispering into his ear.

"Why up top?" he asked as he rolled in her direction, his tired eyes prying open.

"It's just something I need," she said, her voice louder as she tried to stir him.

He sighed as he looked at her. "You're dressed."

"Yes. Can you please bring me up top? I need you to do this for me," she said.

"Okay," he said as he sat up and tossed the blanket off himself. Shaking the last remnants of sleep, he slipped into a pair of jeans and a t-shirt. Grabbing his leather jacket, he followed her out of their unit.

Tala glanced down at the quiet City Center as they made their way down the stairs that overlooked it. Once they reached the first floor, they took the secure elevator back up until they reached ground level.

They stepped outside of the small entrance into the quiet morning, where not even the breeze dared to blow in the city that mourned. Down the street, the beautiful park was all but destroyed by the airstrike, buildings opposite it only half-standing, smoke still rising from their remains. There was devastation all around her, and she took a deep breath, the cold filling her lungs, grounding her.

Reaching for Kane's hand, she stepped into the vacant street, out of the shadow of The Village entrance, and looked up at the sky. The sun was rising in the east, casting a soft, orange light around as it pushed above the horizon.

Closing her eyes, she felt the first traces of sunlight on her face. Her heart was full, a tapestry woven with the fibers of sadness, pain, and even joy. In that moment, she didn't want to grieve, she wanted to celebrate that little life. It had been small and tiny and short-lived, but it wasn't insignificant. Its impact was big and momentous, and she would forever be changed by it.

Life was fleeting, there one moment and gone the next. Death was a thief, eventually claiming everyone when their time came. And only he knew when that was. Her heart felt a profound ache deep inside, but she was not standing in the darkness alone. She had Kane, who shared in her loss, and a whole family that loved and supported them. While she would never hold that baby in her arms, she would always feel it in her heart. Even death could not take that away from her.

That baby was as beautiful as a fresh morning sunrise, and in that moment, she was going to watch it come up in all its breathtaking glory and let it flood her soul. With the dawning of every new day, she would let the sunshine bring peace to her heart. Somewhere, that baby was safe, and eventually, their time would come when they would finally meet. Until that day, she would look to the morning sky and smile. She would let it wash over her, restore her, fortify her, and she would let it remind her of the deepest kind of love.

There was something healing about watching the sun climb higher into the sky. To other people, it was just a sunrise, but to her, it was both a hello and a goodbye.

When the sun finally reached above the trees and crested the top of the buildings around them, she turned to Kane and gave him a hopeful smile. "This is what I needed, and I'm better for it."

He was quiet as he studied her.

"I'm far from okay, but I'm better," she said, her voice a little stronger.

He dropped her hand and slipped his arm around her, pulling her close. His body was warm beside her. Despite everything, they still had each other. And that was something to celebrate.

Tala was restless during breakfast, the thrum of people in the City Center loud. She had grown accustomed to it, all its liveliness as people readied for their day, but now it just seemed to echo in her head, giving her a headache. Her mind was on Thias's message that was waiting for her.

"You're giving me anxiety," Vi said with a frown from across the table. "The way you can't stop moving your body and your eyes are frantically looking around the room."

"Sorry," Tala said, then took a bite of her granola.

"When do you see Vulcan?" she asked. Her blue eyes were wide and filled with concern. She knew, just as the others did, that a message from Thias wasn't going to be good.

But Tala was prepared. His last one took her by surprise, but she was ready now and would not be caught off guard.

She glanced at the time on her palm pad. "Fifteen minutes," she said, looking up to see everyone's eyes on hers. "It's just a video."

The table was quiet, and she caught Maverick's gaze. Unlike the others, who wore their worry, there was a look in his eyes that she couldn't read. She reached beneath the table, giving Kane's leg a small squeeze, then he slipped his hand into hers.

"At least tell us this," Declan said as he turned to Kane, knowing he'd seen it, "does he take responsibility for the bombing on Hatfolk?"

Kane had given them no details of any of it. Even Tala was in the dark, but he gave them a slow nod of his head.

"I wish I could watch it with you, Tal," Vi said as she straightened in her chair.

"I don't," Mila said quietly. Declan reached for her, slipping an arm behind her and pulling her a little closer.

"He's a narcissist on a power trip," Maverick said, and Tala was reminded that he'd seen Thias's first video message. "Every time we fear him, we put him higher on his pedestal."

"A narcissist with an arsenal behind him," Declan said.

"His day is coming," Maverick said. "Mark my words."

A chill ran down the length of Tala's spine. She couldn't help but wonder what that day would look like, and who it would be that would ultimately depose him. If anyone.

"It's time," Kane said, his voice low, though everyone at their table heard him, their heads turning in his direction.

Tala stood, taking her empty breakfast tray in her hands.

"Good luck," Mila said with sadness, and Tala felt a tug at her heart. She understood the depths of Thias's evil. She'd suffered at his very hands, forever carrying her scars.

Tala, Kane, and Maverick made their way to the fifth floor in silence. And when they were asked to wait outside Addox's office, the quiet lingered between them there too. While she felt her nerves coming to life inside her, she focused on her breathing. She could control nothing about Thias, about what was in his message, but she could control herself. She wouldn't give him the power of being able to do so himself.

"They're in the conference room," Selene finally said, and the three of them perked up.

Rising to their feet, Kane and Maverick fell in stride behind Tala, following her down the hallway to the last door on the left, their footsteps echoing with each footfall.

Tala wasn't surprised to find that it wasn't just Addox who waited for her in the room but Ash too. Without being prompted, Tala took a seat on the same sofa she always did, Kane beside her, and Maverick in the same nearby chair. This was becoming routine for them.

"I assume Kane has briefed you on the message," Ash said.

"Some. Not a lot," Tala said. "Though I already have my suspicions about it."

Ash nodded, and Tala's gaze flickered over Addox as he silently stood in the corner, arms folded across his chest. He looked on edge as he kept his gaze averted.

Unlike before, when every reason not to watch Thias's message had circled through her mind, she could not find one now. "Let's get this over with," she said.

Ash pursed her lips, then pressed play, everyone looking to the digital wall.

Like he had been in his last video, he was sunk back in a deep chair, and while his body said he was comfortable, there was something in his eyes she'd never seen before. Was he distressed? A moment later, however, it was gone.

"Tala, Tala, Tala. Tsk, tsk. I'm disappointed in you. I'm disappointed that you chose the Rebels over me…" She listened as his words unfolded, his voice filling her brain.

Of course he was disappointed.

Of course he had been the one to call off security.

Of course the airstrike was his doing. And of course he put the responsibility on her shoulders.

"I have a proposal for you, Tala… But I will only, and I repeat only, talk with you. And you will come to me. I will let you into the city. If you want to stop the bloodshed, and I know you do, you will do this. See you soon, little sister."

There was a time in her life when coming head-to-head with him would have sent a chill to the depths of her bones. When it would've sent her running. When it had sent her running. But this was not that time. She now better understood how he played the game. That's exactly what all of it was to him, a game, and what she would have to remember was that he would try to win any way that he could. There were no rules for him.

All of her advoprops had been just rhetoric, and now the time for action had come. Maybe all the struggle up to that point had been preparing her just for this. Because in that moment, she knew, unequivocally, that it was time to fight fire with fire, and she was ready to meet him head-on.

Tala rose to her feet, the room silent as they waited for her to say the first word, to take the first step. She was more ready than she ever had been before. If he wanted her, she would go, to finally put an end to everything or die trying.

"I'm going back to Columbia City," she said resolutely.

Kane was on his feet in a moment, followed immediately by Maverick.

"Then we're going with her," Kane said, his voice hard and stern as he locked eyes with Maverick who nodded as he folded his arms. There was no room for negotiation.

"That's a suicide mission! This is what he wants. He wants you in his territory where he can control everything," Addox said, his voice loud and tight, his face reddening. He turned to Ash for support. She looked at him only briefly, then at Tala.

"We're going to need one hell of a plan," Ash said. "But let's go to Columbia City."

Unlike the last time Tala had agreed to go back to the Republic, there was no gleam in Ash's eyes, there was no smile on her face.

TWENTY-FOUR

"Are you crazy?" Mila asked in exasperation. "You can't go back there. Do you remember what you went through just to get out? And don't forget about the things he's done… Ronin, me, Kane, your baby…" she said, her voice growing quiet, her sentence falling away.

Tala slid closer to her on the sofa as the two of them sat in the quiet of the fifth-floor lounge. "Of course I haven't forgotten. I never could," she said gently, her hands unconsciously finding her belly. She swallowed back her rising emotion as she moved them back to her sides. "Those are the very reasons I have to go. Thias has to be stopped."

"And it's not just you, you're taking my brother with you," she said.

Tala was quiet, feeling Mila's heartache, understanding her fears.

"Damn it!" Mila yelled. "I could really use some of Kane's awful whiskey. Now I get why he drinks it."

Tala cocked a confused eyebrow.

"Never mind. I just don't understand why it has to be you," she said as she looked away. Her voice was filled with anger, it was on her face and in the tension in her body. "There are armies fighting him right now. Let them take him out."

Tala sighed. There was no way to make her understand. But she had to do this, she had to face him. She had to stop him. She may be meeting him on his terms, but she was smarter now, understood him better, and he underestimated her. He was so centered on his own superiority that he would never see her for who she was and what she was capable of. And that was going to be his downfall.

"I have lost so much to him," Tala said, choosing her words carefully, "but if I can't face him, if I can't stand up to him, everything and everyone I love will always be at risk. I need to fight him, or I'll end up sacrificing everything that matters to me. I can't let him destroy the best parts of my life. I won't let my dreams, my future, be the price of doing nothing." And if she wasn't able to stop him, if she lost to him, then she only hoped that those she loved would someday understand what she had been willing to sacrifice herself for. Though she kept that thought to herself.

"There's nothing I can do to change your mind, is there?" Mila asked in defeat.

Tala somberly shook her head. She knew the life she wanted, and she was determined to be courageous enough to fight for it. Both her heart and her mind knew there was no turning back.

Mila's shoulders dropped, and there was sadness in her eyes. Tala understood. There were no guarantees, and they both knew it.

She was afraid. How could she not be? But this was her time, and her belief in her mission was stronger than her fear. She wasn't trying to be noble. She wasn't heroic. She was selfish. Her motivation wasn't the people, but rather *her* people. She would face him because there was no other way to keep her people, her forged family, safe.

There was a little piece of each of them in her, and that was to be her armor for what was to come. And she wouldn't be alone. She'd have Kane and she'd have Maverick beside her, and she trusted no one like she did them.

Tala tossed and turned in the quiet darkness, Kane fast asleep beside her, undisturbed by her every move. Finally, she sat up, tossing the blankets to the side. She slipped out of bed, then quietly left their unit. She wandered the empty corridor, its silver light paling the bare skin of her arms. When the lounge came into view, she couldn't help but feel a little bit at home in its dark serenity.

She took a seat on the sofa. Sinking into it, she pulled her knees to her chest and closed her eyes. In the stillness, her mind wandered back to another time, to another life.

"Look, it's a baby bird," Tala said. Now that she'd lost both her two front teeth, she spoke with a slight lisp. She clasped the small bird, its feathers brown and white with a hint of orange, in the small of her hands. Its dark, beady eyes moved in all directions, watching her.

"Where'd you find it?" Thias asked as he dropped to the grass from a low-lying branch in the old oak tree that stood in the back corner of their yard. It was large and sturdy, wide and tall, with a full maze of branches, and they both loved to climb it. Because Tala was smaller, she was always able to go higher than him, and he hated her a little bit for it. Though she did learn the hard way, by a rock to the back of her head that had left a large welt, not to patronize him about it.

"I think it fell," she said, peering up through the labyrinth of limbs and leaves. High above her, she spotted the nest snuggled between two converging branches. "From there!" she cried out.

Thias approached her, brushing his hands together to clean off the traces of bark from his palms. "Give it to me," he said, snatching it from her.

"Careful," she said. "You'll hurt it."

Thias clasped his hands around the bird. It fit perfectly in them, one hand cupping the bottom and one over the top. He brought it close to his face, his shaggy blond hair falling into his eyes. He exhaled a large puff of air from his mouth, his bangs blowing to the side.

"Well, hello there," he said as he surveyed the bird up close.

"I bet it fell learning how to fly," Tala said as she bounced on her feet. "Give it back, give it back, give it back," she whined.

"It's sick," he said flatly. "And its family won't want it now that you touched it."

"Really?" she said, her eyes wide. "Is that true?"

"'Course it is," he said with a shrug. "Don't doubt your big brother. I'm older and far smarter."

"Whatever," she said with an eye roll. "I'll nurse it back to health if it's sick," she said with a wide, toothless grin. She turned on her heel and took off in a sprint toward the house.

"Where're you going?" he called after her.

"It needs a nest!" she yelled over her shoulder just before slipping inside the patio door. She hustled through the house, her father yelling at her to slow down. But as soon as she passed him in the living room, she darted quickly up the stairs, taking two at a time.

In her bedroom, she dug through the bottom drawer of her dresser and pulled out an old t-shirt with paint stains on it from an art project gone wrong, then she went to her closet. Scaling the built-in shelves, she reached for a box from the top shelf. Back on the floor, she dropped to her knees, then dumped her things from the box: a half-uneaten roll of fruity chew-candy, a bottle of red nail polish that belonged to her mother, a necklace made of rainbow beads, a homemade birthday card from Rory Cafflen that was covered in colorful glitter that had contaminated everything else in the box, and then lastly, a fluffy ball of white thread all knotted together. Tucking the t-shirt under her arm, she reached for the knotted ball, which had been used last Halloween as a cobweb decoration she stretched across her window, then headed back downstairs.

Tala pulled apart the ball, creating a hallow impression in the middle as she made her way back across the lawn, a bounce in her step.

"We can make a nest for it!" she exclaimed. But as soon as she reached Thias, she came to a sudden halt, her smile quickly falling away. She looked at the bird, still in his hand, now lifeless, its head turned at an unnatural angle.

"What'd you do?" she cried out, tears springing to her eyes.

He shrugged. "It was a lost cause."

"No!" she yelled as she dropped the shirt and the threaded ball. She reached for the bird, taking it from Thias. She ran her finger gently over the feathers on its back, soft and smooth to the touch. "You killed it?" she asked, her tears falling down her cheeks.

"Oh, get a grip. You don't need to cry like a baby. I was helping it out. It's not like you knew anything about caring for baby birds. It was doomed the moment it fell out of that nest," he said as he turned away from her.

Tala's bottom lip trembled as she looked at the dead bird in her hand. Was he right? Would she really never have been able to nurse it back? Her heart felt broken as she looked at the little lifeless bird in her hands. Reaching down, she picked the t-shirt back up and gently wrapped it around the bird.

Digging through her mom's gardening tools in the garage, she found a spade, then made her way back to the tree in the yard. Beneath the strong limbs above, she quietly dug a small grave, her tears running silently down her face, her little shoulders heaving, then carefully put the bird, still wrapped in her shirt, in the hole and covered it back up.

"I still can't believe you did that," she said as she wiped her tears on the back of her hand, gazing up at Thias, now high in the branches above her head.

"Whatever. You're the one who touched it. Its mom never would've taken it back after that. I was putting it out of its misery. You should thank me really. Besides, you have to learn that you can't save everything," he said, then looked away. Reaching for another branch, he climbed higher.

The cold crept up Tala's spine, and her body quaked with a shiver. She wondered how she had gone her whole life and never seen it. There had been a constant push and pull in their relationship that had been completely controlled by him. He had used his position as her brother as a mask to hide his true intentions.

He put her in cadet training to finish secondary school, his show of force over his young and rebellious sister. He took away her MF case and classified it above her head but then cast her to make the National Statement because she'd been the one to make the arrest. He'd lied to her all those years about how their parents died, asserting he was sparing her the heartache of the truth. He cleared her after her lie detection analysis, keeping her from certain punishment. He shot Ronin when his gun had been aimed at her the entire time. He called off security when she rescued Kane.

The list went on. He controlled every situation to his own liking, his own purpose.

And then there were all the times when he'd skirted responsibility for his actions and masterfully turned the finger of blame away from himself. There was a time, not so long ago, when she had resented herself for believing his lies. But she couldn't fault that version of herself anymore. There wasn't a point in hanging on to all of it. It was time to forgive herself for not knowing any better, for lacking understanding, for not having perspective, for not believing in herself.

There was an art to his manipulation; he was an adept master of deception. He knew how to read his audience, to sculpt his words, to form and shape the reality he wanted people to see. His power was unique, beautiful but wicked.

At one point, she thought she'd somehow lost him, that they'd lost each other. She didn't know when he'd become the version of himself he was now. But the truth, she could now see, was that he had always been this person. She hadn't lost him after all, she was finding him. And what she was doing now was taking her life back.

Life was about timing, and hers had come. The life she wanted was on the other side of this last fight. Her dreams were not fickle and they were not feeble, and they were worth giving everything she had for. What was coming was going to inevitably come, and she had to be prepared for when it did.

All that she'd lost left a heartache deep inside that would heal in time but never leave her, and she was made stronger because of it. Thias had put her through hell, and now she would look his fiery vengeance in the eye and smile because she was no longer afraid of those flames.

Tala's head jerked up at the sound of feet shuffling across the floor as Kane stepped into the lounge. He was heavily shadowed, making his dark skin even darker, but she knew him. He ambled across the room and took the seat beside her on the sofa.

"I didn't mean to worry you," she said quietly.

"I figured you were here," he said, his head tipped to one side, and he frowned. "You okay?" he asked. "Maybe that's a terrible question to ask right now," he added quickly.

She reached out, taking his hand. It was soft and warm to the touch, and she smiled. "I'm okay," she said with a nod. And it was the truth. "I'm ready for this. Is that weird? Being ready to forge into battle against my own brother? What would my parents think of us?"

"I don't think so," he said, his fingers curling around hers. "And hopefully, they would see that you're doing what you have to."

"I'm not naïve. I know it's going to be dangerous; it won't be easy," she said. Even in the darkness, their eyes still found each other.

"Doesn't mean it's not the right choice. We do this together," he said.

"I couldn't do this without you," she said. "You're what makes this worth it. I can either spend my life running, or I can put a stop to this. You and I only have a future when this ends. Otherwise, we'd spend our lives always looking over our shoulders. And we deserve so much more than that."

He took a breath as he rose to his feet, giving a tug on her hand.

"What're you doing?" she asked as she gazed up at him.

"Just… stand up," he said, tugging again. He had a smile on his face, and even in the darkness, she could see that it reached his eyes.

She stood, her head only coming to his chin. There was something in the way he looked at her that made her breath hitch.

He took a small step backward, putting space between them, but didn't turn to leave.

"From the very moment our lives converged, something in me shifted. I couldn't explain it then, and I can't explain it now," he said, his voice low and steady. "I'd never shown anyone other than Max what I could do, but for some reason, I never hesitated with you. You were a stranger who was somehow familiar."

Tala remembered that night, the night they first met, at the warehouse near the river when she had come to at the sound of his voice, her body broken. And he had healed her.

"There was something about the way you looked at me," he said. "You weren't afraid. I'd spent all of my adult life building walls around myself, to protect myself and my secret, and with one look, you took them down. You saw what I'd been terrified to show anyone. You saw me, and you weren't afraid."

That night she had been in shock, bewildered by what she'd seen. And maybe she'd been frightened at first because she couldn't explain or understand it, but he was right when he said she'd never been afraid of him. Something deep inside had whispered that she was safe with him.

"There was no future for me, I had no dreams. I was always going to be what I was. I was always going to live in a secret bomb shelter and be provided for by Max because I couldn't exist," he said. He ran his hand over his head and cleared his throat, the silvery moonlight from the virtual windows catching in his eyes. "And then you came into my world, and I found myself wanting things I never thought I would. Things I didn't think I deserved. You," he said with a tip of his head as his hands slipped into the pockets of his pants.

"I want to give you the world. I just didn't know how before. But now we're here, we're outside the Republic, we're together, and when I look to the future, you're what I see. Tala, you're my dream."

She felt her heart quicken and her chest tighten. Her breath shook as she took a deep breath, and goosebumps raised across her skin.

"I never understood how a single person could affect another like you have me. You have consumed me in the best possible way."

His eyes held hers as he lowered himself to his knee. "I promise to love you wholeheartedly until the end of time, and then, even after that." Though his voice was steady, she could hear the emotion in his words. He pulled his hand from his pocket, a small ring that glinted in the moonlight held between his fingers, and her breath caught. "Tala Alexander, will you marry me?"

In that moment, the world stood still and everything fell away but for the two of them. Her heart was in her throat, pounding with an excited flurry. He was right, their lives had converged and something greater than both of them shifted, bringing together the least likely of people. But he was her match in every way. He was both her home and her adventure. Theirs was a once in a lifetime kind of love, the kind that didn't just live in the heart, but rather in the depths of the soul.

A smile that she couldn't contain spread across her mouth as she brought her tingling hands to her face. Tears pricked at the back of her eyes, and she nodded, wildly and profusely.

"Yes," she said, on a hurried breath, her voice thick. "A thousand times, yes."

His smile mirrored hers as he rose to his feet and reached for her left hand. Gently, he slid the ring onto her finger, gliding it over her knuckle, putting it safely and perfectly into place. She couldn't pry her eyes from it, two thin bands entwined together, a thread of tiny diamonds along one strand catching the light. This was them, their lives woven together. He was her forever.

With tears in her eyes, she met his gaze, then reached for him, wrapping her arms around his neck, pulling him to her. She pressed her mouth to his. She kissed him hard, with an ardor that lived deep inside.

He slid his hands under her, easily lifting her, and she wrapped her legs around his waist. She pulled back, their eyes finding each other, and she laughed, he laughed. Their happiness was genuine and crazy and intense and overflowing. With him, she felt complete. Their joy was pure and flowed like a river between them, filling them up.

She kissed him again, the first kiss of the rest of their lives.

TWENTY-FIVE

Tala and Kane spent the morning entwined together. In the quiet peace around them, wrapped in his arms, she could almost convince herself that the world wasn't falling apart. She could almost convince herself that all they needed was to pack a bag, and they could simply walk out of The Village, go anywhere, and start a new life together.

None of that could be further away from her reality. But she wasn't going to let it stand in the way of their bubble of perfection. She would live in it as long as possible.

"Think if we lie here long enough, the world will just forget us?" she asked, her head nestled in the crook of his arm.

He let out a breathy chuckle. "If only it was that easy," he said, his fingers dragging across her arm. "We deserve more than just a mediocre life."

Tala craned her head and kissed his neck, and he pulled her closer. "I keep telling myself it's just another mission. Then I realize it's my brother, and I'm conflicted. I hate that I'm conflicted because there isn't any gray where he's concerned."

"Why can't it be both? I mean, it is both, just another mission and your brother. As he's repeatedly demonstrated, family isn't inherently good just because they're family. They're still people, and they make their own decisions," he said. "It's the fact that he's your brother that gives you an edge. You know him, his tells, what makes him tick."

"I'm not sure I know what makes him tick. If I did, I'd like to think I could've put a stop to this a long time ago," she said.

"What I'm saying is that if anybody knows how to handle him, it's you."

She nodded, understanding what he was saying. The truth was, she knew she was already in his head. She was what was standing in his way of total control. And he was spiraling.

A knock came on their door, and Tala sighed. Kane untangled himself from her and slipped out of bed. He ambled across the room to the door with a sigh and opened it to see Max standing opposite him.

"Do neither of you respond to your messages anymore?" he asked as he rolled his eyes.

Tala sat up and reached for her palm pad, surprised to see the string of unanswered messages. Addox, Maverick, Mila, Max, Vi, Addox again, and a new alert.

"When Addox couldn't reach either of you, he came looking. I said I'd track you down. He wants to see you both at ten," Max said.

Kane glanced at Tala and frowned. "Guess the real world found us."

"There were more bombings in the Republic," Max said.

Tala felt her heart drop. "Where?"

Max combed his fingers through his shaggy hair, slicking it back, then nudged his glasses. "They targeted the Mississippi River cities of Providence, Jackson, and Clara City. The major border crossing bridges."

"They're trying to curb the number of people trying to get out of the country," Kane said.

This was just another show of power for Thias. He was trying to force her hand. Violence was the strongest tool in his arsenal, and he was applying maximum pressure. If the current crisis proved anything, it was that his regime would stop at nothing to remain in power.

What form, she wondered, did he expect her to come to him in? Did he still see her as his naïve younger sister, or had his opinion of her elevated in the months since, when he saw another side to her? There was one thing she knew for certain, and that was that he still saw himself as superordinate to her. He always would.

He thought he was forcing her to come to him. But she was choosing this. His rapid escalation revealed more about him than she was sure he intended. His superiority complex was a psychological mechanism of defense meant to counter his true fear. It wasn't just about losing control of his people, it all stemmed from his fear that in the end, the truth would be that he was inferior, that he didn't matter at all. Everything was threatening to unravel before his eyes, and she was the catalyst. She yielded far greater power than he knew.

Even as she sat there in her bed, a plan was being devised by the leaders of the U.S. She was ready, and it made her eager, but until the time came for her, she told herself she would be present in her life with those who mattered. She wasn't going to wish away one moment between where she was and where she was going.

"His reckoning is coming," she said. "But until then, we won't be his casualty." Her eyes met Kane's, holding his gaze, and she nodded. She tossed the blankets off, yawning and stretching her body.

"Can I tell him?" Kane asked, a smile curling on the corner of his mouth.

"Tell me? Tell me what?" Max asked eagerly.

Tala laughed and nodded.

"Did you do it?" Max whispered as he leaned in closer to Kane.

"I did," he said.

"What'd she say?"

"Do you really not know the answer to that?" Tala asked as she stood, then dug through the dresser for something to wear.

"I didn't want to assume," he said, his eyes wide, his voice high. "I mean, I never saw this guy as the marrying type, but look how wrong I was about that."

Tala smiled. "Of course I said yes. I'm going to shower. Then I have some friends I need to talk to." She met Kane's gaze, saw the light in his eyes, and it stirred the happiness in her all over again. She turned and stepped into the bathroom. Closing the door, she pressed her back to it, letting it support her, and she sighed.

In that moment, she was filled with joy and excitement, and it scared her. She had the gnawing knowledge that there was a lot that stood between them and the future they wanted. She wasn't afraid of facing Thias, she was afraid of losing the dream that lived in her heart – a life with Kane.

Max insisted on getting a celebratory drink, but since it was too early for the tavern, he and Kane settled for the coffee shop while Tala met the others for breakfast at the café on the second floor.

"Not that I don't mind changing things up," Declan said as the four of them wedged into a large booth, Maverick pulling up a chair at the end, "but what's the occasion?"

The rest of the table was quiet, all their stares fixed on Tala, and she felt heat rising in her cheeks.

"Please don't tell me this is some last-hoorah before you go charging back into the Republic," Mila said. Though she tried to keep her voice even, Tala once again saw the sadness in her eyes, and she felt a pang of guilt all over again.

"No, that's not what this is," Tala said, pushing it away. "I have happy news to share."

The table fell quiet again, and Tala's eyes flickered between each of them. Her heart wasn't just full because of Kane, it was full because of these people too. Despite the broken places in her heart, these people made her strong.

"Kane and I are getting married," she said as she held up her left hand. She could feel the happy, dopey smile on her face, and she didn't care.

Mila reached across the table, snatching Tala's hand, bringing it to her face. "Oh my goodness!" she exclaimed, her eyes glinting as she studied the ring. "This might be the happiest I've ever been for you," she said with a smile, releasing Tala's hand. "And I'm only a little jealous."

Declan's head snapped in Mila's direction, and Maverick straightened, though she paid neither any attention.

"When did this happen?" Vi asked, a smile on her face to rival Mila's.

"Last night," Tala said, and she felt the same excited tingle in her fingertips as her mind wandered back. It was one of the most defining moments of her life.

Declan looked pleased, too, though not giddy like Mila and Vi, but it was Maverick's gaze that caught her attention. A small smile tugged at the corners of his mouth, but it was his eyes that spoke to her. They had happiness in them, they had joy. Of all the people that surrounded her, it was Maverick who had known her the longest. He knew better than all of them what she was made of. They both knew her life's current chapter was coming to a close, and the look he gave her told her that he would fight just as hard for her future as she was about to. He would make sure she could write her next chapter.

"Hello? Tal?" Vi snapped her finger in the air, bringing Tala's mind back to the present.

"Oh!" she said as she realized everyone's eyes were on her again. "Sorry. My mind got away from me."

She looked to Vi who was still smiling, her lips punctuated in bright red, like when they first met, the waves of her brown hair falling over her shoulders. "I asked if I could make your wedding dress."

Tala smiled as she let out a sigh. "We've made no plans. I want to get through this other stuff first," she said, and as soon as it was out of her mouth, she regretted it. The last thing she wanted hanging over their conversation was her upcoming mission. The sudden tension that settled around the table was palpable.

"I just mean, I'm not sure what a wedding will look like. I want something small and intimate," she said with a grin that was more forced than anything, but her friends needed to be placated in that moment. She couldn't let them know that she felt it too, the uncertainty of what lay ahead.

"So, elope," Declan said as he stroked his goatee.

"No," Vi said adamantly, shaking her head. "She's going to come back. They're going to come back. And when they do, we're going to make sure they have the wedding they want. Big, small, or otherwise."

Tala looked at her with gratitude. While the tension seemed to ease with the conviction in Vi's voice, Tala could still register Mila's heartache. She wished there was a way to comfort her, to put her at ease, but there were no words. Just as Tala was being tested, so was Mila, and she would have to let her go. She was thankful for Declan and Vi who would help get her through.

After breakfast, they made their way out of the restaurant and diverged. Maverick was going to get in a short run in the gym, and Mila was taking Declan up into Hatfolk to help in the school where she taught, now doubling as a shelter for those displaced by the bombing. They'd been there every day since, and Tala thought it did Mila good to have something to distract her, to redirect her focus away from what was coming.

"Want to get a little shooting practice in before you have to meet Vulcan?" Vi asked as the others disappeared.

Tala nodded. Like Mila, she needed a mental distraction as well. And going to the shooting range was likely to give her just that. "That sounds like the best therapy I could ask for right now."

Vi let out a chuckle as she looped her arm through Tala's. "I can't believe you're getting married. I mean, it seems to be the thing these days for people our age. Though I will likely be single for life," she said with a dramatic sigh. "I might be the last relationship hold-out. Not that I'm actually holding out.

But please let me make your wedding dress. I already have so many ideas running through my head."

A small gasp from behind caught Tala's attention, and she glanced over her shoulder to see Wren in stride behind them, her eyes wide and her jaw slackened. As their eyes met, Wren swiftly spun on her heel and turned down the nearest hallway, disappearing as quickly as she had appeared.

"She's going to go sulk," Vi said with a pleased smirk.

Tala let out a small laugh. She almost felt sorry for Wren. But then she remembered the drama she seemed to always stir, and that feeling was fleeting. "Let her sulk. Let's go."

The shooting range was empty, aside from the two of them. Like she had been doing with Maverick, Tala checked out two guns, a standard handgun and one much smaller.

She chose her bay, then put on the safety glasses and muff, and reaching for the standard gun, she took position. Unlike in the beginning, when all the steps of firing a gun seemed foreign and overwhelming to her, she found herself going through them naturally, instinctively.

"What pisses you off?" She heard Maverick's voice in her head. *"Channel it."*

But this time, it wasn't about what angered her that came to mind, it was what she stood to lose that filled her brain. There was so much uncertainty, and she knew that if she let her mind go there, she'd get lost in the mess, in the unknown, in the what-ifs. She needed to focus on her goals, not her obstacles.

Tala sucked in a deep breath, exhaling slowly, feeling her shoulders fall, then fired.

Every shot she fired went exactly where she'd intended it: chest, chest, chest, forehead, forehead, forehead. She emptied her magazine, then turned to see Vi watching her with a knowing smile.

431

"That-a girl," she said when Tala removed her muff.

"Mav worked with me. A lot," Tala said as she swapped guns, taking the small one that nearly fit entirely in the palm of her hand. "Do me a favor," she said with a pause as she looked away. "Look after Mila. When I'm gone, I mean." She shifted her gaze, stealing a look at her.

Vi was quiet for a moment, studying Tala with her beautiful blue eyes that reminded Tala of her own, of her mother's actually. "Declan told me what happened to her," she said after a long pause. "I understand why she's afraid."

Tala nodded. She and Mila had never talked about Declan's reaction to her story, to seeing the burn scars that were still evident of the torture she'd endured, faint as they were now. She wasn't sure they'd ever go completely away. Just like the two bullet wounds that had healed, she would carry them with her.

"Of course I'll look after her," Vi said. "Dec and I both will, whatever happens."

Tala pressed her lips together, frowning. The weight of realization settled on her as it dawned on her that this could really be goodbye. There were no guarantees, as life had shown her. She'd just made a painful goodbye, how could she make any more?

"You know, I show it differently than she does," Vi said slowly. "And while I understand why you have to go, it doesn't mean it's easy."

Tala nodded. "What if I can't do it?" she asked quietly. She didn't want to admit her fear. She wanted to be brave and determined and let those be her driving emotions. But deep down, the fear was still there. It was real.

"I wish I could stand here and tell you unequivocally that you will," Vi said. "But I can't. I believe in you, I believe that you can do this, but that's not really the same thing as saying that you will. The way I see it, you can't have success unless you're willing to fail. That's what sacrifice is, isn't it? It's having the courage to do what's right because it's right. No matter the price.

We can't have everything without risking it all. Maybe being brave and afraid go hand in hand, two sides of the same coin."

Tala considered this. It irritated her that she had any doubt in her mind at all. She'd been trained as Militia Forces, elite military, and she'd forged into danger without a second thought more times than she could count. So why the fear now?

Because it all mattered so much more than anything else ever had.

Tala took a deep breath, letting her lungs fill, and reminded herself that she was going to be present. She didn't want to spend her time in a frenzy, worrying about the things she couldn't control.

"For what it's worth," Vi said, "I do believe you have what it takes. You're strong enough to face it all."

"Thank you," Tala said, her voice low. "I'll have to keep that in mind when they have me parachute out of a plane over the city." She laughed, letting the tension in her shoulders relax.

"Would you really do that?" Vi asked with exhilaration on her face.

"Who knows?" she said with a shrug. "Let's just shoot." Tala turned back to the target on the opposite wall and raised the small gun. With a brief mental check, she fired.

Tala met Kane in their unit before it was time to meet with Addox. She collapsed onto the sofa after him, dropping her head into his lap. She smiled up at him through her lashes and thought to herself, as she often did, how good-looking he was, and like he often did, he made something stir deep in her belly.

"What?" he asked as he looked down at her, dragging his fingers through her hair splayed across his legs.

"Nothing," she said with a shrug and a smile she couldn't hide.

"Your cheeks are red." He grinned.

She let out a small laugh as she rubbed the inside of the ring on her finger with her thumb. It felt foreign, yet perfectly comfortable, like it had been made just for her to wear.

"How was your coffee?" she asked. She liked this, just the two of them, the quiet, no tension between them, no heavy hearts. Just them in a moment of contentment.

"It was good," he said, and she could see the joy in his eyes. "It's been strange all these months not having Max around."

"Think he'll go back to the Republic? Whenever that's possible?" she asked.

Kane shrugged. "He doesn't know. His work is there, even if it is for the government. But if the Republic fails to exist, who knows what that'll mean for him. For any of us."

Tala wondered what that would look like, a life without the Republic. With the world at her fingertips, what would she choose to do with her life?

"Think our group would disband if that day ever came?"

"Maybe," he said.

She reached up, running her finger along the scruff on the side of his face, tracing his jawline.

"I want to think about the future," she said in a whisper, "but I'm afraid to do so."

He nodded. "I understand. But when everything's unknown, anything's possible. Right?"

"Yeah," she said as she gazed up at him, their eyes meeting, holding each other. She thought back to the first time she'd ever seen those eyes. When they belonged to a stranger who had saved her life. When she'd woken up on the pavement outside that warehouse, so long ago, did her heart feel sure of him because it recognized them, even if her mind didn't immediately know them?

Their meeting was no accident. They were meant for each other. Not that it would always be easy, but it would always be worth it. And she would always fight for him, for them. Thias was her road to walk. While both Maverick and Kane would take it with her, it was ultimately up to her to go the distance.

Tala's pocket buzzed from her palm pad, then she heard Kane's spring to life, and she swallowed hard. Their time of quiet solitude had come to an end. Tomorrow was calling.

Tala and Kane met Maverick outside the leadership offices. She saw the same look in Maverick's eyes that she did in Kane's which was the same gnawing in her gut. None of them knew what to expect. Her emotions were coursing through her veins, and she slipped her hands into her pockets to steady them.

Selene rose briefly behind the desk, brushing a heavy curl away from her eyes. "Someone will be coming for you," she said, eyeing Kane like she always did. Tala couldn't help but crack a smile as they took a seat.

"Someone's coming for us?" she asked as she glanced at Kane, then Maverick.

Maverick leaned forward, his elbows on his knees. "I'm just eager for some details. I hate being in the dark."

Tala nodded, feeling it too. She hated all the anticipation which only strained her nerves and played with her mind. The echo of heavy footfalls started in the distance, growing louder with each step, making their way toward them. A moment later, a woman whom Tala knew immediately to be a soldier for the Unified military in her gray camo fatigues appeared from around a corner opposite the direction of Addox's office, of the conference room.

"Alexander, Ryan, Sergeant Sanders, follow me," she said, her voice sharp.

Tala and Maverick caught a glance at each other as they rose to their feet. Quickly, they followed behind the soldier as she led them down a foreign hallway. It was long and wide, and curved to the left, Selene's desk quickly disappearing behind them. There wasn't a single door nor virtual window in sight. Just an endless, empty corridor.

They finally came to a double door with a security panel in the wall. Without a word, the soldier pressed her palm to the screen, then entered a code. A second later, it lit up green, the doors clicking as they unlocked. She opened them and stepped aside, holding the door while each of them slipped past. Once inside, Tala heard the door close, the click as it locked, and she looked quickly over her shoulder as the soldier straightened to attention, her eyes looking past Tala.

Tala turned around, then felt her mouth drop as she looked out over a colossal oval room, lit dimly in a dark blue light. Rows of digital screens, four high, each at least five feet tall and wider than Tala could span with both arms, circled the entire perimeter of the room. Some screens were filled with detailed maps, others had grids, graphs, and numbers. Some played silent video footage.

"Holy…" Maverick mumbled under his breath.

"Yeah," Kane said, the same shock in his voice.

"There have got to be hundreds of screens in here," Tala said.

"Five hundred twenty-eight, to be exact," a woman said. Tala turned on her feet to see Victoria walking toward them, her stilettos clacking on the floor with each step.

"President Merritt," Maverick said, snapping to attention, automatically bringing his left hand to his brow in salute.

Tala straightened. She'd never saluted Victoria before, but she was a president and suddenly she couldn't help but think maybe she'd been too formal with her all these months.

"At ease," she said with a look at him. She was dressed in a fitted black dress with a belted waist, and even in the blue light, her hair was still copper-red, smooth and sleek, hanging to her shoulders. There was something very dignified about her, the way she stood, the way she looked, the way she spoke, her voice like velvet, kind but firm. Her eyes flitted between the three of them.

"Welcome to the PDCC," she said. "The Panorama Digital Command Center."

Tala's eyes wandered in fascination. In the middle of the oval room was a second-level balcony, and a glass enclosed third level above that. Rows of desks, three-deep, circled the room, two people to each, a hologram computer screen for each one. A few heads turned only briefly in their direction.

"We've expanded and upgraded this room over time, but this here was the main reason The Village was ever created," Victoria said with pride, a glint in her eyes. "It was the most secure facility in the entire United States before the Great War, arguably one of the most secure facilities in the world. While our headquarters is Camp Washington, we run everything from here."

"What're we doing in here?" Kane asked as he shoved his hands into the front pockets of his jeans.

"There are things," Victoria said, "that you need to know before going on this mission."

Tala cocked a brow as she glanced furtively at Kane.

"Ah, Colonel," Victoria said, turning as a man approached. He wore a hardened expression, his square jaw set. He was dressed sharply in a charcoal military dress uniform with insignia down the jacket sleeves and multicolored ribbons across his chest. "Tala, Kane, Sanders, this is Colonel Thornton."

Maverick once again snapped to attention, raising his hand in salute.

Colonel Thornton nodded. "At ease, Sergeant."

"Colonel Thornton is with Special Forces and will be overseeing your mission into Columbia City," Victoria said as she began to walk away, waving them along.

Tala looked at Maverick, tipping her head toward the Colonel. He gave her a furtive nod as they followed, walking along the curve of the room, the oversized screens to their left, each filled with data she didn't understand, until finally coming to a stop. In shades of dark and light blue, a map of the Republic of Columbia filled an eye-level screen, cities and major roadways lit up, all their lines looking like fractured glass.

Victoria turned to face them, her eyes, now dull and dark in the dim light, fixing briefly on Tala. "We have been putting countless hours into planning this mission, Operation Libertas," she said. "It has been a long time coming, and we are more than prepared to act, we are more than prepared to get you safely into the city."

"Safely?" Tala asked skeptically, almost cynically. Getting out had been anything but safe, how could they guarantee that going back in?

"That's right," the Colonel said. "A large team isn't going to be able to get anywhere near the Central Government building with you. President Alexander was clear about that. We're pushing our luck having you two with her." He looked at Kane with an unreadable expression. "I know you don't have any military training, but I understand you can use a gun and are good in physical combat. Captain Vulcan lobbied hard on your behalf."

Tala couldn't mask her surprise at this.

"Now," Colonel Thornton said, his eyes glancing between the three of them, "I'm confident we can get you to Columbia City. With limited complication."

"How?" she asked, still dubious.

"To begin, we're going to disable the power grid," Victoria said.

Tala's head snapped in her direction. "The power grid? The *entire* power grid?"

She nodded, her face deadpan.

"Is that even possible? It's thirteen hundred miles to the capital from here," Maverick said flatly. "You'd be blacking out the entire country."

"Yes, we would. And it's more than possible," she said. "For over a decade, we've been positioning ourselves throughout the Republic through Project Electrum, an international collaborative enterprise which has always been designed to target the power grid, among other critical infrastructure vulnerabilities."

Tala's jaw was slack. She was at a loss of words.

"I think I can shed some light on this," Elias said, approaching from the side, startling Tala. She turned to him, meeting his piercing gaze, a chill running through her body. He gave her a slow nod in hello.

She swallowed hard. "What is Project Electrum?"

"Before I was governor," Elias said, "I was a businessman. I owned a company called Headwater Electronics. We manufactured replacement parts for small electronic devices. I did well for myself. The political climate between the Colonies and the Republic at the time was strained, for many reasons that I won't bore you with. The Republic's biggest and most vocal dissenter at the time was Lakewood Colony's Governor Franklin."

Tala folded her arms across her chest and shifted on her feet as she listened.

"Fifteen years ago," he continued, "I was approached with an offer. Both highly lucrative and incredibly risky. It was two-fold. First was an investment opportunity overseas. I was introduced to Liu Wei, or Liu Zong Cai, whom I'm sure you're more familiar with as Ambassador Liu."

Tala straightened as she recalled the Chinese man Vaughn introduced her to at President Royer's birthday party. He'd asked her about a collection being exhibited in the museum. He'd sat at their table for dinner.

She nodded. "I know who he is."

"Liu Zong Cai owns a very large electronics manufacturing company outside Beijing called Accelerated Tech. It is also the parent company of many smaller companies that appear to have no affiliation with each other. Unless you know where to look. And I," he said with a brief pause and a smirk, "am his invisible partner. The second part of the offer was to depose Governor Franklin, then to be his replacement."

"Why you?" Kane asked, his voice gruff. He took a small step closer to Tala, their arms brushing against each other.

"Aside from my money, because I shared an equal dislike for the Republic. Though my opposition wasn't quite so public. And I already had good standing in the community as a business owner. I was groomed for leadership for the sole purpose of quieting the tension between the Colonies and the Republic, to sustain an alliance," he said.

"If you opposed them, why would you work with them?" Tala asked.

"So that ultimately I could work against them," Elias said calmly. "You see, it wasn't just anybody who approached me with this offer, who introduced me to Liu, who practically voted me in as governor himself. It was Jameson Alexander."

Tala's breath caught. "My father?" she asked, her mouth agape.

Victoria used a small remote in her hand that Tala hadn't noticed to pull up a photo of Jameson on the screen, replacing the map of the Republic. Tala looked up at the solemn face before her and felt an unexpected rise of emotion inside. She hadn't seen that face in eleven years. Growing up, she'd always been told she looked like her mother, but as a fifteen-year-old girl, she'd always dismissed it. Seeing her father now, she couldn't help but see a small reflection of herself.

"I…" she stammered with confusion, "I still don't understand. My father was director of Militia Forces for the Republic. Are you trying to say that he wasn't loyal to them?" The words sounded as preposterous out of her mouth as they did in her head. When she thought of her father, he was only ever working, a true patriot. He was an Alexander, the Republic was his legacy.

"Jameson became disillusioned with the Republic at a young age," Elias said. "I only ever knew him as a freethinker. He rarely accepted an idea or notion without all the information and careful consideration."

"No. No," she snapped, her voice rising. "I know my father. He was loyal to the Republic. It's what got him killed."

Elias took a slow breath. "It was your father who organized the Rebels, who brought them together with those who were displaced and still believed in the United States," he said patiently.

"See for yourself," Victoria said calmly as she clicked the remote. A new image appeared on the screen. A younger Jameson, though still undeniably him, surrounded by a group of young men and women holding what Tala had come to recognize as the American flag.

"But," she said, her thoughts swarming in her head. They were dizzying, and she reached out to Kane. "I found a journal entry of his. I know his handwriting. He made it very clear how he felt about the Republic," she protested as she recalled the scanned document she'd found on Thias's computer… *they are willing to make the hard choices… The Republic of Columbia is the future.*

"My father's rhetoric seemed to be some of the inspiration for Thias," she said, goosebumps raising across her skin. She pulled her arms around her waist, hugging herself. Thias's cold words were burnt into her mind, imprinted in her memory. She could hear them in her head like he had just spoken them:

"We have to be willing to make the tough decisions."

Assassinating President Royer, she knew, wasn't a tough decision for Thias. He knew what he wanted, and nothing was going to stand in his way.

"There was an incident about three years into his position as director of Militia Forces, when Jameson's allegiance with the Republic was questioned, and it required an elaborate coverup," Victoria said. "Did it ever occur to you how a handwritten journal entry survived the fire?"

Tala looked at Kane, his expression hard, but she saw the conflict in his eyes.

"The Republic tracks communication from their leaders, and Jameson used an encrypted device to make contact with someone in the Rebels' organization. His transmission was picked up, and less than twenty-four hours later, he noticed a break-in at your family home. It was his immaculate attention to detail that raised the red flag as he noticed his safe had been moved. Just enough to catch his attention," she said as she tucked a strand of hair behind her ear.

"The Rebels launched into action to do damage control, to shift suspicion away from him," she continued.

"It was fabricated?" Tala asked.

She nodded. "And planted in a safe-deposit box in Columbia Central Bank. It was meant to be found. And that's how it survived the fire. It wasn't in your house," she said. "This situation was the first time we were able to put into action Project Electrum. By that time, the project was two years in the making."

"What is the project?" Kane asked. "You've mentioned it more than once, but you've yet to say what it is."

"Project Electrum was the entire reason Elias and Ambassador Liu went into business together," Victoria said. "Accelerated Tech produced high-level internet routers that were then purchased by the Republic, due to a government contract negotiated by Jameson. In two years, they were everywhere, in all levels of government.

"Those routers had vulnerabilities programed into their firmware, malware capable of being triggered remotely. Through this access and sophisticated artificial intelligent viruses, we can acquire data and credentials for anyone who synced to them at any time. Each router allows us to access sensitive information on entire networks rather than having to hack individual devices and computers." While her voice was steady, her eyes were alive. "This gave us the ability to control the information used in the investigation against your father."

Tala opened her mouth to speak, but nothing came out. She once again looked up at the image on the screen before her, her father not just holding the flag, but draped in it. There was something about him in that photo that was different than what she remembered. Sure, she saw the same deep blue eyes, the sandy blond hair, the long face and slightly hooked nose, but there was something bright in his eyes, in his smile. His face lacked the taut expression she knew him to always have. This was a look she'd never seen on him before.

"Are you trying to say that Accelerated Tech has been filling the Republic with compromised routers for over a decade?" Maverick asked, speaking for the first time.

"That's exactly what we're saying," Elias said with a rare smile curled on the corner of his mouth. Much like his wife's, his eyes had a gleam in them.

"Am I to assume that Reformed China isn't really the ally the Republic believes them to be?" Tala asked, thinking back to how friendly the ambassador and Vaughn had been with each other.

"No one is," Elias said with the shrug of a shoulder. "For a very short window of time, the Republic of Columbia was synonymous with hope, progress, with prosperity, and for those reasons, it rose very quickly to power. It was a favorite for the people, as well as other countries looking for allies. They became a force to be reckoned with. But has it occurred to you why no one has come to their defense since its conflict with DeSoto began? Or when the rebellion within its borders started? The Republic is a tyrant, and it has alienated itself from everyone else. People simply try to play nice to keep the peace. But even as we speak, some of the countries they believe to be their biggest allies are quietly working against them."

"Most of the routers in the Republic have been dormant, waiting on a command from a virus designed to exploit the vulnerabilities within their firmware," Victoria said. "Others have slowly been probing networks, collecting information, analyzing data, and planting custom sub-viruses and trojans into computers and networks for many years." She used the remote in her hand to bring up another map of the Republic, small markings in both red and green scattered throughout the country. "Each red X you see on this map is the location of a power plant or facility. We have accounted for every magnetohydrodynamic, nuclear, solar, and fusion plant in the country."

"And all power plants are federally owned and operated," Tala said, the picture becoming clearer. "It allows the government to control all electricity." She recalled the nightly scheduled blackouts in each sector of Columbia City. "You compromise one, you compromise it all."

"I get the others, but how do you cut solar?" Maverick asked.

"Excess solar is pumped back into the power grid because of the high electricity demand. It's not stored. We send a reverse power surge into the solar parks and it damages the installations, rendering them useless," Victoria said. "The goal isn't to destroy for the sake of it. We'll need as many resources as possible to support and sustain the people after the Republic's fall."

"And what about the Militia Forces bases?" Maverick asked, stepping up closely to the map.

"The bases are marked in green, and they all run on power grids separate from the civilian grid," Victoria said.

"After Accelerated Tech, Liu and I created ConnectSys, a subsidiary company that produced next generation military-grade routers that have been used specifically for MF bases and facilities," Elias said.

"So you cut power, but there are bound to be facilities that are backed up with generators. What's to stop them from still locating us and scrambling jets to intercept us, or even retaliate and bomb another civilian sector?" Maverick asked, crossing his arms, his expression hardened.

"We have infiltrated all utility and telecommunication networks, as well as all control systems. When we trigger those A.I. viruses, we will then have the ability to intercept all communication. Remote access will give us operational control to interfere with early defense warning systems and take down signal defense. They will only see what we want them to see," Victoria said. "In addition, it gives us unilateral control of all military networks, bringing all installations to a halt."

"Until their tech agents figure out how to close these backdoors," Maverick said, but his words barely registered with Tala.

"Don't worry, we have people on the inside too. Bombs destroyed us last time. This, this is a different kind of warfare. We're trying to spare as many lives as possible," Victoria said. "The Republic thinks the world is run on hardware, but the truth today is that it's run on software. This will be an attack they never saw coming."

"If you had all this access when Kane was abducted, why didn't you use it then?" Tala asked, edge in her voice.

"This infiltration allows us to target the whole, not search for a needle in a stack of needles," Victoria said, holding Tala's gaze. "Our technology was never meant to be used in that capacity."

Tala looked back to the screen, but her father's face was gone, replaced by the map. Her mind was reeling with all the information just thrown at her. How was it that the people who'd raised her, that she'd lived side-by-side with for most of her life, turned out to be nothing but strangers to her? A decade after their deaths, Tala was discovering a new side to all of them. Jameson, Brit, Thias, Tala: who were each of them really? No one was on the inside who they played on the outside. Defiance ran thick in their bloodline.

"He really did all this?" she asked, her voice quiet, not entirely sure anyone heard her. Except for Kane.

Victoria reached out, placing a gentle hand on Tala's arm. "This was his life's work. He wanted a better world." Her hand fell back to her side, and she frowned. "You should know that Jameson, he was the first recognized leader of the United States after the Great War. Before him, we were all just pieces. He brought us together."

"Does my mother fit into this at all?" Tala asked. She was afraid of the answer, afraid she already knew. Brit had worked for the Republic while her husband, Tala now knew, worked against it.

"She doesn't," Victoria said. "Her career, her work, it kept her from ever knowing the truth."

"And yet he died at the hands of the Republic because of her," Tala said. There was never any justice. The Republic just took and took and took. She looked at Kane, his eyes soft as they fell over her, and he reached out, brushing a strand of hair out of her face.

He turned to Victoria, gave Elias a quick look. "All these years you've been quietly preparing the battlefield." His voice was deep and strong.

She nodded, her lips curling into a knowing grin. "And now we pull the trigger."

TWENTY-SIX

Kane rested his hand on the small of Tala's back as they left the secured offices, Maverick on their heels. They walked in silence, each of them no doubt processing all the information that had been thrown at them. He still wasn't sure what he would say to her about the revelations regarding her father. It was something none of them saw coming, and he knew her head was swimming. There were too many secrets buried among her family. He'd hated his father, but at least he knew who he was. Tala would never truly know her parents.

After they left the PDCC, they were taken to a briefing room. It was a large room, though nothing compared with the command center, with detailed maps of Columbia City on large screens, and a 3D digital image of the city that Colonel Thornton was able to manipulate. There, he precisely laid out the comprehensive operational details and directives to them and the other elite soldiers of the first wave of the attack.

Operation Libertas would be conducted in three waves. The first targeted top Republic officials: Chief Justice Mikel Murdo, Interim Chancellor of International Affairs Lev Patton, and President Thias Alexander. For the second, tactical teams would simultaneously raid all government facilities throughout the country, including the Central Government building after Thias was apprehended, as well as all leadership residences. The third wave had the largest scope with both land and air assault as Unified and coalition troops, launching from points around the Colonies and neighboring countries, would seize control of all Militia Forces facilities and bases. And it would all happen in rapid succession.

There didn't seem to be a single detail unaccounted for. Kane had never seen anything like it in his lifetime. He was sure the Republic of Columbia would be left spinning. But there was a gnawing deep in his stomach as he wondered what came next. Win, lose, or draw, what would be left?

He glanced furtively at Tala. Short wisps of hair had fallen loose from her ponytail and now framed her face. Her expression was a serene one. Without anything to say, he simply reached for her hand. She took a breath, looking at him, then gave him a small smile. They both knew it wasn't a real smile, it wasn't a genuine smile. But it was something.

"You guys hungry?" Maverick asked as the three of them descended the stairs that overlooked the City Center. It was the first time any of them had spoken since leaving the mission briefing. A glance at the nearly vacant atrium below told Kane they'd missed lunch.

He felt his sudden hunger at the thought of food. "Yeah."

"Think I'm going to grab something from the convenience store," Maverick said, still in step behind them. "I need to spend some time with Mila after that."

Kane nodded and looked at Tala. "What do you want to do?"

"The convenience store is fine," she said. There was a faraway look in her eyes that he couldn't read, and that unsettled him.

They once again fell quiet, their footsteps echoing off the tile, until they reached the main floor. There were a few small groups of people still lingering in the City Center, but it was mostly empty as they wound their way between the tables, cutting across rather than walking around the giant atrium.

"Kane!" He heard his named called out from behind them as they approached the convenience store's entrance. He cringed, knowing the voice.

Tala squeezed his hand a little firmer as she turned around, quicker than him. Wren made her way toward them at a brisk pace. Her face was tight, and he could hear her erratic heart.

He sighed loudly. "What do you want?" He hadn't spoken with Wren in weeks, and he wasn't exactly in the mood to do so in that moment either.

Wren didn't stop walking until she was uncomfortably close, only feet away from them. Kane could reach his hand out to touch her she was so close. He took a step back, but Tala didn't move.

"What can we do for you?" Tala asked coolly, an impassive expression on her face.

"I'm not here to talk to you," Wren snapped, her eyes narrowing as she looked Tala up and down. Her distaste obnoxiously obvious.

"What do you want?" he repeated impatiently.

"Is it true?" Wren asked, her attention shifting away from Tala and on to him.

He shrugged. "Don't know. I'll need more details about what you mean," he said with a small smirk. Of course he knew what she was referring to, but he couldn't help himself.

"Are you really getting married?" she asked, sounding hurt.

He resisted the urge to roll his eyes. He didn't understand her emotion. He'd more than made it clear how he felt about her. The last thing he wanted was an argument with Tala on the eve of their mission. He glanced at her, trying to read her. Though she didn't look at him, she gave him a small squeeze of his hand.

"Why yes, we are," Tala said. Though her voice was even, she put an emphatic smile on her face that he had to suppress a chuckle at.

"I said I wasn't here to talk to you. You don't deserve him," Wren sneered.

"You don't have a clue," Tala said firmly. "But it's all beyond your comprehension." She turned to him. Reaching out, she ran her hand across his arm. "I'll grab something for you. You can deal with this," she said, cocking her head toward Wren. Then she turned and walked with Maverick into the store.

"Yes, Wren, it's true," he said as he crossed his arms over his chest. "Why does it matter to you?"

Wren looked like she'd just been slapped, and he felt his irritation rising. He couldn't recall ever seeing this side of her before. But the truth was that she'd only ever been in his life for one reason, shallow as it was, and he had never really known her. He purposely didn't get to know people, all people, to protect his identity. But Max had called it. He'd seen it in her, and Kane silently cursed himself for being such an idiot. What he couldn't understand was why she was still holding on to all of it.

"I… I figured your little fling with her would've flung by now," she said as she put a hand on her hip.

He sighed, glancing to the side at Tala as she stood in front of a cooler filled with prepackaged food across the convenience store. "Things with Tala have never been a fling," he said matter-of-factly, turning back to Wren. Her pants were tight and low on her hips, her shirt, more than just fitted, crept up her waist, and her eyes were lined with thick black liner. She was attractive, sure, but she had nothing on Tala, and he couldn't help but shake his head, wondering how he'd been interested in her in the first place.

She grunted under her breath. "I don't get it, I just don't. When we were together you were—"

"I already told you," he said, cutting her off, his voice rising. A few heads in the City Center glanced in their direction. "We were never together. It was a couple times, but we were never together," he said, lowering his voice. The last thing he wanted was a spectacle.

"Because you made it clear that you didn't do relationships," she said sharply.

He clenched his jaw in frustration. They'd had this conversation already, and he was tired of defending himself.

"How'd you two meet anyway? I mean, it's not exactly like you ran in the same circles. I can't imagine some Republic Nameless could've just shown up at the door of her luxurious manor along the bay. The *princess of the Republic*," she said. "So how'd you meet?" she asked, tapping her toes on the floor.

"I don't have to give you a history," he said, his brows furrowing. "The point is that we met. It's never going to happen between you and me. Even if Tala wasn't in the picture."

"I could've made you happy," she said, her anger turning to sadness, her mouth turned down.

"I'm sorry we ever got involved. And it's time you move on," he said. His mother would've told him to be gentle, to be kind, that she was upset, but he was past caring about anything where Wren was concerned.

"Can we at least be friends?" she asked, her desperation written across her face.

He wanted to laugh. It was a ridiculous thought. "I don't think so," he said, shaking his head firmly.

Her shoulders fell, and she looked crestfallen. She turned, looking into the convenience store, and from the corner of his eye, he saw Tala laughing with Maverick about something. Then Wren looked back at Kane, tears welling in her eyes, and she nodded. "You're making a mistake," she said quietly.

"No. I'm not," he said. "And this conversation's over." With his lips pursed, he sidestepped her and made his way toward the store. He heard Wren's shaky breath from behind him, and a moment later, the rapid thumping from her shoes on the floor as she hurried off.

"She looked like you shattered her heart," Maverick said when Kane appeared beside them in the snack food aisle.

"She finally get the message?" Tala asked as she looked up at him, her hands full with two packaged sandwiches, two bottled drinks, and a large bag of pretzels.

"I'd say you really know how to pick 'em," Maverick said with a smirk, "but you redeemed yourself with this one." He nodded toward Tala.

"Let's just say that I've realized how stupid I once was," Kane said as he reached for the drinks, taking them from her. "You're going to drop something."

"It was a fine balancing act," she said. "I had it all perfectly in my grasp."

"Yeah. Okay," he said in amusement as he turned and made his way toward the front counter.

"I see how it is," she said as she followed after him. "Swoop in at the end and look like the hero."

He glanced over his shoulder and smirked, then set the drinks on the counter, Tala putting her things next to them.

"That's what I do," he said as the clerk began to ring up each item. "I thought it was what you like about me. I mean, it's pretty much how we met," he said, eyeing her beside him.

He saw the tic in her jaw as she resisted a smile, but there was a gleam in her eyes that was unmistakable. He loved that gleam.

"Whatever you need to believe," she said with a shrug.

He couldn't help but chuckle as he looked over at her. And for a brief moment, he forgot all that was looming ahead of them.

They took their seats at their usual table in the City Center, right beside the koi stream. Though few people sat at any of the tables, there were still plenty of people passing through the large atrium or walking the perimeter hallways.

Kane opened his packaged sandwich, one slice of bread slightly soggy. But it was better than nothing. Feeling the hunger in his stomach, he took a bite.

"How do you guys feel about the mission?" Maverick asked.

Kane and Tala looked up from their food, but neither of them spoke. He wasn't sure how to respond. Was this the time for encouraging words? Was this the time for uncertain goodbyes?

"Oh, come on," Maverick said, cocking his head to the side. "You're both thinking it. I'm just the one to finally come out with it."

"I think I've underestimated the United States," Tala said as she reached in the bag for some pretzels.

Maverick nodded in agreement. "I've never underestimated the Unified military. I've been all over, to bases other than just Camp Washington. Some in Pacifica, some in Tahari. But this infiltration into their computer networking, it's both impressive and disturbing."

"Where does the power start and stop? Where do the rights of the people begin and end? And who determines all that?" Kane asked, his mind spinning all over again as he sunk back in his chair.

Tala and Maverick went quiet, exchanging glances. There were quiet murmurs of conversation coming from a few tables away, and Kane looked briefly in their direction. Two older men in a deep discussion, blissfully unaware of what was to come. He envied their ignorance, their ability to sit at that table, not giving their safety and liberties a second thought.

"It begs the question," Maverick said between bites, "is there really such a thing as freedom, or is it just some utopian ideal?"

There may be some truth in that, Kane thought, but if there was no such thing as freedom, then what was he fighting for? What was it that he was risking his life for? What was the point of it for any of them?

He looked at Tala beside him and remembered the moment he realized he loved her, standing on a pier at a beach in Walhurst. It had been a warm day, but windy. It was the way she looked at him, her eyes as blue as the sky, that was arresting. It took down every wall around him. She'd leaned into him, her body against his, and it was that one simple movement that had completely undone him. He'd lost himself in her that day. Or perhaps he'd found himself. Maybe both.

In the Republic, there was never a chance for them. A future where they were free to be together was what mattered to him. This war meant many different things to everyone. But all it took was having just one person worth fighting for. Tala was his person.

"Hey guys." Kane looked up, shaking his thoughts from his head as he saw Max approaching. He couldn't help but smile at the sight of him. The world as they knew it was in rapid evolution, but Max, he was exactly the same as Kane had ever known him to be. He was steadfast, and there was something comfortable in his familiarity. He was the other person in his life worth fighting for.

"Where've you been?" Kane asked, sitting upright.

Max shrugged. "My unit. I can't use that computer in the secured offices anymore, but they gave me a tablet. I've been working on some stuff," he said. Though his voice was casual, Kane picked up the slightest rise in pitch, and he immediately knew Max had been up to something. He was working on more than just *some stuff*. With the others around, however, he kept his curiosity to himself.

Max took an open chair beside Maverick. "Sandwiches?" he asked, reaching for an empty container. "The chicken salad was better." He let out a nasal laugh.

"I imagine most things would be," Maverick said as he pushed back, away from the table, crumpling a napkin in his hands. "Sorry to bail on you all, but I'm going to find my sister before I need to get some sleep."

"I'll come with. For just a little bit," Tala said as she glanced at Kane. Maybe he wasn't the only to pick up on the change in Max after all. She placed her hand gently on his shoulder as she stood, giving him a small squeeze.

"I'll find you later," he said with a half-smile as he looked up at her, and she nodded.

"I know they're all good people," Max said when Tala and Maverick were out of earshot, "but it's just easier to be around everyone when you're here too."

"That's because you're antisocial," Kane said with a smirk.

"Not true," Max said defensively.

"It's true," he said with a nod. "Now, you going to tell me what you've been up to?"

"I can't hide anything from you," Max said.

"Nope."

"Well," he said as he leaned forward, his elbows on the table, "with you going back into Columbia City, I did some digging."

Kane raised a brow. "What kind of digging? Where?"

"The kind that let me know what risks you're walking into. Thias's computer," he said quietly under his breath.

"What?" Kane's mouth dropped. "How… how'd you manage that?" Max knew nothing about the hacked routers, which meant he'd managed to get into Thias's computer on his own.

"It wasn't as hard as you'd think. If you know what you're doing," he said flatly. "I told Tala once that there weren't many things I couldn't do on a computer. I didn't realize you needed to be reminded of this."

"But how? And why?" Kane imagined the number of people worldwide that could accomplish this could be counted on one hand.

"With a little bit of digging, I got the email address of his assistant. I spoofed a bogus job application that was bugged with a very elaborate, very nasty virus, so when she opened it, she opened her computer up to me. Then all it took was an email she sent to Thias. Boom. With a little Max-designed decryption software, I got into his computer."

"Sometimes, I think you're too smart for your own good. And sometimes I wonder how you and I are even friends. I've got no skills like you," Kane said, impressed.

"Brains and brawn," he said with a shrug. "My mental acuity, you're physical capabilities. It's what makes us the perfect duo."

"So, what'd you go digging for?" Kane asked.

"I wanted to know what he knew about you. We don't need a repeat of the things that happened with the chancellor."

"I think it's safe to assume that whatever Vaughn knew, Thias likely knows too," he said. "He had his own go at me."

Max wore a grim frown as he nodded. "I dug so deeply into his computer, looking for anything relating to you or Project Magnar. I don't think they know the extensiveness of your abilities. No one anticipated everything they turned you all into in that experiment. And I know for certain they don't know your identity. How's that even possible?"

Kane folded his arms across his chest and gave Max a knowing look.

"I thought they… did things to you," he said, swallowing hard, his voice falling.

"They did," Kane said flatly. So much had happened since his captivity that everything he'd gone through seemed small in comparison. Though it really wasn't. It was simply easier to push it away. That wasn't the first time in his life he'd been brought to the edges of hell. And he'd gotten through then. He had managed to hold out on them. He survived, again, and that was what mattered. "They found me to be a very… obstinate person," he said. He really didn't want to elaborate. He didn't want to relive those memories.

"Gee, I had no idea," Max said with a welcomed smirk to lighten things. "You really gave them nothing? Not even your name? You were there for almost four days."

He let out a deep sigh. Despite himself, his mind wandered back. In the beginning, he was dosed with just enough lithium to keep him lucid, but under control. Who was he? How'd he know Tala? What was their relationship? Where was Tala? How'd she get involved with the Rebels? What was the UR's plan? Without the answers he wanted, Vaughn's frustration rose, and his temper flared. Kane was drugged more and more, and he recalled his interrogation between bouts of consciousness. "I told him only what I wanted him to know. I was turned into a super-soldier, remember?" he said. "Turns out, I was made to hold up in tough situations."

"Maybe," Max said. "Though I think you had more of that in you before your transformation than you give yourself credit for."

Ismet would undoubtedly agree. "So he doesn't know who I am, and he kind of knows what I can do."

"You have to be so careful," Max said, a look of desperation flashing in his eyes. "He's going to know you'll try to go with her."

"I'm not letting her go alone," he said sternly. "You're not going to talk me out of this."

"I'm just saying you need to—"

"Be careful," Kane said with a clipped voice. "No more or less than any of us going on this mission. I get it, Max. But this is war. And battles aren't won from the sidelines."

Max's shoulders fell, and Kane instantly regretted his harshness. Max had known him longer and better than anyone ever had. He'd been by his side when they were boys, had hidden him for years in his pod, being his every lifeline. If there was someone who deserved to be worried about him, it was Max.

"I'm sorry," Kane said quickly.

"No, I understand," he said, gazing through his glasses at him. There was something in his eyes that put Kane on edge. Max had never been one to pity him, ever, but there was a way he was looking at him now that he never had before.

"I also have some other information," Max said after a moment. "The two guys you escaped the Republic with…"

"Gerrit and Burke," Kane said, nodding.

"It was their sister's husband who'd gone missing?" he asked.

"That's right. Corban Young."

"I found him," Max said.

"What?" Kane straightened in his seat. "Where? Is he alive?"

"Think so. He's in a work camp near Alexandria. I found a record of him in one of the ordnance factories. He's being detained as a political prisoner."

"Political?" Kane couldn't hide his exasperation. "He was looking for car parts for crying out loud."

"The point is, he's alive."

"I need to tell them. I need to call them," Kane said.

"I can make that happen," Max said.

"Good. Anything else you found in that computer?" he asked.

"Just what I went looking for. He's the president, there's an endless supply of info. What else was I supposed to be looking for?"

"Just making sure," Kane said as he pushed away from the table, then stood, Max doing the same. "You know," he said as they made their way across the City Center toward the stairs. "You are every bit the genius you say you are."

"I know," Max said with a shrug. While his face was impassive, there was a smile in his eyes. "Think I'll be able to go back into the Republic after all this?"

"You'd still want to?" Kane asked.

"I don't know anything else. Besides, if it's not the corrupted mess it is now, why not?"

"If things go as planned, the Republic will dissolve, be absorbed by the United States. That's the future we're fighting for," he said.

"Democracy, elected leaders and all, huh? That's a world that seems too good to be true," Max said. "Though in my experience, things rarely go as planned. If ever."

Kane was quiet, knowing too well that he was right. Maybe that fact alone was what created the dread that was gnawing at him deep inside. But even if Max was brave enough to say it aloud, Kane still wasn't.

On the fifth floor, they entered the living quarters and made their way down a quiet hallway to Max's guest unit. It looked exactly like the first unit Kane had stayed in with Tala when he first arrived at The Village. It wasn't all that unlike the one he was in now, just with bunks rather than a full-size bed.

Max took a seat on the sofa with a tablet in his hand. In less than a minute, he looked up, a victorious grin on his face.

"That was fast," Kane said, sitting beside him.

"Public numbers are about the easiest thing in the world to locate," he said dully, handing the tablet to Kane as he pulled out his palm pad.

Nervously, Kane dialed the number Max found. It rang three… four… five times, and Kane's shoulders dropped. It was the one thing he could think to do to repay them for all they'd done for him, and now he couldn't even reach them to tell them.

"Hello?" a voice said just as Kane was about to end the call. A moment later, the video connected, and Kane was looking into the eyes of Marina as she peered out from beneath a head of dark curls.

"Kane?" she asked, her mouth going slack at the sight of him.

He nodded and grinned. "Yeah, it's me. How're you?" It seemed awkward to try to make small talk, but he also didn't know how to launch right into what he knew.

"I… I'm fine," she said, her surprise still etched across her face. The camera on her palm pad shifted, and Kane saw baby Iris, who had more than doubled in size, perched on Marina's hip. Sometimes it felt that time was standing still, but looking at the baby, who had been nothing more than a newborn months earlier, the passage of time was unmistakable. "Guys!" Marina yelled out, her mouth too close to the palm pad, and Kane recoiled slightly at her loud voice.

At first, there was silence as Kane waited patiently, the camera focused not on Marina or Iris anymore but rather across the kitchen. Kane could make out a stockpot on the stove, a sink full of dishes.

The sound of footsteps filled Kane's ears, faint at first, then quickly growing louder until Burke came into view.

"Kane?" he said, his surprise mirroring his sister's.

"Hey," he said, nodding.

"Man, we thought we'd never see you again," Gerrit said, appearing beside Burke.

"Marina still there?" Kane asked.

"I'm here," she said, turning the camera toward herself for a moment, just long enough to give a small smile.

"You still up north?" Burke asked.

"Yep," he said.

"Still with your girl?" Gerrit asked with a smirk.

"Definitely," Kane said as he grinned.

"Good. At least all our efforts weren't futile," he said with a small chuckle.

"What can we do for you? I doubt you've called just to catch up," Marina said, though the camera remained on her brothers. She was just as he remembered her, no-frills, right to the point.

"I have some news. About Corban," he said.

"What?" Marina gasped, the camera whipping around to face her.

"A friend of mine found him registered in a work camp. Near Alexandria, in the Republic," he said.

"He's alive?" she asked under her breath, and Kane nodded.

"Do you know what he's doing, what the conditions are like?" Gerrit asked, his voice somewhere in the background.

"Does it matter?" Marina snapped. "You're sure he's alive?" she asked. Her eyes, pooling with tears, met Kane's through the camera.

"According to the most recent information he is. He's working in an ordnance factory," he said. "But I don't know the conditions."

She nodded as she took a deep breath that shuddered when she exhaled. "What do we do? How do we get him out?"

"Mare, there's no way of getting him out," Burke said. "It's not like we can stroll up to the factory and ask for his release."

"What was he arrested for?" she asked, ignoring her brother.

Kane was quiet, unsure how to answer.

"It doesn't matter," she said after a brief moment of silence.

"Is anyone doing anything about what's happening?" Gerrit asked. "We've heard things. Bombings in the Republic. Clara City was hit hard. But also that Militia Forces have been pushed back out of DeSoto. Pacifica and Tahari and Mazanada are all helping. Do you know anything? You have to know something. We've seen Tala Alexander's messages that have broadcasted." There was an urgency in his voice. The camera was turned back in his direction. Both brothers wore hardened expressions on their faces.

Kane swallowed. The last thing he wanted was to get their hopes up. But maybe some hope, even just a little, would go a long way. Marina had been without her husband for months. Baby Iris had yet to know her own father.

"There are plans," Kane said cautiously.

"But you can't say more than that," Burke said. It was a statement, not a question.

"No," Kane said.

"People talk," Burke said. "There are whispers. It's all bigger than the Revos," he said quietly, as though it were dangerous to say aloud.

Kane pursed his lips.

"I told you I wouldn't get involved," Marina said as she turned the camera back to herself. "I didn't help you because I was afraid. But you followed through. You did as you promised. You found him." He heard the regret in her voice. He saw it on her face.

He shook his head. "You helped me more than you could imagine," he said firmly. "You didn't have to run out and pledge to the Revos to still make a difference. And I'm grateful."

She nodded. "We're all going to have to decide sooner rather than later where we stand," she said as she adjusted Iris. "I know where I'll put my allegiance." She straightened her back, her chin lifting.

"I promise to play my part," Kane said after a moment. "To do whatever I can to get Corban back to you. For you and for Iris. I swear to that."

She pressed her lips in a line and gave him a grim smile. "Know that I'm more than grateful for what you've done already. I don't regret anything I did for you. Thank you, Kane. Good luck and stay safe." She turned the camera away from her, back to Burke and Gerrit.

"Yeah, good luck, man," Burke said while Gerrit let out a deep sigh and gave a single nod of his head.

A moment later, the call ended and the screen on Kane's palm pad went black. He looked up at Max who was watching him closely.

"What if we fail and nothing changes?" Kane blurted out before he could stop himself. He couldn't contain his worry anymore. "Who holds Thias accountable then?"

"We can't afford to think like that," Max said. "And you seem to be overlooking one very important factor in all of this." He gave his glasses a nudge back up the bridge of his nose.

Kane cocked his head in confusion. "And what's that?"

"That you were made for this exact thing."

It took him a moment to understand. "A super-soldier," he said after a minute.

Max smiled, a conspiratorial look on his face. "Exactly. The irony is that you're a weapon being used against the Republic. I don't think revenge could be any sweeter."

Kane couldn't help but let out a low laugh. Max was right. And there was a lot to want revenge for.

"Thanks for coming," Addox said when Kane stepped through the doorway of his office. He motioned toward the seating area, the virtual windows along the wall showing a calm, sunny day outside. Not even the smallest boughs in the trees moved, birds flying from branch to branch. The snow on the ground melted now.

"I wasn't sure if you'd come or not, after our last conversation," Addox said as he sat. He leaned forward on his elbows, closing a small amount of distance between them as Kane sat opposite him.

"I figured this was not a good time to be stubborn," Kane said, crossing his arms.

"I didn't think you knew how not to be stubborn," Addox said. His voice was light, but his expression was indifferent.

"And you're one to talk?" he asked.

Silence fell between them, their gazes locked together. Kane almost forgot how much of their mother Addox had in his eyes. It was easier to always look past it, but in that moment, it was unmistakable. There was a reflection of her in them as Addox looked back at him.

You'd hardly suspect they were brothers if you didn't know. The only things they seemed to have in common were their facial structure, thanks to Ismet, and that they were incredibly headstrong, also thanks to Ismet.

"I'll be in the PDCC tonight and tomorrow during Operation Libertas," Addox said. "Even though I'll have no operational control, I'll be following the situation from here."

Kane wasn't sure what to say to that. Did he want his brother to monitor the mission? Did he even care? Either way, it wouldn't change the outcome.

"Tell me something before you leave," Addox said. "I spent years looking for you, and when I had my suspicions about what'd happened to you, well, it ate at me. I thought I should've done more back then. What I want to know is if you have any regrets. If you could go back and do it all over again, would you?"

Kane took a moment to respond. "Choosing to do or not to do something over again and having regrets aren't necessarily the same thing," Kane said, clearing his voice, sitting up straighter. "Regret is what you have over your own choices. I had no choice in the things that were done to me.

"But the truth is, I'd have to say no to both of those questions. I was a cocky, stubborn kid, but I think those attributes are what got me through my years in the research facility. Ismet would've been an ass whether I was a good or bad kid. I don't regret being the latter. And as for what was done to me, well, it was one of the worst things ever, and I'd never wish it on anyone. But it made me who I am, and it brought me to where I am. It's how I met Tala. And I'd never change anything that would change that."

Addox went quiet as his gaze fell briefly to the floor, his shoulders sagging. "You know, I envy you," he said after a minute, looking back up. "I know your life's been hell, but what you and Tala have, that'll never be me. I know there are no promises, but if the both of you get through this mission, you'll go on and live a life together. At least, that's my hope for you."

"I don't dare think about that, hope for what I want on the other side," Kane admitted, his voice was hoarse as he spoke. "The only thing I can do right now is focus on the job. Nothing will ever happen until that's over. And I don't dare test fate."

"Destiny doesn't guarantee forever," Addox said quietly. "I get it. I'd like to tell you I'll look out for her if something happens to you, but she's already got people for that."

Kane nodded. "Still means something that you would."

He didn't particularly like Addox, though he certainly didn't hate him. Not anymore. He'd done what he had to to survive in life just as Kane had. He couldn't fault him for that. As they sat in silence, Kane couldn't help but wonder if maybe the best thing their parents had ever given them was each other. They were brothers, for better or worse. They didn't have to be friends. There was already a bond between them that could never be severed, and maybe that was all that mattered.

That afternoon, Tala and Kane got their unit as dark as they could so they would be able to get some sleep, the only light in the room coming from the virtual window on the wall opposite them. Tala eased into bed beside Kane, neither of them at all tired but knowing they needed to sleep. She rolled to her side, facing him. He took her in, the somber expression she wore, the contours of her face that he'd long since memorized. He reached out, running his thumb gently across her cheek, over her jaw, then down the side of her neck. Her skin was soft and smooth, and he felt her goosebumps raise beneath his touch.

Were there words to be said in that moment, or did their silence say it all?

In the quiet between them, he could hear her slow, shallow breathing, the steady, rhythmic beating of her heart, and his fell into sync with it. Everything was uncertain. But of one thing he was sure, and it was that he had no regrets with her. He wouldn't regret loving her as he had. He wouldn't regret falling for her when there had been no chance for them. He wouldn't regret everything it took to get back to her. He wouldn't regret giving her the part of him he would never give to anyone else.

He was changed because of her, and he could never go back to the old version of himself. His life would always be defined in one of two ways — before her and after her. A part of him was ready for the next step, to be met on the battlefield, eager to put an end to the conflict. But he feared what that end might take with it. Was this the last day of life as he knew it? The sun would rise in the morning, but that didn't mean it would be a new dawn.

He suddenly felt fragile, standing on the edge of the unknown. Addox was right when he said destiny didn't guarantee forever. He thought the dream lay on the other side of tomorrow, but the truth was that he had lived a thousand dreams already, each in the blink of an eye, each because he knew an extraordinary love. He'd wholly given his heart to her. She was his world, in the morning and night and in all the stars, and should he lose her tomorrow, he would be buried with her, and all that would be left of him would be the shell of his current self. He realized, in some distant part of his brain, that perhaps it was loss that was the flipside to love, to go from having to not having, from full to empty.

He swallowed hard, but the ache was still there. "Say something," he said as he realized the silence had dragged on.

She opened her mouth to speak, then paused, as if deciding against what she was about to say. She took a breath. "My father," she finally said.

Of course Jameson would be one of the things on her mind, along with the million others he knew were swimming inside her head.

"I remember the first time I met Victoria," she said. "She mentioned knowing my father, mentioned he helped Elias politically. But it seemed like such an afterthought in that conversation. Everyone turned out to be a stranger to me. When I look back, I'm no longer sure what was real in my life." Though he could hear her sadness, it didn't seem to overwhelm her.

"I think your parents were brave," he said honestly. He wasn't trying to placate her. He knew she didn't want to be coddled. "Your father wanted a better world. And your mother, well, in the end, she tried to make things right. And how could they have told you any of it? You were young and they were protecting you."

"The thing is, my whole family, including Thias, has only ever acted on what we've believed," she said.

"But when you act with others in mind, willing to put yourself aside for the greater good, acting selflessly, that's the noblest thing we can ever do," he said.

"Maverick asked if there was such a thing as freedom," she said, her voice quiet. "I have to believe that while it may never exist in its purest, most complete form, that giving the power to the people by giving them a voice, their independent ability to choose, that that's the closest we can bring ourselves to a free world. Freewill should be a natural right as we are all born with the ability of freethought. That's a society I want to believe is possible, and I want to play my part in creating that. I've always acted on behalf of my people, my life as MF, all those advoprops. This will be my final fight for them."

He found that there was something moving about her love for her people. As long as there were people like Tala, there would always be someone willing to fight for what was right. The things he knew unequivocally about freedom were that it was expensive and that it was only born from courage. He saw it in Tala, in Maverick, in all the soldiers who had been in their mission briefing.

A change was coming, and all that was left now was to find out which way the wind was going to blow.

"I love you," he whispered, their gazes holding each other in the dimness. She leaned forward, pressing her forehead to his. They were so close he could feel her warm breath on his face, and he closed his eyes. He wanted to linger in that moment as long as possible, letting it imprint in his mind, on his heart.

He wasn't sure how long they'd lain like that, quietly breathing the same air between them in the stillness of the room, but slowly he pulled away. His eyes opened, catching hers, and he swallowed hard the emotion he felt deep inside.

"We need to get some sleep," he finally said. His voice hoarse from a dry throat. It was really the last thing he wanted, but he knew he had to be sharp. They would be back up and out of The Village even before most people went to bed.

Tala reached out, grabbing hold of his t-shirt. "Not yet," she said and tugged hard, pulling him to her. Letting go of his shirt, she slipped her hand around the back of his neck, sending a chill down his spine. Before he could give anything a second thought, she crushed her lips to his. In an instant, he came undone and slid his arms around her, pulling her against him, then kissed her deeper.

TWENTY-SEVEN

Tala stood in the open doorway of the hangar at the small airport just outside Hatfolk with eight Unified Special Forces troops, in addition to Colonel Thornton, Kane, Maverick, and six chopper pilots. It was late, just after midnight. While there was a cool breeze, the outside temperature lacked the bite of winter, reminding Tala it was now early spring. Northern cities still felt the chill of winter on many days, but warmer ones were coming for them all.

The headlights of four vehicles approached from across the apron. Tala already knew who to expect even before anyone exited the large, black vehicles. First were two military guards, followed by Victoria and Elias. Two more guards came from the second, along with presidents Graham Walker and Lana Xavier. From the third vehicle, Fischer Hutton emerged, towering over the guard beside him. And Otto Fulton, Teagan Blakley, and one more guard stepped out of the last vehicle. Each of them was dressed warmly in wool and fur, looking smart despite the early hour. They greeted each other kindly as they made their way toward the hangar, giving Tala nods of hello. When everyone had passed, she turned and made her way back into the brightly lit building where the team and the Revos' leaders were already waiting.

"Delta team, attention!" Colonel Thornton yelled out, his voice booming over the murmuring crowd.

Tala rushed to join the others in a line, straightening her body, standing a little taller. All together, the troops, including the colonel, Kane, Maverick, and her, saluted the leaders before them.

Victoria's mouth was pressed in a firm line, her eyes scanning each soldier. Tala couldn't pinpoint her expression which seemed equally pensive and morose. She waved her hand at the colonel.

"Commander," he said with a nod at her. He turned toward the team. "At ease," he said. There was an audible breath taken from each of them, almost in collective unison.

"Delta team, you've a large task ahead of you," Victoria said, her voice loud for such a small person. Her copper hair was sleek, curving inward, framing her face, and she wore a black coat that hung to the middle of her thighs, the pointed tips of her black stilettos peeking out from the bottom of her slacks. "Few would envy your mission if they understood the risks involved and what was at stake. But you have been chosen, individually selected, because you are the best of the best. Exemplary in every way, and I know that you eleven are more than capable of succeeding in your task."

Tala gave a sideways glance down the line of Special Forces soldiers, five other men and three women. She couldn't help wondering about each of them. Who were they? Why specifically had they been chosen? But this wasn't a social gathering. They had a job to do. Whoever they were individually no longer mattered. They, all eleven of them, were a team, and they had to work as one if they were going to succeed in their mission. They were no longer a who but rather a what. They were Unified troops. They were Delta team. A chill ran down Tala's spine, and she looked back to Victoria.

"Today is history in the making," she said, her words like liquid as she paced before them. "We have been preparing for this day for many years, patiently waiting for our moment. We are poised and ready for action."

Tala couldn't help but think of her father, the image of a young Jameson Alexander holding an American flag. She swallowed hard, silently wondering, as he had been one to set this in motion, would be proud of the role she was about to play in it? An unexpected and sudden urge to please him washed over her.

They'd never been close. Not like she had been with her mother, but standing there in that moment, she couldn't help but feel a surreal connection to him that her mind couldn't wrap itself around. But it was there, nonetheless.

"Today is the end of the Republic of Columbia. Today is the end of the inequality and oppression. Today is a new beginning," Victoria said firmly. "Fight your fight. Then come home." Falling silent, her arms hanging loosely at her sides, her eyes once again skimmed the line of them, then paused, lingering briefly on Tala. She gave a furtive nod of her head, then looked away. She turned toward Colonel Thornton, starting in on a hushed conversation with him that both Graham and Lana joined.

Tala looked at Kane, and despite the heaviness weighing on her, the corners of her mouth curled into a small smile at the sight of him in uniform. The entire team wore black fatigues and heavy combat boots. Not unlike her former Militia Forces uniform, they wore a tactical frag jacket engineered to help protect against bullets, shrapnel, and even plasma charges. It was heavier than the one she'd worn as MF. The webbing across the front held extra magazines for their assault rifle and the handgun strapped to their leg, along with two flashbang grenades and two stun grenades. Conformity was a new look on him.

"Tala," a voice called from behind her, and she turned to see Otto Fulton, governor of Lincoln Plains Colony, approaching her. When they'd met at the summit, he'd been dressed in a blazer and tie, but now he looked far more casual in a fitted t-shirt and dark denim jeans. She wondered how he wasn't cold with the hangar doors open. There was something about the look in his eyes, small and beady, that reminded her of that first meeting. She couldn't help but feel that he looked at her with a strange sort of reverence.

"Are you ready?" he asked. The way he said it seemed less patronizing and more like he already knew that she was, like he expected nothing less from her.

She nodded, looping her thumbs through the straps on the sides of her frag jacket. "I am," she said firmly.

"I understand you've been apprised of the history of the Revos. Of the new United States," he said. "And I imagine it came as a bit of a surprise."

"A bit?" she scoffed under her breath. "I'd describe it more like being hit by a ton of bricks."

He let out a laugh as he slid his hands into the pockets of his jeans. "I knew him. Jameson. You could say that he recruited me. Though it took little convincing," he said, his voice gentle. "I believed in his vision from the very beginning."

With a glance at Otto's bare arms, Tala saw the black lines of ink peeking out from beneath the cuff of his sleeve, and she sucked in a breath as she shifted on her feet.

"I know you lost him when you were young. Before you ever had the chance to really know him," he said. "See, when we're children, we only know our parents as just that, parents. We don't see them for the people that they are. That comes later in life when we become adults too. You never had that chance," he said sincerely, "the opportunity to discover the kind of people your parents were. And I'm genuinely sorry for that. Now it's up to us," he said, motioning toward the others in the hangar, "to those of us who knew him to share his legacy with you.

"He was a brave man who took great risks to build a better world. While he chose this, you've been kind of thrust right into it all, starting with that warehouse in the city. Who would've thought a single arrest would unfold into all of this? I see in you what I saw in him. You're a freethinker. It's why you challenged your orders in the very beginning. I admire that in you," he said with a subtle smile as he rubbed his hand along his jaw, matting his thick, graying facial hair.

"I know you know what's at stake in this mission. We're standing on the precipice of a great transition. But it's evolution, not revolution. You're like a stone dropped into a still pond. It doesn't matter if you're large or small, the effect is the same. Ripples. So small at first, but growing, expanding, eventually disrupting the entire pool. All from a single stone. Your only job is to set this in motion. The rest is up to us and those we have tasked in the waves following yours. Your father was the best. That's what I wanted to tell you. You were made for this. So, do me this one favor, in the name of Jameson... finish it."

Tala held his gaze for a moment, his words sinking into her, burrowing into her mind, settling on her heart. *You were made for this.* Looking back, she couldn't help but feel certain that none of it had been chance, but rather a destiny that guided her one step at a time to where she was now.

"I think you're right," she said. "I know you're right," she amended because it was the truth.

"Delta team," Colonel Thornton called out, his voice echoing around them. Tala craned her neck toward him as all conversation in the hangar fell quiet. "Attention!"

Like the other team members, Tala was quick to find her place in line, snapping to attention as the colonel walked slowly in front of them. He held something in his hands clasped behind his back. His square jaw was set in a hard line, and his eyes narrowed. After walking the length of them, he turned and began making his way back down the line. Mid-way, he stopped and turned, squaring himself to all of them.

"Once you are airborne, I will assume operational control from the PDCC alongside your commander-in-chief and president, Renegade," he said as he tipped his head toward Victoria. Tala didn't dare to even move her eyes as Colonel Thornton looked over each of them. "Triple Play," he said, calling the first wave of the mission by its code name, "is just one part of Operation Libertas. But you are the tip of the sword. People will live a better life tomorrow because of what you will do today. You are not fighting just any battle, but rather *the* battle. You are not fighting just for your life, but for *all* life. Today, you are no longer three countries, you are not Rebels or Revos. Today, you are the United States," he said sternly, unflinching, his gaze not wavering. Slowly, he approached them, his eyes taking their time as they roved carefully over each of them.

With Kane at attention on her right and Maverick on her left, Tala's pulse raced. She felt her adrenaline building. But she held her position, her eyes fixed forward.

"Please put out your right hand," Colonel Thornton said, his voice not booming but not gentle either.

The team followed his instruction, each one extending their hand. The colonel began pacing before the line again. Reaching the end, he stopped in front of a woman who Tala only knew as Rover. She was tall and muscular, her thick black hair pulled back into a braid like Tala's. It was easier than a ponytail when they wore their protective headgear.

After a moment of Colonel Thornton staring directly into the unflinching eyes of Rover, Tala saw his shoulders drop as he placed something in her open palm. Next, he moved to Mamba, the woman beside Rover, who was nearly a head shorter, hair as blond as Tala's. Like he had done with Rover, he placed something in her open palm, then moved down the line. One by one, he moved to each of them, though Tala couldn't see what he was giving them. She didn't dare move her body even a centimeter to catch a glimpse.

Soon, Colonel Thornton stepped in front of her, squaring his shoulders to her while his eyes bore into hers. But she didn't move. She didn't even breathe. She simply stood as stiff and erect as possible, her muscles tight. Finally, he reached out, putting something lightweight in her palm, then moved on to Maverick. Holding her hand still, the feeling of something scratchy against her palm, she kept her eyes focused ahead. After Maverick, there was one soldier left, a stocky man with skin dark as night who Tala knew as Hornet.

The colonel retreated from their line and went to stand beside Victoria. The hangar was eerily quiet as the leaders looked over each one of them. A dropped pin could've been heard in the silence.

Standing among the rest of Delta team, Tala didn't feel like anyone special. She didn't feel the weight of the Republic on her shoulders. She didn't even feel like an Alexander. She was simply a soldier. And she had a job to do.

"Our time has come," Colonel Thornton said, his voice ringing loudly in Tala's ears. "Defend freedom, fight for liberty, and wear Old Glory proudly. At ease."

Each soldier in the line relaxed, the relief palpable as everyone looked down at what had been put in their hands. An embroidered patch, a simple black and white American flag, with a fabric adhesive backing.

"It goes on the left shoulder," Maverick said in a hushed voice as he slapped the patch onto the plush spot on the shoulder of his fatigues.

Tala stared down at the flag in her hand, an unexpected surge of emotion in her. She'd been so distracted with coverups and secrets, with plots and lies, that she'd almost forgotten what it was that had truly set everything into motion. Otto was wrong, at least partly, about what had started it all. It wasn't because she had wanted to challenge an order, it wasn't because she thought she was being lied to. It began because she had believed there was a threat to her people, to her country, and she had taken an oath to protect both at all costs.

Staring at the patch in her hand, she couldn't help but realize that she had come full circle. She had chosen a life committed to the preservation of others, and now was her moment, the one she'd prepared herself for long before her world had spun out of control. While her mind still wavered because it was where doubt lived, her heart was ready in a way that was so tangible.

A smile tugged at the corner of her mouth as she looked up at Kane who was studying her intently, his dark eyes fixed on her. She inhaled sharply, then exhaling slowly, she reached around and stuck the patch to her left shoulder, near her heart, near the phoenix ink on her skin. This was what it was to be born again. This was the resurgence.

High above the ground, their military chopper, followed by the two others, glided quietly through the cover of night as it made its way to the border. Tala strained against her harness to catch a glimpse out the window, the height in the air in the chopper oddly less frightening than in an airplane. Passing over small towns, Tala could see the faint flicker of lights below, which meant they were still in the Colonies. The power grid in the Republic wouldn't be brought down until they were nearer the Mississippi River, the border between the Central Colonies and the Republic of Columbia.

Like the chopper she and Maverick had taken to Michigan City, these were custom engineered for stealth capabilities. They moved through the darkened sky unbeknownst to anyone on the ground, and that was how they would infiltrate the Republic, arriving in Columbia City at dawn.

Their pilot, Mountaineer, and her co-pilot, Werewolf, spoke between each other as they monitored and made manual adjustments to the near fully autonomous chopper, where a simple voice command could redirect it entirely. Tala sat between Kane and Maverick, their tactical helmets on the floor, wedged between their boots, their weapons secured at the base of their seats. She glanced at Kane, his eyes closed, his head tipped back against the seat. The slow and steady rhythm of his breathing told her he was sleeping. It would take them almost five hours to get to the city. She couldn't blame him for wanting to get some rest.

As she closed her eyes, the images of Mila and Vi appeared in her mind, their goodbyes playing back to her as if on a reel. There hadn't been much to say from any of them. Their sad eyes seemed to have the conversation they couldn't bring themselves to have aloud. Mila wore her heartbreak on her face, Vi was more stoic, and Declan was a surprising mix of both. But it was Max who caught her off guard. He was filled with emotion. It was hard to watch his goodbye to Kane.

It had been harder to walk away than Tala thought it would be. She had told herself she would come back to them, but looking at each of them, Mila with her deep brown eyes, Vi's large and striking blue eyes, she knew that was a promise she couldn't make. Instead, she decided to remember what they had in each other. To remember what existed between hello and goodbye. Their friendships had been a beautiful thing. They had guided her, supported her, loved her. They had given her a safe place to call home where she was free to find herself. No goodbye could tarnish that.

With renewed emotion running through her, Tala opened her eyes. She looked across Kane and out the window. Off in the distance, she spotted a small town, its lights flickering into the night like stars. Then they were suddenly plunged into darkness, the world going black. It had begun.

"Firefox 1 to Black Cat 2, Mountaineer here. Just crossed into RC airspace at 234.6 knots, maintaining cruising altitude 6800 MSL," their pilot said.

Tala craned her neck for a better look, but the world outside was nothing but a heavy black cloak, not even the moon in the sky.

"Black Cat 2 confirmation, now in RC airspace," a voice from over the radio filled Tala's ears.

There was a brief silence, then the radio sprang to life once again. "Echo 3, entering RC airspace, increasing altitude, present position 3.6 miles on Black Cat 2's six."

"Copy that. Out," Mountaineer said into her radio. Once again, the cab fell into silence.

Tala sighed, dropping her head back against the headrest. She slid her hand onto Kane's thigh, though his body didn't respond to her touch. She was glad he was able to sleep and knew she should too. But her mind was too busy.

Mostly, she wondered what it was going to be like to see Thias again.

"Can't sleep?" Maverick's quiet voice asked, catching Tala by surprise. She turned to face him, just able to make out his features. There was so much of Mila in his face, or maybe she was in his. The familiarity was comforting. With hers and Maverick's training and Kane's skills, she knew their team was capable.

"Too much going on up here," she said, tapping the side of her head with her finger.

"You were always like that before something big," he said quietly.

"That's true." She nodded, thinking back. "Do you remember Aerial Assault Training?"

Maverick let out a small laugh. "How could I forget? I really thought you wouldn't make it. I specifically remember thinking, finally found something Tala Alexander isn't good at."

"Fooled all of you," she said haughtily, smiling. "Even finished in the top five."

"That's only because three-quarters of your class failed AAT the first time around," he said.

"Well, that should still speak to my abilities, that I could even pass on my first try."

Maverick nodded. "A valid point."

"I did, however, think that rucksack was going to flatten me before the end of Initiate Day. What did that thing weigh, like fifty pounds?" she said.

"Forty."

"Close enough. We had to haul that damn thing everywhere we went," she said, recalling her torturous two-week aerial training while in the academy.

"It wasn't your strength and endurance that made me question whether you could finish, it was your fear of heights. You were so distressed when it came time to rappel down the Tower," he said with a chuckle under his breath. "I thought you'd just refuse right there, and then you'd have been done."

"I kind of forgot all that. It was the heights on our drive in the mountains to Camp Washington that got me then too. I still remember what that sergeant in AAT said as I stood up on the Tower, looking down to the ground, fifty feet below—"

"Fifty-six, actually," he interjected.

"Even worse. Anyway, he told me that I could think and think about how high up I was all day and it would get me nowhere. Fear is conquered by action." She smiled to herself, her mind taking her back to that day six years earlier. It had been overcast but hot, the dead of summer, and she'd been sweating through her training uniform that entire afternoon. It wasn't until she'd stood on top of the Tower that she noticed the breeze. Though it did nothing to cool her down. Her anxiety had been sky-high at the prospect of rappelling down the vertical wall. In the end, she did it. The first female in her class to complete it, and it felt like a true victory. Though nothing in that training course was easy, probably the most difficult work she'd ever done, it all seemed a little downhill after the Tower. It wasn't that she'd suddenly gotten stronger or more agile after that task. It was the shift in her mindset and the fortification in her confidence, and that made all the difference.

"Because my MF assignment was in the city, I never used those skills. The first time I've come up against anything that we learned in that training was when I was escaping the Republic. I had to fast-rope down a mooring line from a ship," she said. His face was heavily shadowed as he looked at her.

"The irony being that you'll use those skills again today when we rappel that elevator shaft," he said, referring to their mission once inside the Central Government building. "They trained a combatant that will be used against them," he said.

"They trained both of us," she said quietly.

"And they made their super-soldier," he said with a nod toward Kane. "You know, it's never easy to go up against an enemy. That's what we're all about to do. But I think it's even harder to go up against someone who's personally hurt you. Someone you once loved. Especially when it's your brother."

Tala took a deep breath and relaxed her shoulders. There was truth in Maverick's words, and she nodded in agreement. "The longer I've been away from him, the more distance there is between us. Metaphorically speaking. When I see him, I'm sure my heart will need to be reminded more than once that he means nothing to me anymore. But my head knows, undoubtedly, that he's a terrible person. That anything I thought was good in him was all manipulation. The Thias I knew never really existed. He was merely a figment of his own orchestration."

"I'm proud of you, Tals," he said as he gave her a small nudge with his elbow. "When we were first reunited, I thought you'd been hardened. And maybe you have been a little bit, but mostly I think you've been strengthened."

Tala looked at him, finding his eyes in the darkness, and she smiled. "Can I ask you a question?"

He nodded. "'Course."

She reached out, settling her hand over his as it rested in his lap. "If we walk away from all of this, if we see the other side, would you escort me down the aisle on my wedding day?"

Maverick was quiet for a moment, the only sound around them coming from the pilots in the cockpit. He slipped his free hand over hers, grasping it gently. "I absolutely will do that."

Maverick and Tala fell into comfortable silence. Kane still asleep, she leaned against him, as much as the harness would allow, dropping her head to his shoulder. She listened to his slow and steady breathing. Outside, a partially obstructed moon appeared in the sky, lighting up small traces of snow on the ground below. She listened to the steady chatter between Mountaineer and Werewolf, and the intermittent exchanges between choppers, Firefox 1, Black Cat 2, and Echo 3.

Their flightpath followed along the 32 freeway that spanned all of North America, from east coast to west coast. Approaching Michigan City, they cut slightly south to avoid the blacked-out city. Sometime between Michigan City and Weston Port along the southern shore of Lake Erie, Tala began to doze off, waking only when her head would loll off Kane's shoulder.

Tala's eyes fluttered open as she felt small nudges against her arm.

"Time to wake up," Kane whispered near her ear. "We're about forty-five minutes from Columbia City. Need you alert."

Tala could swear only fifteen minutes had passed since she'd closed her eyes, but if they were so near the city, she knew it had been much longer than that. She yawned as she sat up straighter, a crick in her neck. Rubbing away the stiffness, she looked around, everyone in the chopper alert.

"Take this," Maverick said, holding a white pill in his outstretched hand.

"Vitality pill?" she asked. She hadn't seen those since she'd left the Republic.

He nodded. "You didn't sleep much."

"No, I don't want one," she said, pushing the pill away. "I'll do better on my own adrenaline." While they were wildly popular with most people, Tala always felt a little jittery on the rare occasions that she took them. Even if they were meant to enhance alertness and better focus, she knew she could rely on her own body more.

"I don't like them either," Maverick said as he pocketed the small pill.

"Morning," Kane said as she turned toward him. He was bright-eyed and gave her an encouraging smile.

She reached for his hand, taking it in hers, lacing her fingers between his. Turning forward, she stole a glance out the front windshield, daybreak on the distant horizon. A ribbon of yellow and orange beginning to brighten the sky, clear and cloudless. It looked like a world of possibility, ready for anything, the clean slate of a new day. Tala felt anticipation tingling in the tips of her fingers, the pull of sleep long gone.

The time seemed to pass equally slowly and quickly. In one moment, it dragged on endlessly, and in the next it seemed to be gone in the blink of an eye. Eventually, the dense thicket of forest below gave way to the outer city limits, Columbia City appearing in the approaching distance, it's high-rises standing like sentries at the threshold. The sight of it sent a chill down Tala's spine and raised goosebumps across her arms.

"All right," Maverick said, releasing his harness. He reached for a small plastic pouch in the side cargo pocket of his pants. "Comms in."

Their harnesses releasing automatically, Tala and Kane put the tiny bead just inside their ear. The three of them reached for their tactical helmets, securing them with a strap pulled tightly below the chin. The last pieces of gear to be put on were their fingerless gloves and protective eyewear before they reached for their weapon.

With a quick tap of the bead in their ears, their comms came to life, and Tala exchanged glances with both Kane and Maverick.

"Delta Triple Play 1, team leader Lancer to base-ops," Maverick said. Long gone was his gentle and jovial voice. He was stern and serious now. "Locked and loaded."

"Lancer, this is base-ops Hawkeye, we copy." Colonel Thornton's voice echoed in Tala's ear. Only seconds later, both Delta Triple Play 2 team leader Granger, and Delta Triple Play 3 team leader Wintergreen confirmed they were also in ready position.

"Black Cat 2 separating from the flock. Out."

"Echo 3 has visual on L.Z. Separating from the flock. Out."

"This is Mountaineer, Firefox 1," their pilot said. "Decreasing speed to forty knots, inbound approach at 2500 MSL. We have a confirmed visual on our L.Z."

Up ahead, Tala could see the tall, triple twisting spires of the Central Government building standing high in the sky. Its iconic black sphere, the cynosure, like a pearl in an oyster, was clutched tightly in the heart of the three towers.

Below, the streets were as congested as Tala remembered, even at the early hour, the crowds of pedestrians like liquid moving down the sidewalks, traffic filling the streets. She couldn't help but wonder what kind of havoc the blackout was creating. Looking out at the cityscape, nothing seemed to be any different than when she'd left. The botanical gardens of the Vertical Village housing buildings were still brown and wilted from the winter. Cranes still stood beside partially constructed buildings that seemed to have made no progress in the many months that had passed. Maybe a result of the taxing costs of war.

As they neared their destination high-rise, their chopper slowed drastically, hovering more than flying, as the south tower disappeared below them.

"Turn and descent," Werewolf said with a nod at Mountaineer as they eased to the left, then continued to decrease altitude.

Maverick pulled hard at the door, sliding it open, wind rushing into the cabin. He crouched near the open doorway, watching as they dropped from the sky, his assault rifle clutched firmly in his grasp.

Tala turned to see Kane behind her right shoulder. He wore a hardened expression, his jaw set, and his dark eyes caught hers. Though neither spoke a word, their glance was enough.

Ready.

You've got this.

I love you.

Tala swallowed hard and turned back toward the door. The edges of the helipad on the top of the Central Government building south tower appeared out the open doorway, and only moments later, they landed comfortably on their L.Z.

"Firefox 1, settled," Mountaineer said through the comm.

As soon as they came to a stop, Maverick leapt from the cabin, his feet hitting hard on the ground. Without even a breath of hesitation, Tala followed after him. When her feet hit solid ground, she took off in a jog, her senses on high alert as she ran from the helipad to the single rooftop doorway, taking cover on its right side, Maverick on its left.

The air from the rotor blades whooshed around them, the sleeves and pant legs of her uniform flapping, stray wisps of hair whipping around her face. Kane approached with a pry bar in hand, then took position behind Maverick. With the power down, the security panel at the door wouldn't work. They'd have to access the building through force.

Firefox 1 lifted from the helipad, and Tala gave it one last look before it would disappear completely.

"Base ops, Delta Triple Play 1 is pouncing cougar," Maverick said, telling Colonel Thornton they were ready, his voice loud and clear in Tala's ear.

"Lancer, hold your position," Colonel Thornton said.

They waited, the seconds ticking by. The sun, unobstructed in the eastern sky, was warm on Tala's face, a sure sign of spring. Her heart raced in her chest, and she felt her blood pumping through her veins, but her hands were steady, and her mind was clear.

"All Delta Triple Play teams in position," the colonel said. "Go on Renegade's command."

There was a brief pause before Victoria's voice filled Tala's ear. "Teams, engage."

Maverick reached for the doorknob, attempting to turn it. He gave a quick shake of his head.

Kane stepped around Maverick, the pry bar in hand. He easily wedged the flat tip in the small crevice between the steel door and the jamb. Kane gave a hard, minimal-effort tug, the door loosening. With a single swift kick, it swung open, and he quickly stepped behind Tala as Maverick moved into the doorway, his gun raised, its buttstock wedged against his shoulder. He gave a quick nod of his head as he stepped through it, into a dark stairwell, then waved a flat hand for them to proceed in a line behind him.

Tala's gun was grasped firmly in her hands in the ready position. Sucking in a sharp breath, she stepped through the open door. She could feel Kane close on her heel as she followed behind Maverick, light on her feet on each stair.

"Stop!" someone yelled as Maverick rounded a corner below her. The voice was deep and loud, echoing through the stairwell, reverberating off the walls, and she knew instantly that it was not Maverick's.

Tala no longer had a visual, and a moment later, she heard a gun fire.

TWENTY-EIGHT

At the sound of the gunshot, first one, followed by a second, Tala pulled a glow stick from the side pocket of her pants, pressed the tip to activate the neon, then tossed it down to the landing at the bottom of the stairs, offering limited light in the dark stairwell. She descended the stairs with caution, Kane behind her. Her heart was racing in her chest, blood rushing to her ears, drowning out the echo of her footsteps in the narrow stairwell as she approached the corner Maverick had just slipped around when he disappeared.

She glanced at Kane, raising her fist in the air as she came to a stop on the bottom step.

"All clear," Maverick called out. Tala took a breath of relief. "Situation neutralized. The viper's dead."

Tala exhaled as she stepped around the corner, a Militia Forces agent with a bullet mark square in the middle of his frag jacket, a second fatal shot to the head.

"Hawkeye to Lancer. Respond."

"This is Lancer," Maverick said.

"Backup power to the building's surveillance system has been cut. We have no visual of your team. It's likely only the cynosure has any generator power. Prepare to proceed blind," he said.

Maverick glanced at Tala. They already knew the stairwells in the building wouldn't be safe as they'd be easy to defend, easy to pin their team in, and their execution took this into account, but base-ops was to remotely monitor the building for MF while the team made their way to the cynosure. Now they would be on their own. And Tala was certain Thias knew they were there. The blackout made them nearly invisible coming in, but it had also announced they were coming.

Tala pressed her mouth into a line as she gave a single nod of her head.

"Copy, Hawkeye," Maverick said a moment later. "Nothing changes. The aim is the elevator shaft," he said to Tala and Kane.

"Right," Kane said. "Let's go."

The three of them fell in line, Maverick leading them as they continued their descent down the stairs.

At the bottom of a second flight, there was nowhere to go but through a single door, a large number 125 on the wall identifying the floor. Tala reached for the doorknob, and with Maverick's go-ahead signal, she opened it. They stood in silence, watching Kane as he listened for even the slightest of sounds. A moment later, he nodded, giving them the all-clear. Maverick was the first through the door, followed by Tala and then Kane.

Knowing the layout of the building, the three of them moved as one down the corridor toward the elevator bank. With the power down, the hallways were dim, only the morning light from outside streaming in through the windows to light the way. And the air was stagnant, stuffy. They approached every door along the corridor with vigilance, only to find each office they passed empty.

"This is unexpected," Kane said, his voice hushed.

"I agree," Maverick said as they slowed, then came to a cautious stop. "There's no one here."

"It was evacuated," Tala said. Thias had been serious when he said he'd let her into the city. But this was no time to let her guard down. She was on his turf.

There was a stillness in the air, the silence pressing on her as she looked around. All she could hear was the sound of her breathing and the beating of her heart. In the faint half-light, a wave of unsettlement came over her and a chill ran down her spine.

"Let's keep going," Maverick said as he turned, then continued down the corridor.

Reaching the end, they were met by an intersecting hallway. Maverick came to a stop, raising his arm, his fist clenched. He and Tala turned toward Kane again as they waited for an all-clear. A moment later, he nodded to them both, then Maverick rounded the corner to another empty corridor.

When they came to a halt at the next one, Kane gave a small tap on Maverick's shoulder, then held up a finger and pointed to the left. Maverick dropped low, Tala on his four o'clock, both with their guns ready.

Slowly, Maverick crept forward, just enough to catch a small glimpse around the corner, then quickly pulled back. He held up two fingers confirming as many vipers to the left. He gave a silent nod at Tala, then pumped his fist… one… two… three. Both stepped around the corner, and with a clean shot from each of them, the two MF agents dropped to the floor with a thud.

Once again, they moved as a pack, like liquid, down the hall and repeated the same protocol when they reached the next corridor. The elevator bank came into view, and they approached swiftly, cautiously. When Kane gave them the all-clear, Maverick took up a defensive position on one side, Tala on the other. Kane took the pry bar, which had been looped at his hip, and wedged it between the double doors of the elevator. With a tug, the doors cracked apart, wide enough for Kane to slip his fingers between them. Using his strength, he pried them apart from each other, exposing the dark, empty shaft, one hundred twenty-five stories to the bottom.

"Lancer to base-ops," Maverick said in his comm, "Triple Play 1 has breached the elevator."

"Lancer, you're confirmed. Proceed."

"You're up," Maverick said to Tala.

Her gun gripped firmly in her hands, she positioned herself in front of the elevator bank for cover-fire for any potential vipers while Maverick and Kane slid their small packs off their backs. Opening the bags, they pulled out three coiled ropes and three harnesses.

While they set up the rappelling gear inside the shaft, Tala remained in her ready position, her head on a swivel. It was warm in the building, and beads of sweat were forming along her hairline. It was amazing to her how her mind could be a chaotic frenzy of thoughts in the quiet moments of her life, but as soon as she was in the field, her mind was instantly stilled and her senses flipped to over-drive.

A glance to her left, she saw only Kane's feet as he climbed into the shaft to secure their ropes.

The hairs on Tala's arms instantly stood on end, and she snapped her head to the right, feeling the presence of someone approaching before even hearing them. A moment later, she picked up the steady, rhythmic thumps of approaching footfalls. Multiple footsteps, each hitting at different times, one set heavier than the other.

She stood quickly, then slid to the other side of the elevator bank, her back pressed against the wall. She peered over at Maverick, winding her finger in the air to hurry them up. She strained to listen to the sound of the approaching footsteps as she tried to gauge their proximity. She had one chance.

Her gun lifted, the butt pressed snuggly against the inside of her shoulder, she took a deep breath, steadying her hands as she gripped it tighter. Letting out a heavy exhale, she stepped around the corner of the elevator bank and fired a shot. One MF yelled out, then dropped to his knees as the second fired a shot back at her. She pulled back to safety around the corner just as a plasma charge went past.

"Hostiles. South tower. South elevator bank. Hundred twenty-fifth floor," one of the agents reported over his comm, and Tala cringed as their position was given away.

Crouching lower, she rounded the corner a second time, firing her gun twice, hitting the second agent in the forehead, his body instantly collapsing to the ground. The first one scrambled to his feet, the wind knocked out of him from her shot to his chest, stopped by his frag jacket. With an unsteady hand, he fired at her, and she felt the heat pass by her cheek, the plasma charge nearly missing her.

Sucking in a sharp breath, she fired her gun again, the agent falling to the ground, a bullet wound in his shoulder, his gun dropping from his hand.

Tala moved swiftly down the hallway as she approached him. She quickly kicked the gun out of his reach as he stumbled to his feet once again. He charged at her, his arms wrapping around her waist, knocking her backward into the wall with force.

There was instant pain in her side as he punched her in the flesh, just below her rib cage. She jerked her knee up, hitting him low in the abdomen, below his vest, then smashed her elbow into the base of his neck. He grunted, his arms falling loose from her waist.

Tala thrust her palm up, into his face, his nose breaking. An instant stream of blood ran from it as it cocked unnaturally to the side.

Finding his footing, he punched her, pain exploding through her jaw, the metallic taste of blood in her mouth. He swung at her a second time, but she dodged him, his hand colliding with the wall. Turning her body, she drove her elbow into his chest.

She stumbled on her feet. Before she could turn around, the agent's body suddenly slumped to the ground at her feet, his neck at an aberrant angle. She looked up to see Kane beside her, and she knew he'd snapped it.

"We've got to go," he said, his eyes wide.

Tala reached for her gun, wiped at her bloody lip, then jogged down the hall after him, back to the elevator bank where their rappelling gear was all set.

"Harness," Maverick said, holding out the black straps for Tala. She quickly stepped into them, then pulled them tight and buckled them at her waist.

Kane clipped a carabiner with a rope looped through it to her harness, then did the same to his.

"He reported our location," she said, her eyes briefly meeting his.

"Then we've got to get out of here," he said as he ushered her to the open elevator.

Tala slung her rifle across her chest, then gave a firm tug on her harness and the rope attached to her. Reaching for the rope above her, she eased her body into the shaft, her feet falling away from the floor as she dangled above the hundred twenty-five stories below her, a thrill running through her.

"You're good," Maverick said as he eased himself into the shaft beside her, followed quickly by Kane who had a flashlight in hand.

Gripping the rope with shaky hands, Tala used her feet to push her body off the wall of the shaft, easing herself lower with every kick. Reminding herself not to look down and thankful the shaft was black as night, she picked up her pace as the three of them made their way down twenty-five stories.

Tala's heart was hammering in her chest as she stole a glimpse at Maverick, his face heavily shadowed.

"Just like the Tower," he said, knowing her fear.

She swallowed hard. Kane was behind her, but she didn't dare steal a glance back at him, afraid of throwing her body off course as she bounced herself over and over again off the wall, her body dropping lower with every kick-off.

"See," Maverick said after a minute. "It's not so bad."

"Ha," she said nervously, wiping at the sweat that had gathered along her brow. The air in the shaft was hot and stifling.

"This is our stop," Kane said, his voice deep as he shone the light on the 100 on the wall. He clicked it off and stored it.

The three came to a halt in the blackened shaft, the light from the open doors above them so far away. Using the pry bar, Kane opened the doors with ease. A brief look down the empty hallway, he then swung his body through the opening. He pulled himself onto his knees across the floor, then unhooked his harness.

Getting instantly to his feet, he reached a hand out to Maverick, pulling him out of the shaft. As soon as his feet were stable on the floor, he unhooked himself, then Kane turned for Tala who was just out of reach.

Using her legs, she kicked her body off the wall, swinging toward the open doors. Kane was quick, grabbing her outstretched hand before she swung away. He pulled her through the doors, her feet finding solid ground, then she, too, unhooked herself.

"Lancer to base-ops, Triple Play 1 is pouncing cougar, ready to proceed to the den," Maverick said, updating their progress to the PDCC.

"Affirmative, Lancer," Colonel Thornton said.

"Renegade to Lancer," Victoria said, her commanding voice filling Tala's ears, "you're in a red zone now. Stay alert."

Maverick's finger waved between Tala and Kane, confirming they both heard the warning. Red zone, danger zone.

"Shit!" Kane yelled.

Before Tala could respond, three MF appeared, two from around the left side of the elevator bank, the third from the right, pinning them in on both sides.

"Don't move!" one of them said, a menacing scowl on his face. He was unfamiliar to her, tall and stocky, a heavy five o'clock shadow.

Then Tala's breath caught as her eyes found Agent Kassis, standing to her left, just past Maverick. She looked hard into his jet-black eyes just above his plasma gun that was aimed specifically at her. It seemed like a lifetime had passed since she'd seen him last, since she'd worked side-by-side with him at Command, since she'd killed his partner. She shuddered as her mind recalled the blank, lifeless look in Bishop's gray eyes just after she'd shot him on the day of the Annual Address. She hadn't hesitated then. Just as she knew Kassis wouldn't hesitate now.

Tala's hand flexed, her fingers wrapped around the grip of her handgun strapped to her leg, her rifle still strung across her chest. Behind her right shoulder, she could sense Kane's proximity to her, could feel his tension. She was desperate to make eye contact with him, to know what was running through his head. He was no doubt assessing the situation, the best way to take down three MF at once. He was strong and fast, but even this was an impossible situation for him by himself.

"Don't even think about it," the agent to Tala's right said as he eyed her hand on the gun. He was well over a head taller than she was. "Hands to your sides! All of you!" he spat, his eyes darting furiously between the three of them.

Tala could only see Maverick in her peripheral, and she released her grip on her gun, dropping her hand to her side the same time he did.

"You shouldn't be so predictable, Alexander," Kassis sneered. He was enjoying this. As was the agent beside him. They'd never been adversaries like she and Bishop had, but they also hadn't been friends. She could see the way he looked at her now. He saw a traitor, and he was staring revenge for the death of his partner in the face.

"The blackout? That you guys?" Kassis asked, his eyes shifting to Kane and Maverick before finding their way back to Tala. "How?"

"Is this a social call for you, Kassis?" a deep, stern voice asked, and Tala's chest tightened as she craned her neck to see Captain Kole as he appeared to her right from around the corner. Holding a plasma gun in his hand, he stepped between her and the towering agent, the same hardened expression she'd only ever seen on him, his mouth turned down, a deep furrow between his brows. She swallowed hard at the sight of him, her mouth going dry.

"Been a while, Alexander," he said coolly, his eyes meeting hers as he adjusted his suit coat.

She gave him a small nod, realization dawning on her. There were now four of them to their three. Thias was so close she could almost feel him. But she wasn't going to get close to him now, not with Maverick and Kane. If she surrendered, there was a chance they'd take her to him. After all, it was her he wanted. But that would mean leaving Kane and Maverick behind, leaving them with the MF. That wasn't an option. This was it, she thought. This was how it would end, practically before it even began.

Her mind went to the patch on her left shoulder, her father's vision, all those people counting on them. She was about to let them all down, and it opened a pit inside her.

Everything in her life seemed to come to a head in that moment. Every person she'd known, every choice she'd made. It all led her to that very moment, and what was it all for? So that she could come so close but still fail? Did it even matter that she tried?

"This is quite the case of sibling rivalry," Kole said, the corner of his mouth twitching, as if into a small smile that faded as quickly as it had appeared.

"Let them go," she said, her eyes meeting his. Her lip was tight where the blood was now drying. "This is about me. Let them go, and I'll come willingly."

"No!" Maverick snapped as he gave her a sideways glance. Kane took a step closer to her. She could feel the heat of his body, or maybe she just imagined she could. Either way, she felt him so near to her.

"You're supposed to have come alone," Kole said, his gaze hard and piercing as though he was speaking to her through the fury in his eyes.

"And so I should have," she said in agreement. The truth was, she'd been warned. Somewhere in the recesses of her mind were the reasons why she couldn't have come alone, but in that moment, Kane and Maverick suddenly in jeopardy, she knew she'd been reckless.

Kole's eyes flickered briefly to the handgun holstered on her right leg, her hand instinctively going to it, brushing along the handle.

"My orders are to bring you in, all of you, dead or alive," he said, his gaze furtively dropping again to her gun. "Though President Alexander would prefer if you were alive." His eyes were fixed on her. It took her a moment to realize he was blinking at an irregular frequency. Faster than usual.

She was silent as she looked back at him, trying to keep her face impassive. She couldn't pinpoint what it was, but the hairs along the back of her neck stood, as though charged by a current in the air.

"Just let them go, and I won't put up a fight," she said, though with less heart, her mind swimming. She felt the eyes of the other three agents on her. She had to keep Kole talking. Nothing would happen while they were talking.

"You were one of my best agents," he said, his eyes flickering once again to her gun as he took two small steps to his left, the agent beside him in clear vision of her now. "There were people who thought you didn't deserve your assignment at Command, because you were a woman, because you were an Alexander," he said, his eyes blinking faster. "But none of that ever mattered to me. You'd earned that spot. Until, well, until you decided to go rogue."

He glanced at her gun again before catching her gaze, and her thumb brushed along the easy-snap of the holster.

"I know that's how you see it," she said. It felt as though the air around her was collapsing in on them, and she felt a trickle of sweat run down her back. With the tip of her nail, she pressed against the snap, feeling it disengage.

"Ha!" Kole said, his eyes going wide, though never faltering from hers. "You wouldn't describe this as rogue? I can give you three reasons why that's exactly what you've done." He stopped his erratic blinking, his gaze leveling. "One. You disobeyed practically every order both your director and I gave you. Two. You killed one of your own."

Tala sucked in a sharp breath.

"Three."

Even before he had finished saying the word, back-to-back plasma charges pulsed through the air as she pulled her gun from the holster. With a single, clean shot from Tala, just past Kole's shoulder, the MF agent dropped to the floor. She turned, Kassis and the other agent to her left now both on the floor as well. Kassis coughed, shot in the neck, blood spewing from his mouth as he let out a low, guttural groan. His hand went instantly to his wound.

Kole approached him, swiftly kicking the plasma gun out of his free hand. He stared down at him as he twitched, coughing harder with more blood. Kole extended his arm, firing a single shot of his plasma gun to Kassis's head, his body going instantly limp.

He turned and looked at Tala, the same hardened expression on his face as always. Maverick and Kane were at her sides in a moment, their guns gripped firmly in their hands as they pointed them at Kole.

"I was hoping you were smart enough to pick up on my cues," Kole said flatly as he holstered the plasma gun at his waist. "And Sanders, it's nice to see you're alive." He tipped his head at Maverick.

"What the hell is going on?" she asked, casting a side glance at Maverick who looked as uncertain as she felt.

"You think you're the only one who can read the writing on the wall?" Kole asked, unfazed at Maverick's and Kane's guns. "I was a little late to the party, but I got there. And right now, I'm an asset to you for two reasons."

Tala's eyes roved over the three dead MF agents, then back up at Kole. This wasn't the captain she remembered, and her mind was spinning. She turned to Kane, knowing he was the best one to read him, to gauge if this was real.

"Maybe getting to this floor was a walk in the park," Kole said, "but this is the presidential floor. There are MF here. Everywhere. Lucky for you, I called them to the west tower. Though some are still here, of course. I can get you to the cynosure."

"The other reason?" Kane asked, his voice clipped. Tala could see he was scrutinizing him closely, intently.

"He knew you'd come," Kole said, not so much as a glance at Kane. "He's got a contingency plan."

"What is it?" Maverick asked.

"There's a bomb," Kole said.

Tala straightened.

"Not just any bomb. A Macro-CPB," he said.

Tala felt her jaw fall. "I…" she stammered. "I thought those were just theoretical."

"Apparently not in the Republic," Kole said.

"Someone want to fill us in?" Kane asked with hurried impatience.

Tala turned toward him, unable to hide the fear in her eyes. "A macro centrifugal profusion bomb."

"There's no way," Maverick said, shaking his head fervently. "No way."

"You think I'm lying?" Kole snapped.

There was a brief silence among the four of them as Tala looked at Kane. She felt her panic charging its way into her mind, she felt it tighten in her chest.

"Where's the bomb?" Kane asked.

"Does it matter? You'll never get to it in time. That thing would decimate the entire city. There'd be nothing and no one left," Kole asserted.

"Where's the bomb," Kane repeated, his voice taut.

"West Oxwick. Miles Park, near the East River," he said.

"As centrally located as anything can get around here," Maverick said. There was a fear in his eyes that Tala had never seen before.

"I can get to it," Kane said.

"How? That's miles away," Kole scoffed.

Tala was quiet as she studied his eyes, dark and deep with their tiny golden speck. Those were the eyes she'd built a home in.

"Lancer to base-ops," Maverick said.

"Hawkeye here. What's going on?"

"I've got three dead vipers and an olive branch," he said, Kole being the olive branch as a possible defector. "Has information. A Macro-CPB."

"In the city?" the colonel asked.

"Affirmative. Miles Park."

"Lancer, this is Renegade. Is the olive branch credible? We have no intel on this and no teams anywhere near Miles Park."

Maverick sighed as he looked at Tala and Kane.

"Renegade, this is Phoenix. Olive branch seems credible," Kane said.

Until that very moment, until Kane spoke, somewhere in the back of her mind, Tala could convince herself that it wasn't real. That the bomb wasn't real. His words hit her like a sledgehammer, knocking the wind from her lungs. It was the bomb everyone and no one wanted. It was whispered about, always rumored but never confirmed. Who dared to build something powerful enough to end the world? In less than a hundred years, every lesson the Great War should have taught them had disappeared into the ether.

Evolution, not revolution, as Otto had said. It was evolution that was going to be the end of everything.

"I can get to it," Kane repeated. She heard his desperation this time, and she wasn't sure who he was trying to convince at that point.

"We have no intel on how to disable it," Colonel Thornton said. There was urgency in his voice.

This was what Thias wanted, Tala realized. He was determined to beat her at any cost. He was willing to go down too, so long as he could take her with him. She suddenly felt sick to her stomach. She looked away, taking slow, steady breaths through her nose, fighting the rising bile.

"Merlin," Kane said after a moment, like it was the most obvious answer. "Merlin knows. Or he can at least find out. He can get into Outlaw's computer," he said, referring to Thias.

"Phoenix, there is no way to get that intel in time. We don't know how much time we're working with," Colonel Thornton said. "Our goal is to capture Outlaw. That's how we prevent this bomb going off."

But they were wrong. Tala knew it, Kane knew it, Maverick knew it. Thias's plan wouldn't allow for his capture without his bomb exploding.

"You know I'm the only chance we have," Kane said, looking to Maverick. He was appealing to him in a way he couldn't to Victoria or Colonel Thornton.

"Lancer, do not let him leave. Triple Play 1, you have a mission," Colonel Thornton nearly spat in their ears.

"As team leader, I have situational control," Maverick said, standing a little straighter. His lips pursed in a line, he fixed his gaze on Kane.

Tala looked between the two, a conversation happening between them without a word.

"Go," Maverick said sternly.

Kane turned toward Tala, and she felt her throat constrict, the air suddenly sucked from the room as she felt a pang of panic rise inside her. Her heart pounding, her hands trembled as they hung at her sides.

If there was anyone who could get to it, it was Kane. But why, she felt her heart start pleading with her, did it have to be him? Because he knew the city better than anyone. Because he knew how to stay unseen, how to stay in the shadows even during the day. Because he could do things no one else could.

"Tala," he said gently as he took a step nearer her. The way he said her name stirred fear inside her.

"Don't say it," she said, her voice thick. Her emotions caught in the back of her throat. She saw the nuance of many emotions cross his face, filling his eyes as he looked at her.

"Don't say it," she repeated, her voice suddenly hoarse. She held his gaze, afraid to look away, afraid to blink.

"Phoenix," Maverick said, his voice commanding.

Kane's eyes lingered for another moment. Tala wanted to step inside them, live in them forever, never be away from him. When he dropped her gaze, she swallowed hard, feeling a needling behind her eyes. She willed herself not to cry.

"The stairwell at the end of the corridor should be clear," Kole said. "But the reflection pools outside the towers are all critical terrain. You'd be spotted by MF the second you step foot outside this building."

"The north side is all wooded park," Maverick said.

"There're no doors on that side of the building. For things such as this, I imagine," Kole said as he cocked his head.

"Who said I need a door?" Kane said, his voice deep.

"Go," Maverick said.

"Phoenix," Colonel Thornton's voice boomed through their comms.

Kane nodded, then took a step away from Tala. She reached for his hand, tugging hard. He paused, turned toward her, a breathtaking pain tearing through his eyes. Reaching out, he brushed a loose strand of hair off her cheek. Then with a frown, he dropped her hand, turned and left.

Tala's breath caught. It took only a moment to feel his absence in her bones, and she knew he was gone.

TWENTY-NINE

Tala felt numb as she followed the line, Maverick, then Kole, both ahead of her as they wound through the deserted corridors. Despite the stifling air around them, Tala shivered. She knew she had to keep her mind focused, but her heart was breaking into a million pieces. The air in her lungs felt solid, and despite herself, she felt her mind slipping away.

"Bluebird," Maverick snapped.

Tala jerked her head up, realizing he was talking to her.

"Get your head right," he said. His eyes were lit with admonishment. "You're a soldier."

She silently looked back at him, his scolding feeling like a slap across the face, and she nodded. He was right. This was not the time to fall apart. She bit hard at the inside of her cheek until she tasted blood and nodded again.

"Okay then," he said, his eyes not wavering from hers. She hated the doubt she saw in them. Her grief, her fears, they were to be expected, but they had no place in the moment, and she knew she had to push them away.

"Alexander, you're not being the agent I led. You either get in the game now or you bow out. We can't afford to have you half in this," Kole said, the furrow between his brows deepening.

"I'm good," she said and clenched teeth, assuring herself as much as them.

"All right then. Around the corner, at the end of the hall," Kole said, his eyes flitting between her and Maverick, his plasma gun now in his hand, "is the presidential lobby. It's a large space that circumvents the entire cynosure, spanning all three towers. And it's guarded. The entrance to the president's chamber is through the east tower, to the right of our current position."

Tala nodded, focusing, letting Kole's words sharpen her mind while using them like glue to hold herself together. Listening to him transported her to another time, when she was in the field, when her subject was just another somebody. She clung to that.

"They'll see you even before you get to the end of the hall, and there's nowhere to take cover," Kole said.

"So we'll use you," Maverick said. "A fake-out hostage situation."

"I was about to suggest that," he said as he looked at Maverick, then at Tala.

"Tala, you stay on my six," Maverick said. "Look at me."

She met his gaze, keeping hers steady. She wasn't going to let him doubt her again.

"Tell me you can do this. I need you. Tell me you can do this," he said. His voice was strong, commanding, pulling her further out of herself.

She could do this. She *could* do this. This was exactly what she was trained for. And though her mind wanted to betray her, it was time to tap into her discipline. It was time to level-up. What it came down to now was her mindset. She was determined to prevail, not for herself, but for everyone else, those who came before her, and those yet to come.

And that was enough to fortify her.

Be the stone, she told herself. One ripple at a time. She was so small in comparison to the larger vision. *Be the stone*. But that didn't diminish her role. She had a part to play, a part that was hers and hers alone. No one, especially Thias, would take that from her.

"I can do this," she said, her voice steady, unwavering. "On your six."

Though Maverick's face didn't so much as flinch, there was something that passed over his eyes: fortitude, determination, and more importantly, confidence. He was putting his life in her hands.

He pulled the handgun from its holster at his leg, and while he was righthanded and held the gun with his left, she didn't doubt his aim. He'd trained for years to master his shot. Clutching his rifle in his other hand, the buttstock pressed into his shoulder to steady it, he turned to Kole.

"You're up," he said.

Kole wedged his gun in his waistband at the back of his pants, his suit coat hanging over it. Without hesitation, he turned the corner, Maverick behind him with his guns ready, and Tala behind him, gripping her rifle tightly in her hands. They moved swiftly toward the lobby, the black cynosure visible through a wall of windows ahead of them.

Tala's heart pounded, her adrenaline pumping through her veins with every step she took. The world fell away, and all that was left in her mind was her mission.

"Stop!" a voice commanded as they approached the last few yards of the hallway. An agent held his plasma gun aimed at them. But Maverick stayed steady and pushed forward, keeping Kole, who held his arms in the air above his head, positioned in front of him.

"I said stop!" the agent yelled again.

Tala watched as a second MF appeared beside him, his gun aimed at them as they continued their way toward them.

"Guns down," Maverick called out, his head just above Kole's shoulder to catch a view of the MF. "You've already got six dead agents, don't think I won't shoot him too."

"I don't think he's making an idle threat," Kole said.

"Captain," the second agent said, and Tala caught a glimpse of him, recognizing him, though she couldn't recall a name.

"Now!" Maverick's voice boomed as he gave Kole a hard shove forward, pressing the barrel of the handgun into his back, between his shoulder blades. Maverick stepped out of the confines of the hall and into the lobby, and before Tala could even blink, the loud, deep electrical blast of a plasma charge from an unseen shooter filled her ears and Maverick dropped to his knees with a loud grunt.

Tala's breath hitched as she stepped around Kole, firing at the two agents before her. The first dropped to the floor, a loud moan escaping his lips. She pointed her gun at the second agent just as a third, the one who'd been out of sight and shot Maverick, appeared to her right. She fired once, missing, the bullet shattering the glass of the window across the lobby.

She fired again, this time finding her target. A moment later, she watched from the corner of her eye as the third agent fell to the ground, Kole's plasma charge hitting him squarely between the eyes.

Tala rushed to Maverick as his handgun fell from his grip. Tala heard shouting and the sound of boots on the ground as she dropped to her knees at his side.

He gnashed his teeth as he took his rifle in both hands, firing half a dozen shots over Tala's shoulder just as he collapsed with a loud, grating groan.

She wasn't sure what registered first, Maverick's chalky white face or the blood soaking through his pants, a deep laceration from the plasma charge in his thigh. She had to get him out of the lobby. Kole stepped in front of her while continuing to shoot at the approaching MF. Tala slipped her arms under Maverick's and dragged him back into the hallway, shielded at least by the walls on both sides. He let out a guttural moan as he tried to prop himself up against the wall, his breathing rapid and labored.

Kole kicked Maverick's gun back toward him, then took cover around the corner of the hallway as a plasma charge sailed past. He fired three times, and Tala heard another body hit the floor.

"I need fire support!" Kole hollered over his shoulder.

Tala jumped to her feet. Clutching her rifle, she sidestepped Maverick, stepping into the open lobby as two MF quickly approached from the left. She and Kole fired simultaneously, Tala's shot hitting one in the leg. She fired again, her second shot hitting him in the shoulder, knocking him to the ground.

Kole's shot missed, and the agent fired back at them. Tala spun away from the charge as it hit the wall, blowing bits of it into the air.

"He's yours!" Kole yelled, then quickly ducked into the hallway, away from Tala. She fired at the agent as he rushed toward her while the one on the ground pushed himself onto his knees. He took a shot at Tala, the charge narrowly missing her face, though close enough to feel its heat.

Tala sucked in a sharp breath, steadying her arms as they trembled with adrenaline, then took two quick shots, each one hitting their mark, both agents dropping lifelessly to the ground. The lobby went instantly quiet without the sound of gunfire peppering the air. She turned and stepped back into the hallway as Kole tied his tie around Maverick's leg as a makeshift tourniquet. Maverick cried out, his face twisted up in pain, and Tala gasped.

"Mav," she said, dropping to her knees beside him. "Stay with me," she pleaded. There was so much blood, its ripe odor making Tala's stomach flip.

He turned his face toward her, his jaw clenched, his breathing erratic. "Tals," he said.

"It didn't hit the femoral artery," Kole said, though the look in his eyes told Tala it was still a serious wound.

"You need to hold on," she said to Maverick as she looked at his leg. Thick, red blood oozed from the large laceration, pooling on the floor below him. "You need to hold on long enough for Phoenix to make it back to you."

He groaned again, louder, and nodded. "Finish this," he said, his words labored.

"I'll get him somewhere safe," Kole said assuredly. "Follow the lobby to the right, to the east tower. You'll see the bridge-way to the cynosure. There's power to the security panel. The current passcode is 522T210T."

Of course, she thought, their birthdays.

"He's waiting for you. Do not let your guard down, Agent."

Tala nodded. He might be waiting, but she was ready. She looked back at Maverick, his face growing paler with each passing moment, sweat gathering above his top lip, dripping down the sides of his face.

"Just hold on. Until Phoenix can get to you," she said again. She cringed at the uncertainty in her voice. She wasn't sure Maverick had that long, but she hated for him to doubt too. He needed to hold on to something.

"I believe in you, Tals," he mumbled, his voice trembling and growing weaker. "I've always believed in you. Go," he said, his head lolling back, his eyes closing.

Tala's stomach tightened, and she swallowed hard the emotion rising in her. She nodded. With one last look at each of them, she turned. Steeling herself, she held her gun tightly, the buttstock pressed into the fleshy part of her shoulder near her chest, then eased her way down the hall toward the lobby.

Around the corner, she heard the heavy footfalls of approaching MF. Carefully, her hand found the metal cylinder attached to the web of her frag jacket, and with a quick jerk, she pulled it loose.

She tugged at the pull ring, then tossed the small stun grenade around the corner of the wall, into the lobby. Turning away, she crouched low, her fingers shoved hard into her ears, her eyes closed. The explosion was loud, deafening, and she felt it in her chest. Even from behind closed eyes, she saw the bright flash of the candlepower. A moment later, she was on her feet, rounding the corner. She fired twice, each bullet hitting a staggering and disoriented MF clutching at their ears. Without a glance behind her, she took off in a jog toward the east tower.

Staying light on her feet, sticking to the inside perimeter along the windows, she ran through the circular lobby. It was quiet, too quiet for her comfort, and she ran with her heart in her throat. Through the windows, she could make out the bridge-way just ahead and slowed.

With steady and quiet steps, she eased herself around the curved wall of windows, passing a large administrative desk, an MF coming into view. But she was ready before he was and a clean shot brought him to the floor.

Passing his body, she glanced down at him, recognizing him as part of the Presidential Protection team from when Royer had been president. She felt a pang inside as she realized these weren't just random enemy combatants that she'd killed. These were agents she had served alongside. She turned down the narrow bridge, the walls and floor made of thick glass. Her breath hitched as she glanced down, the ground a hundred stories below. When she reached the security panel at the door, she paused, willing her racing heart to calm.

"Phoenix to base-ops." Kane's voice suddenly filled her ears, hearing him through her comm.

"Hawkeye to Phoenix. What's your location?" Colonel Thornton asked.

"Miles Park. I'm at the bomb. I've got it in front of me," he said, his voice taut.

"Phoenix, it's Merlin," Max said, and Tala exhaled in relief at the sound of his voice. "I've been tearing through Outlaw's computer, and I think I've found something. I'll walk you through it."

Tala gave the small bead in her ear three rapid taps, turning the volume down. She couldn't have them in her head for what was about to come.

Reaching for the security pad to the right of the door, Tala's hand shook. She made a fist to steady it and took a breath, her shoulders falling. Then carefully, she typed in the passcode:

522T210T.

THIRTY

There was a quiet click as the door unlocked, and Tala felt a shudder in her bones. She turned the knob and cautiously gave the door a slow push to open it.

"I've been waiting for you," the cool, familiar voice said as the door opened fully.

Tala stepped slowly into the cynosure, her hand clutching the grip of her gun so tightly her knuckles were turning white. The morning sun streamed gently in through the engineered glass panels that made up the entire room, the polished black granite floor the exception. Her breath caught, her eyes finding his at once. They were the same blue that lived in her memory. But he looked different. His hair was even longer than in his video messages, curling at the edges. There were crinkles in the corner of his eyes and deep lines across his forehead that she didn't remember. He looked older than his thirty-three years of age. But time and distance have a way of changing the way someone looks at things they're used to seeing every day. Maybe he'd always looked this way. Maybe these were signs of due stress. Was he, in fact, not as infallible as he thought?

He sat, looking comfortable, on a black sofa that faced the door where she stood. He was dressed in a steel gray suit and no tie, which was also a new look for him. He was sunk back, an arm leisurely draped along the back of the sofa, a leg brought up, resting on the knee of the other. But while he looked relaxed, his face was hard. She heard the door close behind her, latching.

"Actually, I've been watching you," he said. He sounded distant, detached, and it raised goosebumps along her neck, down her arms.

She glanced to the side. While the cynosure was designed to be unable to see in from the outside, it was possible to see out from the inside, right through the windows and into the circular lobby. He'd watched everything from the comforts of his couch. She swallowed, her mouth going dry.

"I tried to not make it too difficult to reach me," he said offhandedly. His indifference disquieted her, putting her nerves on edge. "Though I'll admit I'm impressed with your performance. I've never seen you in action before." A smile pulled at the corner of his mouth. "All that intensive, elite Militia Forces training. They did well with you. Too bad you're using all of it against us. Against me," he said, tipping his head toward her.

"You didn't leave me much of a choice," she said, finding her voice. It had been months since she'd actually spoken with him. Months that seemed like years. Before leaving the Republic, the most they'd ever gone were a handful of days. But her life wasn't even a silhouette of what it had been. "Someone has to stop you," she said, hearing the bite in her tone.

"And you think you can?" His leg swung off the other, and he rose to his feet, adjusting his shoulders in his suit coat, tugging gently at the cuffs. "I'd like to see you try. But things are bigger than just you and I."

"You mean your bomb? The Macro-CPB?" she asked.

His eyes flared for a moment, then he took a small step toward her.

"That would completely level the city. Decimate everything within thirty miles. Not to mention long-term fallout," she said. She fought to keep her voice level, not to let any of her emotion give her away.

He gave a small shrug. "Sometimes we have to make the tough choices, despite the cost. At any rate, there's nothing you can do about my bomb."

"We'll diffuse it," she said, not as confident as her voice let on. The dismaying truth was that she didn't know the full scope of his strategies. While the new United States had been putting together their plan, he'd been assembling his own.

"We'll see." He smiled and let out a deep chuckle. "You ruined things for me."

"How's that?" she asked.

"I was going to bring the world together," he said. "Mankind is broken, humanity is flawed. People need leaders with a bigger vision, a way to make the machine of the world operate. I, *I* was that person."

"You weren't bringing anyone together," she said sharply. "You were dividing them, setting people against each other. You're suffocating and deprecating the people you've relegated as second-class, your own people, stripping them of their rights. You created unrest because of the social disparities among the population, by taking and taking and never giving."

"Rights," he scoffed. "Rights shouldn't be guaranteed to all, but rather to those who earn them, who deserve them. It's freewill, the ability to choose, that's what divides people. They pit themselves against each other over their differences. I was preventing that. We're stronger when we operate as one."

"That kind of conformity goes against the very nature of humans," she argued. "People can co-exist despite their differences, they can still be treated with dignity and respect. When you give them power over themselves, it gives them purpose. When we have the opportunity to serve ourselves and to serve others, that's how we serve our nation. That's what allows us to thrive."

"I see now that my biggest mistake was not involving you in the politics of it all from the beginning," he said, his voice steep with irritation. "Maybe I could've molded you the right way, suffocated these radical and rebellious ideologies. You've fallen away from our legacy, from what makes you and I important."

"You don't have a clue about our legacy," she said, shaking her head. "It was our father who started this revolution!" she yelled. Maybe it would only antagonize him, but she couldn't hold it back.

He was quiet for a moment, his eyes narrowing. "I don't believe that for a second."

"Of course you don't. But I've seen the proof. And I know things you don't, things you could never understand," she said.

"It doesn't matter anymore, who started what. I'm about to finish all of it. You can't stop what's coming." His vexation ebbed, his eyes brightening with something else, a smile playing on his mouth.

Silence fell between them, and she could once again hear the faint conversation in her comm between Kane and Max as he instructed him, step by step, in bomb disassembly.

"Locate the master circuit board... closest to the power supply... trace the ground wire..."

Looking across the small space between her and Thias, she realized there was more to his smile. It wasn't just mockery because he thought he was superior to them, there was something diabolical in it that told her there was more to it than the bomb. That was just one part of it all. She was suddenly certain something was being missed.

No sooner had the thought processed in her mind, she heard Kane's voice in a way she never had before. Before registering even a single word, she heard his panic, his fear. Her comm erupted in a cacophonous frenzy between him and Max and Colonel Thornton that echoed through her head, sending her spinning.

Tala pressed her finger to the side of the bead in her ear, the volume increasing, her mind catching only fragments:

Activated.

Timer.

Countdown.

Eight minutes.

Enough time.

Disable.

Tell me.

What you see.

Exactly.

An orange wire, a blue, a green wire, a multicolored, a purple, a yellow wire...

"What did you do?" she gasped, the sudden horror of realization striking her, knocking the wind from her lungs. She snapped her gun up, pointing it at him just as she looked down the barrel of his plasma gun.

In that moment, a flurry of emotion ran through her, but two prevailing ones clasped their cold fingers onto her: anger and fear. And Tala knew they were the worst of them all. They had a way of disabling, of paralyzing, of creating doubt, of manipulating reality.

"What did you do?" she yelled again, her emotion escaping her mouth along with her words.

Thias only laughed as he took another step closer. She tried to step back but was halted by the door, the knob pressing into her back. Step by step, he moved closer to her, and she felt panic prodding its way into her mind. She swallowed hard, fighting to keep it at bay as she glanced around the room, unsure of what she was looking for.

"It wasn't that long ago that we stood at a standstill not unlike this one," he said, still making his way toward her, his gun still raised. "My mistake was letting you live." Gone was the smile on his face, replaced by a hardened expression that filled his blue eyes with darkness.

Tala's mind raced, the frantic conversation between Kane and Max still playing in her ear.

"You couldn't shoot me now any more than you could've then," he said. He was at her, and while his right hand held the plasma gun steadily aimed at her, only inches from her chest, he reached out with the other, dragging his thumb along the side of her cheek.

She sucked in a sharp breath, then swung her arm in front of her, knocking his hand with the gun away just as he fired, the plasma charge drilling the door.

She kicked the gun from his grasp, sending it sailing across the room as she thrust the heel of her hand into his nose, feeling it break upon impact. He lunged at her, knocking her backward, her head bouncing off the door, his hands finding her throat. His fingers wrapped around her neck like a noose, instantly severing the breath to her lungs. He lifted her entire body from the ground, the toes of her boots barely scraping the surface of the floor.

With one hand still clutching her rifle, she used her free hand to claw at his arm, at his hands, her nails cutting his skin raw, but his grip didn't slacken. She kicked her leg between his while she slammed the butt of the rifle into the side of his head, and he released his grip as he staggered backward.

Tala coughed as she took heavy breaths, the air burning in the back of her throat. Before she realized he had steadied himself, he kicked her gun from her grip, her fingers crunching beneath the blow from his shoe. She charged at him, pushing him backward, and he punched her hard, his fist finding her cheekbone, a burst of pain flashing across her face like an explosion. She stumbled on her feet, her head spinning.

"Merlin," Kane said soberly in her ear, "the bomb's been customized. The last two wires, they're blue and yellow, not red and white."

The conversation in her comm fell silent, and her eyes met Thias's, cold, hard, and distant, as she realized this was his plan. He didn't care if the bomb was found. He knew that as soon as someone tried to disable it, it would engage the countdown. He probably counted on it. He wanted them to think they could disarm it. But in the end, they would find that he'd outsmarted them, modified things just enough so they would fail. After all of it, he was still in control. This was his utopia.

"Tell me what color!" she yelled, the pain in her face pulsing with the racing of her heart. She charged at him again, knocking him off balance, then turned her hips as she side-kicked him hard in the abdomen, watching him fall to the ground with a thud. Throwing herself on top of him, mounting him across the chest, she punched him in the jaw, his head flailing to the side.

"Tell me what color!" she yelled again, her face only inches from his. She could feel warm blood trickle down her face from her busted cheek. She took a breath and punched him again, his nose still gushing red.

"Tell me!"

Thias laughed, deep and throaty, in a way that was so menacing it sent a chill down the length of her spine.

As she punched him a third time, he raised his hands, blocking her fist from his face. He wrapped his arms around her torso, pulling her to him, pressing her against his chest, then swung his leg, quickly rolling her over, pinning himself on top of her. He was stronger than her, his weight bearing down on her chest.

"Fight me all you want," he said, blood dripping down his mouth, "but I won't tell you. I'll hold out for at least that long." He sneered and then smiled, his perfectly white teeth now shaded pink with blood.

"I don't get you," she said, her head pounding at her temples and behind her eye. Her body felt weak as he lingered above her. "Why take everyone down with you?"

"Not everyone," he said, shaking his head, his eyes fixed on hers. He spoke slowly, emphasizing each word. "Nina and the kids are safe. But all those other people, they don't mean shit to me. It's you, Tala. If I go down, I'm taking you with me. It isn't enough to be just another ghost to haunt your dreams. You're mine. I'll never let you be without me."

She flung her fists up at him, her left just grazing the bottom of his jaw as his hands found her neck again. His grasp tightened, and she tried to take a breath but couldn't. He gripped her so hard she began to shake under his quivering hands, her brain rattling inside her head.

Tala tried to scream, but not even a whimper could be heard from her as she clawed at him, digging in her nails, tearing the flesh off his hands as she dragged them across his skin.

"Bluebird, this is Hawkeye," she heard the colonel's voice loudly and clearly in her ear. "We know you're with Outlaw. Get him to tell us which wire. Whatever it takes. Copy."

There was a brief silence in her comm.

"Bluebird, do you copy?" he repeated.

"Bluebird, respond!" Kane yelled. The terror in his voice made her heart fall. This wasn't going to be it. This wasn't how this was going to end.

"Bluebird, are you there?" Victoria asked.

Dark spots began dancing in her periphery as Thias squeezed harder, his face screwed up in a fury of rage.

Straining her arm around his leg, Tala felt her hand grasp the handle of the gun holstered at her thigh, and for a brief moment, she smiled. She slammed the butt into the side of his face, exactly where she'd hit him before, and his grip slackened though he didn't let go.

Tala's body shifted into action, her mind left behind to play catch-up. Before reason could take over, she pressed the muzzle of the gun into his shoulder and fired.

Thias's grip released instantly, his body slumping over. She struggled to catch her breath, the air filling her lungs, burning with every gasp as if her chest were to combust. Giving him a heavy shove, his body tumbled off her.

"Bluebird," Kane said again with desperation.

"I'm here," she said, her voice strained. "Copy."

Groaning, Thias brought his hand to his shoulder, blood staining through his pristine suit.

Tala fumbled to her feet, the gun still firmly grasped in her hand, aimed at him while she steadied herself.

"Tell me which wire," she said hoarsely as she looked down at him.

He gazed up at her through heavy lashes. "You fucking shot me!" he spat, bloody spit spewing from his mouth.

Tala kicked him hard in the abdomen, and his body lurched as he grunted.

"Tell me," she demanded as she took a step closer, towering over him. With her gun still on him, she reached into the side pocket of her pants, pulling out a restraint cuff. She kicked him again, his body folding over. Quickly, she grabbed his wrist, slipping the cuff over his hand, then tightened it until it pinched his skin. She reached for his other hand, smeared with thick blood as he clutched his shot shoulder, and slipped it into the cuff.

"Tell me which wire," she said and clenched her teeth. They were running out of time, and she was afraid to ask about the countdown.

"Tell me!" she screamed.

Thias laughed.

Tala put the muzzle of her gun to his wound and pressed hard, twisting as she drilled it into his shoulder, and his laugh molded into a grumble of pain.

Tala heard the door of the cynosure open behind her, but she only pressed the gun harder into him. She peered quickly over her shoulder to see Kole entering the room. "Tell me," she demanded.

"I told you," he said between heavy breaths. "I'll hold out as long as I can. Until time runs out. Which it will," he said wryly. "Soon."

Tala stood up, looking at Kole as he approached them.

"Traitor," Thias mumbled, though Kole ignored him.

"He customized the bomb. Switched the colors of the last two wires. One stops all of this, the other blows us all up," she said, wiping at the sweat along her hairline with the back of her hand, smearing the blood on her face.

Kole looked between them as Thias propped himself up against the couch, wincing from the pain with each movement.

She turned back to him. "Tell me!" she shouted as she looked down at him. "I'll shoot you again," she threatened as she raised the gun.

Thias's eyes met hers, the same blue she saw in the reflection in the mirror. Their mother's eyes. It was in that moment that she suddenly registered the scene around her. Thias, her brother, a bullet in his shoulder from her gun.

Looking down at him, a whirlwind of memories crashed through her mind, settling on one long ago. Fifteen-year-old Tala curled beneath a blanket in the captain's office in Command, heartbroken and afraid as she looked up into the assured bright blue eyes of her older brother.

"Tala, I'm going to take care of you. I'll always protect you."

Her heart suddenly felt heavy, her mind trying to reconcile the brother from that memory with the man she saw now. Her mind began to waver, her doubt seeping in between the cracks.

"You can't do it!" he hailed, a hysterical laugh bursting from his mouth. The very sound of it made her anger flare, everything in her vision going red.

She lurched across the small distance between them, putting herself in his face, her eyes narrowing. She reached for him, fisting his thick blond hair and jerking his head back, then pressed the gun to his throat.

"Which wire?" she asked, her voice scratchy as she spoke through gritted teeth.

His laughter stopped, and his smile faded, his eyes leveling with hers. He pursed his lips in defiant silence.

"Are you really going to just let yourself be blown up?" she asked, though deep down she knew it was futile.

"I get to walk away," he said, his voice strained from the angle of his head, from the gun pressed against him.

"What?" she asked, cocking her head to the side.

"I get to walk away," he repeated calmly with a beguiling smile.

Tala took slow, deep breaths as she studied him, searching his eyes for the smallest of tells. No one knew him like she did.

She released her hold of his hair, then stood, stepping back from him.

"I get to walk away, and I'll tell you which wire," he said.

"I don't have the power to make that kind of deal," she said after a moment.

"Bluebird." Kane's voice came to life in her ear again. "Bluebird, we're running out of time. Less than two minutes. You need to do something." There was so much tension in his voice.

"If that clock drops below twenty seconds," Colonel Thornton said, "Phoenix, you are instructed to cut any wire."

"But—" Kane started.

"We've got a fifty percent chance of stopping that bomb from blowing," he said sharply. "That's an order."

Tala took a breath, looking away, her mind racing, pulsing in her temples. *Think,* she told herself. She turned back to Thias. Between his busted lip, broken nose, and the gash to the side of his head, his face was a bloodied mess. But his eyes were as fierce as they'd ever been.

"You don't have to make a deal," he said, pointing at the comm in her ear. "Not with them. They never have to know. You allow me to slip away, and I'll tell you which wire." His voice was smooth as liquid as he straightened his body, adjusting his suit jacket, fumbling with the hem of his pants.

"Alexander," Kole said. She turned, her eyes meeting his, dark and hard, the furrow between them deepening. "Do what you have to."

There it was, her chance to stop it all dangling right before her, and she couldn't understand why she wasn't jumping for it. There were a dozen scenarios that played off the top of her head that would let Thias get away.

"You can move on with your life," Thias said. "Whatever future you want, it's yours. Let me slip away, and you can have it all." His words filled her head, inflating inside her mind, suffocating her voice of reason.

She turned back to him, swallowing hard. The fifteen-year-old version of herself looked at him and saw the last person left in her world, and she'd trusted him with everything she had. She shifted on her feet, the weight of the gun in her hand suddenly heavy.

"Bluebird…" Kane said.

Kane.

He was the one person she wanted to have forever with. A life with him, that was the dream, and she had never been so close and equally far away from it as she was in that very moment.

She let her shoulders fall, sighing in resignation. A smile crept across Thias's face as he looked up at her.

"This is treason," she said.

"Think of all the people you'll save," he said as he readjusted his body, turning partially away from her, his face contorted from the pain in his shoulder.

"True." Tala held her finger to her comm, turning it off. "The chopper taking us out of here flies in autonomous mode," she said after a moment. "My friend Max, I can get him to override it. When we put the chopper down unexpectedly, that'll be your window," she said, meeting his gaze.

His eyes lit up like a fire that burned inside of him, and he nodded his head.

"A deal's a deal," she said.

"Yes, it is. And at the end of the day, you're my sister," he said, his expression serene. "The blue wire."

Tala felt a jolt of energy charge through her like an electrical current as she looked down at him. It was true, at the end of the day, she was his sister, and he was her brother. It's how it had always been, and it was how it would always be.

But they were still strangers.

"I'll never let you be without me." She let his words circle back to her in her mind, a smile curling at the corner of her mouth.

She turned away, giving the comm a tap, turning it back on. "Phoenix, cut the yellow wire," she said.

"What?" Thias yelled. She heard him scuffle behind her.

"You're sure?" Kane asked.

"Cut it!" she shouted.

"No! No!" Thias's hollers were loud and belligerent.

Time seemed to suddenly slow to half-speed, the room expanding around her as she turned back toward Thias, now standing on his feet. She caught the wild, feral look in his eyes. She saw the small gun in his hands in the split second after he'd already taken aim at her. The sound of the deep electrical blast filled her ears. Unable to even take a breath, her body was frozen, paralyzed as she stood in place, her eyes wide with terror and confusion.

In one moment, she was looking across the small distance between her and Thias, his icy blue gaze locked on hers. Then she watched as he dropped to his knees, the gun falling from his hands. The bright red stain on his chest bled through his shirt as he crumpled to the ground. In a flash, the life in his eyes was gone.

Tala turned to see Kole, his arms outstretched as he clutched his plasma gun in his grasp. And finally, she took a breath.

Kole abruptly left the president's office, without a word, leaving Tala in the cynosure with Thias, his lifeless body growing cold. She approached him slowly, with caution, then dropped to her knees beside him. Reaching out, she closed his eyes. She thought about his family, Nina and the kids. They would be okay, she would make sure of that.

Her mind wandered to Kane who had been instructed to stay with the bomb in Miles Park across the city until a special ordnance disposal team could reach him. But no one knew when that would be. The rest of Operation Libertas was well underway, troops pervading the country. There was chaos, uncertainty, confusion. First a nationwide blackout, then troops storming the cities. To the people of the Republic, the sky was falling on that fateful day, and they weren't sure what would be revealed once the smoke cleared. But she knew what her people had in them. They were strong enough to survive. Then with a wave of change, they would do more than just survive, they would learn to live a new life. That was her hope.

As Tala looked at Thias, she could feel his absence, that he was no longer with her in an almost tangible way. And while she felt sadness, she also felt free, the shackles that bound her to him gone. It was time to let go, of the illusion that things could've been different, of all the loss he'd brought upon her. To hang on to him would be to hold herself back. And all she wanted was to step into a future that, until that moment, had only been a dream.

The door of the cynosure opened, and Tala turned as Kole reappeared before her, Maverick clinging to him. Kole supported the brunt of his weight, his leg dragging uselessly behind him. She could see the strain of pain on Maverick's face as he gnashed his teeth to keep from crying out, and she hurried across the room to them.

Maverick was pale, white as a ghost, his eyes sunken and sallow, but he still managed a small smile at the sight of her. She slipped under his arm, shifting some of his weight to her, relieving Kole enough that he let out a deep sigh.

"You did it," he said weakly through dried, chapped lips. She saw his struggle to keep even his head up.

"Well, kind of," she said, her eyes briefly catching Kole's as they dragged him across the room and settled him on the sofa. He groaned loudly as they eased him into a seated position and elevated his leg. Though his pants were black, she could see the large bloodstain, but the wound was now covered by a wadded, black fabric.

"I just fired a gun," Kole said dismissively. "Nothing more."

"And nothing less," she said as she looked up at him. For the first time ever, the furrow between his brows was less defined, almost relaxed.

"Mav, hold on a little longer," she said, trying to at least sound optimistic. He didn't look good. His skin was cold and clammy to the touch, and both his breathing and his heart rate were rapid and erratic.

As his eyes fluttered shut, Kole gave her a slow shake of his head. Tala had to catch her rising emotion and looked away quickly. She wouldn't fall apart now.

Tala wasn't sure how long she and Kole sat locked in the cynosure, Thias's body unmoved from the floor until the scene could be processed, and Maverick floating in and out of consciousness, but eventually, a knock came at the door.

"Bluebird," the familiar voice called out, and Tala's heart practically leapt from her chest. "It's Phoenix."

Tala was across the large room in only a few strides, and as soon as she opened the door, she launched herself into his arms. It was the sight of him, the feeling of his arms around her that brought all her emotions to the surface. Her body shook as he held her, his strong arms never wavering.

"We live to see another day," he said, his voice low and deep, raspy, his mouth beside her ear.

They pulled apart, and Tala found his eyes. There was a happiness in them that translated deep inside her.

"Maverick," she said quickly. "He needs your help." She heard the desperation in her voice. Then she turned to see Kole, sitting quietly beside Maverick.

"I already know," he said calmly to Tala. Kane and Tala exchanged a nervous, uncertain glance. "I was warned by Thias that he could do extraordinary things, that he was likely to be with you when you came for him. Naturally, I don't know the full scope, but I know enough to know he might be able to help your friend."

"Who else knows?" Tala asked anxiously. She could feel Kane's tension beside her. He'd lived his life in the shadows, desperately hiding this secret from the world.

"No one. To my knowledge. I was the one tasked to be in command of the agents in this building. It's pretty sensational. Unbelievable. I can understand your need to keep this information contained," he said as he rose to his feet. Casually, he adjusted the collar of his shirt, then cleared his throat.

"I'm going to step out while you do what you need to. I don't need to be a part of it," he said as he approached. He paused at them, looking between each of them, an impassive expression on his face. Then he left the room.

Kane went to Maverick's side. Glancing at Tala, his concern was apparent, and she felt a tug in her chest.

"Maverick," he said as he kneeled beside him.

Tala went to him. "What can I do?"

"I'm not sure," Kane said, shaking his head. "Hold his hand, maybe. He's lost a lot of blood."

She nodded as he reached for the wadded fabric, now congealed to his bloodied thigh. Carefully, he peeled it back, the fibers sticking to the wound, and Maverick's eyes shot open. He winced as he let out a deep moan.

"This is going to hurt," Kane said as he gave the fabric a tug, stuck in the deepest part of the laceration, exposing the raw, meaty flesh.

Maverick gnashed his teeth, groaning in a guttural way that made Tala shudder. Once the fabric was free, his body seemed to relax some.

"I've got to cut your pants, I can't do this otherwise," Kane said with hesitation. "Tala, find a bottle of alcohol. I'm sure your bother has something around here. I need to try to disinfect it as much as possible."

Tala was on her feet in a flash and at Thias's desk almost as quickly. She rummaged through the drawers, coming up empty with each one. Then she turned toward a large bookshelf, a row of cabinets along the bottom. In the third cabinet, she found what she was looking for. A silver tray, a decanter of brown liquor, though what kind, she didn't know, and four crystal tumblers. She grabbed the bottle in a hurry, knocking over one of the tumblers, sending it crashing to the floor, shattering it into a dozen pieces.

Kane took the large bottle from her, then poured the alcohol over Maverick's wound. He recoiled with a gasp. Kane reached for the knife sheathed beside his handgun, then slowly started to pull at the fabric of Maverick's pants, careful with every move as he peeled it away.

Maverick yelled out, then cursed, and Tala reached for his hand. "Do it. Fast. Don… don't worry about me," he said. He ground his teeth together.

Kane nodded, then swiftly lifted the fabric. Sliding the knife below it, Maverick grumbled in misery, a death grip on Tala's hand. Kane cut the fabric away, revealing the full laceration, deep and long, fresh blood oozing from it.

With the fabric of his pants torn away, Kane poured more alcohol on the wound and then doused his hands with it. Crouching low, he sucked in a sharp breath, then pressed his hands firmly onto Maverick's leg. His instant cries of pain filled Tala's ears. Kane closed his eyes, focusing, breathing deep, steady breaths.

At first, Maverick's cries were fervent, but after only a short bit, Tala felt his grip relax. His hollers quieted, the tension relieving in his jaw, in his shoulders. Kane's hands, which began to quiver with intensity, stayed steadfast, pressed firmly against Maverick's thigh.

And then it was over. Kane opened his eyes and pulled his hands away to reveal only a soft pink line.

Maverick pushed himself up on the couch, looking at what had been his wound, catching his breath, his mouth agape. After a moment, he looked up at Kane, his shock etched across his face.

Of course he knew the truth, but to know it and to see it were very different things, and Tala understood his disbelief.

Kane gave him a small smile as he rocked back on his feet, away from the couch, then stood. "I'm just hoping you don't have an infection. But I guess only time will tell us that."

"I…" Maverick stammered, pressing his fingers to his skin. "That's the wildest thing I've ever seen."

Tala let out a small laugh at that. Wild was absolutely one word for it.

Slowly, Maverick rose from the couch, cautiously putting his weight on both feet, bouncing slightly to test its sturdiness. He was unsteady, and Tala let him support himself against her. She cautioned him to take it easy, that he'd lost a lot of blood, that it was his leg that was healed, not his blood levels restored.

"Thank you," he said after a few seconds as he turned to Kane. "That seems like a feeble appreciation considering what you did. But thank you."

Kane shrugged. "Don't mention it," he said, the corner of his mouth curling into a smile. "I'd like to think you'd have done the same for me."

"Sure, I would," Maverick said, then he smiled and let out a weak chuckle.

It took Victoria four hours to reach Tala at the Central Government building, and she arrived flanked by a team of security agents that wouldn't let her out of their sights. The world as they knew it was going to be a very different place.

Victoria was adamant about transparency over what had transpired. She insisted the people deserved the truth. The world deserved the truth, and so a group of agents meticulously processed and documented the scene in the cynosure. Separately, both she and Kole were questioned, asked to recount what had happened leading up to Thias's death. And lastly, his body was removed from the room, zipped into a long, black bag and hauled away.

"Captain," Victoria said as she approached Kole, her hand outstretched. He took it, shaking it firmly.

"Victoria Barrington," he said, and Tala couldn't help but wonder in what capacity he knew her.

"It's actually President Merritt," she said kindly, though assertively.

His expression was stern as he looked at her. "The president of what, may I ask? Because protocol would indicate that Tala Alexander is the successor for that title."

Victoria's lips pressed into a smile. "Of the United States," she said coolly. "And yes," she said, turning toward Tala, "she does now hold that title for the Republic of Columbia."

Tala felt her heart stop, the color draining from her face.

"What?" she gasped.

"Leadership positions in the Republic are assumed by inheritance," Victoria said.

This was information Tala knew, of course, but had never stopped to consider. But it was true, Thias's death thrust her into his position. She inherited everything.

"And the Republic will need a just leader who can guide them through this next chapter. Tala, you have every capability of doing this," Victoria said confidently, approaching her. She was dressed in a dark teal suit, the blazer cinched at the waist by a chunky belt, the trousers cropped at the ankle. Like she always did, she stood tall in her heels, poised and flawless as ever. She reached out, setting her hand on Tala's shoulder.

"Our other leaders are en route as we speak. President Alexander," she said without irony, tipping her head toward her, "I do believe it's time for you to address your nation."

Waves one and two of Operation Libertas were executed swiftly and successfully, without casualties to the Unified tactical teams. It was, as had been expected, the third wave that met the most resistance when all Militia Forces facilities and bases were seized, though the number of soldiers and aircraft outnumbered MF by more than five-fold. There were some places where the conflict was ongoing, but the resisting MF forces were falling back, and it was only a matter of time before their inevitable surrender. The operation was being hailed a victory, Unified and coalition troops effectively requisitioning their targets, though there were casualties on both sides. While Tala wanted to grieve each one, she knew, she understood, that wasn't what any of them would want. Mourn, yes, but also celebrate their triumph. They willingly and valiantly gave their lives defending freedom, defending their country, even if it didn't yet have a home. No victory would have been possible without their sacrifice. To be a soldier was to put aside one's life so that others could live, so that others could thrive.

Tala stood nervously at the podium in the private press room in the Central Government building. Because the State Media building hadn't been fully secured, it was decided to keep the address to the public a private event, only one highly vetted camera team allowed in the room.

The incomplete triangle that symbolized the Republic was removed from the wall, Tala watching proudly as it was taken away.

Kane, who stood like a sentry to her left, just out of the camera's shot, didn't seem to share any of her anxiety. He looked both calm and composed.

She'd addressed her people many times in the advoprops she'd made over the past several months, yet as she stood beneath the bright lights of the small room with security agents as her audience, there was a swarm of frenzied butterflies in her stomach. She pressed her hands to her thighs to steady them as she glanced down the line. Victoria stood to her right, along with presidents Lana Xavier, Graham Walker, and Stella Pierce of DeSoto. Beside them were Jasper and Ash. To her left were the governors of the Colonies: Otto Fulton, Fischer Hutton, Teagan Blakely, and Elias Barrington, then lastly, Gemini and Addox on the end.

She reminded herself that she had all the support she could ever need. But to suddenly be the president she'd never imagined being, she felt the enormous pressure that came with not just representing her people, but with leading them.

"President," a young woman beside the cameraman said. "You're live in ten seconds." She began to count down, and Tala felt each number in her racing heart. She could do this, she told herself. She had to do this. *Finish this.*

"Good evening, citizens of the Republic of Columbia, and all of those throughout North America who are watching this broadcast. I am Tala Alexander. I'm here to tell you that former President Thias Alexander has been overthrown and died in an altercation during his apprehension. Throughout the country, government and Militia Forces facilities have been commandeered through a global collaboration and joint military efforts between the Central Colonies, Tahari, Pacifica, DeSoto and, the Unified Revolutionaries, also known to many as the Unified Rebels.

"This is a decisive victory and a major turning point for more than just the Republic, but for most of North America," she said, her body relaxing with every word she spoke. Each flowed easily off her tongue as her confidence and conviction took root inside. "I am pleased to tell you all that the totalitarian regime of the Republic of Columbia has been deposed. I am issuing a decree to any remaining loyalists to lay down your arms, and I am calling for an immediate ceasefire. Unbeknownst to many citizens, it is the United States that has been operating behind the scenes in association with these countries. They have amalgamated to re-establish the former United States of America, and it is my intention as the new Republic of Columbia president to dissolve the Republic and unify with them."

Tala took a slow, deep breath, glancing briefly at Victoria beside her, who gave her a furtive nod of encouragement.

"This transition, however, will not happen overnight, but rather in due course as we repair our nation. The Republic will remain a viable polity until free elections can be instituted and control can be transferred. After many decades, the people will have a voice in their leadership once again. Gone is the power dynamic of the Republic, and in its place will be elected officials who can lead with the people in mind. Leaders who will represent those who have had no voice, who have been silenced by the tyranny of a corrupted government. We will instead look to new leaders who are committed to justice, equality, prosperity, and democracy.

"Over the next foreseeable future, we will focus on mending our community. We will begin with liberating the labor camps and reuniting lost family members across the country and beyond our borders. We will be dissolving the caste system, integrating our population, restoring citizenship to those who've had no legal place within the borders." It was this that tugged at her heart as she thought of Kane. He was one of these people. To the Republic, he didn't exist. And just like that, he had a future that was never possible before. "We will implement a fair pay structure for employee compensation. We will prioritize rebuilding and mending our nation. These changes will all occur gradually over time as we settle into a new role. A better world comes from a better environment in which people live. It is my intention to remain at the head of the Republic to stabilize our society before the changing of hands.

"There has been much upheaval for our people recently, but we are ushering in a new age of freedom and liberty. Together we will rise. We will become a fountain of life. Strong people breed strong people, and that is the nation we will build. It will not be easy. We have a long and steep road ahead of us. But it will be worth it."

Tala felt her shoulders fall, the tension in her body relaxing. She thought of her mother, the choices she'd made in the end to right her wrongs. If it hadn't been for her, she'd never have Kane. She thought of her father, who had long ago set in motion a movement that had the vision of a better tomorrow. She couldn't help but feel that he would be proud of her, and that was an empowering thought. She wouldn't fail him.

Turning her head, she caught Kane's eyes as he watched her from across the stage, a smile curling at the corner of his mouth that mirrored hers. They had traversed the darkness, and now all that was before them was the sun cresting on the horizon. And her heart was full.

EPILOGUE

On that early summer day, it was warmer than Tala had expected. Having spent almost her entire life living in the northeast, with cold winters and humid, moderately hot summers, the California sunshine took her by surprise. The sun somehow seemed closer to them here, and she felt the brilliance of its rays on her bare arms as she rode in the front passenger seat of the car.

Tall palm trees lined the boulevards, towering above the steady flow of traffic below, their green fronds like canopies, swaying easily in the light breeze. There was something about it all that brought pure joy to her, her happiness nearly bubbling up from inside her, and she couldn't help but smile. Couldn't stop smiling.

Kane was quiet, riding beside her, a look on his face that she couldn't quite put her finger on. He was more relaxed than he had been in weeks. They both were. To say the last several years had been busy, challenging, and stressful was an understatement. And the last few months even more so. Three important things had happened. First was the joint drafting of a new constitution, providing distinct protections for individual liberty and justice. And to delineate the framework, functions, and responsibilities of the federal government, with a canon embodying three principal branches for the separation of powers. The second was the signing of the Liberty Accord, officially unifying all the regions that now made up the new United States of America. No longer was it five separate nations. It was one country, comprised of forty-eight states, and she finally understood what the map in Vulcan's office, in the Mirari building, was of. A country lost but not forgotten. As Tala understood it, there had been fifty states at one time, but a region in the far northwest was retained, at least for the time being, by the vast and mostly desolate Hudson Territories. And then there was an island nation in the Pacific that had been self-governing, and its fate as part of the U.S. was still very much unknown.

Lastly was the inauguration of President-elect Victoria Merritt, who had won the presidency by a landslide. With Lana Xavier at her side as vice president, Tala felt confident in the changing of hands.

"Freedom, safety, well-being, and being able to meet the basic needs of every human are the foundation of a cooperative, sustainable, and prosperous society. Our environment, economy, community, and people are what and who we live to serve. To be free is to be happy, and to be happy is to build a better world for all. We are a government established by the people, for the people. For all people," Victoria had said as she addressed the country only three days earlier. For a brief moment, Tala's and Victoria's gazes had swept over each other and their eyes brightened. There was a mutual respect, a silent understanding of reverence and gratitude between them that only they could understand.

Tala was content with the work she had done to begin restoring the Republic. It was a job she'd never wanted, but one she stepped into anyway, and with her head held high. It had never been about the designation, but rather, she wanted to make an impact for her people. Under her direction, and with the support of many others, a lot had changed during her tenure. But she was ready to move forward with her life, to go in her own direction, distancing herself from politics and stepping away from roles in the military and security forces. She wasn't entirely sure what she wanted to do next but was in no rush to figure it out either. For the time being, she was simply going to rest. Something she'd never done a day in her adult life. Life was short, time precious, and she wanted to spend it with those she loved most.

Cracking the car window, Tala inhaled deeply the fresh air, tinged with a subtle hint of saltiness. She turned her face away from the sun, her eyes settling on Kane, the smile that seemed to never falter still playing on her mouth.

"You're happy," he said, smiling back at her.

She nodded. "I am."

"Here, put this on," he said, his hand outstretched, holding a black cloth. "Over your eyes."

"What?" she asked, her brows lifting in confusion.

"Just take it," he said.

Apprehensively reaching out, she took it from him, still looking skeptically at him. "Why?"

He gave her a small shrug. "Please?" he said, his deep voice gentle.

She sighed loudly, then brought the cloth to her face, covering her eyes and securing it in the back, trying not to tie her hair in with it as she knotted it to make sure it wouldn't fall loose.

"I thought we were meeting everyone," she said, her world now a blackout, though she could still feel the sun, warm, borderline hot, on her skin. Vi and her boyfriend, Erik Tan, had flown to southern California two days earlier with Mila and Declan. Tala liked Erik, who seemed a natural addition to their group. He was a DeSoto national who'd gone to Columbia City with an organization helping to integrate the Nameless back into the general population.

Max had debated for days whether he had the time for even a short getaway or not. Then at the last minute, he'd been assigned as a lead software developer for a new program for counterterrorism, which was a promotion for him, and he argued it wasn't a good time to drop everything for California.

It had been months since Tala had seen Maverick, but she'd known long before they planned their trip that he wouldn't join them. For a while, he'd floated around bases for the Unified military, which he mostly enjoyed because of the variety of places he went. It wasn't until six months earlier that he'd sewn on his new rank as a first sergeant for the officially established U.S. military and finally received long-term orders, bringing him to Texas with an aviation regiment. It took him a bit to settle into his role but liked what he was doing. It was Texas that he didn't care for, complaining regularly that it was too humid and too hot, the combination brutal. And then Tala would gently remind him that it wasn't even the height of summer yet, and he would grumble even more. He was planning leave in early fall for Mila's wedding, giving Tala just one more reason to look forward to it.

"We are," Kane said. "But first, patience."

"That's never been one of my finer attributes," she said.

He chuckled. "Oh, I know."

Sighing, Tala dropped her head against the back of her seat, her shoulders falling. With her sight suddenly gone, her other senses shifted into hyperdrive. Of course there were the sounds of the wind from the open window and the steady hum of traffic, but the salty air seemed to only get stronger, the sweet scent of blooming flowers blending with it. The car slowed, then made several turns, and Tala could hear the clacking of what sounded like scooters on the sidewalks, conversations that they passed too quickly to make distinguishable, laughter. For a short minute, Tala picked up the aromatic smell of bar-b-que nearby.

After another few turns, they suddenly came to a stop, the car immediately shutting down. With the breeze no longer blowing through the car, the heat of the sun seemed to intensify almost instantly, reminding Tala that her naturally pale complexion would likely require copious amounts of sunscreen.

Tala's door opened, and she felt Kane's hand slip into hers, warm and soft. "Follow my lead," he said, and she could hear the smile she knew was on his face.

She walked blindly, only Kane's hand to guide her along the paved ground below her feet. Whether it was a road, a sidewalk, a parking lot, she didn't know. In the distance, she could make out the faint sounds of light traffic, then laughter, squealing. There were children nearby.

"Step up," he said, slowing his pace while Tala fumbled her foot, feeling for the step. The last thing she needed was to trip and fall on her face or sprain an ankle. This was the first proper vacation she'd ever taken.

"One more," he said.

They came to a brief stop and Tala heard the sound of a door unlocking, opening, then Kane gave her a small tug. Stepping into the building, she was met by a rush of cool air, her nose catching a hint of citrus.

She walked, what felt aimlessly, Kane guiding her every step. She was growing impatient, though she was filled with anticipation rather than irritation.

"Okay," he said, bringing her to a stop.

"Open eyes!" a little, giggly voice said, and she couldn't help but smile at the very sound of it.

Tala pulled the cloth loose, freeing her face. Her skin along her hairline where the fabric had been was now damp. Blinking several times to bring the world into focus, she realized she was standing in the middle of a spacious great room. Someone's house.

To her far right was a kitchen with rich, dark cabinets, a white island in the middle, all with marbled stone countertops. Beside her was a large dining table with a bench along one side and four other chairs tucked neatly around it. And to her left was a large living room, an oversized gray rug filling the middle, resting on the black wooden floor. There were two white sofas with colored throw pillows and a matching chair, and on the far wall was an oversized fireplace set in ebony slate stone.

"This… is gorgeous," she said as she looked around, spotting a staircase to go up and one to go down. "But, I don't get it. Where are we?" she asked, turning toward Kane.

"Is us house!" James announced proudly as Kane held him in his arms. His eyes, dark with a golden fleck like his dad's, were wide, his happiness sparkling in them.

"What?" Tala gasped, her head snapping in every direction, taking it all in for a second time. When she turned back to Kane, she knew her face was screwed up in confusion and disbelief.

He smiled as he gave her a slow nod of his head.

"This… this is ours?" she asked, her mouth agape.

"Yes!" James declared. "Is us house, Mommy," he repeated, still beaming.

Tala felt a surge of emotion, her eyes moving between Kane and the room she stood in. Then her breath caught. Not sure how she missed it at first, she walked across the room to a wall of floor-to-ceiling windows, the deep blue ocean spreading out before her.

Without noticing it, Kane opened a door, then pulled Tala onto the balcony that wrapped around the back of the house. Tala was mesmerized by the sight before her, the water and the sky blending into one. The tide was high, large waves swelled, curling with whitecaps at the top before collapsing back into themselves. She watched breathlessly, the constant rising and falling, feeling each crashing wave in her pulse.

She turned, tears prickling at the back of her eyes, and looked up at Kane who was watching her, James bouncing in his arms.

"A house on the beach," she said quietly, remembering her dream so long ago.

"You didn't think I'd forget, did you?" he asked, a gentle smile on his face, his eyes lit as brightly as the sun high in the sky.

She was at a loss for words, and he reached for her hand, his fingers lacing between hers.

"Come," he said, tipping his head toward the sea.

She couldn't remember walking, descending the stairs, kicking off her sandals. But the moment her feet slipped into the hot sand, her toes disappearing beneath thousands of little white granules, she was sure that was something she'd remember for the rest of her life.

"I want ta wun," James said, wiggling in Kane's grasp. Of course he did, who wouldn't want to run through all that freedom? The nearly endless beach, the foam and water of each wave inching across the sand, the infinite sky and ocean before them.

Tala slipped James's shoes off, tossing them beside her own, and Kane set him down. He squealed as his bare toes touched the sand.

"Is hot!" he said, then laughed with delight. As soon as Kane released his hold, James took off like a rocket, kicking up sand as he raced across the beach, as fast as his little legs could carry him.

She reached for Kane's hand, then leaned into him, resting her head against his arm, and she sighed. "I'm not even sure what to say," she said, talking over the roar of the waves.

Looking up at him, she felt her heart swell, the tears returning in her eyes. Nearby, she heard James's giggles and squeals as he called after a seagull, imitating it as he chased after it.

"Think she'll like it too?" she asked, looking down at her swollen belly as Kane's other hand smoothed across it.

His eyes met hers, small wrinkles in the corners as he smiled at her and nodded. "If she's anything like you, she will." He leaned forward, pressing his mouth gently to her forehead, kissing her. "So, tell me, what are we going to do with all this future?" he asked, motioning at all that was around them.

Tala took a deep breath. One day, she had told herself, it would all make sense, she would discover who she was, what she was made of, what her heart wanted. This was it. Life, with all of its imperfections and lessons learned the hard way and inevitable struggles, with all of its beauty and joy and laughter. All its seemingly insignificant moments that would end up being the most important ones, the million memories made along the way. The quiet moments and the loud ones, the calm and the chaos. And all the love that could fit in the confines of a single heart.

She and Kane had built more than a life together, they'd created a small world within its own universe just for the four of them. They were the gatekeepers, holding the madness of the rest of the world at bay. And they woke each morning, ready to create the first day of the rest of their lives.

ABOUT THE AUTHOR

Originally from small-town Minnesota, Nicole currently lives in the greater Salt Lake City, Utah area with her husband, two children, and a very fluffy dog. She is a graduate of the University of Minnesota, Morris. In addition to having an addiction to writing, she is an avid reader, a baseball enthusiast, and has an affinity for novelty coffee mugs.

Find on social media:

Facebook.com/AuthorNicoleAhles

Instagram: NicoleA_Books

ALSO BY NICOLE M. AHLES

Convergence

Resurgence

What I Am Made Of

The Cape House